I0614620

Levi Samuel was born in 1986 in Elk City Oklahoma, though he was raised in Springfield Missouri. While in high school, he discovered the game, Dungeons and Dragons, as well as a Live Action Role Playing group, where he truly discovered who he was. Graduating high school, he joined the Army, but quickly realized that wasn't the life for him. He returned home and went to work in manual labor jobs. Being a quick study, he became a skilled tradesman in a number of fields, but the quest for happiness and purpose evaded him. In 2008 he became a father and has raised his daughter by himself ever since. In 2009, he decided to write a book, which was the start to a lifelong and rewarding career. His first book was published in 2013 under a penname. He's since established a laundry list of qualifications and achievements. Levi lives with his daughter and their cat, Alona.
Please subscribe to my newsletter for first access to all new content. http://eepurl.com/dxRUvL

What you hold here is the product of several years of growth. This was his first completed book, though it's since been revised many times and is far from the original concept. Whether you enjoy this book or not, leave us a review at any online retailer. Reviews help open the door for other readers, as well as teach the author new ways to entertain.

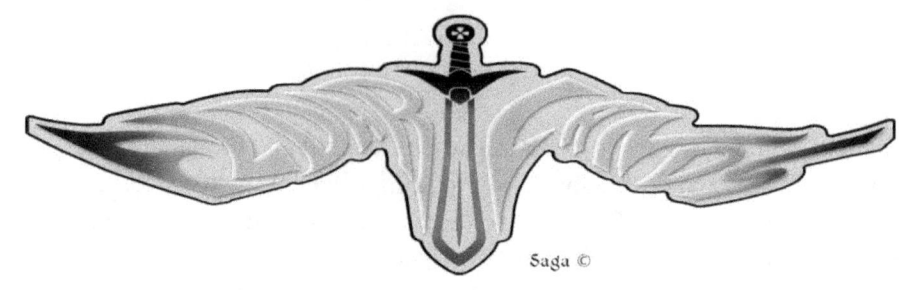

Saga ©

Heroes of Order Trilogy

by Levi Samuel

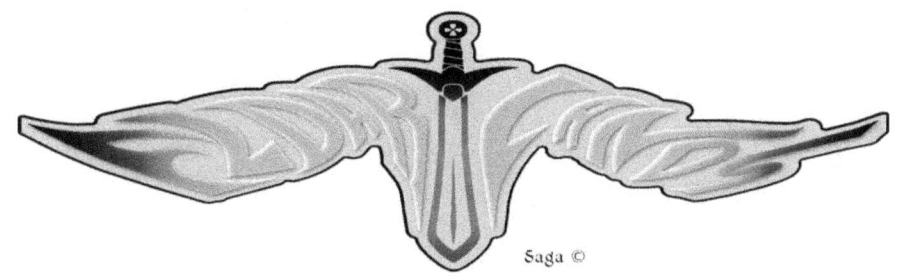

Saga ©

Heroes of Order Trilogy
Volume Three

IZARYLE'S KEY

Levi Samuel

PUBLISHING

ELDARLANDS©
Heroes of Order Trilogy – Volume Three

IZARYLE'S KEY
Eldarlands Publishing
Copyright © 2015-2019

The story, cover art, and illustrations by Levi Samuel.
Edited by Edward Gehlert
Foreword by Edward Gehlert

Genre: Fantasy / Series

ISBN: 1-7321471-4-0
ISBN-13: 978-1-7321471-4-0

Find all the author's projects at http://www.LeviSamuel.com

Foreword

When I was asked to write the foreword for Izaryle's Key, not only was I deeply touched, but also more than a little nervous. I have known Samuel for many years and consider him a friend, peer, and an amazing storyteller.

The feeling of being deeply touched stepped in when I realized that he valued my thoughts enough to consider me his friend and peer; the nervousness reared its ugly head when I thought to myself, "Crap, what if I screw this up? What if I can't convey my thoughts properly?"

The funny thing about my fears, about my nerves getting all jumpy, is that it is the same fear almost every writer faces when they sit down to tell a story. Those of us involved in this crazy industry have, at one point or another, questioned why they're working on a novel, or an article, or on a... whatever.

To me, the act of writing is a daring adventure in and of itself. As authors, we get an idea in our heads. We plan out the trip our characters are going to take: What will they face? What will they overcome? What will they need to help them on this excursion? From idea, to planning, to executing; all of these are ultimately in our direct control. What happens after keyboards are finished clicking is another matter entirely.

We send our creation out into the world. We sit on the sidelines while people share in the journey with our characters, the children of our imagination. We take praise, but we also take criticism. We can be filled with pride, or just as easily feel our stomachs knot up when a reader points out an inconsistency with our tale that we missed. Every emotion the human mind can comprehend assails us during this entire process.

How can we separate the stress and unwanted, or unfounded, emotions from the joy we have while practicing our craft? The simplest answer is, use those feelings. Use whatever feelings you have to breathe life into the story; make the obstacles real to the reader. Make the elation of successes as real as the struggles themselves. Make the journey as believable as possible. If there are giant cows with wings in the fantasy world you are creating, bring them alive and send them soaring across the sky for your audience to see.

Levi Samuel has mastered these skills. He has overcome whatever fears on writing he may have had. His world is alive. It is a living, breathing environment with a history as rich as the one we walk around in during our daily routines. The struggles of his characters will pull at your heart. You easily find yourself cheering them on, hoping that they will find their own peace in a world torn by war and power hungry armies.

In this story there is a small group of friends that are struggling against the unknown. They each have their own skills and knowledge which complement those of their brothers-in-arms. They may bicker and chide each other, but at the end of the day they have their comrade's best interest at heart. Together, they are not afraid to march into the future.

That also describes what it is like to work on a project with Levi Samuel. I trust the man with my life, the lives of my family, and with any task he says he will do. Honor is still alive. It is nurtured by Samuel and is imbued in his character and in his characters.

This series has held my attention and has made my work days fly by. The use of imagery allows the reader to exercise their imaginations in ways that will leave them begging for more.

Something tells me that Levi Samuel is busying himself crafting more adventures for us to share in. Something also tells me he is fearless about the journey. I will happily march into the unknown with him anytime he asks.

Edward Gehlert
Author, Children of Enoch Series
8/10/17

I would like to dedicate this book to my brothers, Brian and Justin.

To Justin for staying up late with me after D&D nights to help me think through interesting plot twists and always encouraging me to keep working.
And to Brian for being an asshole who never likes anything I write. It's your nagging that makes me question myself and inadvertently what makes me better.

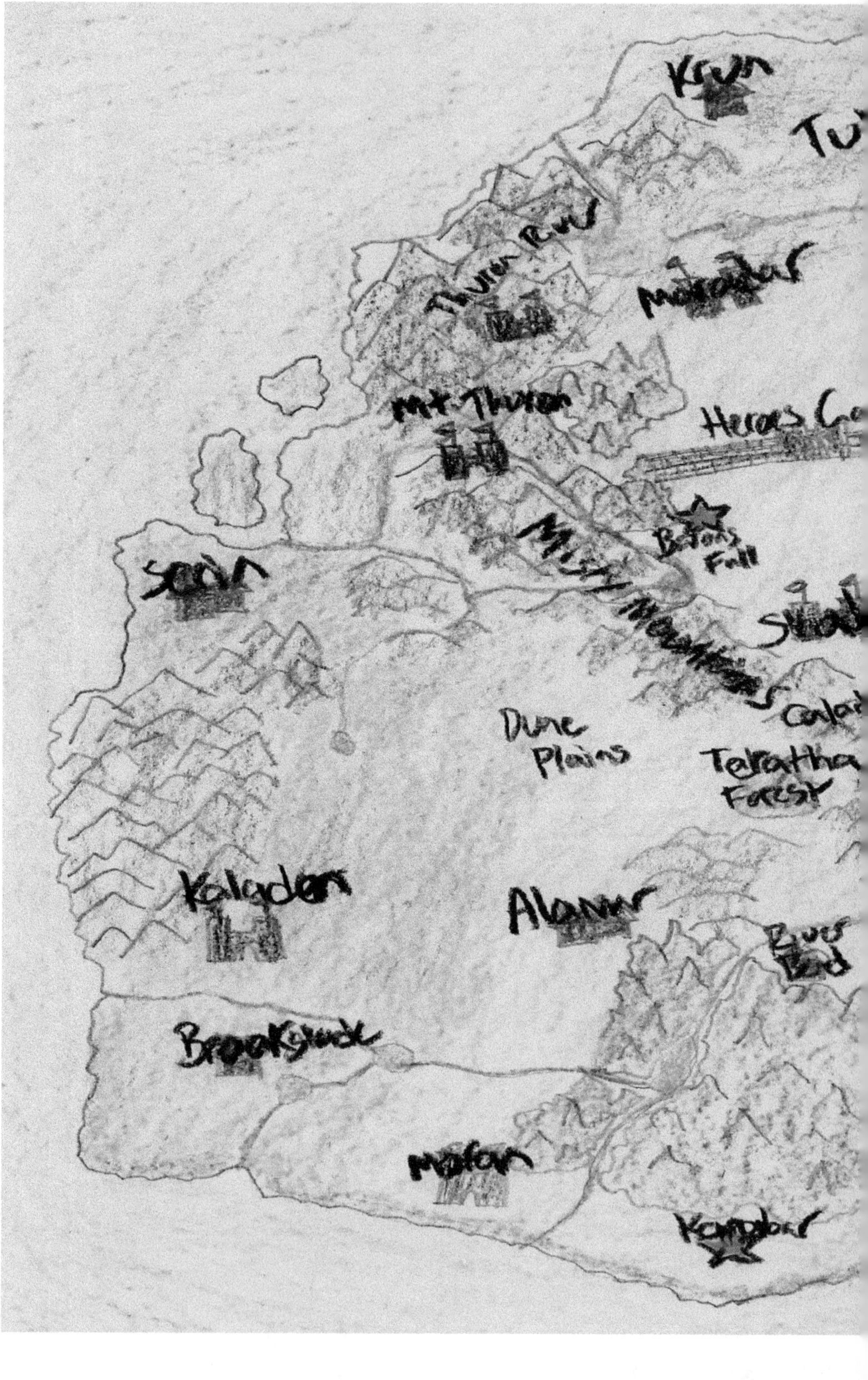
Mt Thuren
Misty Mountains
Dune Plains
Kaladen
Alanar

Tulgar

Tolgrimm

Barkwood

Vale

Gate

Bodgull

Paladir
tha
t

Dyrod
Rise

Amonwell

Ravengale

Canyons
of Amonr

Durnol
Hill

Drundale

Megield

Faye

Contents

Chapter 1
Dark Tidings

A sweet smoke drifted throughout the pub, filling the nostrils of all within. The barroom chatter blocked out coherent conversation more than a few feet away. Gareth tipped his tankard back, finishing off the golden liquid within.

"Maev, be a doll and bring me another."

Without pause, she swooped the empty mug off the table. Giving him a telling smile, she turned and rushed off toward the bar.

Gareth watched her leave, studying the way her hips moved beneath the form fitting deep, red dress.

A moment later she returned, replacing the tankard. "You keep staring at me like that and you're gonna' have to buy me dinner."

He glanced up with a hidden smile. "Who says we need dinner? I'm just here for dessert."

"Follow me then," Maev grabbed his arm and pulled him from his seat.

Gareth followed closely behind, anticipating the night's adventures. *I wonder how she'll be? Reserved? Aggressive? Violent? How many came before?* The questions piled, answers promised to come. Hearing a familiar voice around the corner, he slowed. Peeking through the cracked door, he paused just out of sight, searching the room under the stairs for the men within.

The young lord of Shadgull was wrapped in a black cloak, as was his best friend and adviser. Gareth thought for a moment, recalling the man's name. *Jam, Gem, Jem, that's it.* They were locked in debate against a lowly looking man. The expression on his face suggested he didn't wish to be in their company.

"Don't play me for a fool. I've searched high and low. If it were here,

I would have found some evidence to support your claim."

Erik was growing tired of dealing with the rogue. He'd spoken to every low-life the kingdom had to offer and none of them had yielded the slightest creditable information. There was little chance this man was any different.

"Aye, My Lord. It is." The rogue reached into his cloak.

Jem sprung forward, pointing a dagger at the man's throat. "Do you know who you're talking to? Remove your hand slowly."

The rogue cautiously took a step back, slowly revealing a rolled parchment. The edges were darkened and burned away, suggesting it had been pulled from a fire.

"Forgive me, My Lord. I forget how quick I move sometimes." His hand shaking, the rogue extended his arm and handed the scroll to Jem. Disarmingly, he backed away.

Jem unrolled the parchment and looked upon its contents. Shifting, he turned and showed it to Eric.

Gareth felt his heart skip a beat. The depiction of the kris was perfectly proportioned. Even the blended black and purple colors along the blade matched. There was no mistaking that weapon.

"How'd you come by this?" The young lord adjusted his stance, allowing blood to flow evenly through his legs.

"I saw it myself. 'Bout a year back."

"You comin'?" Maev leaned over the banister, impatiently awaiting the bald warrior.

Gareth took a deep breath, stealing a final glance at the dooming image. Such dangerous rumors circulating wouldn't help him or the Order. Demetrix would want to know about this as soon as possible. But at such a late hour, there was no sense in waking the lad. And he had pleasures to attend. *I'll tell him first thing in the mornin'*. Smiling at the bar wench, he pivoted on heel and rushed around the railing after her.

Eric glanced at the door, hearing movement too close for comfort. Giving a subtle nod, he said everything he needed to.

Jem approached the door and pulled it open just enough to peer out. Seeing nothing out of the ordinary, he closed and latched the wooden barrier. Returning to his lord's side, he gave a reassuring nod.

"You say you saw it yourself. Where'd you see it?" Eric raised an eyebrow, awaiting his answer.

"Marbayne, My Lord. The day the dreuslayers returned. It was tucked in the big one's belt. I was gonna' take it when they walked through the parade but I couldn't get close enough. Too many wardens guarding 'em."

Eric rubbed the stubble growing on his shaved chin, processing the information. "Marbayne, you say?" Glancing at his oldest and most loyal friend, he gestured. "Do it."

Jem sprung forward, thrusting his dagger beneath the man's chin. He was dead before he hit the ground.

"It seems things just got a lot more complicated. Jem, contact the Black Lotus. Have a two-thousand gold bounty placed on Demetrix's head. Pay half up front and half when the job's done. I don't foresee them succeeding, but it should keep the dreuslayers distracted enough to slip a spy into their ranks."

"As you wish. What do you want me to do about this one?"

"Leave him. We were never here. Release one of the thieves from the stocks and backlog his release two days ago. When people demand justice, we'll hire the border wardens to pick him up. I've no problem letting Marbayne clean the mess up for us."

"Do you think it wise to bring them into the mix? I've seen some of their methods. I doubt they'd willingly execute a man claiming to be innocent without complete certainty."

Erik's eyes beamed, daring the man to question him again. "Did I stutter? The more stress we put on Demetrix, the easier it's going to be to get someone close to him. But if it makes you happy, pay the thief enough to keep him happy the rest of his days. When the charges are brought, tell him we'll clear his name if he confesses. All we have to do then is turn our backs."

"What about the money, My Lord?"

"What money?"

"The money to pay the thief. Won't people question where he came up with it?"

"He's a thief. Everyone knows where his money comes from. He simply scored a good haul, and probably murdered this man for it. Thief to assassin isn't a far leap."

"It shall be done, My Lord."

Maev opened her eyes, stealing a quick glance upon the sleeping man beside her. His snoring was deep, yet peacefully rhythmic. She carefully sat up, hoping he wouldn't wake. Placing her bare feet on the cold, wood planked floor, she stood and grabbed her dress. Shaking the wrinkles free, she quickly tossed it over her naked form and laced the bodice. She sat gently on the edge of the plush bed, giving him a light prod, ensuring he was still asleep.

Gareth snored louder, refusing to budge.

A sadistic smile formed on her lips. She didn't expect the sleeping powder to work so quickly. Leaning over the unconscious man, she removed the false jewel set into her ring, exposing a tiny needle. She would have to be quick and precise to prevent rousing him. Selecting the soft skin on the underside of his arm, she carefully pricked his flesh, watching a single drop of blood roll from the wound. Keeping the needle lodged, she fumbled with her coin purse and retrieved a small glass vial from the near empty compartment. A faint red liquid rested in the bottom, sloshing against the sides from the minor movement. Pulling the cork stopper from the top, she retracted the needle, bringing a drop of blood with it. Carefully, slowly, she watched it fall into the liquid and dilute throughout. Replacing the stopper, she swirled it, mixing the two together. The liquid turned a faint golden tone and released a soft radiant glow. She wiped the excess blood from his arm, holding pressure to stop any future bleeding.

Maev waited a few minutes, content it had stopped. Quickly, quietly, she rummaged through the dreuslayer's belongings, searching for the one item he carried at all times. The round leather badge was easy to identify, sewn onto a sash made of dreualfar skin. Maev poured the golden liquid over the etched trident, letting it soak into the material. No sooner than the last drop disappeared into the leather, the badge let out a faint glow. It faded away in no time, leaving it as it once was. She tucked his belt away and bundled his clothing to look as if they'd never been touched. Confident in the ruse, she quickly made for the door.

Footsteps echoed along the ashlar hallway, slow and methodical. He walked the abandoned corridor without concern, taking in the bare walls of the citadel. Running his fingers along the rough stone, he brought his hand up and swept his lengthened silver tinted hair behind his slightly pointed ear. The massive doorway loomed ahead, awaiting his entry.

The masterfully carved twin doors swung open and crashed into the walls on either side, inviting him in. Stepping into the room, he kept his eyes locked on the shadowed figure upon the ornate throne at the far side. A single beam of light shown through the round window near the top of the wall, depicting a demonic face onto the stone floor.

"The infamous Ra'dulen. I wondered when you'd come for me." The voice was pleasant to hear, yet the authority behind it commanded respect.

"Well, I'm here now. Since you know who I am, you know what I'm here to do. Your fortress has fallen, Tycondus. Your sharliets and orcs have been defeated. It's just you and me now."

The newcomer drew his blade, letting the curved edge slide against the sharpening stone in its sheath. It echoed throughout the grand chamber.

"Perhaps. But I didn't get where I am by working with others. Rezerik and Inyalia were weak. Do you really think you can single handedly defeat us all?"

The seated figure stood, revealing his full height. Stepping into the beam of light, his elven form towered nearly a foot over the trespasser. His muscles flexed beneath the scaled shirt, stretched to capacity by the bulk beneath. Two thick horns protruded from his forehead, curving up and toward the rear, much like those of a ram. The elven nightking reached down, drawing twin daggers from his waist. The jagged blades glowed green, highlighting the many hooks in the razor-sharp edges. They were clearly made for inflicting as much damage as possible. "If you're ready for death, let's begin."

Ra'dulen leapt toward the massive figure, bringing his curved longsword down in a single, powerful strike. Anticipating the nightking's reaction, he let the momentum carry him. Tumbling over his right shoulder, he sprung back up, delivering a second attack.

Tycondus flicked his wrist at the last moment, easily deflecting the strike. Spinning around, he crossed the twin daggers, locking the longer blade between them. Rolling his wrists, he forced the sword low, exposing his attacker's chest. With blinding speed, he unhooked the sword, letting it hesitate against the change in pressure for the briefest moment. Refusing to delay, he sliced with both blades, watching them tear into the molded armor. The hooks ripped several large gashes in the thick, blackened leather, but it wasn't deep enough to reach flesh. The nightking hissed. He hadn't expected the armor to be enchanted against such attacks.

Ra'dulen felt the pressure against his breastplate. He knew another direct hit would result in its complete failure. He had to get his opponent at a distance. The shorter weapons would hinder the use of his sword and he was no match for the demonic elf's speed. Tumbling past the mutated creature, he rolled his wrist, twisting the curve of his blade upward. Seeing the opening, he raked it across the older nightking's leg. Finding his footing, he spun around and positioned his sword in front of him, gaping the distance.

The keen blade cut deep into his leg. He felt the streaming blood trickle from the wound. It didn't hit any arteries, but it would slow him drastically. Anger threatened to overcome him. But such emotion would provide no favors. Forcing it aside, he stepped toward the man, daggers unthreatening, at his sides. The younger nightking was over-stretched, making any sort of thrust impossible. Tycondus casually walked toward him, feeling the curved tip of the sword press against his chest. The metallic scales of his shirt bunched beneath the pressure, rendering the blade unable to penetrate. Continuing forward, he rolled his wrist, hooking his dagger over the spine of the blade and pulled it to the side. Stepping into the man's threat range, Tycondus lashed out, aiming for the weakened breastplate.

Ra'dulen watched his sword go wide, unable to separate it from the hooked dagger. The elf was upon him before he could recover. Anticipating the attack, he blindly drew his own dagger, throwing it up to block the incoming blade. To his relief, he heard the metals ring out. Refusing to waste the opportunity, he rolled the small blade, dislodging both from their owner's hands. The weapons hit the ground, breaking away from one another and sliding across the polished floor. Ra'dulen broke free of his enemy's hold. Wasting no time, he dropped and spun on his knee, extending his sword. It sliced into the nightking's other leg.

Unable to withstand the force of the blow, the demonic elf's leg buckled, and he toppled to the ground. *I've had enough of these games.* Catching himself, he slammed his fist into the ashlar, unleashing his god-like powers. The force carried into the stone and mortar, sending a wave of energy throughout the room.

Ra'dulen felt the power erupt, rippling out toward him. Straining against his perception, he spotted the energies inside the stones, moving too fast to be blocked. The weaves spider-webbed out from the source, diluting the further they traveled. They were like bolts of lightning shooting through the sky. *It smells of arcane!* Springing from his knees, he leapt into the air, flipping his sword around. Applying as much force as he could, he stabbed deep into the base stones, burying the blade several inches. The web crackled outward, jumping to the embedded weapon. The young nightking watched the energies hit the edge of his enchanted sword and shoot wide. As if his weapon sliced through the blast it split in both directions, missing him entirely. He ripped his sword free, displaying an unnatural amount of strength. Tumbling toward the immobile nightking, Ra'dulen closed the distance and brought his sword down to finish his opponent. The unwelcomed ring of steel against steel sent disappointment through him. His eyes focused, finding the parried blow. The larger elf strained the single hooked dagger overhead. It was locked against the edge of his heavier blade, forcing the sharpened metal into the mutated elf's hand. To his surprise, the exposed flesh wasn't bleeding. It was clearly wounded, but no blood pooled around the ever-growing gash.

The elven nightking's arms trembled beneath the force, weakened moment by moment. He felt the burning in his hand, but there wasn't much he could do about it. The weaker he became, the closer deadly edge moved toward his skull. He had to do something and fast. Setting his feet, he forced the damage from his mind, choosing to ignore the pain. Lunging forward, Tycondus slammed into the younger man's chest. The bite of steel called out from the back of his legs. He hadn't been fast enough to avoid the blade's fall, but it was better than death. His sturdy horns pressed into the younger nightking, carrying him toward the far wall.

The curved sword slipped from his grip, leaving him empty handed. Ra'dulen, helpless to the force carrying him across the room, brought his fist down against the muscular elf's back. It was no use. He couldn't get any leverage. And that made his enhanced strength next to useless. Crashing into the wall, air escaped his lungs, forcing panic to set in. Instinctively, he held his breath, calming his mind in preparation for his body to reclaim lost breath in short spurts. A second blow from the thick horns slammed into him. Had his breath not already been lost, it surely would be now. Sucking in through his nose, he recovered from the initial impact, regaining his composure. He hadn't noticed the lack of pressure against him. From the corner of his eye, he spotted a wicked green blade rocketing toward him.

The nightking thrashed his head back and forth, slamming his horns into the man. If he could disorient him, he could land a solid blow while he was defenseless. Seeing his dagger lying at the man's feet, he snatched it up, ready to land the final blow. He stabbed in, aimed for the man's ribs. Moments before impact, crushing pain shot through his wrist. He glanced down, seeing the man's reddened knuckles locked around him. He was much stronger than he looked.

Ra'dulen squeezed, hearing bones crack beneath his grip. Twisting, he rolled the elf's wrist, watching Tycondus' fingers loosen.

Unable to keep hold, the nightking felt the blade slip from hand. His free hand launched for it but it was too late. The man already had it in his grasp.

Lost in the comfort of the grip, Ra'dulen stared at the ebbing green blade. It fit his palm perfectly, cupping his fingers in the semi-soft leather wrap. If there was such a thing as perfection, this blade qualified. Rolling the perfectly balanced weapon, he struck. It passed through flesh and bone as if it were cutting air. Had he not seen the hand hit the ground, he would have believed the attack a miss. Freeing himself from the wall, Ra'dulen laid a shallow slice along the elf's collar bone. The wound cauterized instantly, refusing to shed a single drop of blood. Several thin, jagged lines spread from the wound, wrapping their way around the elf's neck and shoulder, disappearing beneath his clothing.

The pain was unbearable. It wasn't the ordinary pain he'd grown accustomed to over the years. That was child's play. This was much worse. It felt like his flesh was being burnt from the inside. Like his insides were boiling everywhere the magic spread. He couldn't think of anything except the pain, unable to give it voice. A sickening pop echoed from his legs and he collapsed to the floor, helpless to the man towering over him. Tycondus could feel the magic coursing through his veins, spreading beneath his flesh, working ever closer toward his heart. He knew he didn't have much time. Once it reached his bloodstream, he was done.

Ra'dulen casually encircled the dying nightking, laying another shallow gash across the elf's back. The scales and rings split apart as if they were cloth, revealing pale-white flesh beneath. The throbbing veins of blackened liquid spread before his eyes. Ra'dulen laid another slice along his shoulder blades, watching a greenish-black ooze seep from the fresh wound. It quickly scurried back inside, escaping the air and sealing itself inside, as if it were alive.

Leaning over the nightking's shoulder, Ra'dulen whispered into the long, pointed ear. "Three down, four to go." A smile formed across his lips, celebrating victory over the defeated demon-elf.

Quivering against the pain, Tycondus glared up at the arrogant man. *How dare he mock me? I am a nightking. Even in defeat, I'm due respect.* Forcing every ounce of will into his final words, he spat his defiance at the man. "Izaryle has graced me. Another will take my place!"

Ra'dulen encompassed the fallen nightking, taking position in front of him. Staring into his fading eyes, he took pleasure in his success. "And I'll kick his ass too!" Springing forward, Ra'dulen laid a deep gash across the nightking's throat, holding his head upright by the thick, curved horns. He closed his eyes and inhaled softly, sucking through his perched lips. A wispy gray substance rolled from the sealed wound in the nightking's neck. It floated upward, drifting toward the young nightking. Sucking inward, Ra'dulen took the essence into himself, feeling the power wash over him. Dropping the dead nightking, he watched him collapse to the floor.

Shivering from the surge of energy, he shook the tingles down, letting the chill in his spine settle. Stepping over the body, he grabbed his sword off the floor and returned it to its sheath. Looking around, he located the dagger's twin and his own. They rested across the reflected face in the floor, scattered where they'd fallen. Quickly securing them, he took a final look around the throne room. There was nothing left to do here. Glancing up at the single window overlooking him, he waved his hand. The window shattered, destroying the depiction of Izaryle. Colored bits of jagged glass rained down over the room, brightened by the rare beams of sunlight through the parted clouds.

Ra'dulen turned, finding annoyance in the growing rays. Passing the carved doors, he gestured, letting them seal behind him.

Smoke lingered in the air of the broken battlements. The battered citadel doors creaked open, revealing a lone figure at their center.

Looking out over the field of victory, Ra'dulen stepped through the damaged doors and onto the rubble littered landing. Descending the hundreds of steps toward the slate embedded road at their base, Ra'dulen watched the massive armies celebrate their victory.

Humans, elves, dwarves, and a select few orcs scurried about, obeying their individual commands. Piles of headless bodies lay strewn about, ever growing from the fallen combatants. The dark warrior glanced toward the headsman, hoisting the guillotine blade into position for the next execution. He thought it an archaic practice, but he couldn't fault them. The god of death didn't exist in this place. That meant there was no one to claim the souls. Beheading seemed to be the only way to ensure they didn't rise again. And even that it wasn't a guarantee. The corpses of this land were extremely resilient.

Ra'dulen quickly made his way down the dark-gray steps and onto the trampled road leading from the citadel. The embedded slates were cracked and broken in many places, leaving the surface uneven and rough. Stepping onto the softer, but equally disturbed dirt, he watched a young human rush toward him, duty fresh on his brow.

"Lord Ra'dulen, we've received word of a counter attack amassing at Faeorun. The scouts barely made it back in one piece."

Ra'dulen continued walking, ignoring the young man.

Seeing the commander march past, he turned and followed, eager to continue his report, "Do you want to meet them head on or use one of your other tactics?"

Ra'dulen stopped and turned to address the man. "Send the Sleepers. Have them circle behind two miles out. They can group up and flank from the inside." He handed the pair of jagged daggers to the young human and walked off, leaving him to his commands.

The young man stared a moment, watching him move away. Memorizing the orders, he turned and rushed off to add the blades to the other artifacts they'd claimed in the assault.

Ra'dulen paced through the battle-torn lands toward a large tent constructed near the center of their forces. He pulled the flap to the side and entered, spotting a fair elven woman inside. She was dressed for battle, wearing dirt covered leather. Though the only weapon she carried was a single dagger at her hip. Her other weapons rested on a stand beside the entry flap.

"Lady Elalon. What can I do for you today?" He gave a graceful bow, showing respect for the elven commander.

"I see you've managed yet another impossible feat." Her voice carried like a song in the breeze, recalling simpler times to his memory.

"At this rate, the nightkings will be gone by spring. Maybe then your people can experience life without constant fear."

"Many already do, thanks to you." She gave a gentle bow, unmatched in elegance, "Had you not overthrown Idenfal and sent me word, I fear we would still be huddled in the forest city, awaiting a time to attack."

"Nobody should have to live in fear. I'm happy to help where I can."
She froze, lost in his sight.

Taking notice, Ra'dulen stared blankly at her. "What's wrong? Do I have blood on my face?"

"No. You've been consuming their essence again, haven't you?"

"Why do you say that?"

"Your eyes are glowing."

Grabbing a platter of fruit from the table, Ra'dulen poured the odd shaped stack into a bowl and angled the polished silver to show his reflection. To his surprise, his eyes had a dull gray hue radiating from them. "That hasn't happened before."

"You need to be careful. I doubt the nightkings were born evil. They were corrupted by the energies you're consuming."

"I'll be okay. My people are forged of magic. It's my responsibility to manage it."

"I don't doubt your strength. I just don't want to see you lose yourself and, by extension, our friendship."

"I appreciate your concern, but I'll be fine. It's nothing I can't handle. If there ever comes a time when I doubt my ability to control it, I'll stop."

"Okay. Just remember who you are and what you're doing. You mean too much to the resistance. You mean too much to me, to lose you over something foolish."

"Hey!" Ra'dulen snapped. "Before I came into the picture, your people were still hiding in caves. Don't forget that!"

"My apologies. I don't mean to upset you. I just want you to be careful. Demetrix would tell you the same thing."

He took a step back, regaining his composure. "You're right. And no, I'm the one who should apologize. You didn't deserve that. I'm sorry. It's been a long day. I'd just like to rest a—"

A cramping pain shot through his stomach, knocking him to the earth. Clenching his midsection, he stared up at her from the ground, uncertain how he ended up on the floor.

"Are you okay? What's wrong?" Worry showed on her face.

Ra'dulen pulled against the table, getting to his knees. "I don't know. It's a pain deep in my gut, like someone's summoning me and I can't answer. I felt it a few weeks ago, but it wasn't like this. This feels like I have no choice but to respond."

The pain shot through him once again. Keeping himself upright, he turned toward the tent flap. Unable to stop them, the energies wrapped around, swallowing him whole. He stepped through the flap, seeing an entirely different place than he had moments before. He was standing in a dilapidated temple, staring into the ancient mirror. Looking around the room, he checked the thousands of runes he'd scribed in the event of his failure. If he was unable to stop the nightkings, he wanted to ensure they would never be able to step foot into the mirror room.

The pain was nearly gone so close to the mirror, yet it still called to him. He felt an unfamiliar presence radiating from the reflective surface. It felt like a spell of some sort. But none he'd ever seen, or felt. But in these lands, that was no surprise. Only the strongest were even capable of using magic, in large part to the oppressive grip of the nightkings. Casters were hunted and executed. Those in power couldn't risk them rising up.

Focusing on the radiating energies, he found the threads, woven together in a way he'd never seen. Yet he knew what the spell was doing. For the first time since he'd taken the mantle of nightking, he was free of this prison. Taking a deep breath, Ra'dulen stepped through.

Chapter II
Desperate Measures

The stench of dirt and stagnant air lingered in the enclosed space. The black stone walls jogged his memory of the chamber, telling him exactly where he was. An unfamiliar presence drew his attention toward the ancient doorway.

"Thank you for joining me. I apologize for the manner in which I gathered your attention. I thought it best I remain in this realm."

Ra'dulen glared his annoyance at the dark dressed figure, seemingly comfortable in the constricting room. Blackened plate mail covered him from ankle to neck, padded and reinforced at the joints. An engraved hourglass displayed bright against his left shoulder, seemingly alive as if the finite specks of sand traveled from one side to the other and back again.

The young nightking locked his gaze on the broadsword sheathed at the man's left hip, narrowly hidden beneath the partially wrapped cloak. There was no obvious threat. Trailing back to his face, he noted the man's wavy, brown locks and lengthened facial hair. He appeared to be little more than the average warrior, save for one exception. A shimmering aura pulsated around the man. A white beacon in the dark underground, though it didn't put off light. Ra'dulen vaguely remembered his father saying something about a white aura once. But that was so long ago, he couldn't recall the exact words. Fortunately, the library beneath Eisrin was managed by one such as him.

Ra'dulen took a step toward the man, feeling the walls pull at him. He couldn't shake its crippling grip, stronger than any he'd felt before. It was as if the stone was siphoning his essence, slowly draining him. "Speak your purpose, d'zhuni. I've matters to attend."

The armored figure gave a respectful nod. "I thought you'd like to know your brothers have fallen into a trap. There's no stopping it, but this doesn't mean they're helpless. With your assistance I can redirect it, preventing their certain doom."

"They're more than capable of handling themselves. I don't have time to babysit. My responsibilities are in Irayth." Ra'dulen stared into the man's face, his concerned expression somewhat troubling. It was as if the man saw something he did not. "I don't know what you were hoping to achieve. The nightkings must fall. That's the only way I can weaken Izaryle enough to ensure he doesn't come to this world. I cannot weigh the lives of my brothers against every soul on Ur."

The armored man exhausted a heavy sigh, comprehending the young nightking's reluctance. "I understand your concern. Were I in your position, I'm sure I'd make a similar choice. But this is not a simple matter of rescuing them and returning to your throne. If you don't intervene, more than their lives will be lost." He casually approached the nightking and extended his hand. "Let me show you." A moment's hesitation passed, awaiting permission to touch him.

Ra'dulen nodded, feeling the grain of the leather gloved fingers contact his forehead. Thousands of images flooded into his mind. Worlds clumped together, twisted between realities. Timelines and locations intertwined, losing him almost immediately. Small bits began to collect, forming into a single cognitive thought, though not his own. This belonged to someone long dead. And then another took place beside the first. One by one they fell in line, filling his mind with moments long past. The revealed memories played out in his head, leaving a cold sweat clinging to his face. Processing what pieces he could fit together, the young nightking found several conflicting points.

One set of events revealed the world as he knew it, trailing linear from the dawn of Ur to its present day. There was entirely too much detail to fully comprehend what he was seeing, but the highlights were easy to pick out. It was as if those were the key moments that defined the world. They were unique moments in time that the rest of reality was founded on. And just as its comprehension began to settle, everything changed.

Another timeline overlaid the first, tainting its reality. Ra'dulen watched the known events fade away, replaced by the altered variants. One by one they disappeared, carrying him toward destruction on a scale unfathomable to his understanding. Feeling the cataclysm wash over him, the visions faded, leaving him panting and exhausted.

"What the hell— was that?" Ra'dulen asked between labored breaths.

"That was but a glimpse of the danger to which I speak. Your mind is not capable of processing the full extent. Even the fraction I showed you was potentially too much, but you're stronger than most."

The fatigued nightking stood in silence, gathering his strength. Between the room and the visions, he could barely lift his arms. His mind racing, he exhaled softly, calming himself before he spoke. "If I don't go, everything comes crashing down?"

"In more ways than one."

"And if I go?"

"Aside from rescuing your brothers? Should you succeed, everything will be restored as it should be. Though, you've no need to return to Irayth."

Ra'dulen arched an eyebrow, studying the man's statement. "Oh?"

"There's nothing further you can achieve there. The resistance has established a foothold in the northlands. The tide has turned. Without you, they'll continue to grow in strength. But if you return, you'll only stifle their advancement."

"Why would my presence slow them?"

"Ravion, for all you've learned you're still just a pup. You've defeated three nightkings. That's a feat in of itself. No one could have predicted that. But let me ask you a question. What do you think is going to happen when that power you've been sucking up starts to change you physically? What happens when you lose control?" He paused a moment, letting his words sink in. "I can't say whether you'll hold for a thousand years or you'll fall tomorrow. The exact moment eludes me. What I can say is people often respond poorly to one in your position. Many already believe you've been corrupted. Agents of shadow hope to exploit you. And the resistance fears you. I urge you to take a step back and let the events happen as they will."

"I see." Closing his eyes, Ra'dulen straightened his posture. Sighing heavily, he continued. "What do you need of me?"

"It's not just you that needs to act. Your brothers will have their parts to play as well. However, we've hit a small pocket of luck. This is one of the rare instances where you simply have to be in the right place at the right time. Everything else will fall where it belongs."

"Listen here, d'zhuni. I get that you churchy types like to be rather vague in these types of encounters. But bear in mind that you summoned me, not the other way around. So please, can you be a little more specific? If I'm going to take you on your word I'd at least like to who or what I'm looking for. And let's not pretend that I don't recognize the sigil of Ozmodius on your shoulder."

The armored man smiled slightly, thinking through his response. "I work for a group that— surveys certain events." he paused, picking his words carefully. "A particularly powerful being has found a way to evade my organization. This in and of itself is of minor concern. The problem comes in the fact that he's using his knowledge to 'stir the pot', so to speak. Hence the threat we've already discussed. I don't necessarily need you to capture or defeat him. In fact, the less you have to do with him the better. What I need from you is to do what you do. You and your brother have certain specialized skills that few others possess. Therefore, being in the right place at the right time with these skills will be enough to flush him out. From there I'll step in and deal with him."

"Why do I have a feeling that this isn't going to be anywhere near as simple as you say?"

"I'll give you one word of advice. Don't linger on what was. Such thoughts tend to hinder what is and what will be."

"What's that supposed to mea—" A golden light wrapped around him, blocking out all other senses. It grew brighter, near blinding. Spreading out, Ra'dulen saw shadows in the distance. Then it faded, revealing his brothers staring up at him.

Demetrix had puffy bags under his eyes, as if he hadn't slept for days. His shoulder length hair was unkempt and his facial hair had grown unruly. He seemed somewhat out of place in the elegant, green and brown armor wrapped around his restless and crippled form.

Gareth, on the other hand, seemed well rested. He wasn't wearing his customary armor, but his twin cutlasses remained ever at his sides. Something caught his attention, something potent and magical. He could taste the lingering effects of the spell. Searching for its source, a familiar scent wafted past his nostrils. His eyes locked on the kris, completely stealing his focus.

Why does he have that? It should be locked away. Forcing his mind away from the welcoming blade, he sniffed out the magic he'd felt. How they hadn't noticed it was a complete mystery. Its stench was that of honey, begging to be tasted. *If that doesn't scream trap, what does?* Stepping from the light, Ra'dulen found himself standing on the council table.

"What the hell are you doing here? And what's with the hair?" Gareth studied him, lost in the event.

"As usual I'm saving your asses." Ra'dulen jumped from the table and approached the bald man. Reaching beneath his cloak, he ripped the dreuskin sash off his belt. The carved badge, stained in gold and green flashed into his memory. He'd forgotten that he once wore it as well. Studying the badge, he waved his hand over the sigil. A golden rune boiled to the surface, displayed brightly for all to see.

"How'd that get there? Nobody ever touches my badge."

"You went to bed with a girl last night. Did you think to lock it up before hand?" Ra'dulen stated coldly, recalling the lingering images of his brief history lesson.

"Well, no— I was a little exhausted afterward," Gareth paused, thinking it over, "Damn it, I liked her too."

Demetrix couldn't help but smile. "Don't take it personally. It's hardly the first time a girl has tried to kill you."

"No one asked you!" Returning his attention to Ravion, Gareth continued, "What's the rune do?"

"I'm not sure exactly. It's crude, made in haste." He sniffed the badge, as if it were a fine wine giving off hints to its secret ingredient. "It was made with blood from both of you. My guess, it was supposed to activate when the two of you came into contact."

"How'd they get my blood?" Demetrix scratched his head.

"I can't say." Ra'dulen reached down, pricking his thumb on the edge if his sword. Feeling the metal bite in, he pressed the bloody thumb into the badge binding himself to it. Tossing the cursed item onto the table, it disappeared into the glowing, golden light.

Casually, he turned and walked toward the window overlooking the courtyard. Peering out, he studied a bluebird, frozen in mid-flight just outside the window. Its wings were outstretched, ready to carry it elsewhere were it not for the magics holding it stationary. It was close enough to snatch out of the air if he so desired. Ignoring the bird, he looked at the people below, wondering if they were aware of the world around them. It was unlikely. He'd seen the aftereffects of time magic before. Those affected by it never seemed to take note.

Turning away from the stone and wood trimmed window, a statue, carved to his likeness, stood against the wall behind his chair. Slowly approaching, he took in the details of the drastol figure, studying the cold face.

Feeling his brothers' gaze on his back, he spoke. "The curse has already taken hold. There's no stopping it now. However, there is a solution. An alternative you might say. This thing looks nothing like me. I hope you didn't pay to have it constructed." His gaze shifted to the other two statues resting behind their empty chairs. Malakai and Krenin looked near identical to their memories.

"What's the alternative?" Gareth asked, a newfound concern in his voice.

Looking up from his thoughts, Ra'dulen turned to face his brothers once again. "Alternatives don't mean much if you don't know the original path. I don't know the specific details as to how it will happen, but the short form I was able to gather says that neither of you will survive. Shortly thereafter, our world will be lost."

"That's kind of deep. Are you saying the two of us are responsible for the world's survival?" A light smirk formed across Gareth's face.

"Don't be a fool. This is merely a byproduct of your incompetence. The only benefit it offers allows us to reach the core of the problem!" Ra'dulen snapped, marching toward them.

"Call me a fool again and you and I are going to have a long, hard talk." Gareth felt his powers aching to be set free, though he didn't want to use them against his friend and brother.

"Both of you calm down. He didn't know she was going to curse his badge. We've all made mistakes and we've always found a way out. What do you need us to do, Ravion?"

Ra'dulen glared at the larger warrior for a moment longer, daring him to refute. It felt so long ago that they'd fought together. Redirecting his attention toward his younger brother, he let his irritation wash away.

"The details were fairly vague. Basically, we're going to piggyback off the curse. Using its power, we're going to go somewhere else. I don't know where. I just learned of this a little while ago. Either way, it'd be a good idea to grab your gear. I don't know how long we'll be gone."

Ra'dulen glanced at the glowing light, feeling the portal begin to weaken. "We need to hurry. The portal is about to fade."

Demetrix pushed off his cane, limping toward the weapon rack beside the door. Securing his quiver and bow he double checked the arrows and swords concealed within. Snatching his cloak off the hook, he pulled it around himself.

Gareth flung open the wardrobe, letting each moment chew at his anger. He'd nearly forgotten what it was like to let loose. Pulling his armor overhead, he tightened the buckles and snatched his pack off the floor.

Waiting for the others, Ra'dulen pulled a crumpled and folded piece of parchment from his cloak. The black waxed seal was cracked around the edges, but the sigil of a raven remained clear in the center. Silently reading the name one final time, he laid it on the table. Watching them approach, he glanced at the wavy blade tucked into Gareth's belt. Trailing up, he found the larger man's single blue eye. "The dagger has to stay"

"What if we need it?"

"We won't. It's too dangerous to risk taking with us."

"We can't risk leaving it. Erik is searching for it. How long do you think it'll take before he comes knocking on our doorstep?"

"It doesn't matter. I will not allow it to go with us. I'd risk him finding it before allowing it to fall into the hands of an enemy we don't know. Erik is limited by his imagination. He can be manipulated. Some enemies cannot."

Gareth sighed. "Fine!"

Pulling it from his waist, he flicked his wrist as if he were going to launch it into the floorboards from where he stood. To his surprise, it froze the moment it left his hand, floating harmlessly in midair.

"You're not going to need your cane either." Ra'dulen gestured to the gnarled wood supporting his brother.

"But, my leg?" Demetrix stared in confusion. "The healers haven't been able to mend it."

Ravion extended his hand, letting a green light flow from him. It wrapped around his right leg, encasing it in the mystical energy. As soon as it fully encompassed the appendage, the energy faded from view.

Demetrix felt the pain recede. It was still present, but less demanding of his attention, as if his leg had been carefully compressed to pull everything together. Slowly testing his weight, a renewed excitement washed over him. For the first time in over a year he put full pressure on it.

"It's not healed, but it should allow you to move unhindered."

Extending his arms, Ra'dulen let the golden light surround him. It spread to the others and engulfed them all.

"My Lord? I just—" William's voice echoed through the empty room.

Candle light flickered off the canvas walls of the large tent. Several figures stood in the low-light, surrounding a thick table covered by a huge map. Small statues made of aged brass rested in various locations on the marked terrain, denoting occupied areas.

General Tygrell stood at the head of the table, staring intently at the hydralfar directly across from him. His thick, muscular arms bulged against the sleeves of his fitted tunic. His hair was cut short, trimmed flat across the top and tapered to fit his square jawed face. "You realize how insane that sounds, right?"

"I understand it's a lot to take in, but I assure you it's entirely true." The hydralfar reached into his pack and retrieved a thin tome.

Laying it atop the map, he pushed the glimmering black cover across the table, knocking over several of the positioned statues. "General, I've traveled to the far reaches of Ur and back again to bring this book to you. I wouldn't have done all that if I wasn't completely certain in my claims."

Tygrell took the book, gesturing to one of the other dreualfar to repair the damaged markers. Flipping to the middle seemingly unconcerned about what he would find, he stared at the thick, blank pages. Returning his gaze to the figure before him, he closed the book and laid it to rest. "This doesn't offer proof to your claims. For all I know it's simply a blank book. But let's say I believe your story. How does this change anything?"

"If we find the ones who can read it, it'll give us detailed instructions on how to end this war. Once that happens your people will have no need to fight. Izaryle will wash over this land and your enemies will cower in fear before his might. You'll be revered as the general who brought an end to the war and gave your people the status they deserve."

Tygrell looked the pale figure up and down. His clothing was unlike any he'd seen before, but he was extremely fluent in their dialect. That meant he'd spent time with the dreualfar. That was enough to warrant an audience. But to allow him free reign among his army? He was delusional if he thought he could simply walk in and demand such. The hydralfar were no friend of his. They'd spent the last hundred years in a constant state of war against them. No, there was no way he could trust him. Even if he was dreualfar. It wasn't their way. He couldn't trust his own son. How could a stranger expect any different? "I'm sure you believe what you say. But you still haven't answered my question. We free Izaryle, great. The war is over and my people look to me to lead them. That's all after the fact. You can't expect me to redirect my armies on the word of a hydralfar. To do so on no more than that would have me overthrown and executed long before anything you have to offer can come to pass. But I'm not without reason. As ludicrous as your theory sounds, I'll allow you ten men and two weeks. Bring me proof of your claims and I'll reconsider my position. Fail me and you'd better hope my men kill you before I get to you."

The hydralfar smiled. The general was clearly not stupid, but his intelligence was irrelevant. It was his position that was required, not the man himself.

"I see you're no fool, General. I respect that and, please, call me Jorin'otth. I am, after all, trying to build a friendship here. I understand your reluctance. But I can do you one better. Once I've offered proof, I'd like a temporary position as your advisor. Give me three months in that position and I believe you'll see the value in what I have to offer. If you aren't confident and seeing drastic results by then I'll lay my head on the chopping block and you can execute me as a traitor."

Offering his own life for failure? This could work. I wish more had his assurance. Taking a deep breath, Tygrell considered his options, "Bring me proof and we'll discuss this further."

Sunlight beamed through the dark green leaves, scattering random patterns on the forest floor. The warm spring day felt peaceful and bright. It was as if the energy of the day was fuller than it had been, like he season was less exhausted.

Demetrix listened intently to the sound of the leaves in the wind. Searching for any evidence of danger, he froze catching an unusual occurrence. "Do you hear that?"

Gareth glanced around. "I don't hear anything."

"Exactly. A nice sunny day like this. This place should be full of bird chirps and cricket songs. I can't hear anything."

"Maybe our arrival spooked them away?"

"I don't think so. It would have scared them, but even squirrels will stop at a safe distance to bark." Demetrix knelt, picking at a few grains of dirt. Sniffing it, he put a small amount in his mouth. The minerals were heavy and strong. Spitting the remainder out, he brushed what was left off his tongue. "Strange. This dirt is richer than any I've seen before. Wherever we are, it's a pretty safe bet that we're not in Dalmoura."

"It doesn't matter. We need to get moving if we're to find civilization by nightfall." Ra'dulen straightened himself. Hearing a twig snap behind him, he spun around drawing his curved longsword.

The volume was instantly intensified. Thousands of black-skinned alfar roared into view. They paused at the peak of the ravine, seeing the three at its base. Worn and rusted blades caught the briefest reflection of sunlight, disappearing in the dulled metals. Refusing to delay, they charged the steep floor, rolling toward the lone warriors.

Gareth reached across his body, drawing his twin cutlasses. A wide smile found its way to the forefront, baring his teeth for the approaching horde to see. "This is more like it!" Excitement and rage fueled him. He swung at the first to reach him. Intent directing the blade, it cut with ease, sizzling as it passed. His target burst into flame the moment the blade made contact.

The dreualfar screamed the moment the flames reached his skin.

Gareth brought his other sword across, slicing into the wounded creature's chest. It fell silent in the burning rags. Without pause, the one-eyed combatant spun around, stabbing both burning blades into another of the attacking foe.

Demetrix whipped his bow over his shoulder, feeling the trained wood arch from the motion. Instinctively, he hooked the string over the notched limb and took aim. Before the bow could reach peak draw he had an arrow nocked ready to fly. The slender wooden shaft flexed from the force of the released string and launched forward. It caught the wind, spinning toward its target. The iron tip sank into the rough leather armor, stabbing deep into the approaching dreualfar. He watched it topple, lost under the approaching mass.

"It sure would be nice if I had some sunstones right about now." Gareth slashed, cutting through two dreualfar in a single swipe and stabbing a third.

Ra'dulen arched his curved sword, slicing through two at once. He spun around, drawing his dagger. The tiny blade bit into another, dropping him to his knees. As if it were a trained skill, he sucked in lightly pulling the tainted energies from the wounded dreualfar. The wispy gray essence floated up through the wound making its way to his face. A reassuring calm washed over him. It was as if a longing thirst had been quenched.

Feeling energized, Ra'dulen kicked the now dead dreualfar into the charging horde, watching the lightening skin disappear beneath the flood. "I don't think sunstones will do you much good."

"Why's that?" Gareth thrust his sword forward, sending an invisible force into the approaching ranks. They flew backward, violently crashing into the others. Flipping the blade around, he stabbed another, glancing to his left.

"The sun's out. They don't seem to be hindered by it."

"Well isn't that just fuckin' great? The only effective weapon we have against them and it's useless now?" Gareth caught one of the dreualfar in the corner of his eye. Focusing his will on the single being he tightened his grip around the sword, squeezing the air around the creature.

The helpless black-skinned alfar froze, unable to react to the force securing him. Trapped beneath a heating grip and an unseen barrier, he cried out seeing the skin on his arms start to blister. In a heartbeat, he burst into flame and exploded into the others. Flaming chunks of meat and bone barraged them igniting clothes and melting flesh.

A high-pitched horn echoed from the tree line, ringing a familiar memory in Ra'dulen's mind.

The dreualfar slowed to a halt. Cautiously, they turned to inspect the source. The outer ranks dropped from a volley of well-aimed arrows.

Ra'dulen looked to the top of the ridge seeing a sight he never imagined he'd see. At the peak of the ravine, an army of dalari waited. They stared intently at the entrapped army of dreualfar and, by extension, the three at the core. The archers, comprised of both hydralfar and dalari stared down their arrows, ready to release their next volley.

Ra'dulen was lost in the sight having never seen so many of his people at once. Much less fighting beside the creatures responsible for their near extinction.

The army swept forward like the tide rolling in. Hundreds of arrows released in sequence, finding their trained marks. A wave of swords and spears washed across the rear lines, decimating several hundred in one fell swoop. The dreualfar fell before them in droves.

The two armies tore at each other, seeming to have forgotten about the three in the middle of their rank.

Ra'dulen watched the battle, lost in his memories. He felt his anger rise, conflicted by the sights before him.

"Hey! Hey, Ravion! We have the upper hand!" Gareth's voice echoed over the sounds of battle, alerting him to his stagnancy.

Glancing at the joyful warrior, Ra'dulen came to his senses. Bringing his sword around, he cut into the back of the dreualfar and charged after them. Refusing to offer mercy, he tore into their backsides, slashing and stabbing mercilessly.

Caught off guard by Ravion's sudden charge, Gareth rushed after him, using his abilities to slow the dreualfar's retreat. He took pleasure in their deaths, cycling his rage into joy. He'd learned to focus his powers in much the same manner, though nothing caused pain quite like good old-fashioned, unbridled hatred he held for the dark-skins. Seeing the end of the battle in sight, he reached down and sliced off an ear to add to his collection.

Demetrix fired another arrow, watching it sink to the feathers in one hapless dreualfar's head. It dropped, revealing another in front of it, pinned by the base of its skull. Reaching for another arrow, he sighed realizing he was out. Locking his fingers around the shorter of his swords, concealed inside his quiver, he drew it and pressed the purposely notched hilt against the string. Edge up, he drew, resting the spine of the sword against his hand and took aim. Exhaling slowly, he released.

The sword launched forward with remarkable speed. The tip was just starting to rise as if it was going to lose balance and topple end over end. Demetrix slung his bow and charged after the flying sword. The blade connected, catching its target at the base of its skull, splitting the embedded arrow in two. The curved tip hit the spinal cord and slung-shot upward, exiting the top of the dreualfar's head. Demetrix was right behind it. Grabbing the hilt, he ripped the sword free and rolled into battle.

The gap closed around the three, leaving a sea of bodies and blackened blood. If the already soupy dirt collected much more, there was a good chance the area would begin to fill. Victory cheers echoed seeing the last dreualfar perish.

Wiping the blood from their weapons, the army took position around the three warriors as if they were awaiting command.

One of the dalari stepped to the head. He paused, taking in their sight. "You seem to be out of place. Your armors aren't general issue. And there haven't been any reported deserters. Yet I find your presence questionable. What are you doing here?"

Ra'dulen froze. Hundreds of words flashed through his mind but none formed into coherent sentences. *Did they survive all this time? Where have they been? Why didn't I find them?*

Seeing Ravion's confusion, Demetrix stepped forward. "Greetings, I'm Demetrix Santail. These are my brothers, Ravion, and Gareth. How we got here is a bit of a long story. Perhaps you could do me the favor of saying where exactly *here* is?"

The lead dalari studied the others briefly. Lingering on Gareth, he spoke. "Santail, huh? I've known a few Santail. Surprised to find you out here. Most of 'em stayed in Dranar. Must have been one hell of a party to end up all the way over here." He kept his gaze locked on the bald warrior.

"Can I help you?" Gareth was becoming annoyed by the voyeur.

"Not particularly. Having emissaries of the royal family here is one thing. That's surprising. But not so surprising as having a devonie introduced as a brother to two dalari. The devonie haven't shown any interest in this war. I find it interesting is all."

"I don't know what a devonie is. But what's this war you speak of?"

"If you aren't here for the war, I'm afraid you've been severely misinformed if you ended up all the way out here. Come on, we'll fill you in back at camp."

Levi Samuel

Chapter III
Remnants Past

Birds chirped from the tree tops and dragonflies fluttered passively from one flower to the next. The dense collection of vegetation made it seem like they were in some long-forgotten marshland, but the ground remained firm. In fact, not so much as a mosquito or stagnant odor plagued the deceivingly comfortable landscape.

Ra'dulen watched the dalari commander lead the way through a thick wall of cattails. Exiting the other side, he was in sheer amazement at the sights before him. Had it not been for the commander he wouldn't have thought twice that anything of interest would have been found in such an unexpected area.

Hundreds of rows of tents crowded a massive field. Some stood independent, while others were rigged together making large canvas buildings. Tens of thousands of dalari wandered about the temporary settlement going about their daily lives as if nothing out of the ordinary was happening.

Demetrix followed behind the dalari commander. While an impressive feat, hiding so many in such an innocent location, the magnitude was somewhat lost on him. What truly amazed him was the construction of this encampment. If pressed, it appeared as if the entire settlement could be stripped down and relocated in a matter of hours. That was impressive for any army. He watched the commander lead them through the heart of the city-camp and toward one of the larger collections of tents at the top of a hill.

"All I'm sayin' is we don't have time for this. It's great we found a stash of your people. I feel for ya'. But unless you hadn't noticed, we have a fresh supply of dreu to contend with. We don't need to be making detours," Gareth whispered his discontent to the back of Ravion in a somewhat louder than hushed tone.

Ra'dulen marched forward, keeping his eyes locked on the miracle ahead of him, afraid it might disappear if he blinked. A heavy sigh escaped him. Refusing to glance back he spoke. "And all I'm saying is we don't know where we are. We found some allies which have agreed to offer aid. It'd be reckless to wander aimlessly with no idea where we're going or what we need to do. We have an opportunity to learn some valuable information here. Shut your mouth for a few minutes and you might learn something."

"Whatever!" Gareth stepped from the line and increased his pace, passing the young ranger. Taking position beside the dalari commander, he returned to a comfortable step. "In all this," He gestured to the settlement around them. "Do you have a place to drink?"

The captain nodded at a collection of tents not far from the main path. "Down there. But don't go too far. I've a feeling General Kashien will want to speak with you."

Gareth stormed off, disappearing into the tented landscape.

Reaching the largest tent at the center of the makeshift city, they paused taking in the beauty of it all. What appeared to be several large tents strung together at a distance was actually a single intricate structure that spanned the size of a small keep. The fabric was dyed maroon and inlaid with golden runes. Every entrance held two guards, standing just outside the flap style doors. Each one held a spear outstretched and ready for use if needed. Their armor seemed more elegant than that of the standard warrior. These few stood out, elevated above the other guards they'd seen since entering the makeshift city. Even the guards patrolling the outer levels wore simple garments. These were dressed in what appeared to be court garb, modified for battle. It almost seemed a waste of materials. Something so fine would be tarnished the first time a sword glanced across the polished metal and leather.

"Is Lord Kashien available?" The dalari commander asked one of the guards.

The well-dressed dalari lifted his right foot and placed it behind the other. In a single, practiced movement he spun in about face and stepped through the flap. A moment later he returned and reclaimed his position with perfect precision.

"General Kashien will see you."

As if prompted to obey on its own, the canvas flap parted, granting them entry. The dalari commander stepped through the opening and disappeared into shadow.

Demetrix and Ravion stepped inside, lost in the marvels of what the massive structure contained. The inside appeared to be made of wood and stone. If not for the exterior, there was no evidence to suggest they were standing in anything but the entry hall to the finest castle they'd ever seen. Every so often the wooden supports were adorned by a fixed sconce, lighting the room in flickering firelight. The floor was a polished marble, lined by a maroon carpet to quiet the clap of boots. What seemed odd was the lack of dirt marring the perfect walkway.

A beautiful woman with long brown hair pulled into a tail stepped into view from the far side of the chamber. A light, baggy fabric covered her legs and chest, revealing much of her midsection.

"This way, Captain."

Trendal gestured to the door, silently telling Ravion and Demetrix to lead the way. "Thank you, Kaileen."

The captain waited for them to pass the threshold. Pausing in front of the woman, he stared at her intently as if he wanted to say something further but lacked the words.

"Duty first, Captain." Kaileen smiled. Leaning in, she quickly kissed his lips and darted around him. Marching through the entry way, she left him to follow after.

Ravion and Demetrix stepped into a narrow room. Each wall had an opening at its center and a rack positioned on each side. The center of the room housed a long table covered in rolled furs, scrolls, random pieces of armor, and a variety of other items. A strange assortment of weapons rested upon the racks. Daggers sat comfortably on the narrow arms that protruded from the vertical stand, while longer weapons leaned against the side walls of the overflowing devices.

"Would you gentlemen be so kind as to do me the favor of lightening yourselves of all weapons? You may utilize the shelves if you so desire. All of your belongings will be here upon your return. Any and all spellcasting, including clairvoyance is strictly forbidden. You may experience moderate discomfort as the walls have been inlayed with dark crystal."

Ra'dulen removed his sword belt, laying it across the scattered items covering the table and stepped through the opening on the far side. He didn't need a guide. The draining stone he felt in the crypt was already pulling at him. It made him feel constricted and weak, as if his body was being squeezed by an invisible grip. Though the vice-like feeling was nothing compared to the hunger growing inside him.

Demetrix removed his quiver and hung the strap on one of the many hooks. Resting his bow beside it, he waited patiently for invitation.

Trendal stepped through the opening, taking position in front of Ravion.

Gesturing toward the doorway, Kaileen waited for Demetrix to join the others. She quietly followed him. Stepping around the group to the head, Kaileen whispered a quiet incantation. Gesturing, so the others couldn't see the details, she scribed a collection of runes in the air. The faded blue inscription grew brighter and began to split apart into a larger doorway. The sounds of battle echoed through the magical opening. Refusing to wait for the door to quit growing, Kaileen stepped through.

A toned, shirtless dalari parried a sword slice, locking the opposing weapon between his own and the fur-lined floor. Rolling into his opponent's arm, he knocked the failed strike away from him and extended his sword toward the fully armored figure. Narrowly raising his blade, the armored figure blocked the incoming attack and staggered back, regaining his balance.

Demetrix was amazed by the simplicity of the room. It was mostly open, save for a few chairs resting beside a small wooden table near one of the walls. A decorative bed rested in its own little cubby off to the side. A full chest of drawers and a large mirror sat beside it. In the main chamber an ornate throne made of polished and lacquered wood sat opposite of the entrance, demanding attention from all who entered. A heavy layer of dust had settled over it, suggesting it hadn't been used for quite some time. Demetrix guessed it was designed to make visitors feel intimidated.

"If you gentlemen would give me a moment, I'm nearly finished here." Kashien spoke between strikes. He acted as if the battle was little more than mild exercise, allowing his focus to drift elsewhere.

Ra'dulen couldn't help but feel a kinship toward the man. There was more to him than met the eye. More than simply being dalari. He could taste the magic inside them man, similar to his own, though less diluted by darkness.

Expecting his opponent to take the bait, Kashien swung low. Steel on steel rang out. Using the recoil to his advantage, he sprung allowing the motion of the blade carry him around. Spinning on his heel, he launched a powerful attack at the armored man's side.

The armored combatant clinched his sword, absorbing the impact as best he could. His wrist couldn't take another blow like that one. Loosening his grip, he tried to adjust to the shirtless attacker's position. He was off guard and rapidly losing balance. A second attack dislodged his sword, sending it clattering uncontrollably from his hand.

The loose sword hit the ground tip first, slicing into the massive fur rug. It flexed against itself but remained lodged firmly upright. Kashien took a step back, allowing the man to reclaim his dignity.

"Reclaim your weapon. There's no honor in attacking an unarmed opponent."

The figure stepped forward, plucking the weapon from the ground. Raising it, he charged, tip extended and ready to pierce flesh.

Kashien sprung forward, slamming his blade against the other. The edge slid along the other, ringing out when the cross-guards met. Staring defiantly into the helmed face of his opponent, he smiled.

Twisting his torso, Kashien ripped his sword away. Feigning left, he flipped the longsword and rotated it behind his back. His arm flexed as far as the joint would allow. Carrying momentum, he released the blade, catching it with his right hand. The tip shot out like lightning, displaying an array of red sparks against the thick armor. It sunk deep into the metal, burying itself in the side of the iron breastplate.

The armored figure glanced at the sword protruding through him. Looking back at his lord, he crumbled into a pile of empty metal and leather.

Kashien sheathed his sword and snatched his tunic from the back of the chair at the edge of the rug. The dark blue fabric shimmered as he pulled it on.

"My apologies for the delay. What may I do for you today, Captain Trendal?" Kashien tipped the empty chair on its back legs and spun it around to take a seat.

"My Prince." Trendal placed his right arm over his chest and bowed low before his future king.

Realizing the man's station, Ravion and Demetrix glanced at each other and back to the prince. Bowing as the captain had, they offered the proper respects.

"Arise. I've no need for formalities here." Kashien gestured to the throne, implying he had no interest to sit upon it.

"As you wish, My Lord." Trendal stood and glanced at the men behind him. Gesturing them to approach, he returned his sight to the prince and continued. "We came across these men a few miles south, near the edge of the Teratha Forest. They have a third, a devonie. He's at the tavern. I told him to stay close if you wished to speak with him."

The young prince looked the two dalari up and down. "Interesting." He stood and approached Ravion, "The two of you have the look of House Santail, but your armor and dress isn't of this region. From where do you hail?"

His eyes were locked on Ravion. There was something odd about the young dalari.

Ra'dulen could smell the power radiating from the man. While it wasn't the type he craved, it made him hunger for its sweet aroma.

"We come from a land known as Dalmoura. We were brought here through magic, by no control of our own. If you happen to have a few maps, we'll be happy to be on our way. Though, I'd like to read up on your people's history, if possible. Dalari are extremely rare where we're from." Ra'dulen explained, bowing his request.

"Also, it seems you're in the middle of a war," Demetrix interjected. "Any details on what we can expect to encounter would be greatly appreciated."

Acknowledging the younger man's statement, Kashien considered their requests. "You may remain here as long as you like. Though, as you put it, we're in the middle of a war. If your blades are needed, I won't hesitate to call upon them so long as you remain among my men. As for the information you seek, I'm afraid books are in short supply and the few maps we have don't mention a place called Dalmoura. While our history is fairly common knowledge among our people, we'd rather it didn't fall into the hands of our enemies. Give me some time and I'll see if I can come up with a historian to answer your questions. Now, if you gentlemen would be so kind as to leave us. I'd like a moment with my captain here."

Kaileen spun and headed for the door. Waiting for the others, she stepped through and wiped away the spell, watching the doorway disappear.

Gareth stepped through the doorway into what he could only describe as a joke. The fact that the walls were made of canvas made no difference. If it weren't for the few bottles on the shelf and the stack of whiskey barrels, this would have been little more than a stable built around a countertop lined in stools. Even the straw on the floor made him feel as if the place would be better suited for livestock. Though it didn't matter. So long as they had ale, they could call it a palace for all he cared. "Barkeep, ale!" Gareth called out, taking a seat. He glanced around the shack, surprised to find the place empty, save for himself and the barkeep.

The dalari behind the counter nodded and went to work filling a wooden tankard from one of the casks tapped behind the bar. Careful to keep from spilling it, he set it on the bar and slid it across the table to the large man sitting across from him.

"What brings you to these parts? Thought the devonie weren't getting involved in a war that 'wasn't their problem'?"

Gareth sighed. That was the second time he'd heard of these devonie. As if he should know anything about them. "Figured I'd act like the dalari and stick my nose in other people's business. What do I owe ya' for the drink?"

The barkeep chuckled at his remark. "Don't worry about it. First one's on the house. Any more and it'll cost ya' a copper per, or half a day's rations."

"I'll keep that in mind. What can you tell me about these devonie everyone keeps going on about?"

"You serious?"

"Don't I look it?"

"I— Uh— I guess I just assumed you knew about them since you are one."

"I know the name now. That's about it."

"Ah, well, I don't really know what to tell you other than, like the dalari, they're one of the eldar races. Supposed to be good with powers of the mind or something like that. Can't say I've ever spent much time around them. I guess there was a point when we all traded. But those days ended long before my time. I heard rumors the emperor sent an emissary to meet with them when the dreualfar attacked, but they were turned away. Said they weren't cleaning up our mess. Other than that, I'm afraid I don't know much."

Gareth swallowed a large gulp of the foamy, bronze liquid and stared into the reflection inside his cup. "Don't suppose you'd know of anyone that knows how to find them?"

"Can't say I do."

Gareth heard footsteps outside the canvas tent. He didn't have to turn to know who was approaching.

Demetrix placed his hand on his friend's shoulder and took the seat beside him.

"Where's Ravion?"

"He wanted to look around. Said he'd meet up here pretty soon."

The barkeep gave a questioning glance to the young dalari.

"Something sweet. Please and thank you."

"Does he seem different to you?" Gareth kept his eyes locked on the reflection in his cup, feeling his anger grow at the tarnished image.

"A bit. You remember how it is over there. We spent a little over a year in that hell. Ravion's nearly doubled that. I'd say he has every right to be a little temperamental. If you'll remember, it took me about six months to shake the depression when we got back."

"I don't think it's depression he's suffering from."

"Oh?"

"Don't worry about it. Just keep an eye on him." Gareth downed the remainder of his tankard and slammed it on the counter. Standing, he turned and disappeared through the canvas flap.

The majestic gates radiated a white glow through the leafy green terrain. Armored guards marched across the allure, mindlessly making their rounds.

From the overgrown forest's edge, a unit of dreualfar watched, awaiting orders from their commander.

"What are we doing here? There's no way the ten of us can break the wall. I doubt we'd even get to the other side before the alarms sound."

"Patience. All will be revealed in due time." Jorin'otth stated calmly, watching the gate. He was growing tired of the constant questions. If it hadn't been for the general giving them express orders to follow his command he had no doubt they'd slit his throat the first chance they got. Not that the option was out of the question. They were dreualfar after all. Such was their nature. Hearing a wagon creak along the forest road, he held his finger up to silence the growing restlessness of the group.

The wagon reached the gate and slowed to a stop. The cover appeared to be made of a glimmering silk and the wooden frame was bleached white and sleek. Everything about it screamed it was made by the hydralfar. The wagon master stood, exposing himself as one. Reaching behind him, he pulled a horn and pushed it to his lips. Giving a soft, gentle blow, it echoed out, playing like music on the wind.

"It's time," Jorin'otth announced, reaching beneath his cloak.

"You're crazy. There's no way we can take the wagon so close to the wall. The archers will have us before we get close!" The hulking dreualfar insisted, gesturing to the others. It was clear they shared his opinion.

"Relax and trust me. This will probably be the easiest thing you ever do." Jorin'otth pulled a bronze rod from beneath the dark brown robes and flicked it toward the ground. The rod extended into a full-sized staff of half a lacquered wood. A pair of oblong orbs rested upon the crest, joined by a thin bridge of what appeared to be quartz. Finite grains of sand swirled inside the ornament and the wood pulsed from base to the head and back again, seemingly decayed in spots only to be renewed a moment later.

The gate slowly cranked open, revealing a small glimpse of the majestic city beyond the wall.

Returning to his seat, the wagon master gave a firm whip to the reins, urging the twin horses onward.

Jorin'otth stood and slammed the staff into the ground. A wave rolled out toward the city, halting the wagon where it sat. The horses were frozen, mid-step. The guards watched from the top of their post, unable to move.

"Let's go." Leaving the staff where it stood, Jorin'otth stepped from the trees and into full view of the guards. Pausing, he turned to look upon the dreualfar. "And don't kill any children. We may need them later."

The small unit of dreualfar cautiously stepped from their hiding place, joining the advancing hydralfar on the road. They passed him, roaring to the open city gate. To their surprise, the hydralfar guards offered no resistance.

Jorin'otth reached the wagon. Pulling the rear flap open, he stared upon three hydralfar resting in the back. A woman peeked through the door at the front of the wagon, while two children sat along the padded bench running the left side. One appeared to be around ten, while the other looked as if she hadn't learned the concept of words yet.

Pulling himself into the back, Jorin'otth heard the familiar pop of steel penetrating flesh. He didn't have to look to know the wagon master was dead. Pulling the black book from his pack, he opened to the center pages and positioned it beneath the younger child's hands. He plucked his dagger from his waist and carefully pricked the toddler's finger.

Bright red liquid pooled easily and splattered onto the page. It disappeared as quickly as it marred.

Jorin'otth lifted the book to his face. "Is this a child of kismet?"

The book refused to answer his question.

Sighing, he repeated the process on the other child, a young boy.

This time the book offered response. In the center of its exposed page, a single word appeared on the surface. *Yes!*

A loud crash echoed outside, shaking the wagon.

"What the hell?" Jorin'otth peeked out the back, seeing the dreualfar atop the wall.

Several of the guards had already been run through. The crude assassins were taking turns trying to throw them on top of the canopy.

"If you don't mind, I'm trying to conduct business here!" Jorin'otth shouted, annoyed by the barbaric actions of his loaned soldiers.

Despite the hydralfar's words, they threw another guard from the wall. The broken alfaren body collided against one of the horses. A sickening pop echoed out and the horse collapsed from the unexpected weight.

Shaking his head, Jorin'otth returned to his attention to the boy. Pulling a brown leather bag from his pack, he placed it over the boy's head. Carefully, he removed the child from the wagon, lifting him over his shoulder. Easily, he carried him to the tree line and laid him to rest beside one of the thick trunks. Turning, he marched back toward the city. Passing through the gates, the ground was stained in blood. Bodies were littered in all directions, frozen where they'd fallen. It seemed a waste, but his job was more important than their lives. He just had to be careful. One mistake and his entire plan would fall apart. Marching toward one of the elegant buildings, he stepped through the open door. He was fortunate the dreualfar hadn't made their way into this building yet. Rounding the corner, he saw his prize. But he had to be certain.

Opening the book, he carefully pricked the young woman's finger, watching the drop soak into the page. "Are you a child of kismet?"

As before, the book revealed the answer, granting him confirmation to his query.

Smiling his success, he placed another bag over her head and determined the best way to lift her. She was almost too large to carry. But until the spell ran its course or he ended it, which ever came first, she'd remain frozen. Exhaling sharply, he tucked his dagger and book away and bent at the waist. Pressing his shoulder into her midsection, he lifted and carried her from the house. Reaching the gate, he glanced back at the dreualfar, making their way through the first row of houses. Straining, he carried her to the trees and laid her beside the boy. Quickly, he bound their hands and stole a glance at the sands coursing through the hourglass. He was running out of time. The spell would end soon.

Retrieving the book, he pricked his own finger and fed the thirsty pages. "Do any other children of kismet reside in this city?"

The blank page slowly formed revealed the single word. *No!*

Packing away his effects, he pulled the staff from the dirt and lifted it into the sky. Quietly reciting the incantations, he amplified his voice. "Time is nearly up. Abandon your thirst for blood and return to the trees!"

A moment later the dreualfar filed from the open gate, gleeful expressions upon their gore spattered faces.

Waiting for them to be within earshot, Jorin'otth gestured to the subdued children. "Be extremely careful with them. Your general has use of these two."

Two of the dreualfar picked them up and stepped into the forest.

Jorin'otth waited for his band to disappear before turning to look upon the city one last time. Flexing his fingers, he made a wiping gesture. A heavy gust of wind blew across the road, erasing any footprints they might have left. He couldn't have anyone following them. Turning, he stepped into the tree line and squeezed the grip on his staff. The weapon collapsed, returning to its rod-like state. He tucked it beneath his cloak, hearing an assortment of screams echo in the distance.

Chapter IV
A Secret Weapon

The sheer number of dalari was beyond belief. In this camp alone there had to upwards of ten-thousand. Ra'dulen had searched most of the known world and never once found a grouping of this magnitude. From what Kashien had told him, there were others, many others. How did he miss them? It wasn't as if they were intentionally hiding. Yet the fact remained, he believed himself to be one of the last of his kind. And here they were, living their lives, seemingly unaware of the troubles that had plagued him for so long. Rounding a row of tents, Ra'dulen noticed a fair-sized lake in the middle of the camp.

A few dalari sat along the edge, casting their fishing lures into the water. Another dipped a wooden bucket into the semi-clear liquid and loaded up a small cart. Once the cart was full, he lifted the handles and began pushing the single wheeled device up the incline and back toward the heart of camp.

It felt so serene, so calm. Yet the hunger inside him was growing. He needed to feed soon. Exhaling deeply, Ra'dulen stepped onto the wooden dock and marched toward the center of the lake. Reaching the end, he sat down, dangling his legs over the end. For such a large body, he had no trouble seeing through the crystal-clear water. The muddy bottom was calm and free of debris. Several large fish swam by, minding their own existence. It was as if the troubles of the world escaped their notice.

Of course, it does. They're fish. We complicate our own lives. Ra'dulen thought. Mindlessly kicking his legs, the bottom of his boots skimmed the water. He watched the ripples of the mirrored surface expand away from him.

Gareth crested the hill, noticing his friend sitting at the end of the small pier. It seemed odd. The lake, while large, was free of boats. There was little need for such a device. Shaking the thoughts from his mind, he made his way down to join Ravion.

The echo of boots on wood roused him from his thoughts. Ra'dulen stole a quick glance behind him, seeing Gareth approach. The larger man took a seat beside him.

"Mind if I join you?" Gareth asked after he'd already sat down, as if the answer was irrelevant.

"It doesn't appear I have much of a choice." Ra'dulen stated coldly.

"What's going on with you?"

"What do you mean?"

"You show up, saying we have to come do this thing. You're dressing different. In all the time I've known you, I've never seen you wear anything darker than a deep blue. Yet here you are, wearing more black than some of the assholes we've fought. And don't even get me started on your sword. I know how much that blade means to you. Why go through the trouble of having it reforged into something that doesn't suit you? If I didn't know any better, I'd say you're going through one of those identity crisis things you hear about when mothers are bitching about their daughters."

"I'm fine." Ra'dulen kicked the water, splashing several droplets out over the surface.

"If you say so. You can't say I didn't try."

Ra'dulen could feel the corruption inside Gareth. The hunger was screaming at him. He needed to feed.

"I didn't ask you to try. I didn't ask you to do anything."

"And yet, here I am. Tell me, what are we doing here anyway?"

"We're here because, for the moment, this is a safe place. And they have information we can use."

"I understand they're your people and you want to learn about them. Believe me, I get that. But what do you hope to gain? Sure, they can offer us sanctuary. I'm grateful for that. But in case you didn't notice, we're in the middle of another dreu war. And this time they don't seem to be restricted by the daylight. This puts us on a whole new threat level. We need to be out there killing em. There's thousands of em out there, ready to taste my steel. But instead we're sitting on our asses and lookin' at fish."

"I don't have the answers you seek." Ra'dulen glanced at his hand, noticing the tremors start the take hold.

"We'll that's just fuckin' great. We followed you here because you said we were needed. And now we're stuck here with no idea how to get home, for the second time I might add. And you don't have any ideas."

Launching himself up, Ra'dulen landed on his feet, towering over Gareth. "I never said I don't have any ideas! I said I don't have the answers you seek! Don't put words in my mouth." Realizing his hand was resting on his sword, he took a step back, lowering his guard. "I need to kill something!" Turning on his heel, Ra'dulen marched toward the shore.

Gareth cracked a smile and pulled himself to his feet. "Finally, somethin' we can agree on."

Ra'dulen marched toward the edge of camp, uncaring if Gareth kept up. He passed hundreds of tents and dalari. It would have been the perfect opportunity to talk to them and learn about his people, but he had to sate his hunger. Delaying any longer could prove disastrous. If he was ready to drain Gareth after all they'd done together, what chance did these people stand? Reaching the guard post, Ra'dulen stepped through the wooden gateway and into the forest beyond their hidden border.

Gareth was taken back at how peaceful the forest seemed when just a few hundred steps away he would have been in the middle of a massive encampment. It spoke marvels toward their skill at subterfuge. Though he suspected magic was at work. How else would they have hidden in plain sight like that? He'd seen the myrkalfar employ similar tactics, but they at least made a point to camouflage themselves. This, while similar, was no mere camouflage. Catching up to Ravion, he listened for anything that would signal imminent danger.

Ra'dulen glanced into the trees and sniffed at the air. Studying them for a brief moment, he shifted and started north, "This way."

"There's the scout I remember." Gareth chuckled, watching his friend track the unseen foes.

"Quiet down. They're closer than you realize."

"Good. I've been itchin' for a good fight." Gareth drew his cutlasses.

Ra'dulen closed his eyes. He could almost taste the corruption radiating from them. His nose twitched and his fingers strained. He hadn't realized that he'd already begun to draw. Opening his eyes, his arms shot out to the sides. He could see the strands of darkened energies swirling through the air. He glanced at Gareth, uncertain if he could see them too. If so, he didn't say anything.

"Is this some new prayer or somethin'? I don't recall you being the religious type."

His concerns were silenced seeing a dreualfar fall from the trees. How he missed it, he'd never know. Charging toward the weakened beast, Gareth laid a deep gash across its chest.

Another dreualfar toppled from concealment, and another. In a few seconds, twelve of the dark-skinned creatures were picking themselves off the forest floor. Their blackened skin was patchy in places, as if it had been bleached.

Gareth heard a wicked shout behind him. Spinning around, he saw something he'd never seen before.

Ra'dulen charged, drawing his curved longsword. A deep bellow echoed from his throat. He wasn't sure why he'd done it. He wasn't the battle shout type. But he couldn't deny it felt good. As if a large portion of his aggression was released in the shout, and transferred to his swing. The sword cut into the first dreualfar he reached, slicing the creature in two. Carrying through, he brought the blade up, biting into another. He could smell the corrupted power coursing through them. His hands straining against his sword, he inhaled, pulling the magics from their wounds and into him.

Gareth caught movement on his blind side. Realizing he was overextended and unable to defend, he opened his mind and let his anger release. He could see himself standing there, twin blades embedded in the dying dreualfar. Another was rushing his right side, poised to strike. Gritting his teeth, he reached out, using his powers to grab the attacking creature by its throat. Gareth squeezed as hard as he could, feeling a snap. The dreualfar toppled, slinging dirt and fallen leaves from the ground and onto Gareth's dark colored breeches. Returning to his body, the bald warrior ripped the swords free of the dead dreualfar and blindly sliced at the one on the ground, taking its head off for good measure.

The dreualfar were regaining their bearings. Drawing weapons, they charged the warriors.

A powerful blast crackled through the air. Gareth turned, seeing a large bolt of black energy slam into Ravion's back. It hit, dispersing around the dalari scout and disappeared.

Ra'dulen stumbled forward from the unexpected blast. Glancing behind him, he saw the dreualfar responsible for the attack. A longing smirk formed across his lips. Eyes locked on the frozen dreualfar, he turned to face the caster.

Gareth stared in confusion. Two dreualfar charged toward Ravion, weapons ready to strike. Rather than dealing with them swiftly, Ravion was behind them in the blink of an eye. The caster was suddenly dangling from his friend's outstretched hand.

Ra'dulen stared into the worried eyes of the defenseless caster. Pleasure coursed through him. His arm was locked, holding the dreualfar mage by his throat. Pulling at the power within the creature, he squeezed, watching the wispy corruption seep from its tortured face. He sucked it in, feeling a calm wash over him. All the angst and hunger faded away. He continued pulling, draining every bit of magic the mage could produce. It made him stronger, more powerful.

Gareth stared in bewilderment, both confused and concerned by what he was witnessing. He watched his friend completely drain the helpless dreualfar. There was nothing left but a withered husk, dry and revolting. Something about it felt wrong. He glanced at the remaining dreualfar, frozen in disbelief at the sights before them.

Absorbing everything the dreualfar had to offer, Ra'dulen casually tossed the ruined carcass into the underbrush. Without a word, he stepped over the dried remnants and marched toward the dalari camp.

"Hey!" Gareth demanded, uncertain as to what he was going to say after witnessing such a thing. "What the hell was that?"

Ra'dulen stole a quick glance at the bald warrior. Refusing to stop, he returned his focus to the trail and kept walking. He was content. Nothing was going to change that. His only regret was losing himself in the moment. Had he been thinking clearly, there wouldn't have been any witnesses.

Gareth was taken back at the sight. His friend, his brother, this monster in his body, it wasn't the man he knew. It was something else. It was something with glowing eyes and a complete disregard for life. Even a life as tarnished as his sworn enemy. Gareth turned, facing the stunned dreualfar. Flinging his cutlass, the curved blade toppled end over end and embedded itself into one of the frozen creature's chest. It sank to the hilt, launching the dead beast from its feet.

The others paused, unsure what to do. They were as taken back as he was. Realizing they stood no chance, the remaining dreualfar gathered themselves and ran off into the forest.

Gareth hated allowing them to go free. But something didn't feel right about any of this. Even one such as he retained a sense of honor in combat. That honor was betrayed this day. Marching across the field, he pulled his cutlass free and wiped the blade clean. Returning it to his sheath, he turned to catch up with Ravion. He had some explaining to do. Finding out what was going on with him was more important than claiming a few ears.

The scent of cooked meat radiated through the large stone fortress. The dreualfar general sat in his chair at the end of the war room, enjoying his dinner in seclusion. Firelight danced off the walls, illuminating the heavy wooden furniture taking residence in the chamber.

Watching steam roll from his food, Tygrell stabbed the thick piece of meat and sliced a small chunk from the whole. Bringing it to his mouth, he could taste the spices and remaining blood from the undercooked slab, making a sort of gravy. A knock at the door drew his attention away from his meal.

"Enter!"

A single guard stepped through the threshold, presenting himself fully for the general to see. "General, the hydralfar has returned."

"So soon? I didn't expect him for a few more days."

Tygrell sat his food aside and stood. Approaching the table at the center of the room, he scanned the large map covering it. There were no details he needed to review. He thought it fitting for his enemy to see him on his feet when he arrived. Misdirection was a tool. Rather than enjoying his dinner when the treacherous hydralfar arrived, he needed to be battle ready. It was all a mind game. If the enemy believed him to be ready at all times, it would keep them on edge, and therefore, uneasy. That would keep them weak when time came for battle. And exposing weakness was how wars were won.

"Show him in. Once he's shown me whatever it is he believes I'll find so valuable, I want you to drive your sword through his heart."

"Yes, General!"

The dreualfar guard turned, disappearing through the large wooden doors. A few moments later he returned, escorting Jorin'otth, two bound figures, both seeming young due to their size, and two of the dreualfar unit that had been sent to ensure the hydralfar didn't get off task.

The two dreualfar guided the hooded children to the side wall and took position behind them.

Jorin'otth approached the far end of the table and nodded his respects. "General, I've returned with proof." He fumbled with the buckle on his pack and retrieved the thin black book. Turning, he gestured to one of the dreualfar. "Bring the boy."

One of the dreualfar pulled the child toward the table. Positioning him at Jorin'otth's side, he took a step back, remaining close enough to restrain him if he tried to flee.

"General, if you'd join me." Jorin'otth gestured to the book, laying it on the map covered table.

Marching around, Tygrell watched his guard take position behind the hydralfar. If he knew what was in store for him, he showed no sign. "I don't understand what these children have to do with the book."

"Patience, General. All will be revealed in due time." Jorin'otth unlatched the book and flipped to the blank central pages. He could hear the whimpers of the children beneath their hoods. There was no doubt such an experience was traumatic for them. But a price had to be paid. And they were born to pay it. He ripped the brown sack from the boy's head, revealing his gagged mouth and tear stricken face. He was confused, lost, and unsure of what was happening. Jorin'otth could relate. He recalled his own childhood.

Tygrell moved into position, staring intently at the age-worn pages. "What's this supposed to prove?"

Gently grabbing the boy's hand, Jorin'otth pulled it over the table so the book was directly under it. "Be still. This may sting. If you flinch it's liable to be much worse."

The boy watched him. Why would a hydralfar be working with these monsters? The two were sworn enemies of each other. He wasn't around when they existed together, or even when the war started. But he'd heard the stories. The hydralfar accepted them into the empire. And in return they slaughtered thousands. Trusting the hydralfar's words, he held still, ready for what was to follow. As ready as he could be anyway. It wasn't everyday his finger was pricked, but Jorin'otth had done it many times since his abduction. *What was he looking for? Why was he chosen?* The hydralfar had done the same to Maerie, but he didn't seem to show as much interest in her.

"General, may I please use your dagger?" Jorin'otth contemplated using his own blade, but pulling a weapon, even one as simple as a dagger under such conditions could set the wrong mood for an already unbalanced situation.

Tygrell pulled is dagger. He flipped it around to extend the handle toward the hydralfar. He clearly wasn't stupid. Pulling his own blade could have easily resulted in his swift execution. Releasing the blade into Jorin'otth's hand, he returned his arm to his side, stealing a quick glance at his guard, anxiously awaiting the command.

Carefully placing the edge of the blade against the child's finger, Jorin'otth pulled, watching the beads of bright red fluid form from the small wound. Squeezing each side, he turned the boy's wrist, watching the droplets fall to the page. As expected, the book absorbed them as quickly as they landed.

Silence engulfed the room. Not so much as a pin drop could be heard from any of them. Suddenly, an echoing sob erupted from the bound girl against the wall.

"I've seen enough! What the hell is this supposed to be showing me?" Tygrell stood to his full height, quickly losing patience with the hydralfar.

"As I said, patience, General." Jorin'otth let another droplet fall into the book.

He released the child's hand and lifted the book from the table. "Show me the outcome of this war."

Red dots freckled the page. More and more appeared until images started forming from the tiny speckles. Filling in the empty space a massive battlefield could be seen. Tens of thousands laid dead in the settling dust. Pools of blood gathered in the low areas of the terrain. Upon a hill, overlooking the grizzly scene, an army of hydralfar stood victorious over the defeated dreualfar and dalari bodies. Amidst the massacre, a single form stood, arms raised in challenge to the betrayal.

Tygrell couldn't identify who the lone survivor was, the features difficult to make out in the various shades of red. But one thing was certain, his army lost. And that was unacceptable.

Seeing the general's concern, Jorin'otth quickly asked the book another question. "How do we change this outcome? How do we win the war?"

The image faded, leaving the blank pages behind for all to see.

Tygrell watched for any sign of red. Nothing was happening. Perhaps it needed more blood? "It needs more!" Shoving Jorin'otth aside, he pulled the dagger from his hand and ripped the boy up and over the table. Yanking his head back by his brown braided hair, he exposed his throat.

"No, General, don't!" Jorin'otth pleaded.

It was too late. The blade had already embedded itself to the hilt.

Tygrell ripped the blade free, pulling the child's head back to open the wound as much as possible. Spilling blood all over the book, table, and floor, he dropped the limp body, watching it crumble to the stone slates.

The book absorbed every drop that spattered on its pages. A moment later it revealed, in great detail, a map. The point of interest was marked by an odd symbol. A demonic face encompassed by a full moon rested at the base of a grand mountain range.

"What do we do there?" Tygrell asked, leaning over the book.

Jorin'otth stared at the wasted youth, his crumpled form bleeding out at his feet. He closed his eyes and sighed deeply. "General, with all due respect, the bloodline this book requires to deliver these secrets is extremely rare. We were lucky we found these two so close together. I'd ask that you trust me when I say we need them alive."

Tygrell raised the dagger, hunger in his expression. Contemplating his choices, he glanced from Jorin'otth to the dreualfar guard. Nodding, he returned his focus to the book. "I kill when I desire. But I can see the value this book provides. You have my word, from this moment forward no one will touch your pets until their use is at its end. Now, what is the book showing us?"

Jorin'otth listed the book, asking another question. "What will we find at the location marked by our lord's seal?"

The book rearranged, forming the red dots into a singular shape. Upon the page was an image of an odd-looking stone. An inscription formed over the image, naming it for them to see.

"Dalari Eldarstone? What's an eldarstone?" Tygrell asked.

Again, the book shifted, displaying five small images on the page, complete with a description of each one.

"And what are we supposed to do with this stone once we've found it?" Jorin'otth added, hoping the book would keep up with their questions.

Schematics appeared on the page, detailing a grand machine using the stone as a focal iris.

"Interesting. General, this is what's going to win the war. With this, your numbers will be unlimited. Imagine turning your enemies into allies. As their strength wanes, yours will grow. You'll be unstoppable!" Jorin'otth caught movement out the corner of his eye. Seeing the razor edge of a sword poised to strike, he reached for the rod at his side. Fear erupted inside him. The general was also moving toward him, bloodlust in his eyes. He'd made a mistake. He was too late to understand what was happening. If he was lucky, it'd be a quick death.

To his surprise, the general lunged past him. A sickening pop echoed in his ears, accompanied by gasping cries. Spinning on his heel, Jorin'otth saw the general atop the guard, his dagger plunged into the guard's throat. A sword rested in the dying dreualfar's hand, its intention interrupted. Against all odds, it seemed the general saved him from an unexpected death.

Commotion echoed through the hall outside the door. A loud bang echoed through the wooden barriers and the door busted open.

A lone dreualfar scout rushed into the room, out of breath. "General Tygrell, the dalari—" He paused, taking a breath. "They— they have a— I don't know what to call him. He devoured Maelis. Like sucked his magic, life, and all from his body. Nothing left but a withered husk."

Tygrell picked himself up. Dagger in hand, he approached the intruding scout. "Calm yourself. You say a dalari did this?"

"Yes, General. He attacked our entire unit. Weakened us all by raising his arms. It felt like my insides were being pulled out."

"And how many of your unit escaped?"

"Just myself and two others."

"You there." Tygrell pointed at the dreualfar soldier standing beside Jorin'otth. "Go find the others. I want a full report from each of them."

He watched the dreualfar rush out the door. "And you. You've done well!" Tygrell stepped forward, placing his hand on the young scout's shoulder. Feeling the young dreualfar relax slightly under the embrace, he plunged the dagger into his stomach. "Thank you for bringing this to my attention. But I want you to understand that I can't have you telling the others about this dalari you saw. Such a story would damage moral."

The scout dropped to his knees. A final gasp escaped him and he collapsed on the stone floor.

"Jorin'otth, you've gotten your wish. You're now my lead advisor. I don't care how you do it, I want this machine built. You'll be given command of one of my largest companies. Make it happen."

Levi Samuel

Chapter V
An Unexpected Encounter

Demetrix tipped his tankard back, taking a long draw. It felt good to relax for a bit. Though, in truth he had no idea what he was doing here. Sure, he was curious as to where the dalari had been all this time. But there was time to uncover that mystery. The more pressing concern was Ravion. Gareth wasn't wrong. Something was clearly affecting his brother. The real question was what could they do about it? Setting the mug on the high-top counter, he caught motion out of the corner of his eye. The captain, Trendal he believed was his name, entered the small tavern and took a seat beside him.

"Where'd your friends head off to?" Trendal asked, holding his hand up to signal the barkeep.

"I'm not sure. Gareth was in here a while ago. Ravion wandered off after we left your commander."

"They seem rather on edge. That's nothing new for the devonie. They always seem to be pissed about something. But for a dalari, your brother has something else going on with him."

Demetrix tipped his mug back, swallowing what was left of the golden liquid. Setting the wooden tankard down once again, he pushed it toward the edge of the counter and signaled the barkeep for another. Sitting up straight, he flexed his back, giving a quick glance to the man in his company.

"I've seen that look before." Trendal picked up his tankard and took a small gulp.

"What look?" Demetrix asked, watching the foamy liquid slosh against the side of Trendal's mug.

The barkeep took the tankard and refilled it.

"Run down, tired, the thought of battles past looming overhead.

You're a man who's seen and experienced much. And you haven't quite figured out how to deal with it."

"What of it?" Demetrix took another draw, swallowing much more than he should have. He stared into his mug, watching his reflection stare back. The man wasn't wrong. He was tired. He looked it. But the battle was far from over.

"If there's anything I've learned in my time as a soldier, it's that there's only one way to deal with it. Duty. Force yourself into duty. You won't have time to think about the 'what was' and 'what will be'. I think I've got just the thing for you, if you're interested. There's a group leaving out at dusk. It's nothing difficult, just a scout run checking the southern pass. We're moving camp in a couple days and we need to ensure the way is clear when time comes."

Breaking his gaze on his exhausted reflection, Demetrix looked at the captain. The man seemed earnest in his opinions. But was getting involved in another war the best way to deal with his personal demons? "I'll think about it."

"Very well. If you decide to go, have your gear ready and be at the west gate by nightfall. You'll meet Lieutenant Talaek there. He's commanding the run so you'll need to answer to him. Be sure you pack light, you'll be moving too quickly to be overloaded."

Trendal swallowed the last bits of his drink and set the tankard down. Pushing himself from the counter, he stood and marched out the door.

Swirling the liquid around the inside of his mug, Demetrix watched the clinging foam break free of the sides and rejoin the liquid at the bottom. He couldn't help but wonder why he felt the way he did. He missed Elalon that much was clear. But was that his only reason for the depression he'd felt inside him for months? Had he been simply going through the motions? Living a life of routine tasks and trained responses. There was little to no joy anymore. And yet he continued doing it, day after day. That wasn't living. That was surviving. There was an enormous difference. Perhaps Trendal was right. He didn't know anything about this place. Or even his people for that matter. Perhaps working alongside them would provide answers to both. Pushing the half empty tankard across the counter one last time, he tossed a couple coins beside it and stood. Stretching his legs, he lifted his pack from the ground and tossed it over his shoulder.

A thin trail winded through mounds of overgrown brush, snagging against Gareth's armor. He couldn't be sure he was in the right place. He hadn't traveled far from the camp, yet everything looked different than he remembered it. Suddenly, he was standing inside the massive settlement.

The guards gave him a quick glance and returned to their duties.

Scanning the large road leading toward the center, he saw Ravion marching away. Picking up the pace, he ran after him. Overshooting, Gareth spun, blocking his friend's path. "Hey! What the hell happened back there?"

Ra'dulen paused, studying the concern on Gareth's face. "Don't worry about it. It's just something I learned in Irayth."

"You took a blast straight to the back. That should have killed anyone, or at the very least crippled them for quite some time. Yet you turned and destroyed him on a level even I thought impossible. Something's not right about that!"

"Let it go. I learned a few things to protect myself. That's it. A simple incantation can weaken the infrastructure of most spells. That's why I was able to withstand the blast. As for the other part, what can I say? I've spent enough time with you to know when I have to kill mercilessly."

"I may be a lot of things. And yes, I hate them with every fiber of my being. But I've never done anything like you did back there. There's more going on with you than you're telling us."

"Let it go!" Ra'dulen lost his patience. Side-stepping, he felt his shoulder slam into Gareth as he passed.

Gareth spun from the force, watching Ravion storm off. He thought about following after him. This conversation clearly wasn't over.

"What's going on?" Demetrix approached, adjusting the pack on his shoulder.

Gareth noticed he was ready for travel. If he didn't know any better, the young dalari appeared as if he was going somewhere. "Nothing much. Ravion being his new self. Where are you off to?"

"Trendal offered me a scouting run. Figured I'd take it. I shouldn't be gone more than a few days."

"You sure that's a good idea? We don't know anything about these people?"

"It's a simple run. Apparently, they're moving the camp in a few days and want someone to check the route. Nothing major." Demetrix adjusted the strap on his pack once again, hooking it on the edge of his shoulder pauldron.

"Well, I don't have much to do. Mind if I tag along? Ravion doesn't seem to want any help right now."

"Thanks for the offer, but this is something I need to do by myself. Things haven't been the same since we got back from Irayth. I need to clear my head."

Gareth took a deep breath, thinking through his words. "I suppose I understand." He rested his hand on Demetrix's unencumbered shoulder. "Travel safe. We'll see you in a few days."

"Will do." Demetrix turned to continue toward the west gate. Freezing halfway through his turn, he stared back at Gareth. "Hey Gareth, thanks for bringing me home. I never told you that."

"Don't mention it. I was simply doing what Ravion asked."

"I know. I was irritated at you for months for leaving him behind, but my anger was misplaced. I wasn't mad at you for doing what you thought was right. I was mad because I wanted to stay behind."

"I understand. I was never much the apologizing type. But I understand your reasoning," Gareth chuckled to himself. "Look at all I've done since my wife was taken. I'm the last person to judge under such circumstances."

Demetrix nodded, feeling for the first time that he truly understood Gareth. Glancing at the fading sun, he realized his time was running short. "Thank you, my brother."

"You're welcome. And I'm sorry I took you from a place that became home. Safe travels. Come back in one piece."

Demetrix turned and rushed toward the edge of town.

Returning his attention toward the inner camp, Gareth searched for any sign of Ravion. He hadn't been distracted long enough for the scout to have escaped his vision, yet he was nowhere to be seen.

"What the hell do you mean, we march to Drundale? Who gave the command?" The grizzled dreualfar shouted at the messenger. Small droplets of spit escaped like his words, clinging to his unkempt beard.

"General Tygrell ordered it." The messenger stated defiantly, silently daring the captain to protest. "He says there's some kind of weapon close to your position. Wants you to group up with the twenty-first division. New orders will be given there. And, Captain Vaniar, these orders are not negotiable. The general says you're to obey or face execution for denying his direct orders."

Vaniar clearly wasn't happy about the change, but he wasn't about to argue the point to this scrawny excuse for a dreualfar. Twerp would probably take word straight to the general himself.

"Very well. We'll head east. What's the general want done with the prisoners?"

"He said to take them with you. The Twenty-First is working on something that'll require all that survive the trip."

"Understood." The captain spun, barking orders to his lieutenant. As far as he was concerned, this conversation was over. The messenger was free to run back to kiss Tygrell's ass. He didn't need to grant permission for that. "Lieutenant Hermain, we've got new orders. Get your ass out here!"

A smaller dreualfar rushed from one of the elegant tents comprising the fair-sized encampment. His breeches were halfway around his legs when he stepped out. Pulling them up as he ran, he approached the captain and offered salute.

"At ease, Lieutenant. General Tygrell, the ass that he is, wants us to march east. Keep your cock to yourself and get the prisoners ready to move. And son, your fly's still open."

"Yes, Sir!" The lieutenant spun around, fixing the last few buttons on his breeches and cinched his belt. He ran toward the tent he'd emerged from moments before and disappeared inside.

Vaniar watched the young dreualfar disappear behind the flap. A mild smirk came to his face hearing the dominating orders escape such a frail being. He was still a kid, drinking and screwing each chance he got. A day would come when he'd be forced to take his job seriously. Though a little debauchery wasn't a terrible thing every now and then. He certainly wasn't one to judge.

The confiscated alfarian tents fell with relative ease, collapsing to the ground once their ridged frames had been removed. Several of the soldiers went to work gathering the supplies and packing them for transport. Nearly thirty men, hydralfar, and dalari stood, stripped to their undergarments and tied to a single rope behind the wagons. Their hands were bound and feet secured to long poles, forcing them to step as one or face being drug by the others. Only a few of the humans appeared well fed and fairly healthy. One of the female men and two of the hydralfar women appeared pregnant, ready to give birth any day now.

"The unit's ready to travel, Captain." Hermain stated proudly. He stood across from the rugged captain, refusing to move until acknowledged.

"What? Do you want a compliment or something? Do your fucking job and lead 'em out!"

"Yes, Sir!" Hermain spun around and marched toward the assembled force. "Company! Forward, march!"

The group roared into motion, forming large gaps between the front and the rear. It was clear these soldiers weren't trained in drill. They seemed barely trained to follow simple commands.

Vaniar took up the rear, watching the hundred dreualfar company abandon their station for the first time in six months. He couldn't help but feel the general had information he wasn't releasing. His camp overlooked the main southern road. Any dalari or hydralfar forces passing through were in ambush position before they knew what hit them. To give up such an advantage was either extremely stupid, or there was something of greater value. Either way, it seemed he'd find out which it was once he made the three-day journey to Drundale. Glancing into the evening sky, the thick rolling clouds were dark and ready to release their moisture. *It's rained nearly every night for the past month. Why should tonight be any different?*

As if the gods were listening to his thoughts, heavy droplets crashed to the ground. Within minutes everything was soaked. Water pooled on the ground, unable to be absorbed quickly enough.

The army marched south, rounding the canyon to step foot onto the river road. Water lapped at its edge, eating away the packed soil and stone. They'd have to be careful. If the current had washed away the underside, it was possible the road could collapse under their weight.

Lieutenant Hermain made his way to the front of the unit. It'd only been an hour since they'd abandoned their post and his legs were already tired. Taking a deep breath, he pressed onward, scouting ahead. Staring up at the cliffs above them, he felt as if they hadn't made any progress. They were just now below the camp. He knew no one would have been able to set up an ambush so quickly, but the prospect made him nervous. Watching for signs of danger, he trekked along the road. There was no doubt the captain would have him flogged if he missed something.

Rounding the northern bend, Hermain recalled the ford. If they could cross, it would shave half a day off the trip. Though, he didn't expect such luck. The frequent rains had collected into the river, making the landmarks difficult to recognize against the high waters. It was unlikely they'd be able to cross anyway. Even when the river was down, fording was treacherous. It would have to be traveled slowly. The bank had been salted with sharpened flint to prevent travel. That was the only sure way to force any passing units onto the road and into ambush position. Yet now it seemed their own tactics were working against them.

The rain slowed to a stop, the last few droplets settling where they'd fallen. The gusting winds carried upward, leaving an unusual calm over the terrain. The clouds shifted, allowing the beaming moonlight to pierce. The river bend was fully exposed for the briefest moment, revealing strange shapes at the ford.

Hermain paused, squinting into the darkness. He usually had little difficultly seeing at night, but the cloud cover and rain had limited his distance. It would take a few moments for his eyes to adjust. Something didn't look right. But he couldn't make out what it was he was seeing.

The moon glow reflected off the water, illuminating every detail perfectly. A handful of dalari had gathered at the ford. They clearly hadn't crossed. If anything, they were doing the same thing he'd intended. Hearing the army moving behind him, he saw the whites of their eyes. The dalari knew they were there.

"On your guard! We've got dalari scouts!" Hermain reached for his sword, hearing the swish of a bow string. Three pops shot pain throughout his body. Glancing at his chest, he noticed feathered shafts protruding. Weakness overcame him. Robbed of strength, he dropped his sword and fell to his knees. Tumbling sideways, he felt the freezing waters wash over him. And as quickly as it had happened he was gone, swallowed by the black.

The army roared to life, charging the band of scouts. Arrows flew between the two forces, shot in the dark. An occasional arrow found its mark, dropping one side or the other. The muddy ground and moving clouds made it difficult to anticipate movement.

Falling back, the dalari scouts clung to the riverbank, hoping to find a place to escape the army. They had speed on their side. The army would move much slower than their few. But trying to outrun them would be a dangerous chance. They didn't know how large the force was. If they headed north that would lead the enemy straight toward the camp. That was unacceptable. Better they die here than allow the enemy to trail them back. Crossing the river was to only option, but chances for that were dwindling by the moment.

The dreualfar pressed onward, closing in. It wouldn't be long before the dalari would run out of room to flee. The cliff face wasn't easily climbed, and the risen waters were surely covering the canyon pass. They had them on the run. It was only a matter of time before they could be captured or killed.

Captain Vaniar rushed toward the front line. At least ten of his men had fallen to the dalari arrows. That was unacceptable. Bringing his sword across, he heard the wooden shaft snap and fly off course. A few seconds later and he would have had to pull an arrow from his chest. "Close in, you bastards! Deploy the left flank. Don't let 'em escape into the trees!" He watched several of his men break off, swinging wide around the left side. If they could close quick enough, the dalari would be trapped between the rocks, the river, and him.

Morning light was just beginning the crest the mountain face overlooking the battle. Dense clouds of fog rolled in off the raging river, cloaking the area in a blanket of white. Bodies littered the ground, sprawled where they had fallen.

Vaniar ran his blackened fingers through his overgrown beard, staring intently into the fog. He wasn't sure how many remained alive, if any. It'd been nearly an hour since the last arrow fell. That meant the enemy had either exhausted their supply, or they were waiting for something. He scanned the left flank, seeing his men in position. It was unlikely the dalari were foolish enough to expend all their arrows. That meant anyone seeking to approach was walking to an early grave. But a few spare arrows were no match for a horde of crushing soldiers. Throwing his fist into the air, he silently called his men's attention. Gesturing, his fist shifted into a blade and he signaled forward.

The dreualfar company roared to life, charging into what was left of the mist covered riverbank. Screams and sword slashes echoed from the cloud.

Calmly marching forward, Vaniar stepped into the fog, able to see a short distance ahead of him. It seemed he was right. A few of his men lay dead from well-placed arrows, but his command wasn't flawed. The majority of the dalari laid among his fallen soldiers, cut down from the swords of his men. But a few remained alive. And better yet, they had the dalari in custody.

Vaniar marched to the head, finding the highest-ranking soldier he could. "Sergeant Grunil. Congratulations, you're the new lieutenant. How many were you able to claim?"

The newly promoted lieutenant snapped to attention hearing his name. "All but three fell during the battle, Sir. This one here has the insignia of an officer." Grunil dug his heeled boot into the captured dalari's back, forcing him into the dirt.

Captain Vaniar knelt beside the exhausted dalari. "What's your name?"

Lieutenant Talaek glared his rebellion at the empowered captain. Spitting a mouth full of blood at him, he refused to speak.

Vaniar stood as tall as he could, demanding the attention of those around him. "Lieutenant Grunil, why did you lie to me?"

"I'm sorry, Sir. I'm afraid I don't understand."

"You said there were three survivors. Why do I only see two?" Without pause, he stabbed his sword into the prone dalari's back, glaring his disapproval at his new lieutenant.

"My apologies, Sir. It won't happen again!"

"It better not. Bring me the next one."

Grunil signaled toward the cliff face.

Two dreualfar marched into view, dragging a bound dalari. He wore dirty green leather, trimmed in brown. Even for a scout, he was dressed like a noble. One of the dreualfar carried a broken bow of matching color and an empty quiver. They dropped him in front of the captain, taking guard on either side of him.

Vaniar stared at the wounded dalari for a long moment before speaking. A steady flow of blood ran from his left eyebrow. He'd taken a decent sword slash across the chest, but it appeared as if his armor absorbed most of the blow. What caught his eye the most was a badge hanging from his waistline. It was a gold and black trident set into a shield and stitched to a thin piece of blackened leather, much like that of skin. "And just who the hell do you think you are? You don't look like any scout I've seen."

Demetrix stared intently at the dreualfar commander. He didn't know enough to give anything important away, but it was good to remain quiet either way. There was no sense in forfeiting a potential advantage he might have if they thought him more important that he really was.

Lieutenant Grunil jarred the well-dressed dalari in the side. "The captain asked you a question. You'd do well to answer him!"

Demetrix looked over his shoulder at the younger dreualfar. Turning back toward the captain, he spoke in undercommon, "I am Demetrix Dreuslayer. Highlord of Marbayne. You'd do well to release these men and I. Once my brothers hear of your abduction, I can promise there won't be any place to hide."

Vaniar felt a smile on his face. He found it strange this dalari knew how to speak his tongue, broken as it was. It seemed wherever he learned it, they clearly hadn't mastered the dialect. "Dreuslayer! Marbayne! I've never heard of you, or your brothers. I doubt I have much to fear. Though I do find your warning amusing. Who would have ever thought to name a city such? Tainted beware. That's clever." Vaniar brought his fist down, feeling the dalari's jaw crack beneath his knuckles. "Secure them to the others. We'll learn more once we reach the Twenty-First Division."

Chapter VI
Stolen Magics

Raising the flap to the outside world, morning rays of sunlight assaulted his eyes. Gareth looked around the bustling city camp, surprised by how well adjusted these soldiers had become. They appeared as if they weren't currently in the middle of a war. Life was simple. They went about their lives, day in and day out, seemingly oblivious to the threat right outside their warded borders.

Such a thought was clearly an illusion. He knew full well these men and women were aware of the danger. They simply chose to focus on life rather than the prospect of death. It was an admirable outlook, if somewhat foolish in his opinion.

Reaching into the sky, Gareth stretched his back. He'd grown accustomed to the comfort of a soft bed. The canvas cot he'd been allowed to rest on, while comfortable for what it was, left him tense from the firm pressure it applied. He found it odd. The tent he and his brothers had been granted during their stay had been magicked, making it nearly as nice as their keep back home. What should have been little more than one medium sized sleeping quarter became a fair sized single level house, complete with three separate bedrooms, a fully furnished common room, a study, and a privy. If he hadn't been impressed by the few other tents he'd visited, he certainly was now. It was no surprise they were able to house ten thousand strong in such a small area.

Marbayne's population was just over half that, and the land was nearly twelve times the size. If he was into magic, it'd be good to learn how they cast the spells. Or at the very least, it'd be nice to take a few of these tents with them.

Scanning the massive camp, Gareth memorized the layout. He locked eyes on a blacksmith's forge across the road and slightly diagonal on the left. To his immediate right, a small turbine was set up beside a thin structure. If he had to guess, it was a miniature windmill, grinding grain into flour.

Looking across the city-camp, he recognized several of the tents for what they were. This place was so much more than he'd initially thought. Then it was little more than a large camp. But now that he'd been here a few days, it had everything he'd expect to find in the grandest of cities. And it was a fraction of the size.

Seeing the tavern he'd visited a few days prior, he started that way. He wasn't a part of this war. And while he desperately wanted to limit the number of dreualfar this area held, he knew it impulsive to go into battle alone. And contrary to popular belief, he certainly wasn't a fool. A familiar figure stepped into his peripheral vision. Reacting on instinct alone, Gareth spun around, his hand locked on his cutlass and ready to draw the blade.

Trendal stared upon him, unflinching. A mild smirk was fixed upon his face. It reminded him of the cocky nature Ravion had displayed over the years. Hands folded in front of him, the dalari captain stood tall and proper, as if he had some vital information to convey. "Master Gareth, I wondered if I might be able to have a moment of your time?"

"So long as I'm stuck here, all I've got is time. What do you want?" Gareth locked his blade back into its sheath and released his grip.

"As I'm sure you're aware, a few days ago we dispatched a small group of scouts to a particular region south of here. It's our plan to move the camp in the coming days as we've been here too long already. The enemy is beginning to reference our location. But to undergo such a large task, we have to ensure the way is clear. We want to avoid any unnecessary encounters during the trip. As I'm also sure you're aware, your friend, Demetrix was one of the scouts we sent on this mission. I'm reluctant to say, they should have been back yesterday. While I can't say if they remain alive or not, I urge you to keep hope until we find out one way or another. I'm leading a team after them today and I thought, considering your attachments, you and your friend, Ravion, would like to accompany me."

Lost in the words, Gareth felt his rage build. He'd been looking for a reason to slaughter the dreu, not that he needed one, but now that he had one it was going to be a bloody afternoon. "Give me a moment."

Trendal nodded, holding his position.

Gareth turned and marched the few steps toward his temporary lodging. Stepping inside, he marched through the common room and toward the room Ravion had claimed their first night. Lifting the flap, he stared into the near empty chamber. The only evidence of occupation was Ravion's pack resting on the cot, seemingly untouched. Turning, he made his way back outside. Trendal remained where he'd been standing. "I'll go with you. Ravion hasn't been himself the past few days. I fear he won't be joining us."

"Understood. We depart the west gate at noon." Trendal spun gracefully on heel and marched toward the city center.

Dark blood splattered the leafy underbrush of the dense forest. The morning light made the soupy fluids stand out in contrast against the glossy green leaves and dull brown limbs.

Ra'dulen dropped the withered husk. It cracked, impacting the ground. Glancing at the others littered about the forest floor, he sniffed the air in search of more. To his displeasure, he was all alone. Inspecting his hand, it continued to shake. These few dreualfar weren't sustaining him. He needed something stronger. Something with magic. Taking a deep breath, an unsettling calm overcame him. He knew where to get what he needed. The hard part was going to be reaching it without Gareth getting in his way. Closing his eyes, he envisioned the path to camp.

The magics swirled around him, twisting reality for the briefest moment. Opening his eyes, he was standing on the path, just outside the hidden city-camp. Stepping between the thick, vine covered trunks of two large trees, he was standing at the southern edge, overlooking the makeshift city.

Marching toward his purpose, Ra'dulen snaked through the roads and between tents until he saw what he'd been looking for. Glancing around, realizing nobody was paying attention to him, he stepped through the entrance and found himself standing in a rather large room of dalari.

They were each laid out on individual cots, covered in thick, green woolen blankets. The majority were asleep, but a few appeared cognitive of his presence.

Ra'dulen looked around the triage tent, searching for anyone who watched over the sick and wounded. Seeing none, he approached the closest conscious dalari. Taking position beside the man, he stared into him. "Why are you here?"

The dalari man had an aged look about him. He faintly stared up at the visitor, eyes heavy despite all the sleep he'd gotten in the past few weeks. "Arrow to the chest." A hoarse cough escaped, exhausting him further.

"Don't they have healers capable of helping you?"

The soldier shook his head. Too feeble to speak further, he pulled at his blanket, revealing his bare chest. The wound was festered and yellow around the edges. Black veins expanded in all directions, stretched out across his chest and wrapping around his sides.

"Poison? Do they not have an antidote?" Ra'dulen asked, glancing at the others, starting to take notice of his presence.

Coughing again, the wounded soldier pulled his blanket back over him and fell limp.

"Don't worry. I believe I can help." Ra'dulen extended his hand over the unconscious man's chest. Pulling at the forces within, he watched the wispy strands collect and move toward his throat. It began to escape, slowly at first, bubbling out like steam over a boiling pot. Ra'dulen pulled the strands, taking them into himself. This was stronger, purer than anything he'd found in a while.

The tremors inside him began to subside, leaving a calm and clear resolution. Watching the last bits of blue and black smoke escape, Ra'dulen pressed his fingers against the dalari's juggler. His pulse was weak, but he was still alive. Pulling the blanket down, he inspected the wound. It was closing. The black tendrils were gone, allowing what appeared to be a clean wound to seal.

Turning around, he saw four others staring at him. He was already feeling better. If only he could get it to last for a while this time.

"Who else wants to be healed?"

Mild drizzle made the early evening gloomier than usual. The sun was half visible on the horizon, preparing to retire to the night. The last bits of orange glow illuminated what appeared to be a fork in the distance.

Gareth wandered along behind Trendal and the few others he brought with him. It had been a long and uneventful journey. Not so much as a sprained ankle had granted excitement since they'd set out. Now here they were, out in the open, stranded in the middle of nowhere with night falling upon them.

Trendal stopped at the fork. Kneeling down, he inspected the imprints in the mud. The constant rain had washed away much of the evidence of traffic, but this road was teeming with signs of movement. "I can't make out which set belongs to who. But I'm certain they came this way. It looks like they went to inspect the ford. More than that, a considerable number crossed this point a few days ago. This way." Trendal jumped to his feet and took off at a much quicker pace.

The river roared through the landscape, creating a constant echo in the distance. It was clearly higher than usual, though evidence of its normal level was lost beneath the surface.

Gareth approached the captain, stopping a few steps behind him. A slender wooden shaft caught his attention. Stepping off the wide trail, he reached into the matted grass and plucked an arrow from it. Spinning it in hand, he recognized the fletching. The head had been broken off, and a black stain clung to the splintered grain.

"This belonged to Demetrix."

Trendal scanned the arrow, his vision trailing off in search of something else. "They were discovered here. A large force pursued them east. I'll bet we find many more arrows between here and there." Without another word, the dalari captain darted along the riverside. He pointed to a mound of dirt. And then to the bark of a leaning tree.

Noting the areas the captain had pointed out, Gareth saw remains of arrows, notched cuts from bladed weapons, and the occasional scrap of torn cloth. A battle clearly took place here. But where were the bodies? A battle such as this would have yielded at least a few. "Anyone else find it strange we haven't seen any bodies? Even if scavengers dragged them off, there should at least be a few signs of fatalities."

Trendal slowed, keeping his eyes on the trail before him. "You're not wrong. I'd imagine any bodies would have been dumped into the river. If it's been raging like that for more than a week, there's no telling where they could have ended up."

Reaching the shadow of the cliff face, Trendal stopped. "They made a stand here." He reached down, pulling something from the trampled weeds. The carved wood was wrapped in decorative, thin leather and bound together by thick, green sinew. The two broken halves were joined by a single, braided and waxed string.

Trendal gathered the broken bow, turning to hand it to Gareth. "I believe this belonged to your friend."

Gareth stared at the ruined weapon. Anger flooded him, but there was something else keeping it from boiling over. He felt loss. Like a void had opened inside him allowing his rage to siphon off to less dangerous levels. "He was my brother!" Reaching out, he took the broken bow, certain of its owner. Pressing the two halves together, he wrapped the string around it, tying it into place. Stuffing it into his pack, he glared at the surrounding landscape, searching for any evidence that Demetrix was still alive.

"We'll make camp here. In the morning, we'll inform Kashien of what we've discovered."

Tormented screams echoed through the night, removing any possibility of sleep. Demetrix couldn't help but wonder if that was by design. Keeping your prisoners exhausted prevented them from having the strength to revolt. It also weakened their minds, making them more susceptible to interrogation. He stared across the barred cell to the others littering the room. It was unclear how long they'd been here. But one thing was certain, they didn't look well.

Aside from starving, their features were sunken and pale. What appeared to have once been tanned skin of various shades was now alabaster. Even their hair was leeched of its color. Something dark had been done to these few. Adjusting his position, he realized his backside had gone numb from the hardened floor. Unable to get comfortable, he slowly stood, trying to ease into the change. It was painful, but it had to be done. Leaning against the barred wall, he looked into the other cages about the room. All the humans were grouped into one. They didn't appear to suffer the same afflictions the dalari had.

Hydralfar were in another cell, equally well aside from their lack of food and attention. One of the other cages housed what appeared to be some variant of orc. They looked like the orcs he'd grown accustomed to in Dalmoura, but these were much larger. Like those of Irayth. Only their skin wasn't marred. And instead of gray, they were brown. He'd seen the dreualfar usher a number of the orcs out several times throughout the day. Shortly thereafter, they'd return with an equal number in their stead. If anything, it seemed they were being scheduled as work horses. Which explained why they were the only cage that was fed several times throughout the day. The others were given a single large bowl of slop per cage to share. It was up to the strongest to fight for food.

Hearing footsteps echo down the stone corridor, Demetrix watched the wooden barricade open, revealing several figures cloaked in shadow. They stepped into the dungeon, illuminated by moonlight beaming through the single overhead window. Now that they weren't crowded in the narrow hallway, he could make out their features. The dalari scout he'd been brought in with stood among the figures, weak and disfigured as the others in the cage were. The remaining group was comprised of two dreualfar and one hydralfar. He recognized one of the dreualfar immediately as the one that brought him in.

"Demetrix Santail. I must say I'm somewhat surprised to find you here."

He didn't recognize the voice, nor the face for that matter, but it was clear the hydralfar knew him. Or at the very least, knew of him. He'd been careful not to state his surname, a tactic picked up from Ravion, which meant this race traitor had to either be familiar with him and his brother, or he was a different threat altogether.

"I'm afraid you have me at an impasse, as I don't recall ever meeting you."

"Let's just say our paths have come close to crossing a time or two. But where are my manners? My name is Jorin'otth. And I must say I'm excited about this unexpected turn of events. If you'd be so kind as to accompany my companions, we can begin."

The less familiar dreualfar unlocked the cage door and pulled it to the side. Guiding the weakened dalari into the cell, he removed the manacles from his wrists and shoved him inside. Turning his attention toward Demetrix, he extended the iron bands, inviting the dalari scout to come willingly.

"Why would I willingly subject myself to whatever torture you have in store for me?"

"It's the illusion of choice. You're coming one way or another. I just thought I'd give you the opportunity to do so freely." Jorin'otth removed the rod from his robe and extended it. It elongated into a runed staff with a glass ornament on top.

A strange sensation washed over him. Realizing he was no longer standing in the cell, Demetrix struggled against his bindings, finding his arms, legs, chest, and head strapped to a rather uncomfortable wooden chair. A metal cap was secured to the top of his head and several sharp points pressed into his skull.

He scoured the room frantically, searching for any sign of what just happened. He could see a number of hoses stretching from himself and secured into several hanging stands. From there they connected to the top of a strange looking machine that filled the majority of the room. The top portion tapered out like that of a grain silo, while the middle was extremely narrow and had a relatively small gap where a fist sized stone rested in a clawed basin. The bottom portion was similar in shape to the top, but instead of one set of hoses, several sets stretched to more hangers. The whole thing looked like some monstrous version of an hourglass. He followed the hoses down to six chairs filled by unconscious humans and hydralfar.

"I apologize for the manner in which you find yourself here. I can only imagine the fear such a realization could have on you."

Demetrix followed the words, finding the hydralfar traitor standing over him. "What the hell's going on here?" He struggled against the binding, hoping he could find a weak strap or loose board.

"You're going to take part in a little experiment I've been working on. I've had relative success thus far, but hopefully, with what I know about you, I'll be able to calibrate the machine to your specific genetics. A miscalculation results in what you saw back in the cell. It still works but I can't get nearly as much out of them. I'm hoping that changes now."

"Let me out of here or I swear by the gods that I'll kill you!"

"Come now, there's no need for idle threats." Jorin'otth gently pricked the side of his neck with a small needle-like instrument. Carefully carrying it to the machine, in hope of preserving the drop of blood clinging to the tip, he let it fall into a tiny metal funnel mounted near the midsection. The single drop rolled down and landed on the top of the stone. Jorin'otth began twisting knobs. Several sprockets began to spin, shifting the alignment of the top and bottom pieces. Checking to ensure they were positioned correctly, he pulled a lever mounted on the side and watched in earnest.

Demetrix felt a crippling pain overcome him. Not even his leg hurt as much as this did. It felt like his insides were being ripped out and twisted apart. Nothing mattered except the pain. He was screaming at the top of his lungs, unaware of what was happening, not that he could have controlled himself even if he was.

Jorin'otth smiled his relief. Unlike the others, Demetrix wasn't reacting physically to the draw. Finally, he'd found the secret. This would allow him to extend his sessions with all the others. Which would yield greater results than the single session he'd been able to achieve in the past. One for one wasn't a bad conversion, but why settle for less when you could get twenty to one? Glancing at the glowing blue stone, he watched the siphoned energies travel down the leads and into the beings strapped in the other chairs. Their skin began to darken, turning almost black. Their base features remained, leaving them trapped between forms. They weren't dreualfar. And they weren't what they were before. They were something else entirely. He'd done it. He'd found the secret of creation. If that didn't make him a god, what would? Proud of his success, he released the lever, allowing the energies to retreat to the closest host.

Marching across the chamber, he went to work unscrewing the probes from Demetrix. The young man had granted him astounding results. He had to ensure he was taken care of. If his next experiment didn't yield the expected results, he'd need to use him again.

Demetrix felt the straps release. He tried to fight. Tried to flee but his body was unresponsive. He couldn't lift a finger to defend his own life. *What the hell was that?* He tried to give the thought voice, but it wouldn't comply.

"He's ready to be taken back to the cell!" Jorin'otth shouted to no one in particular.

Demetrix sat there, wondering how long he'd be paralyzed. A moment later two unknown dreualfar appeared on each side of him. They pulled him to his feet, forcing him to half walk. He lost his balance, finding his weight supported by the vile creatures. Catching movement out the corner of his eye, he saw the newly formed beings begin to stir. They struggled against their bindings, fighting to get free.

How could something so unnatural come from me? The dreualfar pulled him toward the door, removing them from his vision.

Against his will, he staggered from the chamber. Taken back at how large this place actually was. The architecture was familiar in many ways to many of the human cities, but it was much cruder. The stone buildings were large and thick. Jagged edges protruded for the curved walls, and the rough oak framework was exposed where the stone couldn't cover. Were it not for the infestation of dreualfar, he'd guess himself to be in an orc city. Which, considering he'd never seen one, made the entire prospect seem foreign. But there was no mistaking orc craftsmanship when you saw it.

Fire crackled in the hearth, occasionally exploding against the chainmail curtain that shielded the flame from the wooden interior of the magically altered tent. A single lantern rested upon the desk, illuminating the large room brighter than a single lamp should have.

Ra'dulen sat at the desk scribing what little information he'd been able to gather since arriving at the camp a few days prior. The ink flowed perfectly from the tip of his quill. There were no globs or overly dry marks in the text, despite having dipped it only once since he began. Laying the quill to rest, he lifted the thin vellum from the stack in front of him and quickly read what he'd just written.

As best I can tell, these dalari have missed many of the major setbacks my people have endured. I've been careful not to raise too many suspicions, as I don't know what that would mean to their society.

General Kashien has been of great assistance, though I've found it somewhat difficult to gain an audience with him. I suppose that's to be expected considering the war we've found ourselves in, as well as his status. I can't shake the feeling that I've met him before. Though I know I haven't. There's not a face I've seen that's escaped my memory, yet I feel a kinship toward him. Similar in nature to the way I remember feeling about Demetrix before I learned he was my brother. Though I can't allow these thoughts to consume too much of my attention. I'm certain he knows more about this dreu army than he's saying. Each time I've attempted to make a connection between the dreualfar and the abundance of dalari in this camp, he changes the subject or mysteriously has more pressing matters to attend. While I don't miss my position, I must admit it was nice having the authority to demand answers when I needed.

In other areas, I believe I made a mistake by allowing Gareth to see me drain that mage. Had I been thinking clearly, I would have ensured he was distracted when I let loose. I won't make that same mistake next time. I need to find a way to evade him. He's become ever watchful since that day. I count the minutes until he shows up to check on me once again. The entire process has become tiring. If only Demetrix were back. Perhaps he'd provide distraction long enough for me to slip away unseen.

This morning, I did something I'm not particularly proud of. The effects the dreualfar have on me aren't lasting as long as I'd hoped. At this rate, I'll have to drain an entire city to keep the cravings at bay. Though I believe I've found a suitable alternative. The wounded dalari have a higher concentration of magics lying dormant inside them. I've found I can siphon it off, which keeps me sated for the time being, while allowing my victim the pleasure of a healthy body.

It's a bit of an unfortunate trade, but we're both getting something out of it so I suppose I have nothing to regret. I just need to ensure I'm not found out. I have a feeling it would be difficult to explain my actions to anyone asking questions.

Feeling the outside breeze wash through the illusionary room, Ra'dulen waved his hand over the incriminating missive. The ink boiled from the fibers and disappeared, leaving a clean page where the writing had been. Quickly grabbing the quill, he paused, watching his hand shake vigorously. Closing his eyes, he forced himself calm. Drawing the tip against the page, he went to work scribbling notes.

"Ravion?" Gareth stepped through the arched entryway. Seeing the dark scout, he walked to the other side of the table and positioned himself so he could look upon the man with his good eye. Unslinging his pack, he let the weight pull against the overlapped drawstrings binding the top together. Reaching in, he pulled the broken bow from inside. The two pieces were wrapped tightly together by the forest green string that had fired so many arrows.

"What happened?" Ra'dulen glanced from the bow and back to his scribble decorated page. Only now did he realize he'd been writing in eldar. Crossing the ancient words out, he laid the quill to rest and stared at Gareth with empty eyes. He saw the man's lips moving, but his attention was elsewhere. The desire to feed was growing inside him. If only there was a nightking here to kill. That would sate him for at least a week. Breaking his distractions, he found the man's words.

"—was supposed to have returned two days ago. Since we hadn't heard anything, we set out yesterday, in hopes of discovering what happened to them. We found signs of a battle at the river's edge and followed it for a while until it ended at a cliff face. There, we found this. No bodies were present. Though the way the river's flowing, there's little chance we would if they were dumped."

"Maybe he should have exercised a little more caution." Ra'dulen stated coldly.

"Excuse me?"

"You heard me. Both of you throw yourselves into dangerous situations time and time again, with no thought to what your actions might bring. I'm tired of being asked to save your asses every time I turn around!"

Gareth tossed the broken bow onto the desk, watching it scatter the pile of loose vellum. "Okay, first off, fuck you. Nobody asked you to do a damned thing. He's your brother and I thought you'd want to know what happened. I don't know if he's dead. I don't know if he was captured. I simply know he was in a fight and lost his weapon. Secondly, what the hell is your problem? You know what, I don't care. Just figure it out and quit being such a dick!"

Gareth grabbed is pack and stormed from the study.

Chapter VII
A Way Out

The chill of the iron bars felt good against the back of his head. The long hair that had once sprouted from the scabbed and bruised areas had been shaved away, leaving short, patchy stubble in its place. Demetrix closed his eyes, allowing the lingering pounding in his brain to fade in the cold. Hearing the cell door behind him slam open, he pulled himself up and stood. Turning to face the now occupied cell, he waited for the dreualfar guards to leave. He watched the large brown orc stagger across the small cell and take a seat on the simple wooden bench the brute used as a bed.

"Long shift?" Demetrix asked, contorting his mouth to pronounce the orcish words.

"Longer than most." The orc replied, pulling the tattered tunic from his torso, revealing a series of new lashes over old scars. "They push us twice as long since your turn in the seat."

"I apologize for that. I didn't know what they're doing was possible. When I get out of here, I'm going to destroy that damn machine. No one should have that kind of power."

The orc let out an audible scoff. "You speak like any of us get free. Only way out is death."

"I'm sorry you feel that way. I understand you've suffered much in this place. But trust me when I say we will get out of here. My brothers won't leave me to rot."

"You apologize too much. Don't be sorry. Be strong. That the only thing that's going to break you free."

"And when I'm free, I'm going to save your people."

The orc closed his eyes and rotated himself to lay on the narrow plank. "Torok Clan beyond saving. If you find way out, get far away.

The creatures you help create worse than their masters. Don't stay for somethin' already dead."

Demetrix fell silent. Partially because he knew how rare sleep came in this place. To deny it to one he considered a friend was a cruel punishment. What was more concerning was the fact the orc wasn't wrong. In the past month, he'd seen things many would have believed impossible. And now that they weren't, it felt wrong to willingly participate in these experiments. What the hydralfar was doing was a crime against nature. He had to be stopped before this army he was building got free. The dreualfar were bad enough. They had no appreciation for life. To release these— these things upon the world, there would be no forgiveness for that.

Footsteps echoed off the stone floor outside the door. A moment later, the reinforced barricade swung open, revealing the dreualfar captain Demetrix had grown to despise. The captain took delight in his pet. He'd been awarded many honors for the capture of one so useful.

Demetrix watched the dreualfar step into the room and stagger up to the cell. He leaned against the bars, the stench of alcohol radiating from him.

"Can I help you, Captain?" Demetrix hated giving the creature such respect as addressing him by his title, but the captain had revealed a weakness to him. If he could exploit it, he would.

Vaniar looked upon the captive dalari, his head bobbing back and forth in a desperate attempt to focus.

"Wha' maks' 'ew so special?" His words slurred, trying to compensate balance.

"I assure you, I don't know what you mean."

"You sho' up, 'dwessed in such fancy armor, demandin' title and 'sthatus. I bring 'ew here and suddenly 'ew're the most valuable 'pwisoner of 'em all. 'Wha maks' 'ew so special?"

"If I didn't know any better, I believe you to be complaining, Captain. Correct me if I'm wrong, but didn't you receive quite a substantial reward from the hydralfar for my procurement?" Demetrix approached the staggering captain, remaining as docile as possible. There was no sense in allowing the captain to lash out over a foolish error of judgement.

"Andsomely rawrded. Wha's ta' stop me from stickin' a sord in yeur gut? All I see is 'anudder dalari. Nothin' special 'ere."

"I'm sorry you feel that way, Captain. I don't know what delusions you have about me, but I can assure you I've done nothing to warrant such disdain. If you have a problem, I'm certain it's of your own making."

Vaniar grabbed the bar, pressing his face between the gap in them. Vaniar spit his discontent at the imprisoned dalari, "'Ew listen here, dipshit. Everyting' was goin' on fine until you showed up and brought me into this shit. Now I'm stuck here. No command. No station. Little more 'dan one of 'ew, stuck in a cage!"

Feeling the salvia splatter across his face, Demetrix took a large step, stopping just out of the captain's reach. "If that's the case, might I recommend you seek employment elsewhere? I hear the dalari army is seeking informants."

Vaniar lunged into the bars, his arm extended, trying to get ahold of the blurry figure in front of him.

Carefully, Demetrix stepped into the angry dreualfar's reach, allowing himself to be pulled against the bars. Calmly, resisting just enough to keep the captain from biting him, he reached through the cell and secured a dagger stuffed in his waist.

"Guards. A little help here. I'm sure Jorin'otth would be furious if you allowed his prized captive to become damaged!"

Two dreualfar burst into the room. Seeing the powerless captain, they grabbed his arms trying to break his hold.

Quickly, carefully, Demetrix snatched the key ring off one of the guards and stuffed both keys and dagger into his breeches. Reaching up, he squeezed the captain's hand between the thumb and forefinger, forcing his grip to weaken. Breaking the hold, he stepped away from the wall, allowing the guards to deal with the intruder.

Seeing his prize escape, Vaniar swung on one of the guards, knocking him to the ground. Rolling his shoulder, he shook the other off and stormed from the chamber shouting. "Dis isn't ober!"

The guards picked themselves up, looking confused as ever. Ensuring Demetrix was unharmed, they took their position outside the room and sealed the door.

"What all that about?" The orc was sitting up, watching the spectacle.

"I'm sorry for waking you, Drog. I'm afraid it was unavoidable."

"Again, you say sorry. Not sorry. Be strong."

"You're correct, my friend. Get some rest. You're going to need it when we break out of here."

Demetrix held up the ring of brass keys for the orc to see.

Dust flew up around his boots with each step. Rain had been scarce the past few weeks and the blistering heat was drying out the once healthy soil. Marching through camp, Gareth approached the command tent, regulating his steps against the subtle incline. Reaching the flap, he pulled it aside and stepped inside.

Trendal sat at an elegantly carved table, reading what could only be assumed as reports. He didn't bother looking up from the stack of tattered parchment. "Good morning, Gareth. What can I do for you today?"

"I wondered if any patrols were mobilizing. Thought I'd accompany them."

"None today, I'm afraid."

"Tomorrow then?"

Trendal laid the detailed notes to rest atop the parchment and stared intently at the eye-patched warrior. "Every morning, you come to me requesting permission to join my men. Tell me, why are you so eager to go into combat, not that I'm complaining. Consider it a professional curiosity."

"I've spent the better part of my life learning the most effective means of exterminating dreu. It's what I'm good at. The more I kill, the less threat they represent to the people of these lands."

"So, you're not secretly hoping you're going to find your self-proclaimed brother on one of these runs?"

"I can't say that. I know he's alive. We just haven't looked in the right place yet."

"It's been a month already, Gareth. If you've grown so accustomed to the ways of the dreualfar, you should know they rarely keep prisoners that long."

"I'm aware of their methods. I spent some time in their captivity myself. I'm all too familiar with their ways. But I can't give up looking for him. At least until I have proof one way or the other."

"Your devotion is admirable. But I'm afraid no more units will be moving until after the new moon."

"You expect me to wait another two weeks before you'll let me go out again?"

"I expect you to exercise patience. We have a lot to deal with here. After your brother's disappearance, we delayed moving the camp. We couldn't risk having our main force out in the open. That delay has resulted in over usage of resources in this area. Our supplies are low, and with this unexpected heat our water supply is drying up. Not to mention the epidemic that's befallen the wounded. Each day more of them are slipping into a coma like state. It started with the mortally wounded but now the affects have taken hold of ailments as minor as a broken bone. We have to see to our own if we're going to win this war. But I promise you, once the camp has been relocated, you'll have plenty of opportunities to exercise your chosen skill set. Until then I ask that you be patient. I'll call for you if I have any reason to send out a patrol."

"I understand." Gareth turned, hastily making his way from the tent. He wasn't happy about the announcement, but he couldn't condemn the captain for looking after his own. Had he accompanied Demetrix in the first place, perhaps he would have been able to keep him safe. Or at the very least he would have had answers. Rounding the corner, he noticed Ravion looking over his shoulder.

Ensuring he was alone, the dark scout ducked through the entrance to the triage tent and disappeared inside.

Gareth watched for a long moment. *What's he looking for? It's almost as if he's making sure he isn't seen. Like a thief in the night.* Something wasn't right about it. Decided on his course of action, Gareth marched toward the large tent. He was going to see firsthand what Ravion was up to. He clearly wasn't going to share his extracurricular willingly. The two hadn't said ten words to each other since he broke the news about Demetrix. And what few conversations they had were brief and pointed at best.

Approaching the wide flap doors, Gareth reached for the draped canvas. Hearing footsteps on the other side, he paused, seeing Ravion step through the opening. His eyes had a faint glow. The same glow he saw the day they found that band of scouts.

"What are you doing here?" Gareth asked, refusing to lower his gaze. The glow faded, leaving the dalari's usual blue iris' showing.

"Checking on the sick. What are you doing?" Ra'dulen snapped, annoyed that the larger warrior had been following him.

"I saw you go in. Figured I'd see if you wanted to do a perimeter check. Trendal says they're moving the camp soon and won't allow any units to move until that's complete."

Taking a deep breath, Ra'dulen let a calm wash over him. "Thank you for the offer, but I have other duties to attend. Perhaps next time." He stepped past the broad man, narrowly brushing his arm.

"Hey!" Gareth spun around, watching the seemingly younger man pause. "You haven't said two words to me in weeks. And suddenly you're too busy to accompany me? What the hell are you doing every day? It sure as hell hasn't been working toward getting us home."

"I don't own you an explanation."

"You don't owe me a god damned thing. But I'm asking anyway, as someone you once called a friend. What are we doing here? In this camp? There's an army of dreu out there. And somewhere in that army, they have Demetrix. Please tell me why the hell we're sitting on our asses here when we could be out there making a difference!"

"Gareth, perhaps you haven't noticed, but we're not home. We can't rush into battle with our heads stuck in some foolish revenge plot. Back home, sure we did some pretty stupid things from time to time. But we had a system in place. If we got hurt, there was always someone that knew who we were. There was always someone to help us. We don't have that here. And until we do, I'm sorry, but I'm not going to go running head long into battle without a care in the world. I have life altering duties I must see managed. If I fail, the world ends. I get that such a higher purpose doesn't take precedence in that tiny little brain of yours. But my decisions affect more than just me. Maybe you knew what that was like once, long ago. But you lost your family. You failed. Don't drag me down that road with you!" Ra'dulen turned and marched off, his anger risen with the outburst. He wanted to feed again. But Gareth was getting too close. He'd have to give him some time to wander off and circle around. That was the only way he was going to be able to return to triage.

Gareth watched him storm off. His anger burned to his core. But there was more than hatred in Ravion's words. What he said had one purpose. And that was to cause pain. This was an attack unlike any other. Gritting his teeth, Gareth watched his once friend fade from sight. Hearing that familiar ringing in his ears, he felt his power grow.

His fist trembled, barely able to restrain the forces inside him, begging to be released. He wanted so badly to let them loose. But restraint was what was needed here. If he let go, this would certainly be Ravion's last argument. His once friend clearly had some issues. Killing him wouldn't fix that. Taking a deep breath, he let his rage simmer. It was a good thing Ravion hadn't stopped. He needed to cool down and seeing the pompous ass the man had become wasn't going to let that happen.

"Wake up!"

Demetrix slowly opened his eyes, seeing the guards standing outside his cell. Glancing at the orc in the cell next to him, he gave a gentle nod, hoping his message was received. Pulling himself to his feet, Demetrix approached the door and turned around. Carefully, he rolled the waist band of his twill breeches, ensuring the hidden dagger would stay tucked away.

The door clicked and squeaked open. The two guards stepped inside to secure the prisoner. Forcefully pulling his arms into place, they locked the manacles around his wrist and yanked him around to face the entryway.

Demetrix felt the cold iron against his flesh. Relaxing his arms, he let the guards drag him into position for transport. The dense stone was uncomfortable against his bare feet, but that was the least of his concerns. Stealing another glance to the only friend he'd made in this place, he was relieved to see Drog nod his understanding.

The guards led the way, guiding him along the dark corridors by the short chains attached to him. They rounded the corner and took him down a flight of stairs, through the wooden door of the stock house. In minutes, they were marching through the courtyard.

The chilled evening air passed through his loose garments with ease. Aside from the extremely light wind break, he may as well have been wearing nothing at all. The muddy ground squished between his toes as he walked, feeling small rocks jab into the bottom of his feet. Approaching the machine hall, Demetrix looked the wooden and steel contraption outside the large stone building. Several orcs were chained to a series of wooden beams, connected at the center on a pivot. They briskly made their way around, completing revolution after revolution.

The ground was worn down nearly a foot from where they'd been walking circles around the guided device. From what his orc friend had told him, the dreualfar were using them to power the machine. It had to be in constant motion, otherwise it couldn't generate enough energy to complete the transfer. If nothing else, that was reason enough to free the orcs. If the dreualfar couldn't power the dark device, they couldn't create any more of the abominations.

The dreualfar guards led him to the reinforced door at the center of the large wall. Several hoses passed through the upper levels, where the stones had been knocked out. Opening the door, they pulled him inside.

As much as he hated being hooked to the machine, and what the dreualfar were doing with the prisoners, it didn't do any good to fight. If anything, he needed to conserve his strength. If everything went according to plan, they wouldn't have the chance to use it on him ever again. Demetrix approached the wooden chair where he'd sat many times before. Carefully, he reached into his waistline and unrolled the top band, securing the dagger. He positioned the blade against the underside of his arm and turned to take his seat, hoping the guards didn't notice. Feigning defeat, plopped down, aided by his guides.

The guards quickly strapped the leather bands. Placing the iron skull cap over his shaved head, one secured the chin strap while the other tightened the pointed screw protruding through the device. Ensuring he was secure, they left.

Demetrix watched the two dreualfar leave. Jorin'otth didn't want anyone else in the room while the machine was active. It made it impossible for anyone but him to operate it. What better way to preserve oneself than being the only one capable of performing the job? Testing his binds, Demetrix was certain they were secure. But he had to check. The chair was extremely uncomfortably, but he'd grown to expected such. Keeping his left arm pressed against the wooden arm rest, concealing the dagger, he slowly walked it closer to his fingers. It needed to be ready when the time came.

Demetrix waited impatiently. Usually the hydralfar was delivering some kind of over-inflated monologue by now. Something was wrong. He'd never been left completely unattended before. Jorin'otth was always awaiting his arrival. Come to think of it, none of this seemed right. The six chairs resting on the other side of the room were empty. What were they going to do with him if not make more of the vile hybrid creatures? Demetrix worked the dagger into his grip and began sawing at the strap around his wrist. He'd have to be careful. Not only was he chancing cutting himself, but if the hydralfar saw the dagger, his hopes of escape were gone. And by extension so was Drog's. The orc had no way of knowing if the escape was compromised. To fail meant granting the orc's execution.

The door swung open revealing a familiar figure.

Captain Vaniar stepped into the torch lit room. A sadistic grin showed through his unkempt facial hair. Slowly walking toward the restrained dalari, his intentions became clear.

Demetrix pulled against the cut binding hoping it would break. He had little chance of defending himself against whatever the vile captain had in store for him. To his dismay, the leather held strong. Pressing his arm against the blade, he felt the metal bite in. A little pain was worth hiding the stolen weapon.

"I guess you're not so special now. Poor little highlord, trapped and all alone. I'll bet you've already begun to wonder what's going to happen to you tonight."

"The thought crossed my mind. Where's Jorin'otth?"

"The general's pet was called away. It's a shame really. You should have known better than to attempt an escape. I can't help the fact that you had to be put down during the fight."

Demetrix squeezed the dagger. *Does he know? Did Drog betray me?* Watching the spiteful dreualfar approach, Demetrix flexed his wrist, slowly working the blade. He hoped the movement wouldn't show, but the dreualfar captain was apparently too focused on his vendetta to notice.

Altering his path, Vaniar approached the machine and started turning knobs. "I hear this thing has to be calibrated just right. Otherwise it leaves the host twisted and deformed. I wonder which one of these is best for you?"

The base began to rotate, aided by gears and counterweights.

"Have you ever seen what happens to someone when there's nowhere for the power to travel?"

"I can't say I have. Though I believe you're messing with things beyond your understanding. Do you really think they'll believe I was killed trying to escape when the effects of this machine are as easily identifiable? They'll know how I died and I'm pretty sure someone will tell Jorin'otth the truth."

"That's where you're wrong. Half the guards served under me. The other half know what's best for them. I'll kill you and no one will be the wiser as to how or why it happened. Let's see, if memory serves, it was this one!" Vaniar pressed the lever, watching several bolts of lightning jump from one hose to the next. It traveled down, reaching the iron cap atop Demetrix's head.

The restrained dalari felt his body convulse uncontrollably. Screaming his torment, unable to silence himself, he felt his vision fade in and out. It was too much. Trembling, he felt the tip of the dagger puncture the wrist strap. Finding what little rebellion he could amidst the shocking jolts, he locked his fist around the blade and twisted. The razor-sharp edge tore through the leather and his arm popped free.

"What the— how the hell did you get that in here?"

Demetrix took aim at the torturous dreualfar. He knew his body wouldn't obey him much longer. He was already going numb. Forcing every ounce of will into this one action, he flung the blade at the lone dreualfar. Unsure if it hit or not, his body gave out and he went limp. If this was death it was soothing. The shocking pain left him and his vision slowly returned as a bright white light. Details began to focus. He was in the room, strapped to the chair. Vaniar lay dead at the base of the machine. The dagger had plunged through his hand and locked it against his throat. Taking a deep breath, Demetrix weakly reached across his body, fumbling with the buckle on his other wrist. In moments, he was free.

Pulling himself to his feet, he stumbled, crashing to the stone floor. He had to get his body in check and fast. If the dreualfar discovered him, all would be lost. Crawling toward the machine, he got to his hands and knees. Plucking the blood covered dagger from the dead dreualfar, Demetrix pulled himself up, using the machine as a support. Bracing himself, he leaned over Vaniar and began unbuckling his armor. He'd need it if he was going to fight his way out. Pulling the armor on, he adjusted the straps and positioned the dreualfar's sword. It wasn't nearly as comfortable as his own, but there was little chance he'd ever see it again.

Looking around, Demetrix knew what he had to do. He grabbed hold of Vaniar's legs, weakly dragging the dead captain across the rough floor. Reaching the chair, he lifted him as best he could and strapped him in place. Laying the cap atop his head, he rushed to the other chairs. The hoses were too short to reach Vaniar, but perhaps he could put them in the machine.

Testing their reach, he wedged the six skull caps into the center cavity and removed the blue stone resting upon the pedestal. The fist sized stone glowed from his touch, granting him a strength he didn't know he possessed. While he didn't know what it was, it was clear the dreualfar didn't need it in their possession. Stuffing it between the layers of armor, he wrapped one of the hoses around the lever and began to pull. The lever slowly moved and sparks began to jump from one hose to the next. Tying it off, Demetrix moved as far from the machine as possible. He wasn't sure what was going to happen, but it was a good idea to stand clear if it exploded.

A loud grinding echoed from the center and the wedged caps began to glow a bright red. Lightning jumped from one hose to the next. The smell of burning flesh filled the room as Vaniar's corpse burst into flame. The hoses pulled tight, straining against the metal hangers holding them off the floor. One by one they broke free, getting sucked into the center of the machine. Growing louder, a vibrant glow grew between the two large funnels.

Demetrix shielded his eyes, unable to look at the bright light any longer. Taking shelter beside the wall, he watched the machine spin faster and faster, ripping the knobs off by the flailing hoses protruding from the center cavity. It was coming apart piece by piece. And suddenly, the entire device exploded, sending large pieces in all directions.

Picking himself up from the rubble, Demetrix noticed the far wall had been blown out. He knew he had to move fast. The dreualfar were certainly going to come and inspect the disturbance and it was best they believe the corpse in the chair belonged to him.

A large explosion shook the walls, sending a blinding light through the small overhead windows. Drog stood from his bench. That had to have been the signal Demetrix told him to wait for. Grabbing the ring of keys from the pile of straw he'd used clean his back side, he reached through the iron bars and stuck one of the keys into the lock. It wouldn't budge. He tried another, and another. Finally, the lock clicked and the door came open. Drog returned to the bench he'd used as a bed longer than he could remember. Flipping the aged wooden seat to its top, he slammed his meaty foot into one of the legs, breaking it free.

Securing the makeshift club, he made for the exit. The outer door had a different style lock than that of his cell. Finding the one key different than the others, he stuck it in the hole and twisted. The lock clicked. He was fortunate in the fact that he and Demetrix were the only two prisoners kept in this room. They were considered high priority compared to the rest. Demetrix for his usefulness in attuning the machine and him for being the chieftain's son.

His father died the day the dreualfar invaded. But so long as he was alive, the orcs would obey their captors. If that leverage was lost, they'd have a full-on revolt on their hands.

Drog was surprised to see the guards weren't at their post. Perhaps the explosion drew more attention than desired. If that was the case, Demetrix would need help. The orc ran down the corridor and skipped the stairs two at a time. Reaching the lower level, he cautiously peeked outside the wooden barricade. The dreualfar were surrounding the ruined building. Flames bellowed from the wooden supports and the generator wheel was broken, one half lying in the dirt while the other hung several feet in the air. At least two of the orcs appeared to have been killed in the explosion. Such was unfortunate, but there was no avoiding it. Closing the door, Drog turned and made his way down the first-floor corridor. Finding the mass cells, he stepped inside.

A lone dreualfar stared at him in confusion, resting against a small wooden stool.

Raising his makeshift club, Drog charged the unsuspecting dreualfar. He brought the jagged wood across the creature's face. Its neck cracked from the impact and it flew across the room, slamming into one of the empty cells.

"Drog?" One of the orcs questioned, pulling herself to her feet.

"We getting out of here. Dreualfar not take our home any longer!" Drog rushed to the cell and fumbled through the keys, finding the right one.

Opening the door, four orcs stepped out and grabbed anything they could use for weapons. Drog looked at the remaining humans and dalari. Only a few of each remained, having been lost from the experiment or corrupted and moved to the training block. Weighing his options, he quickly unlocked the cells and turned to join his brethren. "We kill anything that not friend!"

The orcs grunted their agreement. Charging out the door, they made for the entrance. War cries echoed in the night as the small band of orcs descended upon unprepared dreualfar.

Drog slammed his club into the nearest black-skin, launching the creature from its feet. Continuing through, he ran for the broken generator. He wrapped his large hands over the tiny keys and went to work unlocking the shackles on his remaining brethren.

Demetrix climbed through the hole in the wall. He was relieved to see the orcs in combat. That meant Drog had believed him and there was a chance at escape. Seeing one of the dreualfar just ahead of him, he drew the polished, yet neglected scimitar and drove the blade deep into the creature's spine. It let out a yelp and collapsed. Withdrawing the blade, he searched out his next target.

Morning light crested the tree line surrounding the besieged orcish city. Smoke and dust rose from the destroyed structure. Flames spread to the broken generator and onto the next building. Several dead and dying dreualfar laid in the dirt covered streets, bleeding from various wounds. A number of the orcs had fallen. And a few of the humans had escaped and taken up arms against their oppressors.

Demetrix made his way around the rubble and into the large building opposite the machine hall. Stepping through the door, he froze, lost in the sights before him. Nearly a hundred of the black-skinned hybrids stared at him from their overcrowded cages. Several bodies laid dismembered at their feet, gore and bone displayed beneath them. If he didn't know any better, they'd resorted to cannibalism and picked off the weakest of their number.

The creatures watched him intently, hunger in their eyes. Not one made the slightest movement in the dark chamber.

The sight sent a chill down his spine. Not so much as a blink could be seen among the imprisoned army. Just thousands of glowing, green eyes staring blankly from the dark, locked on his every move. He could feel their desire. They'd tear him to pieces if they had the chance.

Allowing their existence was too dangerous. There was only one thing he could do. But how? Looking around the room, he noticed the torches mounted on the walls. A decent sized pile of straw lay beside the door, used as matting for the cells. A stack of barrels rested against the far wall. A plan came to mind.

Marching across the room, Demetrix stabbed the blood-stained dagger into one of the casks. Retracting the blade, he sniffed identifying it as oil. It wasn't enough to burn them alive. He'd have to bring the entire structure down atop them and hope it was enough weight to crush the cages. One by one, he wheeled the barrels around the room, placing them as close to the wooden supports as he could get. Spreading the straw over the floor, he poured oil from the open cask, making a trail to the door. Securing one of the unlit torches, he located a flint and steel and sparked it a few times until it flared to life. Letting it catch fully, he took position at the entrance. "I know none of this was your fault. If anything, it's mine and I'm sorry you have to pay for my mistake. I hope you're able to forgive me."

Demetrix tossed the burning torch into the oil-soaked straw. The flame travel across the room increasingly fast. Unable to look upon the blank faces a moment longer, he stepped out the door, listening to the first cask explode.

In minutes, a heavy, black smoke rolled from the rafters and the roof ignited. Not so much as a scream echoed from inside the burning structure. Just the roaring fire and occasional pop of a cask.

Demetrix watched the building collapse in on itself. A large explosion erupted from within, sending a wave of energy over him. For the briefest moment, a sense of dread settled in his stomach. Shaking it off, he watched his mistake burn away. The city belonged to the orcs once again. And that meant he was free to return to his brothers.

Chapter VIII
The Clash of Titans

You need more! Take it! It's yours! Get up and take it! Now!
Ra'dulen's eyes shot open. He was lying on the elegant cot in his
sleeping quarters. A cold sweat clung to his forehead. Sitting up, he
glanced around the room, uncertain what he was looking for.

Fire danced from the hearth on the far side of the large chamber. It
provided little more than a faint glow in the darkness.

The whispers crept back into his mind. *You can smell it. All that
power in the air. It's stronger than anything you've encountered in this
world. But you're not strong enough for it. Not yet. You know what you
have to do. It's time to do it.*

He wasn't sure what time it was, though from the feel it had to be
early morning. He'd grown accustomed to the lack of sleep at some
point in the past couple years. It was a weakness. One his enemies could
exploit. The less he had, the stronger he was. Pulling himself to his feet,
he grabbed his tunic from the back of the chair and tossed it over his
shoulders. Quickly pulling his boots on, he grabbed the curved
longsword resting beside the bed and secured it to his side. Time had
come. It was time do what no other could.

Approaching the door, he pushed the flap aside and stepped into the
living quarters. To his surprise, Gareth was sitting in the thick, leather
bound chair, watching the heatless fire dance in the pit. Quietly, he
made for the door. He had nothing to say that hadn't already been said.

"We've been friends a long time. I don't know what's happened to
you and I've reached a point that I no longer care. That being said, if our
friendship ever meant anything to you, I have one question to ask.
Where are you going?" Gareth refused to look away from the flickering
flame.

"Out." Ra'dulen stepped through the doorway and disappeared outside.

The sun was just beginning its rise. A distant orange glow eating away the shadows of the night, illuminated the vibrant details of the canvas tarps and wooden posts of the massive camp. The streets were barren, only a few guards within sight, finishing their nightly patrols.

Ra'dulen scanned their positions. He'd spent the better part of a week memorizing their schedule for moments such as this. Judging from the sun's rise, there would be a shift change in roughly ten minutes. Once the change happened, he'd have just under a minute to make his way from the south side of the command tent, across the trade square, and into triage without anyone seeing him. That would give him about fifteen minutes before the healers made their morning rounds.

Making his way toward the command tent, he kept watch on the guards. There was little to worry about as far as they were concerned. They were simply a precaution to keep in mind. Gareth on the other hand— He'd become somewhat a thorn in his side. He was too nosey for his own good. Once his task was complete, he was going to have to do something a little more permanent than simply pissing the brutish warrior off. Reaching the back side of the command tent, Ra'dulen paused, awaiting the final minutes for the guards to finish their rounds. Seeing their groggy replacements stagger into the open, prepared for the laborious day that was to follow, he darted down the hill and through the collection of tents at its base. Wrapping his way around the side of one of the long canvas walls, he shot across the street and ducked through the unattended entryway.

Hundreds of dalari rested peaceably in their cots. A few lanterns were staggered here and there, illuminating the large room in a soft, blue light. It was calming and tranquil, as if its purpose was to promote healing as well as provide sight.

Making his way to the center, Ra'dulen spun around, taking in the sights around him. It didn't matter if any of them saw him this time. This would be final visit. Raising his arms, he let the siphoning energies erupt from his fingertips. Strands of energy shot out in all directions. He was connected to all of them, and they to him. He could feel the lingering pain inside each one, fading away into nothing. Wisps of blue smoke pooled in the air, drawn from the prone mass of dalari lying throughout the room. It collected into thick, bulging clouds and floated coercively toward the lone dalari nightking. Pulling the power into himself, he could feel his body growing stronger by the moment. Another minute and all of it, the combined power of this ancient race, would belong to him.

Gareth scanned the streets. Not much was going on aside from the occasional guard making rounds, or the random bird enjoying the morning's light by pecking at the dirt. It was another morning, just like all the rest. So why was Ravion sneaking through camp? Following the shell of the man he once called friend, Gareth was careful not to get too close.

There was no sense in drawing attention to his presence. Ravion was too smart for that. He'd simply alter course and turn the entire escapade into a game of follow the leader. Instead, it was best to keep his distance. Maybe then he could figure out what was going on.

Gareth stopped, watching Ravion pause at the edge of the command tent. He was waiting for something. Seeing the guards break away from their usual paths, he knew it could only be one thing. Shift change. As suspected, Ravion broke into a sprint, charging down the hill toward the collected structures comprising up the trade square. Reaching the bottom, he ducked between two of the smaller tents and disappeared from sight. Gareth thought about following, but from where he stood there was no place Ravion could go without being seen.

A moment later, his old friend appeared out of the other side and ducked into the triage tent. This was the second time Ravion had shown interest in the wounded soldiers. That wasn't coincidence.

Glancing at the fresh-faced guards, Gareth made for the second largest tent the camp had to offer. It was unlikely he'd find himself in their aim for inspecting the large structure, but there was no sense in taking chances, at least not yet. Carefully making his way past the trade center, he approached the sealed door where Ravion had been moments before. His hand hadn't fully extended to move the flap when he felt the hairs on the back of his neck stand on end. Something wasn't right. Cautiously pulling the flap to the side, he stepped through. Visions of the past echoed into sight.

Ravion stood in the center of the room, his arms outstretched, drawing huge clouds of stolen power from the sick and dying around him. It was almost as gruesome as what he'd done to the mage shortly after their arrival. In many ways, this was worse. These people hadn't done anything to him, yet he was draining them. The only notable difference was these victims weren't being drained of life. They were being drained of something else entirely. Unable to look at their unexpectedly blank faces, Gareth clenched his fist. He couldn't watch anymore. Ravion had to be stopped. "Ravion Santail, you've betrayed your people. You've betrayed your brothers. By the laws, set forth by The Order, I find you guilty of crimes against the realm. It's time to answer for them!"

Ra'dulen drew the final strands of energy into himself. Dropping his arms, he let the acquired power find its place. Opening his eyes, he stared across the room at Gareth. "Now's not the time!"

The power infused words boomed into his ears, threatening to drop him to his knees. Glowing, pupil-less eyes stared intently upon him, burning into his soul. Though it was more than just Ravion's. Every pair of eyes in the room was upon him, burning white, silently mocking him. Gareth felt his rage boil. Using it, he formed a shield around himself, deflecting the overbearing powers radiating from their amplified host. Resolved, he envisioned his invisible grip flying toward his friend. If he could stop Ravion, maybe he could figure out what he'd done here.

Ra'dulen felt the unseen attack headed toward him. The feeble attempt brought a mild smirk to his face. He had no time for such games. Enwrapping the energies around himself, he vanished in a glow of orange. The watching eyes of his victims snapped shut with his departure.

Gareth felt his grip snag something unseen. He didn't know what. It was firm, but it wouldn't last long. Placing his fingers against one of the drained dalari, he couldn't find a pulse. That either meant they were all dead, or it was too weak to feel. Either way, he didn't have time to determine which. Following his psionic fist, he saw a thin sliver of orange floating harmlessly in the air, trying to close around the invisible hand wedged in its seam. Forcing his will into the invisible hand, he pulled the tear apart, opening what appeared to be a window into the outside world. In fact, it seemed to be right outside the door. Taking a deep breath, Gareth stepped through, letting the hand dissipate. As expected, he was standing right outside the triage tent, not ten feet from where he'd been moments before. Searching the streets, he spotted the dark-dressed dalari, disappear behind one of the tents.

Ravion moved at a full sprint toward the west wall. Seeing a stack of wooden crates beside the road, he thrust his hand forward, launching them from this path. They smashed to the ground, spilling their contents into the road. Heads of cabbage, plump gourds, and a number of potatoes rolled across the path. It wasn't much, but perhaps it'd slow Gareth if he pursued. The warrior would die, but not until his job was finished.

Refusing to let Ravion escape, Gareth charged after him. He was less concerned with the produce and more concerned by the dalari in the street working to clean up the mess. He couldn't slow. If he did, Ravion would be out of sight. Picking up the pace, Gareth jumped. He couldn't explain how, or even why, but somehow, he sprang further than he ever had before. It was as if he reached peak height and simply kept going. Hitting the ground, he was surprised at how soft the landing was. His joints didn't feel the impact at all. And best of all, Ravion hadn't gained much ground, though he was naturally faster. If he was going to catch him, he'd have to cut him off.

Several confused dalari watched in earnest. Strange feats were not unheard of, but to see them first hand would have had the elders in awe. The excitement echoed through the streets, drawing more witnesses to the spectacle. Guards studied the racing men, uncertain as to the reason for their escapade.

Rounding the corner, Gareth realized his old friend had gained ground. Nearly ten feet by his estimate. If he didn't do something quick he was going to lose him. "Stop that man!" Gareth shouted, hoping the guards would balance the quo. To his irritation, they turned to look rather than act. Apparently, they were only useful when they weren't needed. The road to Trendal's tent was just ahead. If he was lucky, the captain would hear all the shouting going on outside his door and investigate. "Trendal, something unforgivable has happened. Get Kashien!" The words escaped him before he realized what was happening. More than that, a response echoed in his mind.

"Understood!"

The booming voice behind his ears was more intrusive than an open door in the backroom of a pub. He felt possessed. For the briefest moment, someone had stepped inside his mind and seen everything he kept hidden from the world. Shaking the unsettling feeling off, Gareth pressed on, seeing the dalari captain rush from his chambers in full battle gear. Sprinting as fast as his body would carry him, Gareth reached the gate.

The guards laid on either side of the road, unmoving and pulseless.

Gareth couldn't see any blood, but they clearly weren't responsive. If he had to guess, Ravion did the same thing to them that he'd done to those in the tent. As if his thoughts were heard, their eyes shot open, revealing those frightfully blank eyes he'd seen in triage.

"You'll never catch me, Gareth!" They sounded in unison.

There was no doubt who the message was coming from. Abandoning the possessed bodies, Gareth burst through the gate. A familiar orange glow hovered steps away, fading from view. Out of options, he mentally grabbed the edges and ripped it open. He had no time to think. Action was the only thing that drove him. Diving through the elongated hole in the world, he crashed into the dirt and foliage of the forest floor. Rolling several times, he came to a stop. Slowly picking himself up, Gareth saw his old friend standing on the edge of a large rock. A dark storm cloud rolled in the distance, moving ever closer to them. Getting to his feet, he realized the rock was protruding out over a towering drop off. They were at the edge of a cliff. Silently cursing his fear of heights, he watched the man for a long moment. "What's all this about, Ravion?"

"I wouldn't expect you to understand," Ra'dulen stated coldly, overlooking the rocky bluff. Turning to face the troublesome warrior, he clenched his fist. "Understanding or not, I can't let you stop me!"

Ra'dulen drew his sword with blinding speed. He charged, bringing the sharpened weapon across. A smiled breeched his lips, seeing Gareth had come prepared. There was no pleasure in an easy kill.

Metal on metal rang out. Gareth strained against the crushing blow, holding the attack at bay. It seemed their friendship truly was over. The Ravion he knew wouldn't have done any of this, let alone tried to kill him. Releasing the block, Gareth rolled out of the way and brought his sabre around. It glanced off Ravion sword, but the empowered scout wasn't ready for his second attack. Gareth fist connected, clapping against Ravion's jaw.

Ra'dulen took a step back and adjusted himself. The punch caught him off guard, but it was nothing he couldn't handle. It simply meant he was going to take some joy in this. Lifting his sword, he charged again, aimed to cut the warrior in half.

Seeing the approaching blow, Gareth charged, ready to parry.

The swords rang out, dislodging one another.

A pressure erupted in Gareth's left kidney. Glancing down, he saw a deep gouge in the side of his armor. Had it not hit the small plate as solid as it did and glanced off, it would have been his end. Turning to face Ravion, the scout held a thin dagger at the ready.

"I'm done toying with you. This ends now!" Ra'dulen pulled the energies around him together and launched a black bolt at Gareth.

Knowing he had no way of deflecting or blocking the fatal attack, Gareth fashioned his rage into a shield. The air around him hardened just as the dark energy exploded, blocking his vision. Before he could raise a defense, Ravion was upon him again.

Ra'dulen swiped with the dagger, adjusting his stance for a powerful attack. His sword materialized in his grip and plunged forward. The tip stabbed deep into the shield surrounding his former friend, but it didn't break. Taken back, Ra'dulen tried to identify the magic. His sword should have cut straight through it. But it was unlike anything he'd seen before. Nothing he had could bypass it. That meant it couldn't be arcane in nature.

The dagger's slash glanced off his invisible barrier, but the thrust had a more damaging approach. Gareth saw the tip headed straight for him. It slowed, narrowly stopping an inch from his chest. Out of options, drew his sheathed cutlass and flipped the blade around to knock the sword away from him. His shield was ruined either way. Charging forward, he sent his psychic grip ahead.

An unseen force slammed into Ra'dulen's chest knocking him from his feet. He brought his sword up, deflecting Gareth's downward attack. Rolling to the side, he hooked the bald warrior's leg and pulled it out from under him.

Gareth crashed to the ground, doing his best to keep ahold of his sabre.

Kicking hard, Ra'dulen threw his weight and flipped to his feet. Sword in hand, he readied a final blow. An unexpected power erupted near him, stealing his focus. Glancing toward the forest, an orange line formed in the air.

It spread wide, nearly consuming the entire forest edge. Over a hundred dalari stood in battle formation on the other side. At their head, Kashien, Trendal and several other officers stood side by side, dressed for war. The orange glow faded behind the army, leaving them standing at the forest's edge. The large unit moved in perfect unison, like a well-oiled machine. They rotated as one, horseshoeing out around the embattled warriors. At once, the unit snapped into position, their weapons at ease and awaiting command.

"I see you've brought reinforcements!" Ra'dulen mocked his prone opponent. Seizing the moment, he thrust downward, aimed to kill.

Gareth rolled out of the way, jumping just in time to avoid another swipe. He kicked out, feeling Ravion's knee buckle beneath the blow. Using the opportunity to his advantage, he swung as hard as he could, knocking Ravion's sword out of hand.

The empowered scout stumbled back a few steps, surprised by the loss of his weapon. Wincing his pain away, he stood upright, ignoring his shattered knee. Ra'dulen thrusted his hands toward one another. A deep blue cloud formed between them. Lightning sparked within the translucent surface, growing larger by the moment. Reaching peak potential, the electrically charged ball launched forward, slamming into Gareth's chest. It exploded around him, sending massive bolts of electricity in all directions.

Several of the dalari were launched back, breaking their formation in several places. A few went to work picking themselves up, while others laid where they'd fallen. The scent of cooked meat and charred flesh filled the air.

Gareth felt his body spasm, but something had protected him. Sitting up, he stared his hatred at Ravion. He was little better than the monsters they'd spent so many years hunting. Spitting a mouthful of blood into the churned dirt, he pulled himself up and grabbed his sword from the dust covered rocks. "In all of this you've made one massive error."

"Oh! And what's that?" Ra'dulen summoned another ball of energy.

The storm cloud was moving closer, nearly overhead. Bolts jumped between Ra'dulen's spell and the approaching cloud, dancing back and forth. Each time the bright energy returned darker than before. A darkness grew over the area, blocking out the sun's rays. Bolts of blackened energy danced all around, seen only by their blue outer edges.

Gareth knew he couldn't survive another direct blast. It didn't matter. It was time to end this. "You made the mistake of bringing my family into this!" Throwing his weight, Gareth launched from the dirt, charging the enemy to everything he stood for. Uncaring if the magic crashed into him, he lowered his head and aimed for Ravion's midsection. He had one purpose and that was to end his once friend. If it claimed his life in the process, so be it.

The energy made his hair stand on end. He was surrounded, entangled in the electrifying magic. Slamming his shoulder into the taller man's ribs, an explosion erupted around them, launching him back. He hit the ground, feeling the jagged rocks tear into the leather plates of his armor. A thick cloud of dust made it difficult to breathe. At least that's what he told himself. In truth, his chest was heavy after such a powerful hit. Laying his throbbing head on the packed earth, he closed his eyes. He needed to rest, if only for a moment.

Ra'dulen picked himself up from the dirt. Glancing over, he saw Gareth lying several feet away, stirring from the explosion. Many of the closest trees had toppled, and the majority of the assembled dalari were scattered among the rubble. It was odd they hadn't involved themselves in the fight. Perhaps they wanted to see how this encounter was going to play out. Though he was surprised they hadn't taken greater precautions to protect themselves. None of it mattered either way. He was the strongest dalari in existence. And soon he would rival the gods themselves. Any part the dalari had in his mission had long played out. For all he cared, they could return to wherever it was they were hiding for all the years he needed them. Summoning another bolt of energy, he took aim at Gareth. Perhaps he could finish them all in one final assault.

A dark storm cloud lingered overhead. It had been there since he set out from Drundale that morning. It left a gloom over the area, but somehow, he was able to feel hope.

Demetrix trekked along the trail leading up the cliff face. Nearly fifty dalari followed in his wake, most of them disfigured and drained of will. They walked because they had to, though it was clearly taking its toll. Looking back to ensure they were keeping up, a massive explosion echoed in the distance.

Eyes searching, Demetrix carefully made his way up the treacherous path to the top of the rocky bluff. Confusion and panic gripped him. Gareth was laying in the dirt. His chest moved rapidly, but he wasn't getting up. Behind him, several dalari laid dead or wounded among the shredded tree line. It seemed a few remained unscathed, but those few were busy trying to help the others. Standing in opposition, Ravion's hand glowed a deep blue. He reared back, as if he was going to launch the deadly spell into the group.

Calming himself, Demetrix searched for any sign of outside attackers. What other reason could there be for what he was seeing? Unable to find any, his vision returned to Ravion. Whatever was happening was clearly beyond his understanding.

Ra'dulen smiled at the defeated forces. His spell was ready. All he had to do was release it. A strange sensation reached him. He could taste the power he'd been searching for. It was closer than ever. It seemed the power he'd be tracking had found its way to him.

Glancing to the cliff's edge, he saw Demetrix standing there. An expression of pain and confusion settled on his face. The younger dalari was dressed in black studded leather, seemingly of dreualfar design. He looked as if he'd aged a few years, though he was still remarkably young in appearance, by human standard anyway.

Though his age, or appearance therein, was of little concern. If Demetrix had the power he sought, he'd take it by any means necessary. Turning to face his brother, he felt the spell in his hand dissipate into nothing. Confused, he turned, directing his focus to the dalari army.

Kashien stood at the head of his men, his sword was extended, pointed at Ravion. Remnants of the dark spell retreated into the blade, offering a warning against continued aggression. A magical wall fluctuated behind him, shielding the wounded dalari from further damage.

Ra'dulen smiled at the general's feeble attempt to stop him. It was going to take more than stealing his spell to end his plans, even if he had a magical blade. *Wait! His blade.* Ra'dulen stared intently, unsure what he was seeing. *It can't be!*

If he couldn't use the sword, he'd have to find alternative means.

Ra'dulen summoned the energy around him. It formed into a long and narrow bolt of a purple and black smoke. Growing corporeal, a long spear took form from the raw energies. What should have been a wooden shaft, was instead a glass-like tube, black as night. Bolts of lightning danced inside the hardened exterior like a sprite trying to find its way out of a vial. Ra'dulen marched toward Gareth. This fight was over. He had but to drive the tip into the dreuslayer's heart.

Gareth's strength had fled him. His mind was blank, unable to process what had happened. He was drained, physically, emotionally. The explosion took every ounce of will to keep from blowing him to pieces. Seeing Ravion step into view, memories flashed through in his mind. *You lost your family. You failed!* The echoing taunts made his fists clench in rage. He wasn't going to let it end this way.

"Never again!" Gareth's hand shot forth, locked firmly around the spearhead aimed at his chest. He wasn't finished. Not yet.

Demetrix stared in horror. *What the hell happened while I was gone?* He had to do something. Gareth was going to die if he didn't. But what could he do? He couldn't kill one to save the other. And he couldn't refuse to act. Torn, he charged toward the pair. As if his body made its own decision, he felt the ground shake vigorously.

Slowing to a stop, he noticed the trees were shrinking. No, that wasn't it. It was the opposite. The ground was rising. The earth around Ravion, Gareth, and himself had torn itself away from the forest floor and was hovering in the air, like their own little island away from the rest of the world. Searching for anything that made sense, he noticed his hand, outstretched and locked around the glowing blue stone. He could feel the power within, urging his will into existence.

Searching all around, he was aware of all things. The dalari on the ground, those that were alive and in pain. He took that pain. Those that were dead, he gave life. Even Ravion, he could feel the desires coursing through him, but he couldn't connect to him. There was something else blocking him, something dark and hungry. And he couldn't feel Gareth.

Pain erupted inside, forcing him to return to himself. His leg hurt, it felt like it was broken once again. Stealing a glance, something strange was happening. Okay, not that strange, but certainly noteworthy. He couldn't explain how, or even why, but he could see the magics surrounding him. The barrier containing his wounded leg was weakening, diverted to keep them in the air. The energies inside him were rapidly depleting, and he was had no way to replenish. Not without stealing that which he'd already given. That was unacceptable. There had to be another way.

Ra'dulen glanced up from his target, seeing Demetrix several feet away. But nothing else was in sight. They were on an island, away from all. Nowhere to run. Nowhere to hide. Suddenly, thick vines sprouted from the dirt, entangling around his legs and body. He tried to plunge the spear into Gareth's chest. Tried to finish the job, but the prone warriors hold was too strong. The vines were robbing him of strength.

Gareth saw his moment. Rolling hard, he pushed the spearhead to the side, watching it stab into the dirt where he'd been a moment before. Refusing to give Ravion another chance, he rolled into the spear, knocking it from his grip. The weapon dissolved into the magics it was born from and disappeared. Gareth slammed his weight into Ravion's legs. He felt the empowered scout topple beneath him. Seizing the opportunity, he threw himself atop of his aggressor. The vines swarmed around him, locking him in place. He couldn't move. He was stuck, staring his hatred into the man beneath him.

Liquid trickled from his nose. Pressing his empty fingers to the source, Demetrix saw the bright red blood flowing from him. He strained against the power he was inadvertently releasing. Just a little longer and they'd all be safe.

A gruesome snap echoed in his ears and he crashed to the hovering island of dirt and stone. Refusing to release his hold, he pushed on, feeling his insides quake from the exertion. He'd saved Gareth. Now he had to save Ravion. He watched the vines engulf them both. Neither could move. Which meant neither could kill the other. Feeling a moment of victory, his vision faded. Sapped of strength, his will evaded him and he blacked out.

Weightlessness took its hold. The vines withdrew, retreating into the ground. Gareth crashed into the earth, bits of rock and soil breaking apart beneath him. Still atop Ravion, he stared into the broken man. He radiated defeat. There was just one thing to finish this. Raising his fist, he hardened the air, turning it into a weapon. He didn't have to look to know his psiblade was present. Staring into the glowing eyes of his once friend, he saw those near absent, blue pupils faintly behind the fading glow. They were nearly hidden from sight, but still there. He recognized those eyes. Not the ones of the man he'd traveled with the past month, but those of the man he'd known for years.

Letting his mind travel into them, he saw a child sitting in a world of shadow. Two bodies lay before him, a man and a woman. Gareth didn't have to ask to know these were Ravion's parents. Something beyond his understanding had happened. A shadow flew past him, and another. He wasn't alone in here.

Returning himself to the now, Gareth screamed, releasing his anger in Ravion's face. Enraged, he brought his fist down. The psionic weapon stabbed deep into the earth beside Ravion's head. Another inch and it would have split his skull wide open. Staring into the defeated scout's eyes, Gareth slammed his forehead down, bashing him in the face. Seeing all resistance fade away, he climbed off the unconscious warrior. His body shook from anger. It took everything not to kill him. Gritting his teeth, Gareth picked himself up and marched toward the forest.

Several of the dalari soldiers moved into his path, spears and swords ready to stop him.

"Move!" Gareth demanded, waving his hand. They flew off the path, launched by an unseen force.

Landing roughly on the rocky terrain, they picked themselves up and started after the bald warrior.

"Don't pursue. We have more pressing matters here!" Kashien ordered, approaching the unconscious Ravion.

Levi Samuel

Chapter IX
A Question of Royalty

An eerie silence filled the room. Even the usual sound of crickets chirping outside was absent. Feeling the smooth blankets covering his skin, Demetrix slowly opened his eyes, unsure where he was or how he'd gotten there.

A faint blue glow pulsed weakly against the ceiling, bringing a comfort unlike any other. The scent of pine reached his nostrils, alerting him to his own lack of scent. Patting himself, he realized the stolen armor he'd taken from the dreualfar captain was missing, replaced by thin garments made of silk. His skin was clean and what little hair that remained from his imprisonment had been trimmed and evened.

Taking a deep breath, Demetrix sat up realizing how easily his attire slid across the matching blankets covering the down bed he was upon. Looking around the dimly lit, well-furnished chamber, he froze seeing Kashien at the foot of the bed.

"My apologies, Lord Kashien, I didn't realize you where there!" Hoping to offer the proper respects to the dalari general, Demetrix pulled himself up, feeling every muscle in his body tense in protest.

"Stand down, my friend. You've been through quite enough since we last spoke. We also took the privilege of mending your leg. The damage was quite severe, but we were able to pick up trace elements of the magics used to keep it together. After that it was as simple as reapplying the spell. I was hoping you might be able to answer some questions for me."

Demetrix fell back against the bed, letting the tension in his body return to its less painful state. "I'm in your debt, My Lord. I'll answer however I can."

"Nonsense. It's I that owes you my gratitude. Without you, my men wouldn't have returned and we wouldn't have the slightest idea as to what was happening until it was upon us. Though I'm pleased for your cooperation. I'll try to be brief so you can get your rest."

"Take your time. I've rested long enough and you've shown me more than enough hospitality."

"You did a great service for my people by freeing them from captivity. In some parts of the world such a deed would warrant a life debt. Seeing you cleaned and rested was the least I could do. But, if you'll allow me, I'd like to hear your side of what happened on the scouting run. As I'm sure you're aware, we were going to move the camp. Unfortunately, we couldn't risk such a large endeavor until we were certain the way was clear."

"There isn't much to tell honestly. We were checking the river ford. Learned that it had been salted. Before we could redirect, a unit of dreu came upon us. Truth be told I don't know how we didn't hear them coming. It was storming and there was plenty of cloud cover, yet they found us before we could evade. We fought them off for hours, but eventually our quivers ran dry. It didn't take long for them to overrun us after that."

"Tell me about the prison. My men said they used some kind of machine?"

"One unlike any I've seen before. They used the orcs to generate lightning, which as best I could tell, drained us of life and gave it to the other prisoners. It twisted them into some kind of dreualfar hybrid. They were building an army."

"Were?"

"I destroyed the machine before I left." Demetrix paused, recalling his actions. "I killed their creations, too."

He lowered his head. He didn't want to see the judgment that was sure to be in the general's eyes. There was enough of that in himself. It didn't matter if they were twisted abominations of their previous selves. He'd committed genocide against them and that was unforgivable.

Seeing the young dalari's withdraw, Kashien leaned forward in his chair and spoke in a calm, delicate tone. "I have a fair idea how you feel, but I need you to believe me when I say you did the best you could in an impossible situation. You managed to save your people and the orcs you were imprisoned with. You can't help what the dreualfar did. They have no appreciation for life. Were I in your position, I would have made the same decisions."

"I thank you for the reassuring words, but I'm the one that's going to have to live with my choices."

Kashien took a deep breath and leaned back, interlocking his fingers and laying them to rest on his stomach. "You're not wrong. But for what it's worth, I believe you did the right thing. We have no idea what such an army would have been capable of. But if they were even half as corrupt as the dreualfar, it could have quickly turned the tide of this war to the dreu's favor."

"Exactly. We don't know what they were capable of. For all we know they could have been a peaceful ally. But I never gave them the chance to prove otherwise. I destroyed them while they were caged like animals and unable to flee. I destroyed them because I found them unsettling. Letting them live was a risk I didn't have time to contemplate. They're dead and I'll have to live with that."

"It is possible their minds remained their own, though highly unlikely. The magics it takes to twist someone, as my men described, has a greater impact on the mind than it does the body. And you've seen what it did to the body. Still, I understand how you feel." Pulling himself up, Kashien stood and approached the table resting beside the bed. Reaching into the drawer beneath it, he continued. "Can you tell me a little more about the machine? You said they used the orcs to generate lightning. From what I know about the arcane, it takes a bit more than simple lightning to transfer life from one being to the next. However rare, there have been a few instances where such a thing has been done successfully, though each time there's always been a catalyst between the source and the host. Was there anything like that? This perhaps?" Kashien turned, holding the glowing blue stone so Demetrix could see it.

"Yes, actually. It was in the center of the machine. I thought it was simply a way to focus the energy. I took it, hoping it would slow their ability to build another one. Where did you find it?"

"It was in your hand after you collapsed."

"Collapsed?"

"Yes, you— Do you not recall the fight between your brothers?"

"Fight? I— I remember climbing the cliff face when I heard an explosion. When I reached the top, I— Shit! Where are they?" Demetrix threw the thin blankets off his lap and jumped from the bed. Every muscle in his body strained against him. He wanted nothing more than to relax a while longer. But his brothers needed his help.

"Slow down!" Kashien sat the stone on the table and held his hands out, hoping the young dalari would listen. There was so much to say in such a brief time. "You need to rest."

"With all due respect, Lord Kashien, they were at each other's throats. I need to find them before they cross a line they can't come back from."

"Demetrix, sit!" Kashien's voice raised to a commanding tone. Realizing his own volume, he gestured calm, directed at both Demetrix and himself. Continuing, in his low, reassuring tone, he approached the weakened dalari and placed both hands on his shoulders, "Rest, please. I'll explain everything. Your brother isn't going anywhere."

Stealing a glance at the inviting bed behind him, Demetrix carefully took a seat, letting the tension in his mid-section strain until it found comfort. "You said brother. Does that mean one of them is dead?"

"Not necessarily. Ravion is resting in the next room. Unconscious, more accurately. But there isn't much that can be done for him. At least not until you understand what's happened to him. The other, Gareth if my memory serves, left nearly a week ago. We haven't seen or heard from him since."

Seeing the excitable dalari return to bed, Kashien stepped to the table and grabbed the blue stone once again. "What do you know about our people?"

"Not much I'm afraid. I was separated from my family when I was barely old enough to walk. I didn't find Ravion until about fifteen years ago. Even at that age I didn't know he was my brother until much later."

"I suppose I need to start at the beginning then, again as briefly as possible. Long ago, when this world was new, the gods created the eldar races. There were five sets. The dragons, the elementals, the devonie, the d'zhuni, and the dalari. We were the originals before all other races. In fact, the majority of the other races stemmed from us, the alfar anyway. Orcs and dwarves came from the devonie, and so forth, but that's not pertinent to my story. The eldar races as a whole were equal in all ways, but our forms were frail compared to those of the dragons or elementals, so in return the gods made us the protectors of magic. We were entrusted with the arcane arts. It's that purpose that makes us glow blue. That's the innate arcane energies stored within all dalari. Along with our creation, there were five stones. This—." Kashien held up the glowing blue stone. "—is the dalari stone. It has the ability to influence our kind on a monumental level. Death, injury, magic, nothing is out of the question when it comes to this stone. At least that's the myth behind it. Though I can tell you from firsthand experience that it's powerful. I've seen it one other time in my life before now. I believed it had been destroyed. Which means the others are still out there and this world is in more peril than I'd thought."

"I appreciate the knowledge you're imparting, but what does this have to do with helping Ravion?" Demetrix inquired.

"As dalari, we have the ability to store and manipulate arcane energies far greater than any other spellcaster. What would be impossible for a studied human wizard is but a matter of learning to us." Kashien took a deep breath and returned to his seat, keeping the eldarstone locked in his fist. "Your brother learned how to absorb these energies. He learned how to steal them from other beings, similar to the way this stone allowed the dreualfar to drain energies from you. It wasn't your life it was robbing. It was your magic. That's what twisted my men. They were drained beyond their capabilities, which began robbing from their life. If Ravion chose to, he could create the same monsters you destroyed. Only he wouldn't need a machine to do it. I've seen our kind take energies before. With the right spell, anyone can do it. But only our kind can do it through sheer force of will. It can be done safely in small doses, not that I'd recommend trying to learn. It's kind of like a tankard of exceptional mead. Once you empty the contents, you want another. But what happens when your belly is full and you keep drinking? You get sick. That's what Ravion has done. He's consumed more arcane energies than anyone I've ever heard of. That much power has a tendency corrupt even the most devout. In simpler terms, he's addicted to magic. He needs to consume it. The more he consumes, the more he needs. And when he can't find a source, his body begins to shut down."

Demetrix stared blankly at the dalari general. He didn't know how to process what he'd heard. Playing through every scenario he could think of, he finally spoke. "Is there any way to help him?"

"Under normal circumstances I'd have to say no. I've seen magic addiction many times in my life. Most never recover. Their bodies shut down and die. The few that do are rarely the same person they were before. But Ravion isn't just any dalari. And you just happened to find the one artifact that has the ability to help him." Kashien held up the eldarstone.

"What do you mean Ravion isn't just any dalari?"

"The hard truth of the matter, after what he did we would have put him to death. That was the plan for him. At least it was until I found this." Kashien drew the curved longsword from his side, displaying it.

"Ravion's sword? What's that have to do with anything?" Demetrix sounded puzzled.

Kashien flipped the blade around and extended it to Demetrix, hilt first. Free of its grip, he held his hand out. Another blade materialized in his grip as if he'd been holding it the entire time.

Studying the two swords, Demetrix instantly realized the similarities between the two. In fact, Kashien's weapon looked identical to the way Ravion's used to, before the blade had been modified and curved.

"I feel like I'm missing something. You have the same sword, so what?"

"Exactly. They're the same sword. They're both the sword of House Santail. Your brother's sword is the same weapon, but much older."

"You're saying they're the exact same weapon. Like same metal, same leather, everything?"

"Yes, exactly. That sword shouldn't exist." Kashien gestured to Ravion's blade. "It's not possible without the influence of a particular deity that's been known to take interest in mortal affairs from time to time."

"You don't seem to be too upset that Ravion modified his. If it's as old as you say, I'd have thought you to take offense by that."

"That? That's nothing. The sword conforms to its owner's desire. As desires change, so does the blade."

"Why would having the same weapon spare Ravion's life?"

"I'm the son of Ashlan Torcavious and Marcus Santail. Making me the first Santail heir to the throne. As there's never been another, and the sword can only be bound by the head of House Santail, that means Ravion is royalty after me. I suppose by extension, you are too. That makes Ravion third inline for the throne. You would be fourth inline, that is unless Ravion has children where you're from."

"None that I'm aware of."

"By our laws, no member of a royal house can be executed without first being granted trial by the ruling emperor. As we're an ocean away and in the middle of a war, my time is better spent here than carrying out an execution in Dranar."

"I'm thankful for that. Though it seems like an awful lot of circumstance. How do you know your men won't seek their own justice?"

"I trust them. And they trust me. Besides, in his current condition, it's unlikely he'll live till morning anyway."

Demetrix broke his gaze on the prince and stared deeply into the etchings along Ravion's blade. "Do you mind if I see him? You said the stone can help. If there's any hope it can save him, I'd like to try."

Bits of ceramic exploded against the wall, sending jagged pieces scattering across the stone floor. "What do you mean they escaped and destroyed the machine?" General Tygrell fumed, glaring angrily at the hydralfar before him.

Jorin'otth kept his head low, hoping to avoid the enraged general's wrath. "General, one of your men, Captain Vaniar, he went against my express orders and took one of our more valuable prisoner from his cell. I don't have the details as to exactly what happened, but we've lost Drundale. The orcs have reclaimed it and bolstered their numbers from the surrounding clans."

"Gods damn it! How many did we lose? And please tell me someone took Vaniar into custody. That sorry excuse for a dreualfar has been a thorn in my side since General Elgar fell."

"Vaniar was killed during the escape. As were most of the hybrids, Sir. We believe a few escaped, from the evidence we found. But we have no idea where they may have run off to. Only a handful of your men made it out, and those were the few patrolling the outer wards."

Tygrell gritted his teeth. His fists were wrapped so tightly, his knuckles were turning white. "I wanted to kill that son of a bitch myself." Marching to the map table in the center of the room, he plucked a dagger from the mountain city where Drundale had been. "Guard, get in here!"

A scrawny and underfed dreualfar stepped through the door. "Yes,

General?"

"Send missive to all the commanders. From this day forward, any dreualfar that abandons their post, under any circumstance, is to be executed on sight. I won't have cowards under my command."

"It will be done, General!" The guard snapped to attention and offered salute. Backing from the room, he pulled the door shut once again.

Tygrell exhaled sharply, forcing his anger to subside. "Now, Jorin'otth, what do we do now? I don't suppose you can build another machine?"

"Apologies, My Lord. Even if we retook Drundale, the eldarstone was lost in the battle. Without it, the machine will kill anyone we put in the chair. But there may be something else we can do."

"What's that?"

"Do you remember that scout that said the dalari have someone that can siphon magic?

"Vaguely."

"If we can find that one, we won't need the machine or the stone."

"How do you figure that?"

"If he's as powerful as the scout said, he's beyond his own control. All we have to do is feed him. After that it's as simple as using a counter spell. I swap the supply with a prisoner and let him build our army for us."

"Where would we find him? Unless you've forgotten, I killed the scouts that encountered him. And that was almost two months ago, near Riverbend. Even if he's moving with the main dalari army, a lot of ground can be covered in two months."

"Don't worry about that, Sir. I'll consult the book and see what I can find on our friend. Maybe it'll have some alternative options for us."

"Get to it. I don't want to see you again until the tide of this war has shifted to our favor! And Jorin'otth, consider yourself warned, I won't suffer another failure. If we have another incident like that of Drundale, it'll be you that suffers my wrath."

"As you command." Jorin'otth bowed low and backed to the door. Spinning around, he stepped out and disappeared into the corridor.

Chapter X
Personal Demons

Gareth traipsed through the overgrown woodland, watching the flourished stands of ivy and decaying wood crunch beneath his boots. He was hot and sticky. What had been blazing heat the previous few days had tempered into dense humidity lingering in the air. The seemingly unending forest had shifted. Instead of plump trees and thick underbrush as far as the eye could see, the land had changed. There were still just as many trees as before, but now they shot further into the sky.

Thick vines hung down, stretching from one limb to the next. Everything was glossy, like a layer of sweat clung to the surface at all times. The dry, leaf covered dirt was hidden beneath a layer of thick vegetation. The vibrant pedals and heart shaped leaves were thick and heavy, stretched out to absorb the glistening rays of sunlight through the overhead canopy. What had been a musty forest had given way to a temperate jungle full of insects and reptiles.

Gareth swung his sabre, cutting through the thick vines constricting his path. Stepping through the opening, the sounds of rushing water reached him. That was good news. His water-skin had run dry the previous day and he wasn't sure when or if he was going to be able to refill it. Following the sounds, the roar grew louder. Through the massive leaves, entwined around one of the larger trees, Gareth could see a faint rainbow glowing in the mist of the towering waterfall in the distance. He still had a way to go before he could reach it, but he'd found water. That was more than he could have asked for.

Hacking his way ever closer, Gareth stumbled upon a well-traveled path to the water's edge. He could already taste the fresh spring. His mouth was dry and his throat burned from the dust over the past few days. Following the trail, his eyes fell on the large pool at the base of the fall, though he wasn't alone. Stopping himself, Gareth stared blankly at the shimmering figure swimming in the shallows just beyond the plunge basin.

She was beautiful, even from a distance. Her auburn hair was long and stringy, grouped into thick bands from the moisture. Her pale skin glowed almost red in the beaming sunlight.

Realizing what he was seeing, Gareth stared intently. It wasn't her skin that was red. It was the area around her that was. She clearly wasn't dalari. He'd spent enough time around them to know that much. Besides, they glowed blue. She was something else. Something he hadn't seen before. Taking a step closer, hoping to get a better look, he heard a snap echo under his boot. It rang out like an explosion in the dead of night.

Frozen like a dear in torchlight, those bright green eyes glared death into his soul. Before he could raise his arms in defense, something solid smashed into him, obstructing his vision. He wasn't unconscious. He could feel everything. He simply couldn't move. Whatever had him constricted tightly around his entire body, preventing the slightest movement.

Finding the anger he'd been holding onto, Gareth summoned his will, hoping he'd be able to see outside his body. It wasn't working. The harder he pushed, the tighter the wrap got. He was having trouble breathing, though it felt like he was nearly through. If he could push just a little harder, he might be able to break free. Forcing every bit of will into the rage fueled sight, his lungs gave way and he blacked out.

Demetrix stared intently at the shell of the man he'd known for so long. Ravion's skin was pale and chalky. Beads of sweat soaked into the blankets covering him. If it weren't for the thick bed beneath him, absorbing the moisture, there was no doubt the floor would be drenched. Ravion's eyelids pulsed, as if his eyes were darting back and forth beneath the thin layers of skin, constantly in search of something unseen.

Demetrix could feel heat rolling off the unconscious scout. Something had to give soon. Nobody could withstand such torment for long. He just hoped it would be the fever and not Ravion's body that withdrew first.

"How did it come to this? How does someone so strong fall so far?"

Studying the curved longsword, still in his hands, he raised the weapon and laid it lengthwise beside his brother. If he was to die, it was only fitting his sword should go with him.

"He's stronger than I would have thought upon meeting him." Kashien's words were soothing and calm. "It's often the strongest among us that fall the hardest. We don't expect it from them, which catches us off guard when it happens."

Demetrix turned to look upon the seemingly young prince. "He's always presented himself that way. How better to defeat an opponent than by allowing them to underestimate you?"

"A common trait among dalari. It seems your brother was more akin to his people than he realized." Kashien extended the eldarstone, dropping it into Demetrix's hand.

The power rushed through his body. Something was different. It didn't react that way before. His eyes locked on the glowing blue stone, he felt connected to everything. He could feel the life force of every dalari in existence, each one throbbing right there in the palm of his hand. All he had to do was squeeze and he could snuff the light out of each and every one of them. Such power was not meant for a single being.

"You feel it, don't you?" Kashien asked, studying the younger man's face.

Demetrix took a deep breath, focusing on the dalari prince. He was both near and far, strong and weak. It took everything he had to determine what was real and what could be.

"It's everywhere." Beads of sweat ran down Demetrix's forehead.

"I was afraid that might happen. At the cliffs, you used the stone, which opened you to its power. It's also what fatigued you to the point of collapse. You find yourself at a crossroad. You could use the stone to restore your brother, but the stone's power has already touched you. There's a chance it could affect you much the way your brother is currently affected. You could claim ultimate power over our people and become one of the mightiest beings this realm has to offer. Or you could do this one task and walk away. I can't say which will result from its use."

"How would I use it?"

"It takes little more than a thought. Sadly, I can't offer much more than that. I've only seen them used once before. That was one of the darkest days in my life."

Demetrix could hear his heart pounding in his chest. He wanted so desperately to take the power offered to him. He could remake the world. Eradicate the dreualfar for all time. He could even return to Irayth and defeat the nightkings and their armies. The people of both realms would be free of tyranny. Free to live under his rule. He would be their new god king and they would love him with every fiber of their being. And those that didn't would perish beneath his wrath.

He closed his eyes, forcing the thoughts from his mind. He wasn't that person. He didn't want to be that person. Taking a deep breath, he handed the stone back to Kashien and marched from the room. He wanted to help Ravion. But using the stone would result in the loss of himself.

Kashien smiled, seeing the young dalari leave. "Stronger than I thought."

Stepping forward, he held the stone over Ravion. Closing his eyes, he felt the power grow. It wrapped around the unconscious warrior and himself. They were in their own world, secluded from all else.

"Ravion, your brothers still need you. Your people still need you. You need to get up and fight!" Allowing the power retreat back into the stone, Kashien placed the eldarstone into his belt pouch and stepped away. He'd done all he could do. It was on Ravion now. Turning, he marched from the small room, thinking to himself. *Such magics come with a price. It's my duty to pay it. Now all I have to do is make sure no one uses the stone again.*

Tears ran down the child's puffy, red cheeks. He sat in a pool of blood, clinging to his father's cold, lifeless hand. His mother was a few feet away. Her dull eyes stared into him, draining the strength he once possessed.

Ravion was frozen in fear. He was all alone, surrounded by the corpses of the people he'd lost. Beyond that, the smoky and ruined village of Winterhaven stretched a short way, disappearing into shadow.

That's all this place was. A land of shadow and death. He didn't dare stare into the darkness.

Figures moved within, faster than the eye could see. No, it was safer to stay here, in the small patch of dense and gray cloud cover. The one place where the sun didn't dare shine, but the shadows stayed at bay.

Wiping the snot from his nose, Ravion heard something behind him. Stealing a glance, he saw a figure standing at the edge, watching him. The man was faint, but clearly solid. There was a familiarity to him. The plated leather armor and black eye patch gnawed at his mind. He felt like he should know him. But the memory eluded him.

The figure shook his head and turned, disappearing into the dark.

"Wait!" Ravion called out. But it was too late. The man was gone.

One of the phantoms flew past, slamming into his chest. He felt the pain rip through his body, knocking him to the dust and blood coated ground. Looking around, he was all alone. The bodies he'd grown accustomed to were nowhere to be seen. Even those he was holding had vanished. He couldn't recall who they were. There should have been some importance to them, but that knowledge was missing, like everything else. Picking himself up, he knocked the moist dirt from his tattered clothing. The red smeared everywhere he touched, seeming to add more than there was before.

"Ravion!" An elegant voice echoed around him.

"Your brothers still need you. Your people still need you. You need to get up."

He searched the shadows, looking for any sign of company. Suddenly, as if the being had been there the entire time, he saw a man standing a few feet away from him. He was dressed in the finest garments he'd ever seen. The maroon and gold leather was polished perfectly and decorated masterfully by thin metal plates along the seams. A large, beautiful sword hung at his side. Its twin rested in his hand.

"Get up and fight!" The man ordered, tossing the blade into the blood-soaked earth at the boy's feet.

Ravion bent at the waist, lifting the masterfully crafted sword from the muck. No sooner than his hand touched the grip, the blade shifted, shrinking into little more than a short sword. It fit his hand perfectly. Searching for the man, he was nowhere to be seen.

Alone once again, Ravion felt the world around him awaken. Fear grew inside him. But the sword gave him strength. He watched the shadow surround him, closing the gap it had refused to cross for longer than he could remember.

Phantoms flew past, lunging each chance they got. He was going to have to fight. If the darkness touched him, it'd tear him to shreds. Lifting the short weapon, Ravion watched one of the ghastly beings spring from the rolling clouds of smoke, headed straight for him. Tightening his grip, he swung. The blade cut neatly, splitting the misty fabric clinging to the translucent figure's body. It crashed to the ground, showering him in a rain of dust.

Chatter echoed all around, drowning out the slightest cognitive voice among the sea of noise. Some laughed, some cried, some cheered, while others whispered indistinctively.

Ravion couldn't help but feel like he was in mixed company. Emotions filled him, offering hope and encouragement, while others whispered doom and despair. Suddenly, he realized why they flocked to him. He was responsible for their presence. Each and every one of them was here because of him. It was a miracle they didn't all want him dead.

Seeing another phantom flying toward him, he lifted the blade, realizing it had reformed into a longsword. More than that, he was remembering things. Things he'd forgotten. Slicing through the ghost, he spun around and cut another, moving up behind him. The shadows closed in, nearly engulfing him. He had just enough room to move, but even that was quickly fading.

Peering into the darkness, Ravion could see patches of light on the other side. In those patches stood hundreds of dalari. They were the voices he was hearing. They cheered him, urging him to fight. For the first time in what felt like forever, he wasn't alone.

Swinging his sword, he danced in the small circle, fighting off shadows and geists. One by one they fell to his blade, emitting light into his prison. He could see his father staring through the veil. A proud look on his face.

The smoke shifted and swirled, forming into a massive fist. Slamming into the unexpecting dalari, Ravion flew through the air. Landing on his back, the darkness swarmed him. He was the fly just stupid enough to rest over a pond of hungry fish. Agony shot through him, ripping muscle beneath flesh. Another sharp pain erupted in his chest. Clenching at his breastbone, his heart tensed, as if an invisible grip was squeezing the life out of him. Staring into the shadow, helpless to its torment, he noticed something he never expected. A figure towered over him, comprised of shadow. Those large ram horns and masterfully carved daggers were unmistakable.

Wincing through the pain, Ravion clinched his sword, swinging as hard as he could. It passed through the nightking, disbanding his mass. Rolling to his stomach, he climbed to his knees, feeling another pain in his back. He had to stay up or they'd kill him.

Another figure appeared in the darkness beside him. Such beauty was a marvel to behold. How could he have forgotten her? That question would trouble him for the rest of his days.

Senaria thrust her hand forward, blasting through the smoky figures around him. Spinning around, she drew her sword and attacked.

Demetrix sprung from the dust of the dead phantoms, ready to lunge into battle.

A massive cannon blast silenced everything, ripping a hole in the swarm.

Ravion turned, seeing a motley alfar standing on the side of a ship, floating casually in the distance. He couldn't recall any body of water large enough for a ship in these parts. Yet his eyes said otherwise. Squinting into the distance, Ravion noted the red peacoat and bandolier strung across his chest. His identity filled his memory.

A silver cutlass hung from the alfar's hip, its polished reflection burning away the dark. Smoke rolled from the discharged gun, shrouding the newcomer in a wispy haze.

"Hey, ya' ain't killing all those black-skinned bastards by yourself!" Gareth shouted, stepping into view.

One by one, companions joined the battle. Though Ravion knew they weren't really there. Many of these people had never met each other, having come from all points of his life. Though what really solidified that assumption was when Krenin and Malakai showed up.

He was used to the dead being here. But to have the living among them, this couldn't be real. A warmth wrapped itself around him, offering embrace. Glancing down, Ravion noticed his tan vest sitting in its rightful place. It was so much more flexible and open than the black leather he'd spent the past couple of years in.

A heavy breeze picked up and the shadow began to swirl. As quickly as his friends had appeared, they vanished, leaving him to finish the job.

He knew who he was now. That left him in a better state than before. The overhead clouds parted, revealing a tear in the world. Seeing the shadow fleeing for the gap, Ravion glanced at his victims, still on the edge of shadow. The dalari were starting to fade, turning into thin strands of blue wisps. Like a massive spider web, they shot into the cyclone, turning it from a pillar of black to ash gray. The souls were leaving. He knew that now. And that was okay. He'd kept them prisoner long enough. All but three were free to leave. Seeing the nightkings among the spiral, he knew what he had to do.

"Stop!" He demanded. The spiral froze, unable to complete another revolution.

Marching toward the hulking figures of blackened smoke, Ravion ripped them from the rest. He couldn't allow them to escape. They were too dangerous. Closing his eyes, he pulled the collected dark beings into himself, feeling them find their prison. His knees hit the dirt. It took everything he had to force them into submission. They were powerful, that was certain. But he took their mantle. It was his job to ensure they never returned to power. And that gave him power over them.

Panting heavily, Ravion opened his eyes, seeing the inside of a tent. The dark vortex gathered overhead, tearing its way through the wood and canvas. The illusion spells splintered, raining fragments of false wood and shattered spells upon him. The clouds were darkening outside, beyond the exposed roof. Lightning flashed, revealing a brief glimpse of the storm he'd set into motion. It was difficult to tell what time of day it was due to the swirling clouds blocking the sun.

Pulling himself from the sweat soaked bed, Ravion placed his bare feet on the dirt floor, recalling the fur rugs that lined it the previous time he was here. Grabbing his sword, he stood, feeling a strange power flow through him. The hardened blade contorted, as if the ridged metal had lost its firmness.

Lifting it, the wobbly, fluid blade wiggled and popped, returning to its straight edge. Seeing the blade he'd grown to love, Ravion lowered it to his side and rushed toward the door.

Hurried footsteps echoed outside, unfiltered by the large hole in the ceiling. Wind roared to life, battering against anything and everything in its path.

Stepping from the large tent, Ravion looked upon the dalari city-camp in a new light. These people were truly miraculous, if only his mind hadn't been clouded to that fact when he arrived. They went to work securing everything they could. A few of the smaller tents ripped away from their anchors and disappeared into the darkened sky. But it seemed the majority of the storm was happening outside the camp. If the calm in the center was testament, they were in the safest possible place.

Chapter XI
Calm Before the Storm

Flickering lights and the sweet scent of meat roused Gareth's senses. Slowly opening his eyes, he saw the rough stone of a cavern wall. He struggled to sit up, finding his wrist tied behind his back and ankles firmly secured to them. He'd been gagged, though it wasn't nearly as efficient as his bindings. He clearly wasn't going anywhere. It only stood to reason that his ability to talk was of lesser concern.

Fuzzy memories floated into mind. The last thing he recalled was seeing that woman in the river. Throwing his weight to one side, he half rolled, landing roughly on his shoulder and hip. The pain was jarring, but at least he would be able to see a bit more than he could.

A fire danced from the small pit, lined by several large rocks. They'd been piled on opposite ends and were topped by a thick, whittled stick that had been run through some kind of small animal. Gareth guessed it was rabbit, but he couldn't be certain. Hearing footsteps, he strained against his binding, trying to get a better view of the entrance. Or what he guessed to be the entrance. From what he could see, the cavern wasn't overly large, suggesting one, maybe two entrances at most. Either way, it was in his best interest to find out what he was dealing with.

To his surprise, the woman he'd seen at the waterfall stepped through the natural archway and into view. Her red glow flared at his sight, nearly blinding him. She was dressed in simple linen garments, though they appeared to have been crafted recently. There were no stains or wear holes anywhere. Not even a frayed piece of fabric could be seen for that matter. For lack of a better word, they were pristine. Her thick, red hair dangled over her shoulders, revealing a natural curl now that it was dry. But what drew Gareth in the most was her emerald green eyes.

She marched toward him, pressing the heel of her boot into the fleshy part of his shoulder. Giving a firm push, Gareth felt the tension grow on his limbs. They weren't meant to bend that way. Unable to take much more, he struggled against her hold. She released, taking a step back.

Gareth toppled toward her, landing on his stomach once again. He turned his head, watching the woman take a seat on a large stone beside the fire.

"'Eis isn't 'wuite the introduction I ad in mine." He declared over the rag stuffed in his mouth. "I'd hav' 'ought if e 'ere gonna' get to ta bondage so quick, I'd at leas' know your name."

She reached out and turned the roasting animal to keep it from burning. "If I wanted ya' ta' speak, I wouldn't 'ave gagged ya'."

"'Oreplay. I 'an get behin' dat'."

She shot him a wicked gaze, daring him to continue.

Gareth smiled as best he could. It'd been a while since he'd experienced anyone with such resistance. "Wat's 'our name?"

Sighing heavily, she sat up, glaring her annoyance at the subdued devonie. "Mejra, okay? Now please shut up and let me think."

Laying there, Gareth couldn't help but admire her beauty. The fact she was annoyed made her that much more stunning. He'd already seen her naked, so that was out of the way. The true question remained, what was she going to do with him? She could have simply left him there, lying beside the river. She had to have some reason for bringing him here.

Mejra adjusted uncomfortably and sprung to her feet. "Gods, can ya' not think so loud? Haven't ya' learned ta' control yer' thoughts?" She marched around the fire and knelt beside him to remove his gag.

Stretching his jaw, Gareth opened and closed his mouth a few times trying to get his cheeks to feel right after being compressed for gods knew how long. "Thanks, and to answer your question, no. I haven't learned how to do that. I didn't even know that was a thing."

She grabbed a dagger from her waist and hooked the rope securing Gareth's legs. Ripping upward, the braided hemp cut and his legs sprung free.

"Yer' hands and ankles stay tied until I can trust ya'. And by the way, it's extremely rude ta' watch a girl while she's bathin'."

Gareth rolled to his side and sat up, stretching his legs on the dirt and stone floor. "In my defense, I didn't know you were there until I'd already seen you. But what can I say? You don't steal a quick glance at a masterpiece. You study it. You memorize every perfect curve and supple detail until it's lodged in your mind permanently."

"Stealin's stealin'. If ya' wanted ta see me naked, ya' should have asked."

"Huh? Well, Mejra, can I see you naked?"

"No!" She shoved against him, pushing herself to her feet. "Keep it up, an I'm gonna gag ya again." Returning to her stone, she took a seat and lifted the carved stick from the fire.

The meat was a glossy, dark red. The thinner areas near the joints had begun to blacken, but it was far from burnt. Laying the cooked carcass on another stone, she pulled the spit from it and brought her dagger down, cutting the creature into two. Tossing one half over the fire, it landed on Gareth's lap.

He stared intently at the cooked meat. He was hungry, and it looked delectable. But his hands were bound. How was he going to eat?

Mejra grabbed the charred lower half and bit into the juicy creature. Chewing intently, she kept watch on her prisoner. There was mild delight in seeing him so helpless. It was almost pathetic.

Leaning her food against the piled rocks to keep it warm, she stood and circled around behind Gareth. "I'll untie ya' ta' eat. If ya' try anything, I'll blast ya' into next week."

Feeling his hands come free, Gareth grabbed the meat and took a large bite. It was a bit gamy, but the meat had an excellent flavor. Much better than the dry tack he'd had in his pack, days prior.

Mejra laid a water-skin beside him and returned to her stone. Taking another bite, she watched the brutish, one-eyed man devour his food. "It seems I've found a way to shut ya' up."

"Food's good." Gareth proclaimed between unnaturally large mouthfuls. Grabbing the water-skin, he pulled the cork from the top and took a long draw. "There's much to be said about a woman that can cook."

"And if ya' say it, you'll find 'yerself on da' floor again." She gave a light smirk, daring him to continue.

"So, I've got to ask. Why'd you bring me here? You could had just as easily left me. And what the hell did you do to me? I've never experienced anything like that before."

"This area's swarming with dreualfar. If I'd left ya', there's a good chance ya' be dead. Couldn't have that, now could I? As 'fer da' shell, it's useful against our kind. It feeds on 'yer physic energy. The harder ya' fight, the stronger it gets."

"Our kind?" Gareth asked, taking another long draw. He didn't know how long it had been since he'd last drank, and the water-skin was nearly empty.

"The devonie." Her eyebrow raised, curious as to his question. How could he not know about their people? "Ya' don't know wha ya' are?"

"I heard the name a few months ago. But no one could give me much information about them. For all I know, it's just a big ruse. At least until I ran into you. It's a little hard to plan a random meeting."

Laying what was left of her meat beside the fire, Mejra placed her elbows on her knees and leaned forward. "How is it ye' don't know about 'yer people. I looked into 'yer mind when I captured ya', but it was too clouded ta' see beyond the rage ya' keep bottled up."

"There's much about my past I'm unfamiliar with. About twenty-five years ago I washed up on shore. I'd been in some kind of shipwreck. I spent months on that island until finally a ship happened by. The captain took me aboard and taught me the ropes. A few years later our ship was attacked. My captain would have been killed, but I jumped in front of the sword and saved him. I woke up in a small village off the coast of the Reinir Sea. The woman that was tending my wounds was kind and beautiful. She nursed me back to health and the captain came back for me. He named me First Mate and allowed me to marry that woman. I served nearly another five years until I was awarded my own ship and allowed to return home to my wife. That was seventeen years ago. I've no memory of life before that."

"And the rage? It's something we all carry. Some believe it's the source of our power. If that were the case, ye'd be among the strongest of devonie. I've never found another that carries that much hatred inside them. In fact, if ye' were ta' learn how ta' control it, ye'd probably be one of the strongest devonie ta' live."

"My rage is what keeps me going. My wife and son were murdered by the dreualfar." The mere thought of the vile creatures left a sour film in the back of his throat. He could feel his anger building once again, though there was no outlet for it here. He'd have to keep it in check. There was no sense in scaring away the first source of information about these 'devonie' he'd ever found.

Mejra sat back, taking a more sensitive temperament. "What were their names?"

Gareth refused to look at her. The memory of that dark temple flooded his memory. The bloodstained blue dress— his son's cold, pale skin. Thus far he'd failed them. He'd killed thousands of dreualfar. But it wasn't enough. More lived. Once he'd killed every last one, he would finally have his retribution.

"Sorena and Aden."

"Wonderful names. If ya' keep their memory alive, they'll always be with ya'. No matter what's going on in 'yer life, or how ya' feel, I'm sure they're proud of ya'."

Gareth's gaze locked on to her. "You don't know me or my family. Don't presume to!" He knew there was no reason to snap at her, but it made him feel better. Her beauty aside, she was a stranger. His life was none of her concern.

"My apologies. I didn't mean ta' overstep. I simply wanted ta' understand what happened ta' ya'. I can tell ye've trained 'yerself in the ways of our people. But it's extremely crude. If I could find a way into 'yer head, it's possible I could teach ya' a thing or two."

"I'm not some stray that needs your charity. In fact, I'm only here because you tied me up in the first place." Gareth took a deep breath, realizing he was growing angry at the wrong person. Lightening his tone, he continued. "I didn't even get to experience the fun part of being tied up."

Mejra stood and marched toward him. Drawing her dagger, she cut the bindings on his wrist and ankles. "'Yer free ta' leave whenever ya' wish."

"Look, I don't mean to explode at you." He paused, chuckling at his choice of word, considering the comments he'd already made. "My family is a touchy subject, one that's been ruffled lately. I don't mind spending time with a pretty woman. In fact, I quite enjoy it. Bondage and all. But if it's possible, I'd rather not talk about my past."

"Aye, we can do that." Mejra stood, returning her dagger to its sheath. "And now that ye're a free man, what's 'yer name? I can't simply call ya' prisoner anymore."

"Gareth D'Averon."

"Well, Gareth D'Averon, what do ya' say ta' learning how ta' focus 'yer powers?"

A massive roar echoed outside, shaking the ground violently. Several pieces of stone broke away from the walls, tumbling to the floor. The rock piles on either side of the pit collapsed, sending bits of burning ember and ash into the air.

"What the hell?" Mejra rushed toward the entrance, stealing a look outside. "Ya' might wanna' come see this!"

Gareth took position beside her, looking out into the unnaturally dark sky. A near black cloud stretched across the horizon as far as the eye could see. Dark swirls rotated overhead, carrying heavy winds across the land. Trees uprooted, toppling over, while others took to the sky. There was no way of telling if it was day or night. The sky was completely blocked by the unusual storm.

"We need to go back inside. If any of that stuff hits us, we're done." Gareth placed his hand on Mejra's shoulder, urging her to follow. Returning to the hole in the ground, he was relieved to hear her footsteps behind him.

Heavy drops of rain crashed into the earth, leaving thousands of tiny impact craters in the dirt. The walls shook and groaned, threatening to break against the gale.

Jorin'otth listened intently to the wicked roar, tearing at the ceiling overhead. How such a storm came into being, he couldn't understand. There was a fabricated power to it unlike any he'd ever felt before. As if every spell he'd ever learned had combined into one and was released upon the world. Such a thing seemed impossible, yet proof of it was beating on the door just outside.

If only he had a way to collect it. Such a resource would undoubtedly prove useful in the days to come. His plan was nearing completion. He just had to keep the dreualfar general happy until he had what he needed. Opening the book, he pulled a small glass vial from his robes and removed the cork. Pouring the bright red liquid into the pages, he waited for it to disappear before speaking. "How can I harness the energies of this storm?"

The red droplets reappeared into a collection of pictures.

He quickly studied the images, writing the details on a piece of worn parchment. The design was simple enough. He just had to build the device before the storm was gone. Closing the book, he made a list of the materials he'd need. Tucking the folded parchment into his robes, he pulled the wooden door open and stepped out into the wind and rain.

Making his way to the armory, he couldn't help but notice the absence of patrolling guards. It seemed they'd abandoned their posts when the storm hit. That was certainly going to be remedied if he had anything to say about it. Tygrell would have blood if he learned of their cowardice. Not to mention the flaw in security. Anybody could have infiltrated the base while they were hiding. That was unacceptable.

Working his way to the supply house, he pulled the door open, finding two of the dreualfar huddled just inside the door. They were drenched and shivering. He hadn't noticed the air to be overly cool, but he was also a skilled mage. Weather rarely affected him in any regard. He hadn't even realized the shield he'd placed around himself until now.

"Get your asses back out there and stand your post. General Tygrell will have your heads if he finds out about this. And tell the others the same thing. I'll not face his wrath for your failure!"

The dreualfar shot an angry glare at the interrupting wizard. It was bad enough he was allowed to roam free, but to have to take his orders, it was enough to make you sick. Begrudgingly they opened the door and disappeared into the unnatural dark.

Jorin'otth rounded the corner, pulling the wooden door open. Seeing the stairs disappearing into the underground room, he snapped his fingers. A ball of glowing light formed overhead. Carefully, he made his way into a large chamber filled, seeing the strange pieces of metal cluttered about. They were odd pieces, cast of an assortment of colors and thicknesses. The center of the room was filled by a long table. Hundreds of tools rested on its top, slightly rusted from disuse.

Gesturing, Jorin'otth approached the table and set his crude drawling in the center. The glowing orb floated from him and to the lantern resting on the far side of the room. It flared to life before making its way to the mounted torches on the wall. One by one, the glowing ball emblazed four in total before fizzling out, leaving a well-lit room in its wake.

Jorin'otth rummaged through the collection of instruments and devices, searching for anything he could use. Forming a large pile on the table beside his parchment, he went to work crafting a device.

He tinkered for hours, studying the drawing he'd crafted from the book. What had been a pile of random scrap was now four packs resting peaceably beside one another. Each one had a pair of arms extending from the sides, supporting a net made of copper wiring. A thick cable ran from a metal tube at the base of the arms and into a collection of capped bronze tubes. He'd completed his machines. Now he just had to make sure they were going to work.

Slinging one of the packs over his shoulder, he lifted another and carried them up the stairs. Setting them to rest beside the door, he returned, grabbing the final two. Laying them with the first, Jorin'otth opened the door, relieved to see the storm was still in full swing. In fact, it appeared to have gotten stronger. One of the stone walls had collapsed and several of the buildings were missing, little more than foundation stones and rubble where they'd been. He could see where one of the buildings had smashed into another. The pile of mortared stone was scattered about.

Reapplying his shield, conscious of the effort this time, he stepped into the rain. Thick beads ran down the sides of the invisible sphere, battering against the impenetrable barrier. Making his way across the treacherous courtyard, Jorin'otth was relieved to see the dreualfar had returned to their posts, though they clearly didn't share his joy of that fact. Approaching one of the waterlogged black-skins, he felt a bit of short lived remorse for her. She was smaller than most, and just as ugly. But that was the dreualfar for you. Gender was an irrelevant thing. They didn't care who or what you were, so long as you were willing to die for their goals.

"I need eight soldiers to accompany me. Send them to the supply house. I don't care who you find for the job, just make sure there's a guard at every station."

"Yes, Sir!" The female dreualfar offered salute, though she clearly had no love for him. Breaking the respectful gesture, she turned and disappeared into the night.

Jorin'otth turned and made his way back toward the storage building. Stepping inside, he closed the door and opened the one to his immediate right. There was a large store room, complete with a heavy wooden table in the center. The wood was marred by hundreds of deep gouges and stains of red. If he had to guess it was a butchers table at some point, though its original use was irrelevant. Carefully, he gathered his machines and laid them to rest over the red stains.

Hearing the door slam open, Jorin'otth watched a few dreualfar step into the hall. "In here."

Three had found their way to him. As far as he was concerned it was first come, first serve. Those that carried the packs would be protected from the storm, in theory. But just in case, he wanted to ensure he had backup if they didn't survive the initial collection. It was better to let them die and get what he came for than to go out with the minimum and return empty handed.

"Grab a pack. We're leaving base for a while. And don't worry about the storm. What we're doing, you don't have anything to fear."

The dreualfar slung the packs, having difficulty with the odd levers and sprockets protruding from the device.

Jorin'otth made his rounds, tightening the straps and ensuring all the wiring was connected properly. So long as they remained intact, there was little concern.

The door opened again, revealing more dreualfar.

"I don't care who, but one of you, put this on." Jorin'otth held the last pack out for them to see it.

One of the dreualfar rushed past the others and slung the device over his back.

"Once we're out of here, all you have to do is walk. If someone falls, grab the pack and keep moving. General Tygrell is offering promotions to each of you. Keep your heads up and pay attention and we'll be back in no time." It didn't matter if the general knew anything about this expedition or not. He was in charge. And they believed him.

Heading out from the deteriorating city, the group passed the crumbled outer walls and into the surrounding jungle. Jorin'otth couldn't help but feel excitement. If this was proved successful, he'd no longer require the dreualfar to complete his mission.

They marched for nearly an hour into the constant downpour. It was impossible to see anything, even with their heightened vision. Only the occasional lightning flash offered any visibility. Jorin'otth was pleased to see the bolts jumped into the netting as he'd intended. Checking the packs to ensure they were working correctly, the bronze tubes lining the front side were glowing faintly. It was working. All he had to do now was let them fill.

Another bolt struck, hitting the net directly. The scent of charred flesh drifted through the air and one of the dreualfar collapsed to the ground.

"Grab the pack!" Jorin'otth demanded. There was enough static in the air to fill the containers, but it was slow. Direct hits were what he needed. Though it seemed the dampeners weren't enough to contain the charge. If only he'd brought more than eight dreualfar with him.

One of the unencumbered dreualfar charged forward, ripping the odd device off his fallen comrade. Before he could sling the pack over his shoulder, another bolt hit, exploding into the ground. An earth-shattering boom echoed out, sending chunks of dirt in all direction and knocking them from their feet.

Jorin'otth could feel the ground moving beneath them. Picking himself up, he glanced around. The fallen pack was in pieces, the dreualfar along with it. But that was nothing compared to the crack where the bolt had hit. And it was spreading. "On your feet. We have to move!"

The remaining dreualfar scattered in the chaos. One tripped and fell into the growing chasm. He was gone before he knew what happened.

Jorin'otth inched to the edge and peered down. He didn't know how far the drop it was, but there was a thin red line in the distance. There was no way anyone could survive the fall.

"This way!" He ran, hoping the others were smart enough to follow. Seeing a rocky outcropping in a brief flash of lightning, he charged for it. He'd underestimated the storm. If it had the ability to rupture the ground like it had, he needed to find shelter.

Reaching the rocks, he saw an opening. Stealing a glance behind him, only three dreualfar remained. And of those, only one had a pack. It seemed he wasn't going to have the resources to break ties after all. But one full pack was better than none. Stepping into the cave entrance, he noticed the flicker of fire light off the walls in the distance. Cautiously, he made his way forward. Rounding the corner, he saw two figures sitting by the fire. And better yet, he recognized one of them.

"Gareth?"

"Who the hell are you?" Gareth asked, staring intently at the unexpected hydralfar.

Seeing the dreualfar behind him step into view, Gareth's anger boiled. Near falling from the large rock he'd been sitting on, he reached for his pack, realizing his weapons were gone. It was no matter. He didn't need them. Not anymore.

Seeing the bald warrior lunge, Jorin'otth ripped one of the bronze tubes from the pack, pointing it toward the attacking warrior. Popping the cap, a bolt of dark energy shot across the cavern, striking the female in the chest and launching Gareth into the far wall. Forcing the cap back into place, he checked the glow through the sight glass. That one shot nearly depleted half the energy it'd collected.

He pushed the tube back where it belonged, and approached the fire. "Bind them. We just found our leverage to win this war."

Levi Samuel

Chapter XII
Bargaining Chips

Morning light revealed the aftereffects of the storm. Broken tree limbs were scattered across the ground. Their dark green leaves still clinging to the stems, unaware they were already dead. Overturned carts, once full of goods, laid on the roads and in the middle of communal areas. Several of the tents had been torn from their sites and flung where they'd landed, appearing as little more than odd shaped tarps on the ground. The once city-sized camp was in ruin. Thousands of dalari walked the streets, searching for their missing belongings and helping others clean up.

Reports were already coming in. Over six-hundred dalari were missing or confirmed dead in the few hours since the storm ended. The center most part of the camp had been hit pretty mildly, suffering only occasional damage from an airborne limb or crate. It was outer ring that suffered the most. Entire trees had been ripped from the ground and flung around as if they weighed little more than a feather. Numerous bolts of lightning struck, leaving a number of structures burnt to ash. The remnants looked like an explosion had gone off, destroying everything within a thirty foot area. What had been a well-maintained camp was now a field of chaos and destruction. Yet the morale remained intact.

That was more than could be said about the forest surrounding them. It had been leveled down to the smallest sapling. The only thing left was toppled trees and loose brush lying in large, scattered heaps.

Ravion stared intently at the floor. His knee was going numb from the constant pressure, but he wasn't about to adjust. He'd made a terrible mistake, one that had cost too many lives. The least he could do was deal with a little discomfort.

"You have nothing more to explain to me. I understand what happened and I forgive you. If you wish to make it right, help your people recover from this mess. We've delayed relocation too long. Now that this storm has passed, we aren't going to get a better opportunity than this. We need to move before our enemies have a chance to recover." Kashien stared at the top of Ravion's downturned head. He knew the torment the scout must have been putting himself through. But truth be told, the storm was hardly his responsibility. If anything, that blame rested with Kashien alone. He used the stone knowing there would be a price to pay. These deaths were on his hands. "Rise and go find Demetrix. I would have the two of you at my side when we move. Oh, and Ravion, would you please deliver these orders to Captain Trendal on your way past?" Kashien extended a rolled piece of parchment, stamped by a hybrid of what appeared to be both a fox and a wolf.

"As you command." Ravion stood, refusing to drop his bow. Accepting the scroll, he turned and made his way from Kashien's private quarters.

Stepping outside, he couldn't help but feel responsible for the pain and damage these people had suffered from his decisions. He wasn't worthy of being in their company, yet Kashien demanded he stay. It was little more than a formality. Kashien wasn't his commander and he wasn't bound by oath to obey him. Yet there was wisdom behind that smug demeanor. Kashien had seen things that would make the common dalari weep. And his men respected him. That meant Ravion respected him.

Reaching the command tent, he pulled the canvas flap to the side and stepped inside. Muffled noises echoed through the large, magical building. Passing through the war room, Ravion entered the study, hearing the sounds intensify. Reaching one of the three door flaps, he paused outside the one on the left. This close he was able to fully understand the sounds he was hearing. A smile came to his lips.

Clearing his throat, he spoke loud and clear. "Captain Trendal, Lord Kashien sends new orders." He waited patiently, hearing a large amount of hushed commotion within the room.

A moment later, the flap opened and a woman stepped out.

Ravion recognized her as Kashien's personal aide. It was odd to think she was in romantic involvement with Trendal and not Kashien, but that was none of his business.

Trendal stepped through the flap, an embarrassed expression evident on face. "I'd appreciate if you could keep this quiet. Strictly speaking, officers aren't supposed to have relations between one another."

"It's none of my concern." Ravion handed the sealed scroll to the nervous captain. "Though if you'd like some advice, relationships are easier to manage when you don't have to hide them."

"Thank you, Ravion."

Ravion bowed and turned to leave. It didn't take much to understand that was Trendal's way of telling him to worry about his own problems. Ducking out of the command tent, he skirted the debris and obstructions blocking the road. There was so much damage in such a small area. He dreaded seeing what the surrounding land looked like. Making his way to his tent, he stepped inside finding Demetrix sitting in front of the ever-burning hearth. The young dalari was working a piece of leather. It was far from complete, but appeared to resemble his green leather in shape.

Noticing his brother, Demetrix laid the incomplete armor on the table and stood. "You spoke with Kashien?"

"I did. He forgave me, not that I deserve it."

"I think he understood what you were going through. Now we need to find Gareth. There's no telling what happened to him during the storm. If he got caught in it, the chances of his survival aren't good. I scouted about two miles out this morning. Didn't see a single tree taller than a few feet still standing."

"We'll just have to search for him. He's more resilient than you'd think. And when we find him, I ask that you don't stand in his way. I said and did some terrible things to him. If he feels he needs to finish the job, that's his call, not yours."

The younger dalari was at a loss for words. How could Ravion actually think he could stand by and let Gareth kill him? "I can't make that promise."

"I'm afraid you're going to have to. What I did to him specifically, there is no one I've betrayed more. I have to make it right. And if that requires my life, it's my decision to make, not yours."

"Let just make sure it doesn't come to that."

"If it does, I'm asking you as my friend, brother, and equal to please stand down. Think about it and honor my wishes. Either way, we don't have time to talk about it now. Kashien wants to move camp. We set out in a few hours."

The sun reached its peak height. What was once a small city composed of tents and wooden structures was now a large patch of totted dirt. Over ten thousand dalari stood in block formation, awaiting command from their general. The tents were packed in a series of loaded wagons, along with what remained of the supplies. For the most part, everyone carried their personal effects, leaving the community supplies to be transported by wagon.

At the top of the hill where the command tents had been Kashien sat atop his horse, looking out over the army. He smiled at the sights before him. No commander could have been prouder of their army than he was of his. Not only had these few gone above and beyond in their duties, but they'd managed to hold off the dreualfar forces on nearly every occasion. Sure, there had been casualties and lost ground from time to time. But for the most part, they'd proven their worth in battle. Even the few times the hydralfar had joined them on the field, it was his men leading them to victory. Stealing a quick glance at the overhead sun, he knew it was time to move. They had a long trip to their next destination and with luck, any forces they might encounter along the way would still be disoriented from the storm. "Battalion, right face!"

The army moved in unison. It was like watching a mirage. Not a single detail was left out of place.

"Forward march!" He listened to the roar of footsteps, seemingly amplified by the distance. He could feel the ground shake beneath him. In truth, he didn't need to give the command. The individual company commanders would see to that. But it felt good setting them on their path.

Watching them reach the boundaries of the once camp, he secured the reins of his horse, keeping it from running off before he was ready. Turning to the men mounted beside him, he looked upon their faces. Kaileen, Trendal, Ravion, and Demetrix, and several other captains regarded the general, patiently awaiting his command.

"Shall we?" Kashien gestured the group to follow.

They fell in behind the wagons, moving little faster than a slow trot.

They had a four-day journey ahead of them, which at this pace suggested they would travel roughly two hundred miles. That was provided they didn't run into any unexpected problems.

The better part of a day passed with minimal issue. The one concern on everyone's mind was the true extent of the storm's damage. It seemed the further out they got, the more the world had suffered. They stopped for the night at what was once a small human village near the forest's edge.

Little more than loose stone and crumbled buildings remained. There was no sign of any survivors. Settling in for the night, the scent of several camp fires lingered in the air. Tents were to remain packed, which left thousands of sleeping bags sprawled out on the ground.

Demetrix sat beside one of the small fires, working his soon to be armor and listening to one of the dalari play a lute. He wasn't sure exactly what the song was about, having never fully learned to understand eldarspeak, but from what he could piece together, he felt it was about a mischievous god whom enjoyed playing tricks on mortals.

Despite his uncertainty in the lyrics, it was a rather enjoyable tune. Looking up from his work, he could see Ravion leaning against one of the wagons. The young scout appeared lost in his own little world, though that didn't keep him from standing watch over everyone else. Laying the leather on his bedroll, Demetrix stood and snatched up a wineskin.

Making his way toward the wagon, he extended it, offering Ravion a drink. "You shouldn't spend so much time in your head. False thoughts start to make sense."

"I'm just thinking about how we're going to find Gareth. He doesn't know how to get back to camp in the first place. Now that we're moving, there's little more than divine luck that would guarantee a reunion."

"It's never stopped us from looking before. No matter where we are or what kind of trouble we found ourselves in, we always make it home."

"That was in Dalmoura. We knew where we were going. Even in the catacombs, all we had to do was keep walking until we found a way out. No matter where we came up, home was always within a month's ride. I've seen many parts of this realm. It's much larger than most would have you believe. I suppose what I'm trying to say is, I spent over two hundred years searching for you— searching for our people. I explored any and every rumor that came my way in hopes of finding anything. That journey eventually took me to Dalmoura, where some of my questions were answered. But many more remained. And now we're here, among our people. My point is, if I spent that long looking for an entire race of people, how am I supposed to find a single man who doesn't want to be found?"

"You don't know he doesn't want to be found. He left. That's not unlike him, especially when he gets pissed. Once he slaughters a few dreu and clears his head, he'll calm down. He always does. Besides, we're surrounded by hundreds of spellcasters. I'm sure they can find him in a heartbeat. Let's just get to the new camp and then we'll track him down. Now have a drink and relax a little." Demetrix offered the wineskin once again, waiting patiently for Ravion to take a swig.

Demetrix awoke to the feel of tiny legs walking upon his face. Brushing the fly off his cheek, he opened his eyes to the view of a hawk circling overhead. Pulling himself up, he realized he was only half on his bedroll, seemingly having passed out where he laid. Images of the previous night rushed to the forefront of his memory. Looking around, it seemed the majority of the army was packed and ready to begin their march once again, though he was far from the last to rise.

Stealing a glance at the fire not far from him, the white ash held the form of the night's final logs. He had a feeling if he dug down, he could find a few remaining embers, but such search was unnecessary. Grabbing his water-skin, he took a long draw, wetting his throat. Leaning over, he poured the rest of the water on the ash, listening to it sizzle and throw bits of the burnt mineral into the air.

Ravion approached the weary scout, a mild smirk lingered on his face.

"Did you have a good night?" He handed a fresh water-skin to his brother and extended his hand to pull him up.

"The parts I can remember." Demetrix took his brother's hand and pulled, finding his feet. "What happened to you?"

"I went for a walk, didn't feel much like partaking of the festivities. Nonetheless, come on. Kashien wants to meet with us."

Demetrix took another swig of water and handed the skin back to Ravion. He quickly rolled his bed and strapped it to his pack. Grabbing the bundle, he tossed it over his shoulder and followed after the elder dalari.

They marched through the center of camp to the only standing tent among the tens of thousands of dalari. Stepping through the open doorway, they noticed Kashien standing at a large wooden table. A weathered map rested in the center. Several other dalari stood in waiting, casually talking among themselves.

Demetrix recognized a few of the dalari. He'd met most of them within the past few months. But there were a few he'd never seen before. These few were dressed for battle, unlike those he was familiar with. They appeared a bit laxer, wearing little more than common clothing and their weapons strapped to their hips.

"Ravion, Demetrix, I'm glad you could join us," Kashien offered a respectful bow to the two outsiders. "Captain Theo here was just informing me of a large dreualfar incursion to the east. It seems Tygrell has decided to take advantage of the storm's aftermath as well."

The unfamiliar dalari was dressed in black plate mail, trimmed in gold. A blackened morning star hung from a leather strap at his hip and a heavy shield was slung across his back. Despite his gruff appearance, his hair was relatively short, though that didn't hide the massive scar running from his left ear to the crown of his head.

"My scouts tell me they're moving a force, nearly six-thousand strong straight north, and another nearly three-thousand due southwest." The grizzled captain pointed on the map, showing them traveling from what appeared to be an elven outpost less than a week away.

"Does their path appear to intersect ours?" Ravion asked, studying the map.

This land seemed difficult to understand. It had a familiar feel, but he didn't recognize the shape. Which was odd in and of itself as he'd traveled every land known to Ur and never come across this one.

He was one of the few that had traveled to another realm, something unheard of since before the Demon Wars, as the stories went. It was only a short stretch that they could have ended up somewhere the troubles of the mainland never plagued them. That would explain why the dreualfar weren't cursed to the underdark, and why he hadn't found his people after so many years of searching. Yet it still didn't add up. History was known to repeat itself, but why would one land in particular be protected for so long while the rest was left to the throes of time?

"If we continue on our current path, yes. But if we continue due north for another day before shifting east, we should miss them by about twenty miles." Kashien assured the gathered commanders.

"What about the southern band? Surely they're going to discovered we've left the old camp pretty soon." Trendal interjected, denoting a direct path on the map.

Kaileen waved her hand, dismissing Trendal's query. "We shouldn't concern ourselves with that. They were never able to get a solid location on our base. By the time they arrive and discover our absence, we'll be little more than a distant memory. They won't be able to track us. I made sure of that."

"What would you have us do, General Kashien?" Theo placed a small, bronze statue of a valiant knight on the map, due east of the suspected dreualfar base. "My men are held up here. We've enough supplies to last another month, but eventually we're going to have to fall back."

"Take another hundred men with you, along with all the supplies they can carry. I need you to hold position as long as possible. The more information we have of the enemy's whereabouts, the better off we'll be when it comes time to march."

"Understood, General."

"Forgive me if I'm overstepping." Ravion interjected. "But what's the purpose of all this?"

"I'm afraid I don't understand what you mean." Kashien stated flatly, hoping the dalari nightking could elaborate.

"Judging by the map here, the dreualfar base is here?" Ravion paused, making sure his assessment was accurate.

"The bulk of their force, yes. They have several smaller units spread across the continent. But each time we locate one, they move before we can mount an assault." One of the other captains declared.

"I see. Well, from an outside perspective, you're wasting a fair amount of time watching and waiting for the enemy to come to you. You're competing with their resources, which considering they keep moving and taking new territory, are constantly being renewed. If you continue to do what you've been doing, you're eventually going to run out. When that happens, it's only a matter of time before your army falls after a long and tiring wait."

"What would you do to fix it?" Kashien asked, studying Ravion's face. There was validity in his words and an outside perspective was greatly valued. He'd been fighting this war a few years now and hadn't made much progress. In fact, the victories over the other generals had little to do with tactics and more to do with overwhelming numbers. But the humans were unlikely to come again. Once the threat in their homeland was reduced to a manageable level, they pulled out of the fight.

"Take the battle to them. I've been through a dreu war once already. We made the same mistakes you're making now. We sat idle and waited for them to come to us. That works when you're holding land or have no other options, especially when you're trapped and have nowhere to go. But that also means failure results in the end of your people. If it were me, I'd recommend playing to your strengths. Attack in the open with your main force while smaller units make their way around the sides to flank. Once their main base is under siege, you simply form a perimeter guard, keep a fraction of your men out of the fight and ready for an unexpected counter attack. That way if their scattered units are recalled, you have someone ready to contend with them and you keep their reinforcements from grouping up. And at this stage in the game, they're unlikely to suspect a change in tactics."

"You make many valid points. Once we reach the new camp I want to discuss this further. Until then we stick to the current plan. Any other news or advice?"

"Two nights ago, my archers encountered a group near the ruins of Karabar. We were able to eliminate the threat, but we lost five men in the process. It seems the dreu were excavating the darkstone from the dwarven citadel there. We don't think they've unlocked its mysteries, but they certainly have an interest in it" Captain Lawsen reported.

"I'll reassign another twenty of our finest archers to your command, Captain. Lieutenant Roanin, you and your men are going to accompany Captain Lawsen to the Ruins of Karabar. I want you to defend those ruins at all cost. Whether the dreualfar have learned what darkstone can do or not, we can't risk it falling into their hands. As far as I know, the Udurnie are the only ones that have the ability to work it. But breaking a stone into a single batch of arrow heads could prove detrimental in open combat. In fact, if you have the opportunity, I want you to blow up the entrance. Destroy any chance the dreualfar might have of using it as a weapon against us." Kashien glanced around the room. "Demetrix, Ravion, I'll ask you to hang around for a moment once we're done here. Colonel Kaileen, would you be so kind as to hand select the men that will be reassigned?"

Kaileen bowed. "As you command, my prince."

"You're dismissed."

The commanders filed out at once, resuming their conversations. The heavily armored dalari, Theo his name was, pulled a gold lined scroll from his belt pouch and unrolled it. The reflected sunlight made a large rectangle square on the ground. From the square, three other dalari appeared, dressed in heavy armors, much like their captain.

Demetrix turned from the retreating commanders, devoting his attention to Kashien. "You wanted to see us?"

"I did." The dalari general fumbled with the icons marking the map for a brief moment before clearing them away and rolling the large parchment. "I understand neither of you truly belong here and at times that can make one feel unappreciated. In lieu of that, I wanted to personally express my gratitude. Demetrix, not long ago you saved a great many of my men, both by rescuing them from that infernal prison and guiding them back to me, and again when you found your way to us. Many had suffered the dangers of being too close to a battle beyond their understanding, myself included. You remedied that mistake. For that I'd like to offer you something you wouldn't need had you not agreed to accompany my men in the first place."

Kashien marched to the side wall of the enchanted tent and picked up a small chest. The wood was smooth and polished, removing any sign of a seam between the planks. The corners were trimmed and bound in gold, and the lock holding the lid closed had a blue glow to the flat plate, little wider than a thumb. Setting the box on the table, Kashien gestured to the younger dalari.

Demetrix fingered the masterfully crafted chest, unable to find a single flaw in its appearance. Working his way to the latch, hoping he didn't seem too eager to find out what was inside, he pressed his thumb against the plate, unsure how it opened. The blue glow enveloped his thumb and he felt it spring free. Lifting the relatively light lid, he looked into the chest to see a new set of armor, folded and tucked neatly inside.

Pulling it from the container, he marveled how the entire suit fit inside. The design was similar to the armor he'd arrived in, but this was much better. Instead of a few large pieces layered together, there were several smaller pieces, allowing more articulation than he had before. The other notable difference was color. This armor was black, trimmed in a deep forest green. It was beautiful. Studying every detail, he noticed something impossible. The piece of leather he'd been working the past few days was stitched into place and perfectly formed to the rest of the armor. How had they used it when he'd left it in the tent not thirty minutes before? Unable to wait a moment longer, Demetrix pulled the armor around himself and began buckling it into place. It fit perfectly, as if it had been sized for him specifically.

"I apologize for not letting you know about it sooner. We were waiting for you to finish the piece you were working on, and I wanted it to be a surprise. The leather has been enchanted. It's self-healing. If it gets cut, or gods forbid, an arrow punctures it, the leather will start to seal itself as if the damage was never there. Additionally, you'll find that you move quieter and you'll become less noticeable to enemy eyes while wearing it. But an archer is only as good as his bow."

Kashien reached into the chest and retrieved a familiar piece of wood, wrapped in green sinew and brown leather. The bow that had been broken was reconstructed and waiting to be strung.

Demetrix studied his bow. It appeared as if it had never been touched. Every detail was perfect, matching the bow he had months prior, save for one. There was a presence he hadn't felt before. A tear rolled down his cheek. Nothing could have made a better gift.

"I have a friend who wishes to speak with you." Kashien gestured toward the door.

A cloaked figure stepped into the tent. The only detail that could be seen on the dark green fabric covering his armored form was a black sigil holding the cloak shut. It was circular in shape and had a single band encompassing the entire design that traveled around to make a series of orbs and triangles. It reminded Demetrix of a hedge maze.

"Demetrix Santail, your actions in life have not gone unnoticed. I'm here to offer you the greatest honor any archer can hope to obtain. I know now, you're not ready. But when you are, fire this arrow into the sky. Follow it and where it lands, we shall meet again."

Demetrix didn't realize the armored hand was extending a single arrow until it was already within reach. Cautiously, he accepted the missile and looked it over. The wood was smoked and polished. Not a single grain could be seen in the shaft. The arrow's head was unlike any he'd seen before, and the fletching was solid, appearing to be made of some unidentifiable hide, rather than traditional feathers. Even the weight of the arrow was unlike any other. Looking up from the one of a kind shaft, the cloaked figure was gone, leaving the three to their solitude.

"He's what they call a horator. Protectors of the forest. Extremely secretive and selective of their invitations." Kashien responded, seeing the questions in the young dalari's face. "For you, Ravion. While you've had your challenges in your time here, you also saved a great many of my men, though in a less than traditional manner. Every soldier you affected while in your dark trance has made a full and complete recovery. Even those that were fatally wounded or diseased. Somehow, beyond my understanding, you healed them. For that you have my gratitude."

The dalari prince held out a jeweled amulet. The chain was a complex pattern of overlapping rings that seemed to pull against one another, yet defied understanding as none of them were actually connected to those immediately adjoining. The amulet itself was oval in shape. The stone, blue and wrapped in golden wire. Despite its complexity, it was relatively simple.

"You shall never have to look for your people again. With this amulet, you have but to ask and it will lead you to them."

Ravion accepted the amulet, fingering it briefly before placing it around his next. "Thank you, My Lord." He bowed gracefully.

Horns echoed outside, drawing the attention of all within earshot. The dalari assembled into formations, awaiting command.

Demetrix and Ravion made their way outside, seeing the entire army ready for travel. Turning back, the command tent fell to the ground and folded into a small, compressed box.

Kashien picked up the box and stuffed it into his pack. Approaching his horse, he secured the bag to his saddle and climbed up, pulling the reins free.

Chapter XIII
No Place Like Home

Demetrix's backside was growing raw from the stiff saddle. He wasn't used to being in one for such extended periods of time. The sun was rapidly falling on the horizon, leaving a dull orange glow on the world.

Suddenly, horns echoed from the front of the marching army and it began to halt.

Kashien squinted into the distance. "What the hell?" Spurring his horse into action, he fell out of line and charged past the slowing mass.

The remaining commanders, along with Ravion and Demetrix, followed after. There was a dark reflection blocking the path, bringing the forward units to a complete halt.

Reaching the front line, Kashien was amazed by the sights before him. What should have been a great marsh was now a great sea. The massive body of water stretched as far as the eye could see, disappearing into darkness long before the opposing shore came into view. Turning to face his men, Kashien dismounted, handing the reins of his horse to Trendal.

"Make camp. We rest here for the evening!" Marching around his steed, he reached into his pack and removed the small wooden box containing his tent.

"My Lord, is it wise to stay here? We're on a collision course with the dreualfar." Trendal reminded his prince.

"What would you have me do, Captain? We have no ships. And there's nothing west but dessert. Even magic has its limits. Every caster among us would be long exhausted before we moved even half the troops, provided we could calculate the distance to the other side. Not to mention overloading the portals could potentially drop them into the middle of the ocean with no hope for a rescue. Like it or not, we're grounded for the night. Establish a heavy watch on all perimeters. I don't want a field mouse getting within archery range without us knowing about it."

"Yes, Sir!" Trendal handed the reins to both his and Kashien's horses to Kaileen and dismounted. Disappearing into the formations, he went to work establishing patrols.

The command tent exploded from the box and began to raise. Waiting for it to fully form, Kashien took the reins from Kaileen and tied them off to the attached hitching post. Opening the door flap, the tent was well illuminated and fully furnished. Stepping inside, he unrolled his map and began studying the unfamiliar terrain.

Demetrix climbed from his saddle, happy to be on his own feet again. Stepping toward the tent, he fell to his knees, clutching his head in pain. Images flashed through his mind. He saw Gareth, secured to a thick wooden post. The wood was stained red from what he guessed was blood. Gareth appeared in good health, aside from his obvious irritation. The fortification itself didn't look familiar, but there was something in the image he could never mistake. The mountains towering far above the settlement, he'd seen them more times than he could count. The image shifted again. He was staring at an outstretched map. A dagger pierced the thick hide, erect from the table beneath it. The elegant, alfarian blade rested above inked blots on the parchment, reading *Baron's Fall.* He guessed it was a human fortress. That was the only thing that made sense. He knew the site well, though the structure completely eluded him. A glowing blue orb appeared in his sight, though it wasn't nearly as clear as the other things he'd seen. This one, the eldarstone, Kashien had called it, was blurry and seemingly out of place, like it was being recalled through a memory rather than actual sight. The image faded away, allowing him to stare into the churned sand beneath him.

Panting heavily, a booming voice echoed in his head, *Gareth's life for the stone. You know where we are. Be quick, he dies in one week!*

Ravion jumped from his saddle, pulling his brother to his feet. "You alright?"

"No. They have Gareth. I need to speak with Kashien!" Demetrix rushed to the tent and stepped inside, finding the dalari prince leaning against the table, lost in thought.

Kashien had a compass resting atop the map. The roof of the magical tent was seemingly missing, revealing stars, freshly illuminated by the sun's departure. Charts were scattered across the table, aligned to their overhead counterparts. Breaking his concentration, Kashien looked up finding Demetrix standing before him. "You look like you've seen a ghost."

"Do you still have the eldarstone?"

"I do. But do you think it wise to tempt fate? These are forces beyond our understanding."

"I'm aware of that. I have no intention of using it. Jorin'otth sent me a message. He has Gareth. Showed me where they are and told me I have a week to trade the stone or they're going to kill him."

"Jorin'otth? That's the hydralfar responsible for the machine?"

"It is."

"I'm sorry, but I can't give you the stone. It's too powerful. I can't risk it falling into their control."

"What about Gareth?"

Ravion stepped into the tent, clearly confused by Demetrix's outburst. "What's going on? You said they have Gareth. Who has Gareth?"

"The dreualfar!" Demetrix stated, holding both conversations.

Kashien pushed himself off the table, reclaiming his weight. "Ravion, would you do me the favor of stepping out for a moment? Your brother and I are discussing something that could potentially lead you down a dark path and I'd like to avoid that if at all possible."

"Um, okay, I guess." Ravion turned and stepped through the door, taking position outside. Watching the units break from their formations into new, smaller groups, he waited to be invited back in.

"I'll help you however I can with Gareth, but the stone must remain hidden. I'm sorry, but my decision is final. If we're done discussing that infernal thing, are we okay to bring Ravion back in?"

"We are."

Kashien approached the door and pulled the flap to the side. "Ravion, you're free to join us?"

Ravion followed Kashien inside, taking position beside Demetrix.

"You said you know where they are. Is it on this map?" Kashien moved the star charts into a large pile, uncovering the terrain details.

Demetrix leaned over the table, staring intently at the thin lines and shaded detail. Finding the blip marked Baron's Fall, he pointed. "I don't know how I didn't see it before. Kashien, do you have a piece of charcoal?"

Kashien fumbled in a small drawer on the underside of the table. A moment later he returned with a thin, black stick. Handing it to Demetrix he watched, uncertain what the young dalari was going to do.

Demetrix placed the edge of the charcoal against the thick parchment and began dragging it across the large continent, creating a divide line.

"That looks like Dalmoura." Ravion announced. The discovery brought an expression of shock.

He brought the thick, black line down, separating the lower half of the land mass, creating three shapes from the one. "They have him at this Baron's Fall place. Which is—"

"Marbayne!" Ravion interjected.

"Exactly. When I saw the mountains, I knew that's where they were. Which means this ocean right outside is the Reinir Sea between Dalmoura and Negield. And we're somewhere in here." Demetrix pointed to a general area near the thick line.

"I've never heard of this Marbayne. But Baron's Fall was the final battle in the Misty Mountains. The humans constructed a great wall that cut the dreualfar forces in half. After that, Baron Rohein and his men trapped what was left of the dreualfar between the foothills and the wall. Thus far it's been the bloodiest battle this war has seen. Both armies were demolished and Baron Rohein fell to a dreualfar spear, but not before landing the killing blow against General Elgar and effectively ending the war in the northern reaches. It makes no sense why they would reclaim a site surrounded by enemy territory."

"He's calling us out. He knows we'll come if it means saving Gareth." Ravion stated flatly.

"I'm afraid I don't understand."

"This Baron's Fall, where we're from it's called Marbayne. It's our home. He's taunting us by taking Gareth home. He plans to kill him the moment we arrive." Demetrix explained softly, unsure how they were going to rescue him before the trap was sprung.

"I see. We'll, I have no command over you. Either of you. While you're dalari, you aren't of my charge, and therefore the decision is yours. I'll aid you however I can, but the odds aren't in your favor."

"We understand. You have your men to worry about, especially if that six-thousand head army is marching this way. Would it be too much to ask for a handful of men to accompany us? And you spoke of magic travel earlier. Now that we know roughly how far the distance is, is there any way we could take a portal across the sea?" A plan was forming in Ravion's head. The real challenge would be ensuring it came to pass as intended. And it never seemed to.

"I'll allow you to plead your case and request volunteers. That's the best I can offer. As for the teleportation, I won't say it's impossible, but I'll need a fairly calculated idea as to how wide the gap is. Only then could I give you an honest answer."

"The port city of Everik to the harbor at Acron in the Southern tip of Dalmoura takes eight days with favorable winds at four and a half knots. That's—," Ravion paused, calculating the distance in his head. "—around eight-hundred and sixty nautical miles. Add another six days walk to that and Marbayne is—," He paused again. "—roughly a thousand miles away, accounting for the difference between nautical and statute miles."

"I think we might be able to get you close if I have some help with the casting. That's quite a distance to send one person, let alone a group. You'll also need a scroll if you're to return."

Kashien pulled a piece of vellum from the table drawer and laid it on the map. "Give me until morning. I need to make sure this is even possible before I give the okay. Until then I'd appreciate if you'd assist with the defenses and help prepare camp for the evening."

Kashien stood at the water's edge, watching the foamy ocean waves crash into the sand inches ahead of him. Rarely had he taken in the beauty of it all. His life was filled with all kinds of wonders, yet it was this moment he chose to appreciate it for what it was. It was his time to be remembered for something great.

Listening to the tide roll, he closed his eyes and let himself drift away. It was time. He opened his eyes and turned around to face his men. Glancing at Ravion and Demetrix, standing to the side, he spoke. "Our scouts have reported a massive dreualfar threat headed our way. While we outnumber them, do not underestimate our enemy. We're in the open with minimal cover. What few fortifications we were able to construct this past night is all we have. Be ready for whatever they throw at us. Many of you may not live to see tomorrow's sunrise. But fear not, we are not alone. Our ancestors are with us. And gods willing, we will end this war!"

The dalari army erupted in cheer at their general's words.

Raising his hands, the shouts faded into silence. "Our brothers here—," Kashien gestured to Ravion and Demetrix. "—are in need of our aid. An agent of the dreualfar has captured their brother and is holding him in the fortress at Baron's Fall. I've given my blessing to mount a rescue. But these dalari cannot succeed alone. They need our assistance. In such times of peril, I cannot order anyone of you to accompany them. I will, however, ask for volunteers. The dreualfar march toward us while these men march into battle themselves. Both paths will be difficult and casualties are expected, though if you look out for your bothers we can minimize the risks. Let any who wish to travel across the sea speak now. For hesitance only leads to regret!"

Several hands appeared throughout the assembled formations. One by one they stepped from their ranks and formed into a separate unit.

Seeing a hand rise from his officers, Kashien was surprised to see it belonged to Trendal.

The young captain stepped from his place and marched ceremoniously toward the new unit.

Kashien scanned the unit of volunteers. He remembered their faces, uncertain if he would ever see them again. There were several more than he'd expected. He thought maybe twenty at most would step forward, but before him stood just under a hundred and fifty men and women. Before he could finish the first row, a common trait sprang into memory. These few once occupied the triage beds. Every single one of them had been affected by Ravion's lust. Yet here they were, ready to die for him.

Taking a deep breath, he exhaled and returned to his commanding presence. "Volunteers, remain. The rest of you, fall out and prepare for battle. The enemy is expected to be upon us by day's end."

The large formation slowly broke apart. Many returned to their duties, sharpening what few logs they could find, while others dug a deep trench in the sand. Preparation was the only thing that was going to save them in the hours to come.

Kashien approached the unit of volunteers. He couldn't help but feel concern about Trendal's decision. "You men understand the dangers you've agreed to enter?"

"Yes, Sir!" They sounded in unison.

Ravion and Demetrix approached the group, taken back by how many had agreed to accompany them.

"Captain Trendal, as you're the ranking officer among these men, you're reassigned to their command. Your previous unit will fall to the command of Lieutenant Razorius."

"Understood and accepted, General."

Kashien nodded, "Fall out and gather your gear. You leave within the hour."

He watched the volunteers saunter off. Waiting a moment, he locked eyes on his captain. "Trendal, would you speak with me privately?"

"Yes, Sir."

As if he'd never exited the formation, Trendal took half a step back, did an about face, and exited the chaotic group from the rear, avoiding the soldiers rushing to gather their belongings. Reaching the side, he casually approached Kashien and waited for the dalari prince to lead the way.

The two walked a short distance to the command tent and disappeared inside.

"Have I done something to upset you?" Kashien asked, more confused than anything.

"No, Sir." Trendal replied unofficially.

"Then why do you volunteer to go on a suicide mission? The dreualfar know they're coming."

"I'm aware of that."

"If it was something I said or did, I apologize. You're my closest friend. Hell, most days you're my only friend. I just don't want you to make a foolish decision based on some animosity you have toward me that I don't know about."

Trendal chuckled. "Kashien, you're a pain in the ass most days, but you've been that way since we were kids. I consider you a brother and even when you manage to piss me off, I'll still have your back. My volunteering has nothing to do with your command or even you for that matter."

"Kaileen?"

Trendal shot a worrisome glance at the mention of her name. "What about her?"

"Oh, don't give me that. I know full well you two have been spending every free moment you have together. A blind man couldn't miss that. And don't worry about it. You both do your jobs. As far as I'm concerned, what you do off duty is your business."

"It's still against regulations."

"Have I ever been one to give a rat's ass about regulations? You've known me longer than anyone else here. Just because I play the part doesn't mean I don't long for the old days." Kashien placed his hand on Trendal's shoulder. "Enjoy yourself. And be sure to name your first kid after me."

"Yes, Sir!" Trendal snapped a mock salute. "And just for your piece of mind, the reason I agreed to go is because Gareth isn't like us. He's impulsive and a bit brutish, but under that rough exterior, he's loyal. And, like it or not, I consider him a friend. I'm going so I can bring my friend back."

"Just make sure you bring yourself back too."

"I will."

The heat was beginning to rise, creating ripples in the air. The ring of hammers echoed all around and wooden walls began to take form at the edge of the growing trench. Sharpened poles protruded from narrow gaps and soldiers went to work lugging buckets of water from the ocean and wetting the sand beneath the post.

Demetrix waited patiently at the water's edge. He was surprised at how much air could get through the thick leather plates of his new armor. Were it not for the stiffness of the form fitting suit, it would have been easy to forget he was even wearing it. He held tight to the grip of his bow. The unusual presence inside it was growing stronger, ensuring him victory. He couldn't explain what it was, but he knew he could trust it. The quiver strapped to his hip was adjusted and ready for use. He missed having his swords, but the stolen dreualfar blade would work until he could have another set forged. It wasn't even that bad of a blade once he replaced the leather and polished the metal. In fact, it could have passed for a myrkalfar short sword if it weren't so clean.

Resting his hand on the pommel, he heard footsteps approach.

"Are you ready for this?" Ravion's voice was both reassuring and uncertain.

"As ready as I can be. I'm surprised so many agreed to accompany us."

"As am I. Though I suspect I know the reason."

"Why's that?"

"Those were the dalari I drained while I was Ra'dulen. I can feel them. And that means they can feel me. I may have inadvertently tied myself to them."

"Do you think that's something Kashien needs to know?"

"I've a feeling he already does."

Kashien approached the pair, dressed in his battle armor and ready for war. "I'm aware. But that's the least of my concerns at the moment. I ask that you do everything within your power to ensure Trendal makes it back. He doesn't know it, but he's to be a father."

"Really? I had no idea he was seeing anyone." Ravion stated, overly casually.

"You need to work on your lying. It's not very convincing." The dalari prince chuckled.

"I've been telling him that for years." Demetrix retorted, slapping his hand against his brother's shoulder.

"Are we ready?" Trendal asked, approaching the group.

"Aye."

"Fall in." Kashien calmly commanded.

Ravion, Demetrix, and Trendal found their place at the head of the formation. Watching the others align themselves, they stood at the ready, awaiting command.

"Unit, attention!"

They snapped in unison, heels firmly together, and toes at a forty-five degree. Arms were locked to the side, and heads straight forward, watching their general.

"Due to the uncanny nature in which this band has come together, I name you, Guardians of Order. May Corin protect you from his seas and see you safely to the other side."

"Guardians!" One of the soldiers sounded.

The others erupted in shouts of praise at the name.

Raising his hand to calm the group, Kashien pulled a rolled scroll from his waistline and handed it to Trendal. Rubbing his hands together, orange sparks danced between his fingers. Slowly pulling them apart, an orb began the form. It spread wider, opening a window to a green field of waist-high grass. Two other orbs formed on either side of Kashien.

Ravion glanced over, seeing several spellcasters working their hands in a similar fashion.

The three orbs expanded, becoming a single entity. Taking form, a wide doorway stood in the air offering entrance to the field. It quit growing and shimmered majestically, as if it the forces on the outer edge were revolving opposite of those within.

"The gateway is stable. You may pass." Kashien said through labored breaths, straining the keep his hands positioned properly.

"Forward, march!" Trendal ordered and they stepped into the portal, disappearing ten at a time.

Chapter XIV
Flanking Maneuvers

A single beam of sunlight shot through the smallest of cracks between the wooden beams crudely nailed over the lone window. Mildew had formed on the rafters and stone walls from the lingering moisture. The scent of rotten meat and stale air loitered, attracting an assortment of flies and other insects.

Gareth scrunched his nose in a feeble attempt to shoo away the fly that was biting into his flesh. He could feel a trickle of blood running from the fresh wound. Straining against his unseen prison, he couldn't move so much as a finger. Worse than that, he was trapped in his mind. Nothing seemed to help. He thought of his family, of the dreualfar that murdered them. Nothing was strong enough to break free. Feeling exhausted from the constant fighting, his eyelids got heavy.

"Hey, Gareth. Stay awake!" Mejra's voice reached him in the dark room. Normally it wouldn't have bothered him, but the single strand of light kept his eye from being able to focus.

Straining, he could just make out her form against the opposite wall. "I thought they'd already taken you."

"They haven't yet. Ye' need to keep 'yer eyes open and quit fighting da' binds. Ye're just exhausting 'yerself. If we're gonna' find a way out o' this, we need ta' maintain our strength. When they remove da' spell, we can make a break 'fer it, but until then I need ya' ta' stay awake."

"How do you know so much about this? Spells and such."

"Me father required I learn da' arcane arts. He said knowledge is power and if I'm ta' lead our people, I have ta' gain all da' power I can."

"Lead your people? You're a princess?" Gareth laughed at the concept.

"Aye, that's one word 'fer it. I wasn't completely honest with ya' earlier. I said my name was Mejra. And while that remains true, my actual name is Alonia, daughter ta' Tsar Mejra and heir ta' da' devonie throne."

"Well, I must say this is a first. I can now honestly say I've seen a princess naked."

"Gods, is that all ya' think about? Seeing me naked? Ya' must have seen dozens, or maybe even hundreds of women naked. Are we really so different that ya' have ta' compare us?"

"The way I see it, if you've seen one woman naked—," Gareth paused a moment, considering his next words. "—you pretty much want to see 'em all."

Mejra sighed heavily. "Fine, ya' want ta' see me naked? Get us out of here and I'll let ya' see anything ya' like!"

"Anything?"

"Within reason. Asshole!" She scoffed, yet found humor in his timing. Though there was no way she was going to give him the satisfaction of knowing that.

Gareth chuckled, feeling a bit of his strength return. Annoying her seemed to inspire him in ways he didn't understand.

The door at the top of the stone stairs creaked open, allowing blinding light to fill the room. Several boots echoed on the hard steps, moving ever closer. The first two dreualfar to reach the bottom approached Mejra and took position on either side.

"Keep your god damned hands off her!" Gareth shouted, seeing her move into view for the briefest moment.

Stay calm, ya' know what ya' must do. Her voice echoed in his mind.

He wasn't sure if she actually spoke or not. Either way he understood her message. Calming himself, we watched the dreualfar carry her up the steep stairs. Another dreualfar approached him, grabbing the top of his stubble covered head.

"Keep your damned hand off me or I'm gonna' rip it off and shove it up your ass." Gareth spat, feeling his hatred rise.

"Calm yourself. There's no need for such graphic threats of violence." Jorin'otth stepped into view, near glowing in the dimly lit room.

Seeing the hydralfar, Gareth strained against the unwelcome grip. Unable to resist, his head craned to one side, revealing his neck to the captors. A sharp pain stabbed into his flesh. He fought as best he could, unable to escape the puncturing instrument.

"Be still. This will be over in a minute." Jorin'otth assured.

It didn't make Gareth feel any better. In fact, it made him want to fight harder. But what could he do? He was still weak and his body was frozen in some kind of stasis. His options were limited. All but Mejra's plan, which seemed the only feasible one he had.

Jorin'otth pulled the thin needle from Gareth's neck and exposed a small glass vial to the beam of light, inspecting it closely.

The dreualfar released him and disappeared up the stairs.

Stretching his neck as best he could, Gareth realized what they'd taken from him. "What the hell do you need my blood for?"

"That's none of your concern. Just trust that it won't go to waste." Jorin'otth turned to leave, stopped himself, and turned back toward Gareth. Approaching a second time, he looked deep into the helpless warrior. "I must say, I like you better this way. You're gruffer. Some might go so far as to say rabid. But I think that's just for show. I mean, if we're being honest, the last time we met I found you kind of boring and dull. This is certainly an improvement."

"What the hell are you talkin' about? I've never see you before in my life!" Gareth demanded, feeling uneasy by the hydralfar's words. He suspected him of lying, but what would that accomplish? There had to be some ulterior motive for his statement.

"Oh, you don't remember? How precious is that?" Jorin'otth chuckled, both curious and amused by this turn of events. He'd avoided Gareth for so long, believing the bald warrior would remember every detail. If he'd know there was no recollection, he'd have killed him years ago.

"We'll, I'm not one to spoil a lovely surprise. But I will say I'm relieved you survived the island. I wasn't at first, mind you. After going through so much effort to kill you, I wanted it done. But I've had some time to think it over. I'm glad you didn't die that day. Had you perished, I wouldn't have become who I am today."

"I don't know what kind of game you think you're playin', but I've never see you before. So, tell me what the fuck you know or I promise, when I get free, I'm going to bash your skull in with my bare hands!"

"More idle threats. Such a shame!" Jorin'otth turned and calmly walked from the dungeon, humming some unrecognizable tune.

The morning fog was dense and difficult to see through. While the sun was out, it did little to pierce the thick blanket hanging in the air.

From the river's edge Ravion squinted into the distance, trying to make out the dark shadows where his beloved home once rested. It seemed odd being here and not seeing it. Though that didn't tell him where it was, and his list of viable options was rather slim. In fact, of all his theories, he'd narrowed it down to two.

One was a parallel dimension. He'd heard a brief bit about them when he was spending time at the tower and working with the magi. But few seemed to believe they truly existed. In large part because no one had been able to bridge the gap between worlds, or at least no one of repute. The occasional claim was made, but those few seemed unable to provide any form of evidence.

His other theory was even more farfetched. Time travel. It was no secret that time was linear and it was able to be manipulated to varying degrees. But to actually travel through time? The entire concept was a joke. A really bad joke. The prospect was absurd. He'd seen some strange things in his life. But to believe such a thing was possible, he may as well be locked in a big blue box and made to see a doctor. Of course, there were other ways to deal with the mentally insane that didn't involve entrapment.

Shaking himself from his thoughts, Ravion returned to the job at hand. It was no use, he couldn't see anything. They'd traveled most of the previous day and throughout the night. They desperately needed rest. But Gareth was running out of time. That meant they couldn't rest. "I can't see a thing through all this fog. It's good for observing from a distance, but we'll never be able to get close without them seeing us. The hills provide the perfect advantage. You can see any advancing group long before they arrive in any condition. If we're going to get closer we have to find another way."

"How about skirting around and following the wall?" Trendal offered, peering through a leather wrapped sight glass. The cool, humid air left a thick layer of cloudy condensation on the lens, making it next to useless. Wiping it on his tunic, he stuffed it back into its pouch.

"That's no good. While the forest would hide most of our movement once we left the wall, it's too thick to pass without drawing attention to

ourselves. At that, we'd never make it up the hill before they found us."
Demetrix explained, recalling the exact reasons they chose to build their
keep in such a position. "We could climb the bluffs and wrap around the
edge of Mount Thuron. It's not an enjoyable climb by any means, but
once we hit the main road we can gain a fair amount of speed before we
have to take to the rocks again. And I know just the place. It'll bring us
out at the northwest corner. From there we just have to breech the
walls."

"If you think you can remember the pass, I'll follow." Ravion offered,
trying to see through the mist once again.

"This will have to be a small group. If we all make the climb, we're
guaranteed to be spotted. Not to mention the dangers one of us falling
would represent. The bulk of us need to remain here and watch. Only
when we're inside do you charge. If we're lucky the distraction will buy
us enough time to find and free Gareth."

"I'll lead the men along the river to the bend up ahead. We can take
shelter behind the rocks until it's time to march." Trendal gestured to
the piled stone at the mountain's base.

"Understood. Give us until nightfall tomorrow. If we haven't
signaled by then, assume we didn't survive the trek." Demetrix glanced
into the overhead peaks. If lower layers of fog were difficult to see
through. Those above were going to be near impossible, though it was
much easier once you were in them. "I want five men. Any more and
we risk drawing too much attention to ourselves."

Dalari hands shot into the air. It seemed the whole unit wanted to
go.

"Vasquez, Morena, Stot, James, and Bingham. You all have some
climbing experience. You're to accompany them." Trendal ordered.
"The rest of you, get ready to move."

The five picked themselves up from the rocks and crawled toward
Ravion, careful to hide from any observing dreualfar. Reaching the
young scout, they waited patiently for orders.

Ravion felt a bit uneasy. Every time he wandered off to relieve
himself, the dalari seemed to express interest in joining him. It was
becoming more of a nuisance than anything. It wasn't that he didn't
trust them, or even that he couldn't count on them, but their admiration
made him feel uncomfortable.

They were like a pack of younger siblings that wanted to spend every waking moment in his company. "Demetrix, lead the way."

The dalari unit waded down the river a short way and disappeared into the collection of rocks, forming a break in the flowing current. If they hadn't seen exactly where the hundred plus man unit moved, they never would have known they were there.

Demetrix scouted the narrow passages, selecting the most fitting for their journey. Finding a hand hold, he pulled himself up, digging the toe of his boot into a crevice between two rocks. Carefully making his way up several feet he glanced down, seeing Ravion and the others below him. At this rate, they'd do well to reach the mountain kingdom by nightfall.

Making his way into the heavens, the air was getting thick and cold. He was starting to see flurries impacting against his blackened armor. This was going to add another hazard to their journey, though it was one he knew to expect. Finding a small ledge, he took refuge from the constant winds and biting cold. Pulling his cloak around him, he went to work building a small fire in the corner. It would do the men good to warm their hands and take a break.

Ravion reached the ledge, smelling the burning tinder in the air. Climbing to his feet, he approached his brother, hearing the others close behind. "Do you think it's wise to start a fire up here? Once it gets dark, the dreualfar could see the glow."

"We won't be here that long. I plan to reach the summit by nightfall. Warm your hands and rest for a moment. We're high enough. I doubt anyone from the ground can see the glow."

Certain the flame was self-sustained against the intense winds, Demetrix stood and approached the ledge. He hadn't had a chance to look beyond the moment for the past several hours. At this height, he could faintly make out Heroes Gate stretching across the land. It was an impressive structure to say the least, though the cloud cover made it difficult to see more than the occasional patch. Pulling a piece of dried meat from his pack, he turned and glanced up the mountainside, toward the peak. He was still four hours at minimum from reaching Mount Thuron. The sun was going to set in about three. They needed to gain some ground, and fast. If night fell before they found a place to rest, it was unlikely they'd survive the morning.

Seeing the dalari crowded around the fire, he couldn't help but think they were just along for the trip. In truth, the only reason they were here was to provide backup once they moved on the fortress. If it weren't for that, he would have preferred they stayed with the others. "We move in five. Eat what you can and get some feeling back in your fingers. We don't stop again until we reach the top."

The sun was hidden somewhere behind the mountain and the light was getting dim. The occasional patch of flurries had given way to constant snowfall. Rocks were layered in thick powder and difficult to see. Several times now Demetrix had narrowly caught himself from a deceptively loose stone or a slick crevice. Fortunately, they hadn't lost anyone yet. But the day wasn't over. As if the thought forced itself into existence, he heard a commotion beneath him. Glancing down, he watched Vasquez disappear. He didn't make a sound in his rapid descent. He was simply gone. Shaking his head, he returned to the task at hand and reached up, wrapping his frozen fingers around a jagged stone. Pulling himself to the top, he saw what he'd been waiting for.

The ice-covered ground was flat for several hundred feet. Frozen trees stood in the distance, a collection of cedar or pine, he couldn't be sure. The green needles were speckled in white, and large mounds of snow formed at their bases. In the distance, Demetrix could see a large, seemingly white wall, though he suspected it was an illusion the weather was playing on him. The bricked wall stretched to the north as far as the eye could see. The southern corner traveled across the rocky, frozen land and arched over what he could only assume was the Thuron River.

He'd never actually made the trip to Mount Thuron, in large part to their opinion of the occupants to the world below. Living in the mountains, away from civilization, had made them less than accepting of outsiders. Though their problem was more with humans than any other. The numerous threats they'd made against Marbayne during his time as highlord certainly didn't help his opinion of the winged alfarian race. There was certainly a beauty to their form, however their personalities often lacked what most would call compassion.

Making his way toward the wall, Demetrix could see the last remnants of the sun disappear. The bright orange glow was growing dimmer by the second and they needed to take shelter for the night.

Ravion pulled himself to the top shelf. Waiting at the edge for the others, he extended his hand.

One by one they took it, pulling themselves up. The air was freezing up here and sun was fading rapidly. It was going to get much colder extremely quick. Making their way toward Demetrix, they froze, staring blankly at the wall.

"You think we should see if they'll let us take shelter for the night?" Stot asked, amazed by the sheer size of the structure. It towered nearly forty feet into the air and was perfectly flat of what appeared to be some kind of glossy stone. The only texture the wall displayed was where the snow had collected between bricks.

"No. We need to set up camp somewhere we won't draw attention to ourselves. These people don't tend to accept outsiders and would be more likely to take us prisoner than to aid us in anyway." Demetrix proclaimed. "We'll make camp over there." He pointed to the patch of evergreens beside the river. They formed a natural ring, offering concealment on all sides. And the mounds of snow would help disguise them from any passersby.

Making his way toward the trees, he realized exactly how deep the snow was. In just a few feet, he'd already sunk to his waist. That wouldn't be good for remaining hidden. But hopefully the constant downfall would quickly cover their tracks. If not, perhaps Bingham could use some kind of magic to help them. Reaching the trees, he passed through a shoulder high mound and stepped onto a bed of pine needles. To his surprise, there was little more than a thin layer of snow inside the ring. Opening his pack, he pulled one of the magicked tents out and set it in the center. "Bingham, do your thing."

The dalari mage pointed his fingers at the tightly packed bundle. Without a word it began to rise, inflating into a domed shaped hut.

Demetrix grabbed the leather pouch of stakes, and quickly made his way around, ensuring it didn't blow away with them during the night.

Ravion pulled the flap aside and stepped inside, relieved to feel warmth after being frozen for so long. Of course, it was going to make the morning much harder to bear. But comfort was something soldiers weren't often afforded. Perhaps it was best to enjoy it while they could.

The dalari stepped into the tent and got warm. The magical fire was blazing and a kettle was steaming over the top. Pulling it from the flame, Morena lifted the blackened lid, releasing the scent of stew throughout the common room. One by one, they made a bowl and got comfortable. They were going to have to make the climb all over again tomorrow, so it was best to make the night theirs.

Stot took a seat along the wide bench beside the hearth. Unslinging his shield, he laid it across his lap and placed the wooden bowl on top as a makeshift table.

James plopped down beside him, handing over a matching tankard, filled to the brim with a foamy liquid.

Scouting the horizon in the faded sunlight, Demetrix was content they hadn't been seen, though it was best to exercise caution. He glanced at the tracks they'd made getting here. They were already half gone from the heavy winds. And the snow was quickly burying what was left. With any luck they'd go unnoticed. Kicking the snow clinging to his boots against the base of one of the trees, he stepped inside and pulled the flap shut.

The early morning light was multiplied by the layered snow all around them. For the most part, the constant flurries had stopped, save for the occasional dusting off the trees or a heavy wind. The sun wasn't yet visible, but its glow was getting brighter by the minute.

Demetrix stared intently over the towering city wall, watching the steam from his breath rise into the air. Another group of it winged citizens rose into the sky, their feathered appendages flapping vigorously against the harsh winter breeze. Like several before them, they formed into a staggered pattern and disappeared into the northern clouds. He wondered where they were going but it didn't matter. Not so long as they didn't interfere with his plans. Stealing a glance to the fallen tent behind him, he noticed Ravion was nearly ready to travel. Locating the remaining dalari, awaiting command near the mountain's edge, he crunched through the snow toward them.

"Mind your footing. We don't need to lose any more to something so careless as a misplaced step." He reminded them.

Morena stared down the harrowing cliffs, unable to see the ground. "Do you think he fell all the way? Or is he lying on the rocks somewhere?"

Demetrix stepped to the ledge and stole a glance down. "It's hard to say. We inclined quite a bit, so I'd say he's probably caught in the rocks near the landing we took a break. Either way, it's near impossible he survived the fall. And if he did, he's probably since died from blood loss. Did you know him well?"

"We were childhood friends." Morena stifled a tear at the loss of her companion.

Demetrix placed his hand on her shoulder. "Keep your friend in mind, but don't let his fate become your own."

Lowering his hand, he turned away from the group, watching another batch of the winged creatures disappear. "We need to move before another group of seralfar take flight."

Jogging across the deep snow, he approached the ring of trees, seeing Ravion packed and ready. "We need to move now."

"Lead the way."

Making his way through the snow, Demetrix saw the orange glow of the sun on the rise. Racing the fast-moving beam, quickly gaining on him, he ran for the wall, hearing his companions at his heels. He reached the towering structure in no time, just as the sunlight illuminated the unusual material.

Being so close to it, he noticed it wasn't a white stone at all, but rather some kind of iridescent that appeared white from a distance. Placing his hand on the glassy surface, an orange glow expanded around it. "Interesting— It seems the wall picks up the colors around it."

"We need to keep moving. You can study their wall after we've found Gareth." Ravion suggested, pausing behind his brother.

"You're right." Picking himself up, Demetrix made his way along the glossy stone, keeping an eye overhead. He hoped being so close to the structure would hide them. Provided the wall wasn't transparent from inside. But there was little chance of that. If it was, they would have been seen the moment they reached the landing. Making his way toward the northeast corner, Demetrix could see the wide mountain road just ahead. They were nearing their target at last.

Ravion and the others slowed behind him, studying the path from the cover of the corner. It was unlikely the city entrance would be unguarded, therefore making it to the road unseen was going to be a problem.

Peeking around, Demetrix saw the massive city gate half way down the wall, resting atop a large, arched bridge. The Thuron River flowed under it and into the city through a heavy iron grate. Two guardsmen stood at the end of the bridge, paying no attention to the world around them.

Turning to face his companions, he knelt down to describe his plan. "Bingham, do you have any way to make a smoke cloud or some kind of natural looking screen so we can get to the road without drawing attention to ourselves?"

The dalari mage thought for a moment. "I could create a few different variants of mist, but I fear the wind is too strong. It'd be carried away before it could get thick enough to travel unseen. I could amplify the natural weather. A heavy snow should obscure vision just as well as a fog."

Glancing to Ravion, Demetrix nodded his approval. "Sounds good to me. Make it happen. Once we get on the road we'll be able to move much faster, though we'll still have to be weary of the ice for a few hours."

The mage stood to his full height, lifting his hands into the air. His pale skin was red from the constant cold and his lips were a soft blue. It was clear he hadn't spent much time in such surroundings.

Closing his eyes, he began to chant. "Ecaf ym revo lla, daol ruoy ytpme uoy ksa I. Ecarg rouy em dnel, retniw fo stnemele!"

Dark clouds swirled into existence, blocking out what little sunlight had risen. Heavy snowflakes began to crash to the already covered ground. Within moments the area was surrounded in a strong blizzard.

Ravion stared wide-eyed at the estranged caster. "What kind of spell are you casting?"

Bingham shrugged at the question. "Elemental magic?"

"If you say so." Ravion shrugged it off, glancing at the monstrous flakes of snow raining down upon them.

Demetrix peeked around the corner. He couldn't see the guards through the downpour and rapidly shifting winds. Now was their chance. Stepping into the open, he moved as quickly and carefully as possible toward the road. Reaching the edge, he stole a glance back, hoping he couldn't be seen from the gate. Unable to see further than a few feet away, he waved the others over, hoping they could still see him.

Ravion appeared from the speckled white, then Morena. Stot and Bingham were the last to arrive.

Turning on heel, Demetrix led the way, stepping onto the densely packed road. The light layer of snow on top of ice made it dangerously slick. Rounding the bend, he felt it decline slightly, wrapping its way around the steep cliff face.

They followed the road for many hours. The snow had ceased and the humidity was beginning to rise with the heat, though it was still far from comfortable. Reaching a bend, Demetrix came to a stop, looking through the lower hanging clouds to the land below. He could nearly see Shadgull from this distance, though the large capital city was likely much different than he knew it.

Ravion stood beside him, taking in the sight. "She's different than I remember."

"That she is. This is where we need to leave the road. Any further down and we risk being seen."

"Do you think Trendal's waiting for us?" Ravion asked, stealing a glance at the dalari behind him.

"I'm sure he is. He's not a fool. Attacking the fortress without someone on the inside could take days. I'm sure he knows that."

"Ravion, I was wondering. Why'd you stay in Irayth?" Morena asked, stepping between the two.

"How do you know that name?" Re snapped, caught off guard hearing the simple question. He knew these dalari were linked to him but he had no idea to what extent.

"It's a vision. Like a memory, but not my own. I see you in a chamber. You told Gareth to take Demetrix home. Then you shattered the tunnel behind you."

"You have my memories? Why didn't you say something about that sooner?"

"I didn't know. It just popped into my head."

He had no idea how to process the discovery. His life was none of their business, but it seemed there was much that no longer remained solely to him.

Taking a deep breath, Ravion regarded the young dalari woman before answering. "I stayed because I had to. Rezerik wanted me to take his place so he could leave. But the only way he could do that was to make me the new nightking. While we killed him, his mantle had to remain and I was the only one to take it."

Shifting uncomfortably, he turned away from her, staring at the narrow trail Demetrix had pointed out. "This way?"

Refusing to wait for a response, he stepped past Demetrix and on to the rocky ledge.

Levi Samuel

Chapter XV
Defining Fears

Stars twinkled far above the vast wasteland spanning the glistening sea. Dalari soldiers stood patiently behind their fortifications, hands clutched tightly around their weapons. They stared into the darkness, searching for the source of the thundering drum beat.

Kashien scanned his troops one last time, ensuring everyone was in place. The archers stood in position to his left, arrows drawn and awaiting command. The magi were to the right, spells primed and ready. At the spiked wall, the infantry stood behind the support beams, hiding their numbers from the advancing army. A collection of shieldsmen and swordsmen made up the bulk of their number. He was torn as to whether he should implement a shield wall, but the battlements would serve that purpose, at least until the enemy was beyond them.

The pikesmen composed the second wave, their longer pole weapons were able to reach beyond the first group. This gave them the advantage of reach in such tight quarters. Of course, he expected the dreualfar to have a similar formation. That was basic warfare tactics.

Glancing to the south, he could faintly make out the silhouettes of the cavalry in the distance. They were mounted and awaiting need behind the only hill within range. Kashien wanted them out of sight, but close enough to arrive quickly if need arose. They were the secret weapon in this battle. If placed carefully, they could flank the enemy and attack on two fronts. And if the wall fell, it would be the cavalry to pick up the slack and force them back long enough to form a traditional shield wall.

The drum beats got closer, shaking the ground to its core. Tensions were high. Everyone was on edge, unable to see what approached. In all of it they knew one thing. The enemy was close.

"Light fires!" Kashien ordered, gesturing to the torchbearers.

Sparks flared in his peripheral vision. The ground to his left erupted in large, orange and yellow flames. It traveled along the line of oil they'd poured in the sand shortly after the drums sounded. Another flame erupted to his right, not far behind the magi. Stealing a glance, he saw the thick ball of twine, string, and grass they'd crafted earlier in the day ignite.

The multiple flames dulled his vision, but it was just bright enough to see the edge of the enemy forces.

"Prepare arrows!"

The archers dipped their cloth-wrapped arrowheads into the flame, watching them flare up.

"Archers, catapult— Fire!"

Thousands of flaming arrows took to the sky, shooting like little meteorites in the darkness above. The popping of rope and wood echoed through the formations and a large flaming ball took to the sky. Together, they soared into the distance and crashed to the earth.

Kashien watched the arrows strike, taking out a number of the dreualfar forces. Suddenly, the field ignited, exploding in a massive ball of flame. He watched the flame jump across the tracks of oil they'd poured earlier in the day. It was enough to see where and what the enemy was doing. If things continued to go this smooth, the battle would be over before morning.

Hearing a whistle amidst the echoing screams he looked to the sky, seeing only the briefest reflection of light.

"Night arrows, take cover!" Kashien threw his hands over head, forming a shield out of the arcane magics within him.

Watching the sharpened heads hit and glance off, he searched the damage to his men. They hadn't been so lucky. At minimum, a few hundred were hit. He knew the dreualfar were without honor, but to fire night arrows? That was cowardly, even for them.

"Prepare for another volley! Archers, fire at will!"

Another round of flaming arrows speckled the sky, raining down upon the charging dreualfar. Shouts echoed along the battlefield as they drew closer. The first wave collided against the battlements and the dalari spilled out to combat them.

Thick patches of moss clung to the jagged, stone wall. The air was warm and moist. The scent of dirt and smoke filled the air.

Demetrix peered down from his perch, seeing the backside of the wooden fortress, hidden among the trees. Two dreualfar wandered along the forest floor, aimlessly patrolling the fortifications. Glancing at Ravion and the other dalari obscured behind the protruding rocks, he gestured, relaying his findings without word.

Ravion leaded over, whispering the message to Stot. "Thirty yards away, two dreualfar. We move in three minutes."

Stot nodded, relaying the message to the others.

Morena drew an arrow and nocked it on her bowstring. It was going to be difficult to climb with the weapon, but if she could find a decent position she could pick them off from afar. At least until it was time to breech the wall.

Bingham crouched down and made his way closer to the scout. "I have a spell that could allow you to fire while descending."

"Oh?"

"It'll make you fall at a slow rate until your feet hit the ground."

"Okay."

The dalari mage contorted his fingers, silently reciting the incantation. A blue glow formed between hands. It floated from his grasp, settling on her brown, leather boots. They shimmered a brief moment before returning to their dull and weathered state.

"You have but to jump. The spell will do the rest. But only once, so don't waste it."

"Understood."

Demetrix saw his chance rapidly approaching. The dreualfar were farthest apart, one disappearing in the northern trees, while the other headed south. Now was the time. Jumping from his perch, he threw his arm around the tapered rock and kicked out. Letting a freefall claim him, his feet impacted the steep terrain and began to slide beneath the loose pebbles. Balancing himself, he slapped the rocks as he passed, maintaining balance and slowing his speed.

Seeing the next ledge, he unlocked his knees and landed on the hard stone. The pressure was jarring, but he was able to absorb it, though he felt the magic in his right leg strain to keep its hold. Searching the ground, he saw the dreualfar were advancing slowly back toward him. Content they hadn't seen him, he pulled his refurbished bow from his back, stringing it faster than most could nock an arrow. Taking aim, he aligned the shaft with the southern dreualfar. Feeling the wind with every fiber of his being, he adjusted for the mild breeze and released.

The arrow flexed from the pressure and launched into the sky. It arched upward, twisting against the crosswinds. Reaching peak height it advanced onward, angling slightly.

Demetrix watched the wooden shaft plunge into the dreualfar's throat, knocking the creature from its feet. Jumping from the landing, he hit the ground, allowing his body to buckle. He rolled, redirecting the impact and sprang back to his feet, another arrow nocked and ready to fire.

Ravion jumped from rock to rock, balancing himself. He needed to close the gap, but hadn't found a path he could safely jump or slide from.

The dreualfar scout froze, seeing the archer in the distance. The trained shot protruding from his compadre's corpse told him there was little time. He'd never reach the archer before an arrow found him.

Catching movement from the rocks above, he stole a glance seeing a few others racing down the jagged stones.

The archer was trained on him. He had to do something quick or his death wound be imminent. Breaking into a sprint, he dove into the rocks, hearing the arrow plink near his head. He'd bought himself some time. Now he needed to get reinforcements.

Grabbing the horn strapped to his waist, he brought it to his lips and blew as hard as he could. An ear-splitting tone escaped briefly, cut short. A sharp pain erupted in the back of his throat. His mouth filled with blood. Staring at the wooden shaft protruding from the horn, panic began to set in. He was dying. Strength waning, he grabbed the arrow and tried to pluck it from him. It was buried too deep. He could feel the iron head tearing his esophagus. Choking on his own blood, he collapsed, seeing the trespassers move ever closer in his final sights.

Levi Samuel

Demetrix glanced up the mountain, seeing Morena's bowstring reverberating from the discharge. She grabbed another arrow and jumped, nocking it to the string. Her boots glowed a faint blue as she slowly fell to the ground. Seeing Ravion and the others reach the dirt and rock covered floor, he joggled toward them. "Someone had to have heard that horn before it was silenced. We need to get to the wall now!" A sharp pain shot through his chest. His hands impacted the rocky earth, tearing against the sharp mineral. He slammed to the ground, panting heavily. Stealing a glance toward the wall, he noticed a third dreualfar preparing another spell.

Ravion looked from his collapsed brother to the dreualfar. Stepping toward the creature, he extended his hand, pulling at the power within it. The dreualfar mage hissed in pain, struggling against the unseen hook. Realizing what he was doing, Ravion dropped the mage. His heart pounded within his chest. Out of breath, he broke contact with the mage and locked eyes on Demetrix.

Free of the vice like grip, the dreualfar mage went to work creating his spell a second time. His fingers contorting as rapidly as possible, he released the massive spell hoping to cripple them all in one shot.

Seeing the large fireball headed toward him, Demetrix rolled to his back. It was as if his death was happening in slow motion. He was helpless to stop it. Seeing no other options, he glanced to Ravion. The look of defeat was heavy on his face. He wasn't wrong. He failed to kill the dreualfar. And that failure was going to result in their deaths. It was nearly upon him when someone blocked its view.

Bingham charged in front of the flaming ball, using his own magics to protect him. The spell impacted, exploding against the magical shield. Scorching flame domed around him, igniting the ground on all sides. He strained against the brunt of the blast, hoping it wouldn't reach the others. Feeling the spell reach its end, he released the shield. Lowering his arms, he noticed the blackened, charred flesh clinging to him. His hands were useless, little more than jagged nubs. Looking down, he could see his heart beating inside his chest, covered in black soot. The meat and organs were damaged beyond repair. He knew then he was already dead, he just hadn't felt it yet. Turning to face his companions, he collapsed and fell face first into the dirt.

"No!" Morena shouted, releasing her bowstring. The arrow flew true, imbedding itself in the dreualfar's face. The mage tumbled over the wall, landing roughly on the ground.

Landing softly, Morena ran to the still form of Bingham and rolled him over. A tear fell from her cheek, seeing another friend fall.

Picking herself up, she knelt down beside Demetrix, hoping he was going to be okay. "Is anything permanently damaged?"

"No. It just hurt—a lot." Demetrix said, chuckling to himself. He could still feel where the bolt had impacted but he'd be okay. Extending his hand, Morena pulled him to his feet. Rubbing his chest, he turned to Ravion, "What the hell happened? You had him. Then you just stopped?"

Ravion refused to look at his brother. He'd made a mistake. Another mistake. They seemed to be piling up lately. "I'm sorry. I was afraid I was going to lose control. I couldn't risk it."

"Well, your fear resulted in the death of one of our own. You wouldn't have stood for that back home. I won't stand for it here. Get your head right or wait here until Trendal's men show up!"

Demetrix shook his head, hating he had to say such things to his brother. But this was too important to leave to chance. They nearly died because of his hesitation. Such a thing could not happen again. Turning away, he marched toward the fortress. He spanned the distance in no time, reaching the carved trees comprising the outer wall. Pulling a coiled rope from the side of his pack, Demetrix quickly unwrapped it and looped the end. Slinging it around, he released, watching the wide loop launch over the wall snag on the top of the wooden structure. It caught one of the sharpened points, lassoing the thick beam. He pulled as hard as he could, ensuring it was secure. Demetrix lifted himself and kicked off the wall, carrying himself up. He reached the top with ease, peering into the fortified base. It was as if this was his first time here. Nothing looked as he remembered it. This Baron's Fall was not the place he knew as home. Instead it was a human structure made out of wood and iron.

The fort stood three stories tall and had a collection of smaller buildings along the outer wall. The yard was cluttered and piled high with broken furniture and dead bodies. Humans as far as the young dalari could tell. A fire burned in the center, sending an array of glowing embers and spent ash into the sky. But there was one detail that stood odd among all others. The dreualfar were nowhere to be seen.

Demetrix glanced over the wall at his companions, patiently awaiting his signal. Gesturing them to follow, he turned and carefully made his way along the allure, just inside the sharpened posts. Finding a wooden walkway, he skipped down the steps, two at a time. Stepping onto the bare, dirt floor, he looked around. Gareth had to be here, as did the dreualfar. They wouldn't have been guarding an empty fort. The question remained, where were they?

Ravion made his way down the steps and took position beside his brother. He couldn't blame the younger dalari for his words. Were their roles reversed, he would have said something similar. Forcing it from his mind, he swallowed and spoke. "Do you think it's a trap? To lure us here with false promise of Gareth?"

"It's possible, though I doubt it. We got here quicker than most would expect. According to Jorin'otth's message, we still have three days until time's up. They wouldn't lay in wait that long in advance. I'd imagine they went into hiding when they heard the horn. Be on your guard." Demetrix said to himself as much as the others.

"Guys!" James shouted from one of the smaller buildings on the left.

Ravion and Demetrix turned to see what the swordsman was looking at. Inside the wooden structure, what appeared to be a stable at one point, the straw floor was coated in soupy, red gore. At least thirty horses were strung to the rafters, dangling from their hindquarters. Their hide had been stripped and chunks of rotten meat clung to the bone. A sweet scent filled the air. They approached to get a better look.

"This makes no sense. Why would they butcher the horses and leave them to rot? There has to be something more here." Stot offered, taken back by the finding.

Ravion stepped inside, feeling the ground squish beneath his boots. Looking down, the soupy straw bubbled around his feet. Only now did he see the other bodies hanging like the horses.

Hundreds of humans had been stripped of their flesh and strung up to bleed out. A dark alter had been crudely constructed at the center of the stable, drenched in blood. Ravion recognized the dark sigil marking the stone as that of Izaryle. It seemed the dreualfar had learned the secret of the dark god and were attempting to summon his grace. "There's nothing more to see in here." Wiping the stench from his nose, he smashed the alter and made for the door, hoping to never have to look upon such a massacre again.

The dalari made their way toward the large fire at the center of the fortress. The flames danced wildly, but it seemed it wasn't nearly as large as it had been hours before. A large mass of spent wood and bone lingered in the coals, but there was plenty more, waiting to be consumed. A steady pillar of white smoke drifted into the air, disappearing beyond the overhanging trees.

Demetrix watched it fade away, shifting its path in the breeze. An unnatural form caught his attention, hiding among the tree tops. Squinting into the distance, he could faintly make out the details of armor.

Realizing it had been found, the dark form shifted and disappeared. "It's a trap. Ready your weapons!"

A single arrow flew through the air, striking James in the chest and knocking him from his feet. He hit the ground, snapping the protruding arrowhead beneath him. Gurgling on his own blood he struggled to pull himself up, growing weaker by the moment.

Ravion drew his longsword and knelt down beside the dying dalari. "Don't fight it, my friend. It'll be over soon."

He gripped his hand, holding it tight. He couldn't explain why, but it felt like a piece of him was dying, the third piece in as many days. Feeling James' grip go slack, he stood and took a defensive stance.

Several dreualfar roared from their hiding places, encircling the band of trespassers. A horn echoed, evoking a mass of shouts from the outnumbering dreualfar.

An eerie silence overfell the river basin as the sun was beginning to set for the night. The rushing waters stilled, refusing to slap against rock. Crickets silenced. Birds ceased to chirp. For the briefest moment the world was still, neither lingering in the past, nor planning for the future. It was simply frozen in the now.

Glancing at the dalari warrior lying in wait beside him, Trendal noticed the man carving a jagged trident into the left shoulder of his leather breastplate. Stealing a glance at the others, they had the same mark. Something larger than his understanding was at work here. But now was not the time for investigation. Such a thing could wait for their return to camp. Hearing a grading horn blast echoed over the land, natural order took hold again.

The dalari awaited his command, ready to spring from their stations. The water flowed gently, eroding the rocks little by little each passing moment. The crickets resumed their choir. Feeling the breeze return to the world, he knew the time had come. Jumping from the crevice he'd wedged himself into, Trendal listened to the unsettling pitch fade away, recognizing it for what it was.

"Prepare to battle. We march upon Baron's Fall!"

Dalari swarmed from every nook and cranny along the river's edge. Shaking the stiffness from their joints, they formed into a single, solidary force and readied their weapons.

Awaiting the last of his unit to form up, Trendal took position at their head. Drawing his sword, he thrust it into the air. "Charge!" Adrenalin rushed through him, sprinting toward the distant fortress. He ran as fast as he could, his small army at his heels.

They roared forward, battle chants and thundering footsteps echoing against the mountain wall.

The dreualfar patrols froze, lost in the sight of the assembled and charging army. Hearing commands barked, they grouped up as a last defense to slow the advancing attackers.

Taking defensive positions, the dalari clashed against them.

The closest dreualfar were little more than iron kindling beneath the force of a hammer. They washed over them with ease. Reaching the small formation at the wall, they slowed, locking their shield wall in opposition of the assembled patrols. Arrows plummeted toward them, plinking off their shields and sticking in the dirt.

"Archers, fire!" Trendal ordered, listening to the snap of bowstrings. The dalari arrows launched into the enemy force, dropping nearly half in a single shot.

"Fire at will. Wall, advance!"

His archers began targeting the opposing bowmen at the top of the wall while the melee combatants closed in on the ground forces. Pinning them against the wooden gate, the shield wall opened in the center allowing the swordsmen to swarm through. They cut down the remaining dreualfar with ease, awaiting further command.

The dalari captain scanned the flanks. Seeing no other advancing forces, he stole a glance at the archers atop the wall. They were going to have to be dealt with before they could attempt to climb over. Such an entry would take too long and wasn't worth the dangers of taking an arrow in the back. Weighing his options, he made a decision. "Archers, provide cover. Casters, bring down the gate."

Demetrix plunged the tip of his arrow into one of the surrounding dreualfar. Retracting the blood coated head, he nocked and fired, dropping another. Spinning on his heel, the wooden arm of his bow swooped the legs from beneath another. There were so many, and more seemed to be spilling from every opening. Grabbing another arrow, he realized he was nearly out. Just a shot or two more and he'd have to resort to his sword.

The sharpened longsword slashed across two dreualfar in one swipe. Carrying the dexterous weapon around, Ravion deflected a rapier, knocking the thin weapon off course. Spotting his opening, he stabbed deep into the attacking dreualfar, ripping the blade free as another pressed in.

Morena grabbed for another arrow. Worry took hold, feeling the empty quiver. Swinging the bow, the tensile wood flexed and wrapped partially around her attacker. The string went slack for the briefest moment and the wood snapped, thundering out like the crack of a whip. The splintered wood punctured flesh and the string sliced into the black-skinned creature. Drawing her sword, a stout force slammed into her side, knocking her from her feet.

Seeing Morena hit the ground, Stot charged, slamming his shield into the towering dreualfar. This one was taller than most, his muscular frame bulging against his stained, brown tunic. He stumbled back from the impact, finding the massive dreualfar unmoved by the blow. His sword at the ready, he prepared for the worst.

"I'm so glad you could join me. I feared for a moment you wouldn't." Jorin'otth's mellow, majestic voice carried over the sounds of battle.

The dreualfar slowed to a stop, allowing the charismatic hydralfar his words.

"Where's Gareth!" Demetrix demanded. The tip of his last arrow aimed at the traitorous hydralfar's face. He had but to release the string and this threat would be over.

Jorin'otth snapped his fingers, gesturing to the largest building within the fort.

Gareth came into view from the darkened door frame. He stared straight ahead, seemingly frozen. Slowly floating toward the gathering, he stopped beside his hydralfar puppeteer.

"Don't fret for his health. I assure you he's still alive. I just rendered him into an easily managed state. That foolish woman put some ideas in his head and I couldn't rightly have him attempt to escape once you arrived." Jorin'otth turned to the stationary warrior, petting his stubbled head as if to show his dominance over the brute.

Ravion had never seen such spellwork before. It was one of the most complex weaves he'd had the pleasure of inspecting, excluding those of the Irayth mirrors. But he hadn't been able to fully decipher those. They were incomplete, as if the majority of the puzzle was missing. But that was a different type of magic altogether. Compared to those weaves these were simple, exceptionally advanced, but mundane by comparison. The golden threads were wrapped around one other and intertwined like those of a minor time alteration. But this was so much more than that. Studying the weave, he found a thread that hadn't fully sealed. If he could pluck it, it was possible the entire spell would unravel and Gareth would be free. He felt his innate magics grip the thread. Pausing, doubt filled his mind. *It's too dangerous. What if I give in? What if I lose control? No, I can't help anyone that way.* Releasing the frayed thread, he closed his eyes, forcing his anxiety into the pit of his stomach.

"What woman?" Demetrix asked, refusing to lower his aim.

Waving it off as if it was of little concern, Jorin'otth gestured one of the dreualfar. "He was gallivanting with some devonie tramp when I found him."

The black-skinned creature turned and marched toward the large building. Stepping through the doorway Gareth had appeared moments before, he disappeared inside. A few moments later, he returned, carrying a woman over his shoulder. She'd been beaten and appeared unconscious. Returning to his position beside Jorin'otth, he unceremoniously flung her to the ground, watching her limp form roll to a stop.

Demetrix couldn't tell if she was still alive, though it didn't make much sense to retrieve her if she wasn't.

"Now, if you'd be so kind, give me the eldarstone and we'll be on our way." Jorin'otth smiled. He knew full well they didn't bring it. Were he in their position, he wouldn't have. But maybe they were just stupid enough to prove him wrong. It wouldn't be the first time.

Lowering his aim, the young ranger let the tension off his bow, but kept the arrow ready if needed. "First, have your—," Demetrix paused, selecting his word choice. "—men, stand down. I'm not going to hand you a damned thing until I'm sure we can be on our way without them attacking the moment we relinquish the only leverage we have."

"And if I don't? How do I know you aren't just buying time? If I'm to trust you, you're going to have to trust me." Jorin'otth smiled. He already had all the leverage, though it didn't matter. He was finally going to crush them once and for all.

"Not going to happen!"

The hydralfar exhaled softly and slow. There was no need to rush things. He had all the time in the world. "Show me the stone. Once I'm convinced you have it, I'll have them retreat so we may conclude our business."

"Done." Demetrix reached into his new, perfectly fitting armor. Wrapping his fist around the large, blue stone, he brought it into sight. It pulsed in his grip, mimicking that of a beating heart.

Staring intently at the glowing stone, Ravion felt as if he should recognize the mystical artifact. But the stone before him was anything but familiar. In fact, there was nothing special about it at all. Just a simple illusion clinging to a fist sized rock. Suddenly, he understood what Demetrix was doing.

"Tell them to stand down and it's yours, once we have Gareth."

Studying his face, Jorin'otth couldn't find any sign of betrayal. It was a stupid play, giving the stone to him. But he'd never attributed the young ranger with much intelligence anyway. "Stand—."

Sounds of battle echoed outside the wall. Arrows plinked off the parapets, finding the occasional archer. Those who were hit stumbled over the railing and fell to the ground.

"Kill them. Kill them all!" Jorin'otth bellowed, backing out of melee range.

A massive explosion echoed through the fortress, shaking the ground. The reinforced wooden gate buckled and collapsed under the force, sending jagged bits of burning wood into the dreualfar ranks.

Dalari spilled through the ruptured gateway, trampling the debris and wounded dreualfar among it. They clashed against the opposing force, showering the land in a spray of black and red blood.

Seeing his chance, Demetrix drew his bow, taking aim on the cowering hydralfar. Releasing the string, the wooden shaft flexed beneath the force and launched forward.

Jorin'otth felt panic set in. He'd underestimated them yet again. And now the dalari were out numbering his men. Tygrell certainly wouldn't accept this failure lightly. He needed something to soften the blow. Something to evoke the general's mercy. Seeing the glowing stone laying on the ground a few feet away, his plan began to form. He rushed toward it, silently whispering an incantation. Swirling energies wrapped around him, forming a protective shield from all nonmagical attacks. Kneeling down, he secured the pulsing artifact, pleased to have such a relic in his possession once again.

A sharp pain erupted in the side of his face. Jorin'otth stumbled back. Writhing in agony, he extended his fingers, feeling the deep gash in his left cheek. Bright red blood clung to the tips, glossy wet from the graze. How the arrow had gotten through his shield, he'd never know. He had to get out of here. The dreualfar couldn't hold much longer. He had the stone. That was all that mattered.

Gareth collapsed to the trampled ground, feeling his body become his own again. Pushing himself from the dirt, he looked around, seeing the battle waging all around him. He had no memory as to how he'd gotten here, but one thing was certain. He wasn't going to let the dalari have all the fun.

Gritting his teeth, he charged, slamming his shoulder into one of the distracted dreualfar, launching the beast into the dalari shields.

Ravion stared intently at the small hole in the hydralfar's magical shield. The arrow had plunged straight through the spell. It seemed Demetrix's bow had been altered more than he'd realized. Watching the hydralfar hit the ground. Something dark fell from his robes, landing abruptly in the dirt.

Recognizing the loose object, a sudden purpose came over him. He had to get it. It was too powerful to leave lying around, much less in the custody of the dreu. The secrets it contained were not meant for petty disputes between races. In truth, he'd spent too much time within its pages himself. The book needed to be hidden away, some place where no one could use it for personal gain ever again.

Demetrix reached for another arrow, seeing his first shot graze. He'd intended to kill the traitor, but something altered the trajectory. His quiver was empty, save for the arrow he'd been given by the horator. Slinging his bow, he drew the sword on his hip and marched toward the fallen hydralfar. He needed to die. He'd caused too much pain, and influenced too much in this war. Death was the only fitting answer.

Ravion stepped ahead of him, obscuring his vision for the briefest moment.

When it cleared, Jorin'otth was gone.

Gareth punched, seeing his energy blade split the dreualfar long before his fist ever connected. Ripping the beast apart, he spun around, searching their dwindling number. The dreualfar that had touched him in the dungeon was just ahead. Smiling his rage, he marched toward the creature. He'd made a promise. It was time to keep it. The dreualfar never saw him coming. Gareth brought his energy weapon down, severing the arm just below the elbow. Ripping it free with his other hand, he spun around and stabbed the limp appendage into the wounded creature's rectum.

He wasn't content with the lack of penetration, but it was enough to honor his promise. It had caused pain and that was enough. Bringing the psionic blade across, he severed the dreualfar's head, catching it in the air by the stringy, brown hair. The body crashed to the earth, bleeding out.

Carefully removing an ear, he tucked it into his waistband and kicked the severed head, watching it fly across the field. The limp form of Alonia caught his eye, lying among a number of the deceased dreualfar. He approached and scooped her into his arms. She'd been a friend in a time when he had none. The least he could do was see her to safety. And she still owed him some skin.

Ravion stuffed the tome into his pack. Seeing Gareth up and mobile, he turned and marched toward the semi-bald warrior. "Gareth!" He shouted, stopping a few steps ahead of his old friend. Claiming his attention, Ravion took a knee and drew his sword. Flipping it around, he presented the blade to him. "No words can excuse my actions. My life is yours if you'll have it." Staring into the dirt, he refused to look from it.

Gareth stared at the kneeling scout. He didn't know what to say. Not that there was much in the first place. "Get up!" He'd already had the chance to kill him. If he was going to do it, he would have done it then. Besides, his hands were full. Taking the sword would have been pushing his limits a bit. "I'm not gonna' say we're good. I've killed for much less than what you did, but we've been brothers in arms longer than I care to remember. So long as you don't pull that shit again, I'll give you the chance to rebuild my trust."

Ravion peered up at his friend. It was more than he could have hoped for. Bowing his agreement, he got to his feet and wrapped his arms around the larger warrior, grateful for a second chance.

Trendal marched through the shattered gate, observing the carnage that lay upon the other side. A number of dalari had fallen during the battle, but the casualties were few compared to those of the dreualfar.

Seeing Gareth ahead, he marched straight toward the large warrior. "Glad to see you could join the party."

"I had to do something to make you get off your ass and hit the field." Gareth chuckled. He didn't know what it was about the dalari captain, but he liked him.

The battle come to a halt, the opposition dead or escaped. It didn't matter. They had what they came for. Glancing into the sky, Trendal noticed the moon through the treetops. Turning toward the bulk of his force, he spoke in a commanding tone. "Gather the dead. Prepare ours for a proper burial and burn the dreualfar outside the wall. We march for the coast tomorrow morning!"

"Yes, Sir!" The dalari sounded in unison, going to work.

Directing his attention toward Gareth, Trendal reached into his pack and retrieved a small wooden box. "I'll set up a cot in the command tent. You can see to her injuries there."

Gareth nodded his agreement.

Finding a spot near the wall, Trendal opened the box and laid it in the dirt. The enchanted canvas sprung forth and formed into a large shelter.

Gareth carried Alonia toward the tent. She was weak but still alive. With any luck, she hadn't sustained any permanent damage.

Seeing Ravion staring deep into the fire, Demetrix approached his brother. "Everything okay?"

"Yeah. Just thinking."

"Alright. I wanted to say I was sorry for snapping at you before. You've been through more than I'll ever know and I didn't have the right."

"Don't apologize. I've made many mistakes recently. My most recent one cost a man's life. That's unforgivable and you weren't wrong. I failed, but pretty soon I'm going to beat this thing. I'm done failing."

Chapter XVI
Always Present

An orange glow appeared in the air along the trampled beach. It spread, forming into a large gateway. Several dalari spilled out, hearing the sounds of battle all around them. Finding the source, they readied their weapons and took position on the back side of the battlement.

Trendal stepped through the gate, lost in the chaos of the siege. His men stood ready, awaiting command. "There's no time to delay. Charge. Let's cut these bastards down!"

The dalari broke into a sprint, closing the distance. Falling in-line with their brethren, they cut, swiped, and carved a path into the attacking army.

Trendal spotted Kashien on the southern edge of the field, his sword glowing from some spell coursing through the blade.

Ravion stepped through with his brothers. He sighed, seeing the battle engulfed around them. "Why do we always find ourselves in the middle of a war? Just once I'd like to emerge on a beach, surrounded by palm trees."

"Well, you're halfway there. Looks like we're on a beach," Gareth offered, adjusting Alonia in his arms. She was surprisingly light, but the distance he'd carried her was beginning to weigh on him.

Demetrix pointed to a random section of beach in the distance. "And if you wait a few years, I'm pretty sure there'll be a few palm trees over there."

"Yeah and my blue box will rest beneath them." Drawing his sword, Ravion charged into battle.

Gareth turned to Demetrix. "What the hell is he talking about?"

"I've no clue." Demetrix chuckled and drew his bow. Nocking one of his salvaged arrows, he charged after Ravion, firing shot after shot into the dreualfar forces.

Seeing the tents on the back side of the battlefield, Gareth carried Alonia toward them. If he was going to get in on the action, he couldn't do it carrying her. Reaching the tents he stepped inside the largest one, finding Kashien's bed resting against the wall of the back chamber. It was a fancy thing, draped with a canopy top and corner posts. The sheets were made of the finest silk he'd ever seen and the thick woolen blankets were plump and soft. Laying her in the center of the oversized bed, he pulled the blanket over her and turned to leave.

"Gareth?" Alonia's weaken voice called.

Stopping, Gareth turned to find her eyes open and staring at him. Returning to her side, he grabbed her hand and knelt down beside her. "You need to rest. You're in a safe place now. Well, as safe as it can be anyway." She didn't need to know there was a war being waged right outside the door.

"Ya' got us out. I knew ya' could." Her usual strong demeanor was hidden beneath the pain she was clearly suffering.

"I didn't do it alone. My brothers came for me."

"Ya' still found a way out. 'Yer still alive. I'd call that a success." She smiled and closed her eyes, worn from the exertion.

"Don't be dying on me now. We had a deal. I get us out and you hold up your end of a bargain." He smiled, knowing she'd fight a little harder if she was resisting him.

Opening her eyes again, she couldn't help but smirk. "I thought ya' wanted me ta' live. Not give me an incentive ta' die." Seeing his smile, she felt a little better. "Don't worry. Ya' can't get rid o' me that easily."

"Wouldn't dream of it. Rest now. I'm gonna' head out side and kill some dreu. I'll be back to check on you in a while."

Alonia began to close her eyes. Suddenly, they shot wide open, contorting her face in memory. "I almost fergot. I know what the dreu are plannin'. I saw it in the hydralfar's mind when he was torturin' me. They're gonna' block out the sun. That's their big plan. Once it's gone, it'll—." Her eyes fell shut and she passed out, unable to complete the sentence.

Gareth watched her strength fade away. Making sure she was still alive, he pulled the blanket over her and stood. The information she had could wait until she was able to deliver it. Marching toward the door, he summoned his psionic blades and stepped into the morning light.

The smell of smoke and blood reached him instantly. A malicious smirk formed across his face. Seeing his first target, Gareth charged toward the eight-legged creature on the edge of the battlefield. The day was young and he needed to work out some frustration.

Kashien ducked a wild swing. Easily avoiding the sloppy blow. He swung in turn, hearing the glowing metal sizzle upon impact. It cut through the dreualfar with ease, cauterizing the wound instantly. Seeing another pair headed toward him, he thrust his hand out, launching them back into their ranks. Searching his surroundings, he saw Trendal approach the right flank. The captain had only been gone a couple days, but his insight had been missed.

Stabbing deep into the back of one of the dreuki, Trendal ripped his sword free and spun around, severing the creature's head. Stepping over the twitching body, he approached Kaileen. She was ferocious on the battlefield. There weren't many that could best her on a poor day. And today was clearly not one of those.

She flung a dagger, watching the blade disappear into one of the dreualfar. The seemingly metal blade was gone before the creature hit the ground. Summoning the forces around her, a glowing spear made of shimmering color appeared in her hand. Swiping, she knocked three more away and lifted the towering weapon. Chucking it into one of the larger dreuki, it penetrated, tearing a massive hole in its chest. The behemoth fell backward, spasming on the ground.

"I could watch you do that every day and it'd never get old." Trendal spoke, making sure he wasn't in range of a reflexive attack.

She spun around, looking upon her lover. "It's about time you joined the fun. I was beginning to think you were having a better time elsewhere."

"Not likely." Stepping close, he kissed her forehead and deflected an incoming strike. Skirting the blade, he shoved the tip into the dreualfar's stomach.

"Enough distracting me. Your men could be used at the wall."

Kaileen smiled and pushed him away.

"As you wish, my dear." Trendal backed away, looking upon her for as long as possible.

The seemingly dead dreuki she'd run through moments before, began to stir, pulling itself to its many legs.

Trendal tried to shout, but the words wouldn't form. Extending his arm to alert her, it seemed to move in slow motion. He was helpless to stop it.

The dreuki staggered toward his attacker. Within arms- reach, it hissed. A powerful blue glow radiated from its clawed hand.

Kaileen froze, hearing writhing behind her. Turning around, a stinging pain ripped through her body. She looked down, seeing the blackened arm embedded in her chest. The power released, burning her body from within. She felt weak. Her senses dulled. She watched the beast retract its blood covered hand. The sharpened nails had chunks of flesh, meat, and organ buried beneath them.

Squatting low to look into her dying face, the dreuki sprang forward, knocking Kaileen her feet. The arm sized stinger plunged into her repeatedly, refusing to stop even after she was dead.

Trendal felt a storm of emotion swirl within him. He was angry at himself for distracting her. Angry at the beast for taking her. Confusion clouded his mind. *How did I not see that? Why didn't I step between them?* Sorrow bored into his rage induced fit. *Is she really gone? What am I going to do about it? The only thing I can do. I'm going to avenge her!* Feeling numbness set over him, Trendal charged, his sword angled behind him, ready to strike.

The wounded dreuki dug his hooked talons into the limp form beneath him. Squeezing her fleshy limbs, the soft meat tore, exposing muscle and tendon. Unable to take the force, Kaileen's body popped and came apart. Hearing an approaching shout, the dreuki looked up from his work to see one of the dalari flying through the air toward him. The sword was primed and ready. There was no time. It was moving too fast and already too close to deflect.

A single focus in mind, Trendal brought his sword across, watching it cut into the vile beast that was responsible for his loss. Slamming his knees into its mutilated chest, he felt the balance shift. He was now on top of the creature, falling toward the ground. Carrying his momentum through, he sliced again. The blade cut deep into its collar bone. He was certain it was already dead, which was both a relief and a disappointment. He wanted to spend the rest of eternity punishing it for what it'd taken from him. Straddling the fallen dreuki, he brought his sword overhead and plunged it deep into the creature's disfigured face, sinking the blade into the blood-soaked sand and rock.

Exhausted, Trendal rolled from the creature and crawled to Kaileen. Laying his head on her still chest, he held her tight, raining tears upon her.

Three arrows released the bowstring at once, fanning out toward their targets. Demetrix watched the wooden shafts plunge into the advancing dreualfar. The bodies were piling, filling the outside trench to the brim. They were little more than a minor trip hazard now. It appeared the enemy forces were diminishing rapidly. He had no clue how many had fallen, but of the reported six-thousand, there had to be at least a third of that bleeding out in the sand. Sadly, about equal number of dalari among them. But they still had the bigger force.

Another unit of dreualfar made their way toward the broken section of wall. He doubted he could take out the whole group at once, but the more the merrier. Stringing as many arrows as the sight window would hold, he drew back and aimed nearly straight vertical. Releasing the string, the numerous thin shafts flew upward, reaching ballistic trajectory. Momentum shifted, they arched downward, raining into the advancing unit.

Ravion stabbed, ducked, and spun, avoiding an attack while delivering another. He felt good. Better than he'd felt in quite some time. Spotting one of the dreuki, he altered course to intercept. The creature fell before he could reach it. It was no matter, there was plenty to go around.

The overwhelming scent of magic reached him. Ravion searched the air, locating its source. The dreualfar mage was charged, ready to release his blackened bolt.

Bringing his sword across, Ravion watched the blade slice through the threads composing the magical energy. The spell fizzled and disappeared, returning to the nether from once it came. Following through, the sharpened edge bit into the casting dreualfar, cracking his head like a gourd smashed upon rock.

Gareth stood over the fallen dreuki tasting victory in the black blood clinging to his face. It felt good being back in the battle again. But something was different. He didn't feel the rage boiling within him. For the first time in as long as he could remember, he was simply fighting because he wanted to. It was as if the hatred he'd carried for so long was no longer the driving force behind his bloodlust. Not to say it wasn't still present, or that it'd ever go away. But he was certain he wasn't using it. He had a clear head and a single mission. Defeat the dreualfar and see to Alonia.

A grating battle horn echoed from the far side of the battlements and the dreualfar began to fall back. They abandoned those closest to them, retreating as commanded. Nearly half of the dreualfar force had been wiped out and a good portion of the remainder had been wounded.

Seeing the dreualfar retreat, many of the dalari rushed after them, claiming the last few casualties of the long and tiring battle.

Kashien magically amplified his voice so that all could hear over the fading sounds of battle. "The dreualfar retreat. Do not. I repeat, do not pursue. Gather the wounded and help them to safety!"

Smoke lingered in the evening air, carrying the scent of burning flesh. Hundreds of blazing fires burned in the distance, piled high with the dead.

Standing outside his tent, Kashien surveyed his army. They'd lost much in the past days, but they'd managed to force the dreualfar to retreat. While it wasn't a clear victory, it also meant they weren't defeated. That was reason enough to celebrate. His ten-thousand strong had diminished to a little over eight-thousand. And at least a third of those had been wounded during the fight. The healers were exhausted and they needed to a more defensive location. But such an undertaking could wait until morning. Tonight, they needed rest.

"General!" A weak, yet familiar voice sounded from within the tent.

"Yes, Captain?" Kashien turned, finding the reddened face of his oldest friend. His heart broke for the man, knowing what he'd lost. Even more so, knowing she was with child.

He'd contemplated telling his friend, but such news was likely to drive him mad with grief. *No, that news doesn't need to be relayed. Not now, not ever.* It was easiest to attribute the sorrow to empathy, a part of him hurt as well. Kaileen was one of a kind. She'd been an exemplary soldier and officer, as well as a personal friend. It was going to take some time to get used to her absence, but a day would come when the world would suck a little less for her not being in it.

"The devonie woman is awake. Gareth said she has news you need to hear." Trendal held the canvas door open for his general to pass.

Kashien stepped inside, letting his eyes adjust to the ambient light. Marching through the maze of rooms, he noticed Trendal remained at the door. He considered waiting for him, but what could he do? This was something he was going to have to work through on his own.

Trendal stared into the field. Even at this distance, he could see where it happened. His sword remained lodged in the earth, buried in stone. They had to remove the dreuki in pieces to get it off the blade. That didn't hurt his feelings one bit. The sword could remain there for the rest of existence for all he cared. It would serve as a reminder, not to what he'd lost, but to the wonder that was Kaileen. Breaking his gaze on the polished weapon in the battlefield, he turned and stepped into the tent. If what Gareth said was true, all officers needed to be present.

Kashien stepped into his personal chamber, finding Gareth standing over a woman in his bed. Ravion, Demetrix, and several of his remaining officers stood about the room. It was unorthodox having them here, such meetings were better suited for the war room, but the woman was in no condition to be moved. She needed rest and it seemed his bed was as good as any other.

The officers snapped to attention and offered salute, seeing their general enter the room.

"At ease." Kashien approached the bed. He glanced at the door, hearing Trendal enter, taking position beside the others. Turning back to the devonie woman, he knelt down beside her, hoping to make her as comfortable as possible. "I hear you stumbled upon some valuable information about the dreualfar?"

"Aye." Alonia's voice was exceptionally strong considering her appearance. It was a wonder she was able to speak at all.

"The hydralfar workin' with 'em. When he tortured me, I saw into his mind. He's not from 'ere. Nor 'are they." She weakly raised her arm and pointed at Ravion and Demetrix.

Turning her head, she looked to Gareth. "You aren't either."

"Where am I from then?" Gareth asked, confused by her statement.

"The future!" Kashien stated openly.

Alonia nodded agreement.

Ravion lowered his head in defeat of his inner battle.

"How do you figure that?" Gareth's gaze darted from Alonia to Kashien, hoping either could offer some explanation.

"Jorin'otth, as he calls himself, is from a time far beyond even 'yers." She spoke directly to Gareth. "Ya' told me ya' didn't remember 'yer life prior to the island. Jorin'otth is the reason ya' were there. He found a staff that allowed him ta' travel through time. The further he went from 'is own, the more the world shifted in opposition ta' 'is ideals. As a result, he tracked what he believed ta' be the source o' these changes ta' a group called, The Order. Unable ta' destroy 'em as a whole, he resorted ta' breakin' its founders one by one in an attempt ta' keep it from existin'. He tracked em ta' the most vulnerable point in their lives and set things in motion. Fer ya', he went ta' a pirate ship off the coast of North Korenthia. Using the magics he'd obtained, he chained the captain ta' the mast and made him watch as he murdered the crew. In his arrogance, he left the captain alive and sabotaged the ship so she'd go down. He then went further back in time, ta' a small village in Coriath called, Winterhaven. There, he sent a missive that resulted in the entire populace bein' wiped out, with the exception of a few kids."

The room was quiet, hanging on every word. Ravion, Demetrix, and Gareth couldn't help but believe her. How could she know these details had they not been true? It was both a comfort and curse. Knowing why their lives had shifted the way they had did little but raise more questions.

"He didn't stop there. Learnin' some of the children had survived, he made a deal with a dragon ta' wipe 'em out. All but one. A dalari child, little more than a toddler, was promised as payment. The dragon could use the child in his adult years ta' infiltrate the world of men. There he could rise ta' power and force the mortals to worship him as a god. I wasn't able to see the details of the other times he interfered in 'yer lives, but I could tell there were many occasions, always indirect. He was scared ta' get too close. He knew if ya' found him out, ya'd go after 'em. And he wasn't sure he could escape. Then here, when he came across Demetrix, he knew his time in the shadows was at its end. But directin' 'yer lives isn't the most devious thing he's done. Right now, he aids the dreualfar ta' bring eternal darkness ta' the world. Using an ancient book, he's found a spell that will snuff out the light permanently," Alonia paused, recalling the words that lingered in Jorin'otth's mind. "And in the darkness, the dark lord can move unhindered. For reflections are meanin'less in the dead o' night."

Kashien hung on every word. It was like reading a book of prophecy. It took a certain ability to twist words to their most literal meaning and back again to understand even half of what they were saying. But this seemed pretty clear.

Reaching into his pack, Ravion retrieved the black book, bringing it out for all to see. "You mean this book?"

Alonia lifted her head to see the dark binding. "That's the one I saw in his memory. He took it from a hidden chamber, lying on the floor beside a large mirror."

"Where did you find that?" Kashien stood, marching toward the tome.

"You know what this is?" Ravion asked, cradling the familiar book.

"It's the Tomb of Ur. Believed to be crafted when this realm was forged. Legend says it contains every secret this realm will ever know. I believed it to be a myth, having never heard of anyone finding it." Kashien ran his fingers over the shimmering outer cover. A part of him wanted to explore its contents, but such knowledge had a way of corrupting its bearer.

"When the hydralfar fell, after Demetrix shot him, he dropped it. This isn't the first time I've encountered this book. It led my brothers and I into a dark world where this Izaryle is believed to be imprisoned." Ravion addressed Alonia, handing the book to Kashien. It was clear the dalari prince was uneasy about being in the presence of such an artifact, which made handing it to him that much sweeter. "Alonia, is that your name?"

She nodded.

Approaching her, Ravion took position where she could easily see him. "If I were to find the spell the dreualfar plan to use, do you think you could recognize it?"

"Aye. But be warned, I saw what he had ta' do ta' expose its secrets. I don't know if you're willin' ta' pay such a price."

"This book and I have a long-standing history. I don't fear the price. Do you remember the questions he asked?"

Alonia struggled silently, as if she was recalling the exact details of a memory long forgotten. "There were many he asked, but it wasn't until he asked about bypassin' the portals did it show him the spell."

"The portals? Mirrors, maybe?"

"He said portals. But the passage he read aloud ta' the dreualfar commander said reflections. I see no reason why they couldn't be the same. He found the book beside a mirror, after all."

Ravion turned to face Kashien and the book. "If you'll permit me, I'll find the spell they hope to cast."

"Are you sure you're ready for that? After what you've been through I can only imagine the temptation such magic would leave behind."

"I'll be fine. Using this book isn't like casting a spell. That takes focus and some amount of skill. The book is the opposite. It uses blood magic to reveal its secrets." Ravion waited patiently for Kashien to return the book.

"Blood magic can be extremely powerful. If you start to slip, we'll shut you down by any means necessary." Kashien warned, releasing the book.

"Don't worry. I've done this hundreds of times." Carrying the book to the small table beside the bed, he flipped to the middle pages and drew his dagger. Pressing the sharped edge to his flesh, he slowly pulled, feeling the cold steel bite into the meat of his thumb. It pooled around the blade near instantly.

Removing the blade, he dripped the bright red liquid into the pages, watching it disappear as he had so many times before. "Show me how the dreualfar hope to bypass the Irayth Mirrors!"

The book remained blank for a long moment. Faintly, thin red marks began to appear, written in his familiar native tongue. "Kashien, I'll not udder these words aloud, but you need to read this."

Kashien rushed toward the book, hoping whatever it showed would remain long enough for him to witness. Peering into the red markings, he quickly, silently memorized the passage. "We can use this. If we reverse these words." He pointed to a collection on the third line. "We could cause an opposite effect. Rather than blocking out the sun, we could banish the dreualfar from it permanently."

"You're telling me this is it?" Gareth interrupted.

"This is what?" Kashien asked, misunderstanding what his devonie guest was talking about.

"This is when the dreualfar are cursed to the underdark? By us?"

Ravion chuckled to himself, seeing the poetic nature to Gareth's realization. "I suppose it is."

Gareth waited a long moment, contemplating the possibilities. "Well, alright. Let's do it."

"There's one thing we'll need to perform the ritual that I can't obtain." Kashien announced, studying the words.

"What's that?"

"I need you to perform the spell." Kashien stared intently at Ravion, forcing the severity of the request into his gaze.

"Why me? Why can't one of your other casters do it?"

"It says here the spell must be cast by one who has tasted the dark. Unless we can force the dreualfar to cast it for us, you're our only hope."

Ravion took a deep breath. He wasn't ready to cast a spell yet. What if he lost control? What if it claimed him again and he slaughtered them all? But still, if it was needed, he had to do everything within his power to succeed. "Let me think about it. I'll let you know by morning." Refusing to wait another moment, Ravion marched from the room, disappearing past the door.

Kashien glanced at Demetrix. He didn't have to speak to make his point heard.

Demetrix nodded. "I'll make sure he doesn't do anything stupid." Pushing himself from the wall he'd been leaning against, he rushed out the door after Ravion.

Turning to his captains, Kashien made sure he had their attention. "We've been fortunate this night. It's not often we find ourselves with an advantage in this war. But here we are, the enemy's plan within our knowledge, and a counter attack in the works. We come down to the logistics. Gareth, will you and your brothers accompany Captain Trendal and Captain Roark? For the dreualfar to cast this spell successfully, they'll have to perform the ritual at a site where a god has bled. While very few of those are believed to exist, and most are speculated as mere rumor, there is one place I can think that the dreualfar may try to use."

"Durnal Hill?" Trendal asked, joining the conversation for the first time. He'd been lost in the memory of Kaileen, but if this meant they were finally going to end the war, his attention was needed.

"That's correct, Captain. I need you to lead the assault on Durnal Hill. As we all know, the ruins of an ancient temple were buried there several centuries ago. It's believed this was the final temple to Izaryle, but unlike the others that were destroyed during the Great War, this one is believed to be the place where Izaryle fell and was stripped of his power. If the dreualfar hope to cast this spell, that's where they're going to do it."

"As you command, General."

"I'll lead the remainder of our forces to Avlonwell. The majority of the dreualfar force is believed to be held up in the alfaren city. Missives will be sent to Captain Theo and Captain Lawson, as well as the hydralfar army. Last I knew, they were hold up near Dyre Rise. With any luck, they'll mobilize on our position and we'll have 'em flanked from the start. One way or another, we end the war with this final battle. We'll win, or we'll die trying. Let's give 'em hell and make 'em dread the day they chose to take up arms against us!"

The captains shouted their cheers, ready to march into battle that very minute.

Chapter XVII
A Dark Pact

A full moon lingered low in the sky, seemingly larger than usual. Not a sound could be heard from the camp, tranquil with the few torches and dying embers revealed in the low-lit night, with the exception of the rolling tide, echoing along the shore.

Ravion stood at its edge, staring out into the blackened waters. The waves climbed the sand, stopping a few inches from the toe of his boots. There was little more than a few feet between the first row of tents and the cold, salty water. Listening to the dull roar of water, he heard soft footsteps in the sand behind him. Refusing to abandon his focus, he waited for new comer to speak.

"I've never been much of a caster. The few things I remember from Lythus were little more than parlor tricks. So, I can't pretend to understand what you're going through. Or what you've been through." Demetrix's voice was soft and comforting, aimed to inspire rather than coerce.

Staring at the foamy tips of the rolling waves, washing toward him, Ravion let his brother's words sink in. "Do you ever wish you'd chosen a different place to settle?"

"Honestly?" Demetrix asked, not expecting an answer. "No. When I found Dalmoura, I had no idea what was in store for me in the years to come. Granted, those years feel like someone else's memory, rather than my own. But they linger in my head, like flashes of a dream I had long ago. But, no. I don't remember why I chose to go to Dalmoura. I just sort of stumbled upon it. And there I found my brothers. You guys made me feel like I belonged, which was something I'd never really felt those two hundred years I spent in the Forests of Amaylar. It wasn't the land that made Dalmoura my home. It was the people. And if we're being completely honest, Irayth is my home now. When this is all over, I plan to go back. I want to live what's left of my life with Elalon."

Ravion turned from the waters, seeing his brother for what might have been the first time. "I understand."

"That's it? No guilt trips, or 'we need you heres', or 'we have to rebuild our people'?" Demetrix was surprised by his response. He figured such a decision would have at least warranted some repercussions.

Shaking his head, Ravion smiled for what seemed to be the first time in a long time. "No. You've made a decision. I respect that. Besides, Elalon is a wonderful woman whom missed you terribly. I had the pleasure of getting to know her during my stent as nightking. She's a capable and strong woman. Far superior to your ass." Playfully, he punched his brother in the shoulder.

"I don't dispute that whatsoever. I just hope I haven't changed too much before I'm able to make it back to her."

"Believe me when I say she's thought of no one but you. And changed or not, when you find your way back, she'll be happy to see you."

A heavy smile occupied Demetrix's face. He could hardly contain it. "You know, if you weren't so damn smelly, I'd hug you right now."

"I'm surprise you can smell anything over your own funk. How long's it been since you had a bath?"

"Same as you. Come on. Let's test the waters. But you'd best believe, if we see a shark, you'd better learn to walk on water and quick, because my ass is going to be gone."

Demetrix stripped his armor and made for the ocean. They were due for a massive fight in the near future. Enjoying the finer things in life was not to be forsaken.

The morning sun beamed through the skylight, illuminating the unusually large room. It was decorated simply, wooden furniture, a single bed protruding toward the center. What could have passed as fresh picked flowers, where it not for the obvious illusionary water droplets clinging to the vibrant pedals, rested in a vase on the nightstand.

Alonia struggled against the solid foot board, bracing herself for another step. Placing all her weight on her legs was tiresome and painful. But she had to get her body back into shape. The dalari were leaving soon and she couldn't rightly go into battle with them. Not like this anyway. Gritting her teeth, she forced her legs to comply and stepped forward once again.

Hearing someone enter the room, she glanced at the seemingly wooden doorway, finding Gareth standing there. Distracted for the briefest moment, her legs buckled and she crashed to the floor.

Gareth rushed over to help her up. "Are you okay?"

"I'm fine. Just give me a minute ta' get myself up."

Releasing her arms, he took a step back, allowing her to try on her own. While he hadn't known her long, it was long enough to know she was just as stubborn as him. And if he pushed, she was liable to lash out, not that he feared such a thing. In fact, he quite enjoyed it from time to time. But now was not the time for such games.

Straining, Alonia pulled herself up, balancing on her feet. Keeping hold of the footboard, she made her way around and took a seat on the soft bed. "Me damn legs aren't workin' the way they used ta'."

"Give it time. You'll be back to fighting shape in no time."

"I could still kick 'yer arse, even in me current state."

Gareth chuckled at her confidence. Though there was no way she could handle him if he was truly enraged.

"Still thinkin' too loud. Ya' need to hide 'yer thoughts better. Anyone could hear what's in 'yer head. If they do that, ya' got nothin' left to hide and your surprise is blown. And, yeah, I could take ya'. Did it once, didn't I?"

"Okay, you took me down once, but I was distracted. And you got the jump on me. That time doesn't count." Gareth approached the bed and took a seat beside her.

"Of course it does. In battle, it doesn't matter if 'yer enemy knows 'yer comin' or not. When you have the chance to strike, ya' strike."

Alonia let the powers within her manifest. Forming a modified shell, she slammed in into Gareth's body, knocking him to his back.

He tried to move, but the unseen force kept him motionless. He could still move his head and legs, but the rest of him was defenseless. Letting his mind explore, he found Alonia, straddling him. Her fiery red hair hung about her face and her glowing green eyes burned into him, fueling his desire. He wasn't sure if it was in his head or not, perhaps both.

"There ya' go. Ya've locked onto me. Now, look inside. Feel the impulses. Let the surface memories flow. Once ya've got 'em sorted, ya' can search as deep as ya' like."

Gareth stared into her. He was seeing double, though they weren't the same. He could see her physical form, resting atop of him, and her inner self. It was then he realized she was speaking through his mind again. Her lips hadn't moved at all.

Thinking his words, letting them form in her mind, he felt them travel. *You've got me here, nearly defeated. What do you plan to do with me now?*

Alonia pressed her face close to his and kissed him passionately. Breaking away, she whispered into his ear. "I need ta' travel home before the dalari leave for this war. Will ye' come with me?"

Gareth was torn. He desperately wanted what she was offering. But he couldn't rightly abandon his brothers. Not to mention the best chance he'd ever have at making sure the dreualfar remembered him throughout eternity. If he abandoned his crusade, all of it would have been for naught.

Laying fully on top of him, she spoke softly. "Ya've made 'yer decision. Just know, if ya' change 'yer mind, ya' have but ta' find me."

"I can't let this fear control my life. What do you need me to do?" Ravion asked, standing in the doorway.

Kashien stood over the table in the war room. The walls glowed a soft blue, illuminating every last detail.

Ravion felt like this was the first time he'd truly seen the room in all its glory. The magical threads crawled on the walls, floor, and ceiling, in constant flux. Every grain of the illusionary wood was perfectly placed, forming a seemingly natural pattern. No, not illusionary. It wasn't until this very moment that he truly understood the magics his people were using. It wasn't all illusion spells and cantrips. They were standing inside a pocket dimension, tied to the outside world by way of the tent. How had he not noticed that before?

Weapons hung from fixtures, mounted to the support beams,

displayed for all to see. The heavy oaken table that made the centerpiece was relatively clear of its usual maps, which were rolled and tucked neatly upon the shelf. At the edge where Kashien stood, the glimmering black book rested, closed and bound by its leather strap. A stack of vellum was placed beside it, and a quartz vial of what appeared to be ink sat next to an elegant looking quill made from a white feather.

Kashien worked the mortar in his hand, grinding the components within to a fine dust. "I appreciate your courage. If you'd be so kind as to find the spell in the book once again, we're just about ready to begin."

Ravion approached the table and unbuckled the book. Flipping to one of the many blank pages, he removed the bandage where he'd cut himself the night before. Carefully, he spread the wound, breaking the clot that had set up overnight. Almost immediately red beads rushed to the surface. He squeezed, forcing it to pool slightly.

Seeing enough for a few drops, he held it over the flaky page and let the book do the rest. "Show me the how to curse the dreualfar into shadow!"

As before, the blood soaked into the page and returned a moment later revealing a slightly different spell than the one they'd seen before. This time, the wording was different, but the concept was the same.

Kashien quickly read over the text, finding the changes. "Excellent! I'm glad you changed it. I would have missed the top part. There's no telling what would have happened if it didn't get cast exactly right." Checking the powder in his pedestal, he poured it into the vial of dark ink. Swishing is around, the ink began to glow a near red. The glow faded away and the ink returned to its pitch-black tone. "Are you ready?"

Ravion read through the words of the spell. It was simple enough, though that didn't stop the churning he felt in his stomach. He wasn't sure if it was just nerves, or if he was genuinely sick. Either way it was one of the most uncomfortable feelings he'd ever experienced, short of allowing a surge of collected energies explode from his body. Taking a deep breath, he lifted the book and began to focus.

Kashien waved his hand over the quill, watching it float from its stand. Dipping itself in the enchanted ink, the vial emptied, as if the quill absorbed it.

"Thgil eht morf enog eb. Enog eb, taht rof dna. Laitnetop ruoy derednauqs evah uoy, thgin fo dlihc. Ytinrete lla rof ssenkrad eht ni niamer uoy taht ti ot ees I thgir larom ym yb. Tnemegduj tsac ot ecalp ym ton si ti rof. Uoy evigrof I, era uoy sa detpurroc. Thgil eht ni sworg taht lla morf uoy hsinab I. Uoy hsinab I, thgin fo dlihc."

Ravion watched the quill scribble the spell onto the vellum, the blackened ink turned red the moment it found its place on the page. He could see the weaves of magic coursing through the lettering, waiting to be read by someone, anyone that cared to recite the words. Feeling the magics inside himself twist, he dropped the book, watching the heavy binding clap shut. Closing his eyes, he took another deep breath, allowing himself to remain in control. The magic did not control him, but rather he controlled it.

Kashien studied the heaving dalari scout. He appeared to be momentarily trapped within himself, but he was pulling out of it. Seeing the tall warrior return to his former height, he was confident he'd found his control once again. It was going to take some time before he'd truly be comfortable with who he'd become, but he'd get there. His resilience was testament to that. "Go get a drink. Calm yourself. Tomorrow morning, we march toward victory." He suggested to the scout.

Kashien watched him leave. Returning his focus to the magical page, he carefully lifted the scroll and blew across the lettering, ensuring the ink had settled. Rolling it into a tube, he tied a small piece of sinew around the page and tucked it into his belt pouch.

A cool afternoon breeze carried across the sand, bringing with it the scent of cooked meat.

Demetrix looked up from the unique arrow he'd been given, seeing a wild boar roasting over one of the fires. His stomach rumbled from the smell. He couldn't remember the last time he'd had a solid meal. Instead, he'd been living on dried meats, hard tack, and whatever it was the dalari served when in the field. It had a similar taste and texture to food. But he wasn't entirely sure that's what it was. Forcing the thoughts of food from his mind, he returned his focus to the smoked arrow shaft. He couldn't fathom how such an arrow was even crafted. There wasn't a single component on the simple device made of familiar materials.

Seeing the lone dalari, sitting on one of the fallen sections of the makeshift barricade, Gareth approached and took a seat next to him.

"Whatcha' got there?"

"An arrow."

"Well, no shit. I can see that much. Why you lookin' at it like it stole your coin purse?"

"It was given to me by some kind of elite archer. Kashien said it was a horator, whatever that means." Demetrix flipped the one of a kind arrow around and plunged it into his sheath, ensuring it found the divider separating it from the others. "What are you out doing? I'm surprised you aren't spending all your time with Alonia."

Gareth shrugged, "She's great and all, but she's not Sorena. Now, don't get me wrong. Lords know I'd smash given the opportunity. But more than that? I'm not sure I'm wired for the family life anymore."

"That's your call, brother. Just don't let stubbornness get in the way of being happy. And she seems to make you somewhat happy."

"There's certainly a kindred spirit type of thing going on. And she's taught me quite a bit about what I can do. I've still more to learn, but I'll figure it out. I just don't think I could ever really be with her."

"Why's that?"

"Well, somehow, in a way that I won't even pretend to understand, we went back in time. With my luck, she's probably my great-great grandmother or something. And I know you assholes. If I tapped, you fuckers would never let me live it down."

Demetrix chuckled, knowing Gareth was right. But only because he'd do the same were the roles reversed.

"Besides, she wants to go home. Can't say as I blame her after what she's been through. I'd probably want to go home too. Hell, I've been through what she's been through and if memory serves, Marbayne was the first place I went of my own accord."

"Has she healed up enough to make the trip?"

"I doubt it. She's like me. She wants to make it whether she's fully healed or not. Apparently the devonie are a hard headed and strong-willed people."

"You know, I always wondered where you got it from."

"Shut up." Gareth bumped Demetrix's shoulder, knocking his balance off the rough barked log forming the collapsed section. "Knowing she's not healed enough to make the trip, I don't feel right letting her go alone. Gods know what lies between here and there. And

I can't rightly go with her as Kashien has asked us to march in the morning."

"You could always ask if some of the dalari would accompany her. Ravion made quite the impression on a number of them. If he were to ask, I'm sure they'd be chomping at the bit to escort her."

"How is Ravion? He seems better since I kicked his ass. Just further evidence that everyone needs a good beatin' every now and then. It keeps 'em in check."

"You're long overdue, my friend." Demetrix returned the shoulder jab, forcing Gareth to extend his legs to catch himself. "But, Ravion. He seems okay. A little slow to get back in the saddle if you ask me. But he'll get there. He's been through some stuff neither of us could imagine. It stands to reason he'd be a little messed up."

"I suppose. I just hope he realizes how close he was to death. He pushed me further than I've let anyone push. It took everything I had not to kill him."

"I thank you for that. And I understand your position. I won't try to convince you of anything, but I think he'll be okay. He just needs some time to get everything figured out. And from what I understand, he took the first step toward that today by helping Kashien cast the daylight curse."

Gareth nodded, refusing to climb back onto the round beam. Clapping the young ranger on the shoulder, he turned to walk away. "I guess I'm gonna' go find Ravion and see if he can talk to some of those Dalari for me. I'd feel better just knowing she had someone to see her home."

"Do what you've got to do, brother. I think I'm going to grab me a piece of that boar while it's still hot." Demetrix jumped from his perch, his boots sinking slightly into the sand.

Gareth made his way across the encampment, searching for a familiar face. Seeing Trendal, he gave a respectful nod as he passed. The dalari seemed occupied with his thoughts. It would be a crime to rob him of them. Gareth recalled what it was like to lose his love. There was nothing more painful or soul shattering than that. If Trendal was to get through it, he'd have to find his own outlet. And judging from the way many regarded Gareth as little more than a grizzled cutthroat, it was probably best he didn't inspire the man to follow his lead. Passing into the command tent, he found Ravion and Kashien staring over the thin, black book.

"All I'm saying is that book contains the world's darkest secrets. Things even the gods don't want known. We have to be careful not to uncover something we shouldn't know." Kashien pleaded, explaining his desire to close the book and forget about it.

"I don't disagree with any particular part. But the dreualfar have had this book for months. And clearly Jorin'otth showed them how to read it. It'd be foolish to ignore the fact that they probably learned more than a single spell from it." Ravion retorted, holding his ground.

"Just promise me, once this is—." Kashien paused, looking up to see Gareth. "Ah, Master Gareth. What brings you here? Your friend was moved to her own tent this morning."

"I'm aware. I actually came to ask a favor. Of both of you," Gareth's gaze darted from Kashien to Ravion.

"Anything." Ravion replied, closing the book and scooting it away from him. Taking a leaning rest against the table top, he devoted his full attention to his closest friend.

"It's Alonia. She wants to go home. I tried convincing her to stay until she was healed, but she insists. She wants to leave when we set out tomorrow morning. And I can't rightly abandon my post to go with her. I was hoping, you'd be willing to part with a few men that could accompany her? I hear there are a few that have developed some loyalty to Ravion. If that's the case, I'd prefer to send some of them. Matters of trust and all that."

Kashien thought on it for a moment, "It would be wise to send her home with an escort. Her injuries aside, she's the daughter to their Tsar. Showing that kind of support would undoubtedly aid in restoring relations between our two peoples. Besides, what difference will a few men make? Ravion, if you wish, I'll allow you to pick the men. Matters of trust and all that." The dalari prince smiled, mimicking Gareth's words.

"My pleasure." Ravion bowed, showing his gratitude toward the situation. "I'd like to start with Morena and Stot. As I've fought side by side with them, I believe they'd make effective team leaders, considering this group is unlikely to have an officer."

Kashien nodded his agreement. "Consider both promoted. And I'll allow you to send eighteen others, in addition to your lieutenants. That should be enough to handle any threat they encounter along the way, yet small enough to hide as required."

Ravion thought through the dalari he'd accidentally linked. He hadn't learned most of their names yet, but when one came to memory, he saw images of their lives nobody should know. It felt wrong, like he was looking into the most cherished and secret aspects of them. Judging them one by one, he gave a list of names, silently keeping track. They were his trident after all. And any weapon master needed to have full knowledge of their capabilities.

Chapter XVIII
Whispers in Time

"What do you mean, the dalari are marching toward us?" Tygrell shouted, towering over the feeble dreualfar messenger.

"General, Sir—." The terrified messenger stuttered, fearing imminent death. "It's a large force, several thousand strong. The bulk of their force, I'd say. They split at the Dune Plains. A few thousand went south. The rest, east. We trailed the larger group to the mountain range but they disappeared in the Caladine Pass."

"How the hell do you lose an army in a mountain pass? It's not like they could simply disappear!"

Jorin'otth watched the enraged dreualfar from the side wall, hoping he didn't draw the general's wrath himself. He'd failed enough as of late. Adding another strike to his record would certainly result in loss of life, be it his own or the general's. Either way, it wouldn't serve his purpose. It didn't matter if the general wanted him dead. He simply needed time to perform the ritual before tensions escalated. So long as Tygrell used his brain, the very reason Jorin'otth chose him in the first place, his goals would be obtained. A dreualfar victory in this war was little more than a side effect.

"I believe they escaped into one of the old dwarven tunnels, Sir. There's no other explanation for their sudden and unexpected disappearance." The messenger offered, trying to back away without drawing notice.

"Then get your ass down there and find them. I don't care if you have to explore every cavern between here and Alseaol. Find them or I'm going to pluck out your eyeballs and make you eat them!"

"Yes, Sir!" The messenger slinked away, disappearing out the door as quickly as possible.

Tygrell watched him scurry off. He wanted so desperately to kill the weakling. There was no room for such a delicate bloodline in his growing empire. The mere thought of the frail creature breeding made him sick. To continue on in such a state, growing weaker by the generation, his people wouldn't last longer than a few hundred years. Only the strongest were worthy of spreading their seed. It was strength that was going to grind this world into submission. As far as he was concerned, the pale-skins could hide behind their high walls and magic wards all they wanted to. Soon the day would come when the very sun that offered them life would be turned against them. No magic could shield them from that.

Seeing the hydralfar standing along the wall, he felt his irritation rise. He'd proven useful in many cases, but his recent failures were growing increasingly frustrating. It was possible his little pet had reached the end of his usefulness, but there was only one way to be sure. "Jorin'otth, you've always had an answer for everything. Tell me, why should I spare your life today?"

"Well, General, if I may?" The hydralfar gestured, awaiting permission to layout the framework of his elaborate rouse. It was a useful tactic against the general. All he needed was a few complex words and a narrow leap that aligned with the general's goals. Noting Tygrell's silent and waiting posture, he continue. "It's true we've experienced some unfortunate setbacks recently. I've never denied this, nor have I intentionally or unintentionally hidden it from you. We're faced with the unforeseen. It seems these dreuslayers, as they call themselves, have been a thorn in many sides across a number of lands. I won't lie to you, they're exceptionally good at what they do. Especially when their motives are aligned toward a single purpose. I've spent many years in constant study of their methods, for the intention of destroying their order. But these are no mere collection of men or alfar. As you know, the dalari are an exceptional race with many talents unseen to the naked eye. The devonie are much the same way. I can't say if it's luck or simple skill, but each time I've moved against them I've encountered setbacks that were woefully unavoidable. It's as if the gods themselves protect the existence of these few men. But I can assure you, had these dreuslayers never arrived, we would have already ended this war."

"You believe the gods protect them? And that somehow, against all odds, these chosen dreuslayers were brought here to stop us? These three men? You're basing your entire defense on divine intervention?" Tygrell burst into laughter, losing his dominating presence. "Of all the cards you keep hidden in those exceptionally large sleeves, that's the one you chose to play?" He cried through tearing eyes and laughter. "I asked why I should stay my blade, not why I should make the execution swift. You clearly have a death wish, offering such ridiculous theories."

"General, with all due respect, you've never encountered these men. Where I'm from, they're responsible for the largest number of dreualfar deaths ever seen. They don't retreat. They don't submit. And as far as I'm aware, they've never failed in accomplishing their mission. I have no reason to lie about this, therefore, I urge you to take this threat very seriously. Such a boast would do nothing for me." Jorin'otth walked calmly toward the chuckling dreualfar. It was rather annoying, being laughed at, but it didn't change anything. He just had to complete one final task and he could wash his hands of the dreualfar entirely.

Calming his amused senses, Tygrell wiped a tear from his cheek. Still half laughing, he spoke. "That's where you need to check your facts, Jorin'otth. I'm incredibly serious. I don't give a damn who these men are. Whether they call themselves dreuslayers or shit sprayers. They've allowed you to fail. And failure comes with a price. You lost the book. You fell for a simple parlor trick and brought me a false eldarstone. Then you have the audacity to blame all of this on some mythical group that supposedly appears from the shadows to destroy my people. Please, Jorin'otth. I've had lingering shits that were more convincing than that." Tygrell drew the sword strapped to his hip. The thick blade reflected the torch light off the walls. "It's clear your usefulness has reached its end."

"My Lord, your assessment is folly, I assure you. My death will lead to your defeat by the end of the week. I'm the only one you have to perform the ritual at Durnal Hill. That ritual is the only chance your people have."

"Are you threatening me, Jorin'otth?"

"No, General. I'm simply stating a fact. You still need me. Without the ritual, you're on your own. No god to protect you. No weapon against the dalari. You, yourself will perish by the end of the day if you don't let me perform the ritual. This I've seen many times over. There is no alternative."

"Then, my cowardly Jorin'otth, I recommend you get to Durnal Hill and see that the ritual goes according to plan. Just know, if you fail me again, you'll experience a fate unlike anything that can be put into words!"

Refusing to give the general the satisfaction of proper respects, Jorin'otth turned and marched out the door. The time for respect had reached its end. The general was going to have him executed first chance he got. Just so long as he completed the ritual, he had nothing to fear from dalari or dreualfar.

The lone walk along the darkening forest road was eerily quiet. Jorin'otth couldn't shake the feeling he was being watched. Stealing a glance over his shoulder for what had to have been the thousandth time, he paused, searching the trees. The hair on the back of his neck stood on end. The churning in his gut intensified, twisting and squeezing. He thought he was going to be sick. Forcing his resolve, a realization hit him. There was only one thing capable of affecting him in such a way.

His heart raced. He'd been careful and used others to change things. There was no way they found him. Yet the temporal energies swirling in the air said otherwise. How had he been so stupid? He should have known they were on to him the moment he saw Demetrix. That was the only explanation for the dreuslayers' presence here. The churning intensified. It was getting closer. He needed to move now or they'd be on top of him.

A snapping twig echoed in the darkness, ringing out like an explosion in the night.

Refusing to look, Jorin'otth broke into a full sprint, rushing through the crowding trees and overgrown brush. Staying to the road was too dangerous. He'd been found. He needed to take less traveled paths. He had no idea where he was going and using his magics would lead them straight to him. Time was running out. He needed to reach Durnal Hill and complete his task. That was the only way he'd shake the dukes permanently.

A deep ravine laid just ahead.

He prepared to make the jump knowing he'd lose speed if he tried to climb the far side. Reaching the edge, he bent his knees and leapt. Flying across the deep crevice, he crashed into the leaf covered dirt. It sank beneath his boots and crumbled down the steep hill. Kicking at the loose dirt, Jorin'otth reached for a low hanging branch, hoping to halt his descent.

A pale, white hand shot through the leaves, grabbing his arm.

Caught off guard, Jorin'otth jumped, finding almond shaped eyes staring back at him. They belonged to a boy barely old enough to be called a man. There was no way he was out of his first two centuries. He relaxed, allowing the hydralfar to pull him up onto the ledge.

"Thank you for the assistance," Jorin'otth bowed, showing his gratitude.

"My pleasure." The hydralfar looked him up and down, clearly judging his less than pristine dress. Turning toward the brush, he'd stepped through moments before, he signaled. "What are you doing out here? Don't you know this area's crawling with dreualfar?"

Several other hydralfar stepped into the open, revealing themselves to the lone caster.

Jorin'otth counted nine in total, including the one before him. Inspecting their garb, much like they inspected his, he noticed they were clearly dressed for battle. Though they weren't standard hydralfar unit. Their dress was beyond that of the usual scouts, or even officers for that matter. These few belonged to the royal court. Thinking through his options, he came to a decision. "I was aware of the looming threat. That's why I'm here. Could you, by chance, tell me where I might find your commander? I have imminent news to enlighten his ears."

"You're in luck. You happen to be standing in the presence of Jullien the Third. Emperor of the Thirteen Dynasties." The hydralfar that pulled him up bowed, seemingly excited about the use of his title.

Jorin'otth smiled and bowed for the second time. It was as if the alfaren emperor expected him to be in awe of such status. That was the reason he preferred avoiding his people. Their superior attitudes and belittling demeanor never sat well with him. "I suppose the status of commander does not extend beyond that of an emperor." He bowed low once again, feigning interest. "My Lord, if I may be so bold. What do you know of the dreualfar?"

Jullien smiled at the question. He'd never seen this hydralfar before. Who was he to question an emperor? Nonetheless, it was a valid question, to which he didn't have the time to answer. And that secretly meant, he didn't know enough to reveal that fact. "I'm afraid we don't have the time to discuss such a broad topic. If you'll walk with me, there's a gateway to Lorengale just a few miles ahead. My generals await to receive orders."

"My apologies, I'm in a bit of a hurry myself, which forbids me from basking in your superior grace. Would you allow me a brief moment? I shan't be long."

Jullien thought about it for a moment. This lost and dirty hydralfar was an interesting sort indeed. And if he held vital information, it was good to hear him out. "A benefit to being emperor, people will wait for me. You may proceed, so long as you uphold your brevity."

Jorin'otth bowed again, growing annoyed by the ridiculous action. "Thank you, your supreme elegance shall be remembered for eons to come." He silently recalled exactly what was said about this particular emperor in the years to come. "You have been deceived by the dalari, My Lord. They march under the banner of allegiance, but I'm willing to bet they've never told you their dark secret."

"And what secret is that?" Jullien asked, growing uncomfortable with the lingering silence between them.

"Why, the dreualfar, My Lord. The dalari created them, just as they created the hydralfar. Though I'm certain you wish to authenticate this information for yourself. After all, a most noble and understanding commander such as yourself would never take the word of someone they met off the street. Once this information has been verified, I trust you'll bring swift and unforgiving justice to the situation. You are, after all, our lord and savior. To allow the deaths of so many to go unpunished would speak volumes to your reputation. And we can't have that. Anyway, I said I'd be brief, and brief I have been. I'll leave you to your duties, My Lord. Good luck and I look forward to meeting you again."

Before the alfaren emperor could recall him, Jorin'otth marched off into the trees toward Durnal Hill. He was running out of time and meeting the spoiled brat, while productive in his ploys, delayed him longer than he'd intended.

Jullien watched the crude hydralfar rush off, both confused and intrigued by his words. If it turned out the dalari were responsible for the dreualfar, there would be profound consequences. So many hydralfar had already fallen in this war. There was no way he was going to allow another death if this rumor proved accurate.

The thundering echo of footsteps against hardened earth traveled across the sparse woodland. Over four thousand dalari marched toward a single purpose. It was their mission to effectively end the war by any means necessary.

Ravion glanced at his brothers, trekking along beside him. It felt nice belonging to something so powerful. They were united against a force of darkness. And while he'd marched against it before, this time was different. This time it felt like destiny. Hearing the order echo from the front of the assembled companies, he prepared to stop with the rest.

Trendal turned on heel, facing the considerable number of soldiers awaiting his command. Never before had he been the direct superior to so many. Though in truth, his command hadn't changed, just the number of officers that answered to him. Glancing at the assembled captains and lieutenants beside him, he selected what it was he was going to say.

"Dalari and guests!" He announced, looking through the ranks at Gareth hidden among the first company. "As you know, we march for Durnal Hill in an attempt to stop the enemy from unleashing a great evil upon this world. Just over that ridge—," He turned and pointed through the trees, to the large, run-down structure perched atop the next hill. "—we step out of our small existence and we enter into the realm of legends. This battle will never be forgotten so long as dalari live to tell the tale. Keep your weapons up and watch your backs. We're expecting the hydralfar army to join us as we reach the shattered walls, but if they don't show, your brothers and sisters are all you have. Let's take back our lands. Let's take back our freedom. And let's take back our world! Onward to victory!"

Trendal turned and broke into a full sprint. Disappearing over the steep hill, he ran as fast as he could. Reaching the base, he slowed against the steep incline, feeling his breath struggle to keep up. He needed to be the first to reach the ruined city at the peak. He owed Kaileen that much. She was no longer here to kill these evil bastards. It was his duty to ensure first blood was released in her honor.

The assembled dalari army roared, trying to catch up to their commander. He was nearly at the cities edge when they reached the small creek flowing at the center of the wide ravine. Quickly leaping over, they rushed up the hill, seeing hundreds of arrows fly down the hill past them. A few of the dalari were hit, but little could be done about it. The hill was too steep to aim properly. And the other peaks were out of range.

Demetrix saw one of the archers pop into sight, fire his arrow and duck again. He knew there was no way to target him directly, but perhaps he could do something about his cover. Running beside the swarm of dalari, he scanned the broken stone wall, seeing the numerous wood planks sealing off the holes. They'd do little against a full-on assault, but when paired with the steep incline, it was more than sufficient to hold off an attacking army. Reaching into the pocket of his quiver, he grabbed one of the tiny glass vials Kashien had given him before they split ways. Snatching an arrow from his quiver, he pressed the steel head into the formed notch in the vial's base. Tightening the leather binding, he was certain it'd survive the trip. He grabbed his bow, and took aim at one of the weak spots in the wall beneath the archers. There was plenty of space to keep the falling stone from rolling down the hill toward him. Seeing his mark, he released the string. His arrow passed through hundreds of dalari, missing each and every one of them. Impacting the boarded-up stone, a massive explosion erupted, launching dreualfar into the air and crumbing the already weakened barrier.

Dalari soldiers cheered, altering course to the piled rubble of burning wood and bludgeoned bodies. Rushing through the gap, the sounds of battle echoed down the hill.

Ravion peaked over the top, seeing the dreualfar resistance spill from the hole in the wall. There were less than he'd expected, but more than he'd cared for. Drawing his longsword, he charged into the fray, letting his ancestral blade do most of the work. Calming himself, he let the battle predict itself, showing him what he needed to do. Against so many, being prepared was the only way to stay alive.

Attack after attack rained down upon him, yet he spun and danced, deflecting each one. So far no one had been able to touch him, but the battle was young. Trendal dodged a lazy sword slice and plunged his blade into the creature's gut. Shoving it into another, he retracted the blade, knocking another swipe wide. He was surrounded, but the spray of blackened blood made him feel alive. He was honoring Kaileen. That was all that mattered. If he were to die this very moment, it would have been worth it.

Seeing Trendal out manned, Gareth charged, releasing a hearty battle shout. He felt the energy escape him, filling the air ahead.

The dreualfar flew backward from the deadly blast, disappearing beneath the swarming ranks.

Before they could recover, Gareth was upon them, slicing his unseen psiblades. He fought his way to Trendal, thinning the herd.

"Glad you could join me!" Trendal shouted over the sounds of battle. Spinning around, he stabbed deep into one of the dreualfar.

"Wouldn't miss it for the world."

Levi Samuel

Chapter XIX
At Long Last

The air was hot and sticky. Sword clinks and sounds of battle echoed across the vast landscape, carrying on for miles from the crowded hill top. The sun's glow was fading, casting shadow over the battlefield.

Reaching the tree's edge, Jorin'otth wiped a layer of sweat from his forehead. He was out of breath and labored heavily against the trunk of a large oak. Glancing across the deep valley, he could see the dalari army swarming the ruined city. He was too late. They'd already arrived, but that didn't mean he was finished. There was little chance he'd be able to sneak in, but that really wasn't such a challenge. The hydralfar were known to aid the dalari in battle from time to time, especially against the dreualfar. Hell, it was the dalari that came to the hydralfar's aid when the war first began.

Silently contemplating his options, reaching a moment of clarity. He hadn't learned magic for nothing. Cursing himself for not considering it sooner, he recited the spell. The world around him began to shift. Feeling the portal open, he took a deep breath and let it claim him. An orange glow came into view and swallowed him whole.

Stepping onto the dusty and dry dirt, he heard the commotion much closer than it had been. Glancing around, he realized he was within the fractured walls, not far from his destination. The battle hadn't made it this close to the center yet, but it wouldn't take them long. He had to act now or the opportunity would be gone forever.

Ignoring the few straggling dreualfar heading to their deaths, he marched along the stone corridor and found the centermost structure this god forsaken city had to offer. It was much older than the surrounding buildings and held a lingering power that made the hair on his neck rise. Pushing the wooden door open, a rush of stale air pushed past him escaping into the world for the first time in gods knew how long. Jorin'otth stepped onto the dark, ancient steps and hurried into the unknown.

Ravion set his feet, parrying the incoming rapier. Locking his fist around the dreualfar's hand, he brought his sword across and cut into the creature's throat. Movement further in the city caught his attention. He could see a few more dreualfar headed this direction, but that was hardly the worst of his concerns. What he saw wasn't black, but rather pale. He saw Jorin'otth for the briefest moment. And the traitorous hydralfar disappeared into one of the smaller buildings.

"Demetrix, Gareth. We have business to finish!" Refusing to see if they were following, he fought his way through the battle and into the mostly clear city center.

Demetrix followed in his brother's wake, picking off the few dreualfar stupid enough to charge they. They were dead before they hit the ground. "Where are we going? The battle's back there." Demetrix asked, catching up.

"I saw Jorin'otth. If anyone's going to try to cast this spell, it's going to be him." Ravion whipped his longsword around, deflecting one of the attacking dreualfar. An arrow thudded into its skull, dropping it instantly. Letting the creature fall, he continued past, searching for the evading mage.

Demetrix plucked the arrow from the dead creature and returned it to his quiver. There was no telling how long they'd be in combat, and you could never have too many arrows.

Gareth heard his name but couldn't tell where it came from. Punching his bladed fist into one of the black-skinned creature's face, he smiled watching it split, spilling brain matter and blood all over the ground. He noticed Demetrix and Ravion just ahead, beyond the battle. "Where are they going?"

Trendal killed his opponent and turned to see what Gareth was talking about. "I don't know, but I'd wager it's important. I haven't known them to avoid a battle without good reason. You should join them."

"You sure? There's still a lot more of these vile pieces of shit to kill."

"Yeah. We've got this. Go help your brothers."

Nodding his understanding, Gareth turned and charged into the thick mass of enemies. Letting his enraged shout echo, he took joy seeing the dreualfar flee him. Knowing he was the source of their fear brought more joy than he knew he possessed. Cutting his way across the thinning resistance, he broke through the back side of the enemy and rushed after the others. "Hey, wait up!"

Hearing their brother behind them, Ravion and Demetrix turned, seeing Gareth approach.

"What's going on? There's a ton more dreu down there to kill."

"Jorin'otth's here. He went in that building." Ravion pointed to the small shack, perched at the peak of the hill, surrounded by several of the larger structures. Judging by size and appearance, it seemed out of place all alone in the middle of the city. It clearly wasn't much to look at, but the same could be said for the entire metropolis. The words 'run-down' hardly explained the underlying tone.

"Well, if he's in there, I say we drag his ass out and hang him for treason." Gareth smiled at the prospect, taking the lead.

"After everything he's done, I'm not sure I'd agree with giving him a trial of any sort. I say we just kill him and be done with it." Demetrix paused, feeling his ears twitch. "We have company."

A high-pitched horn echoed in the distance, announcing the arrival of the hydralfar. The three paused outside the shack, staring in wonder at the new arrivals on the next hill over. They marched in rows of fifty, creating a perfectly square formation. Their shimmering armor appeared almost white in the fading sun, making their assembled mass glow a radiance that could have lit the darkest cavern.

Reaching the edge of the large hill to the west, they broke formation and charged across the ravine, cutting into any dreualfar brave enough to engage them.

"Great. Now all the dreu-scum will be dead before we get back into the fray." A disappointment carried in Gareth's voice, never expressed before. Letting his uncharacteristically demeanor evaporate, he turned and stepped through the open door. It was narrow, barely wide enough to fit his broad shoulders. Being the largest of them that meant the others would have little to worry about. The air inside the descending stairway was rancid. Not sweet like rotten meat, and not foul like that of a sewer. This was bitter, lingering on the tip of the tongue, like acid that had been cooked into a gas. Only it didn't burn the lungs.

Carefully, Gareth continued downward, seeing the last bit of daylight fade to total darkness. His vision shifted. He was able to see everything. The mold covered stone wall, the jagged and narrow steps beneath his feet, and lastly, the runes scratched into the stone. Running his finger over them, they seemed fresh, as if the mold had been scraped away not hours before. And just as he was beginning to get used to his sight, it went way, leaving him trapped in shadow. "Can you guys see anything?"

"I could for a minute but it's gone now." Demetrix answered, running his hand along the wall to ensure he didn't misstep and tumbled down the steep pathway. "Did you see the runes? What do you think those are about?"

"No clue. Anyone have a torch?" Gareth asked, careful to place his feet before stepping down.

"I have a torch in my pack, but I doubt it'll help. Those runes were a warding spell meant for removing sight. We're trapped in pocket dimension of magical darkness. I might be able to break the spell."

"How would you do that?" Gareth asked, genuinely curious. He'd heard of countering spells prior to their effects taking hold. And on occasion, a studied caster was capable of dispelling the magics of a particular charm or effect. But to break a spell already in motion? He'd never thought of Ravion as the caster type. Though the version he'd had the misfortune of meeting not long ago certainly had no trouble with it. It was strange how quickly and drastically someone could change in such a short amount of time.

Studying the magical threads around him, Ravion picked out the elements of the spell, learning everything it would show him. "I can see energies the spell is made of. It's kind of like hundreds of spider webs woven together into one complex skein. All magic has them. Each one is unique to the spell and the person who cast it. If you know where to look you can usually find a thread that didn't get sealed completely. Once you find it, you can pick it free, and eventually break the effect. The more threads you break, the weaker the spell becomes, until finally it can't hold anymore and the remaining threads give out. When that happens the spell collapses in on itself."

"Yeah, I don't care. If you think you can do it, go for it." Gareth said, listening to the distant battle from the world above. It was faint, only able to be heard in silence. It made him wonder how deep they'd gone.

Ravion took a deep breath, forcing the magics to obey him. He was not going to be controlled by them any longer. Studying the yellow threads surrounding them, he found one that was slightly frayed. Hand trembling, he grabbed hold of it. Sweat was building on his forehead. The spell wasn't beyond his ability, but he hadn't tried anything so complex. Even the curse he'd recorded from the book wasn't this strong, but again, he wasn't relying on the magics inside himself for that. He'd used the book and the enchanted quill to do the hard part. All he had to do was serve as the catalyst for them.

Grabbing at the frayed weave, he trembled, unable to keep his hand steady. It slipped from his grasp.

"Problems?" Gareth asked, impatiently awaiting the return of his vision.

"Give me a minute. I'll get it." Ravion demanded, growing irritated at his unstable grip. Taking a deep breath, he thought through his options. Manually undoing the spell wasn't his only play. He still had one other. Recalling how he'd used it against the other nightkings, Ravion raised his sword. The thin blue threads within the blade danced to the surface, displaying themselves proudly to their master. Ravion could feel a connection to them. It was almost as if they belonged to him, but he knew they didn't. They were a part of the blade, bound to him when he claimed it so long ago. Letting them burn bright, he laid a quick and decisive slice through the air, intent on a single purpose. The blade passed through the yellow webs, slicing them with ease. He smiled at his victory, watching the threads fall to nothing. And just like that, his vision returned.

"About damn time!" Gareth joked, taking another step toward the base. Surprise and concern rushed through him. He was no longer in a stairwell, but instead in a large underground room. How he hadn't noticed made no sense. He was certain they were still on the steps, but these surroundings suggested otherwise.

"You shouldn't have followed me." Jorin'otth's calm voice echoed from the darkness.

"Quit the games and show yourself!" Gareth demanded, summoning his psiblades.

"Why would I do that? You're right where I want you. Away from me and out of my way. Now I can finish this and unleash Izaryle onto this world."

"Why go through all this trouble?" Ravion asked, stepping to the head of the group. "You've targeted each of us in numerous ways. You orchestrated the near genocide of an entire race. And now you put yourself in the middle of a war which has nothing to do with you. I'll ask again, why go through all this?"

"You wouldn't understand and, frankly, it's none of your concern. You shouldn't have followed me here. You'll be the first to die!" Jorin'otth began chanting.

Seeing a pulse of multicolored energy radiate about the room, Ravion knew they had to act quick. If they delayed much longer, Jorin'otth would finish the spell. Searching for the threads, he found them buried beneath a thin cloak. Bringing his sword around, he laid a deep gash across it, watching a hole tear in the room. It spread wider, granting the flicker of torchlight to their surroundings. Ravion looked around, seeing the large dungeon chamber just ahead. They were at the edge of the entry way, at the base of the stairs. The room looked as if a large stone had impacted the middle. A deep crater rested in the floor and pools of glowing red liquid slithered from the outer ring toward the center, like an inverted volcano. Glancing up, he could see a round silo going up into the earth, as if something had crashed into the ground and came to rest here. "Give it up, Jorin'otth. We've escaped your spell!" Ravion shouted.

The hydralfar paused, turning to look at the three standing behind him, armed and ready for combat. "I don't suppose I can barter with you? Perhaps offer you your lives in exchange for turning around and going the other direction?"

"I'm afraid not. It's time you paid for your crimes." Demetrix stated, his arrow trained and ready to fire. It didn't matter how many shields the hydralfar had active, he was certain his arrow wouldn't miss its mark this time. Seeing his brothers ready for action, he released the string, watching the twisting shaft fly toward his target's face.

"Such a shame, but, I suppose all good stories must come to an end." Jorin'otth reached for the bronze rod in his robe. It elongated into the aged, yet seemingly new, wooden staff. Slamming its base into the floor, the red liquid shimmered gold for the briefest moment. Jorin'otth smiled, seeing the arrow stop in mid-flight, not a foot from him.

Glancing at the others, Ravion's sword was raised to strike, and Gareth appeared to be concentrating on something. He clearly wasn't up to any good.

Shaking his head, Jorin'otth walked softly around the room circling them. They were foolish to come after him, though he couldn't blame them. His entire existence was built on people underestimating him. A song echoed in his mind, sounding victory after so many attempts to defeat these three. Whistling his content, he completed his circle and approached the arrow.

Recalling the first lesson his master taught him, he plucked the stationary shaft from the air. Studying the simple instrument, he turned and aimed it perfectly at Ravion's heart. Releasing his hold, it returned to its hovering state, awaiting command. He chuckled to himself, remembering the outcome of an experiment so many years ago.

"It's a simple task. Stop the arrow and alter its direction."

It stopped with minimal issue. And turning it was relatively easy, despite his nose bleeding from the strain of the spell. It wasn't until he released the time stop that he really learned anything new. The fletching end of the arrow launch toward its original destination, embedding itself, feather's first, in the target.

"You lack alteration of momentum. Try it again. But this time, give it a little help."

Returning to the now, Jorin'otth gently pressed his finger against the tail of the hovering shaft, delivering a mild force. It wasn't much, but it was clearly moving toward its new target, be it slow. That wasn't a terrible thing. He didn't want to shove it off course. He continued whistling the tune stuck in his head, listening high pitch echo up the overhead tunnel.

Calmly approaching Gareth, Jorin'otth stepped in front of the bald, battle-worn warrior. It was strange not feeling his breath. His chest refused to rise. He was frozen completely, a slave to time, or the lack of it anyway. He'd finally won. There was no denying that. They'd caused him enough trouble for one lifetime. It was time to end it. There would be no mistakes this time. Raising the staff, he channeled his intentions into the weapon, allowing its power to flow forth.

Both Gareth and Demetrix began to age. Their hair grew long and gray. Their skin wrinkled, developed sickly patches of discoloration. It wouldn't be long now. Aging a body so rapidly had devastating consequences. It'd be a wonder if they even felt it before the end.

Jorin'otth turned to Ravion. Raising the staff, he had a second thought. Having Demetrix's arrow deliver the killing blow was too perfect to pass up, but that was an unneeded risk. The very mistake he'd made so many times before, the one that always allowed them to escape his clutches. Taking a deep breath, he made his decision. Taking position behind scout, he readied his dagger and released the spell.

The keen arrowhead plunged into Ravion's chest. It carried through and exited his back with a pop. A small amount of blood dripped from the embedded metal. Hearing the dalari gasp, Jorin'otth brought his dagger down, stabbing it deep into the base of his skull.

Ravion collapsed in a pool of blood.

Whistling louder than ever, Jorin'otth stepped toward the feeble forms not far from him. They looked so weak and pathetic. He was fairly certain Gareth was already dead, but he had to be certain. The last thing he needed was to have one of them interrupt him in the middle of his spell. Pressing his boot into Gareth's throat, he felt the delicate bones crack and give way.

A weak gasp caught his attention. Glancing over, he saw Demetrix's eyes slowly open. He struggled to move, seemingly flaccid. If he didn't know any better, the weakened dalari broke a few bones during his fall. "And so ends the dreuslayers." Jorin'otth slammed the base of his staff down, letting the capped wood crush Demetrix's skull with ease. Pursing his lips, he blew, resuming his song. Now that he was free of the pesky defenders, it was time to free himself from the rest of this world.

Chapter XX
Outside the Box

Torchlight flickered in the underground chamber, displaying a single shadow on the rough, stone wall. Not a sound could be heard from the lone being, standing over the bodies he'd just destroyed.

Jorin'otth studied them a longer. It didn't feel right. He'd spent longer than he'd ever admit trying to kill the three, in one scheme or another. Yet somehow, they always managed to survive. Kneeling beside Demetrix, he pressed his fingers against the elderly rendition of the dalari he was before, checking for a pulse. As before, it was absent. He was clearly dead, as was Gareth. And there was no doubt whatsoever about Ravion. He'd finally managed to kill them, but it felt anticlimactic.

He expected some huge weight to be lifted, but none came. It was just him, alone in the dark, standing over the bodies of the only true enemies he'd known in his entire life. Truth be told, he felt a slight bit of remorse in killing them. After the fact, anyway. In the moment, it was the only thing he could have done. Now that they were gone, he felt hollow. Like his only purpose had passed. What was he supposed to do now? Aside from complete the ritual and turn the world dark. That was a given. The churning in his stomach intensified, doubling him over. Grabbing his midsection, Jorin'otth stumbled to the center of the crater. He had to cast the spell now or it would be too late.

A golden spray of light erupted near the corner of the room. Opening like a portal, a man stepped out. Jorin'otth didn't have to ask. He already knew who he was. The armor alone said that much.

Meaius stood tall in his blackened plate mail. The hourglass engraved in the left shoulder of his breastplate flowed several grains of sand into the lower portion of the body, but it never seemed to empty. His legendary darkstone bastard sword was outstretched and ready for battle.

Jorin'otth knew his time had come. They'd found him. But that didn't mean his crusade was over. If he could use the staff to kill this duke, he'd have at least a little time before another would come. They'd be too late by then. He'd already be beyond their limited reach. And once the mortal world was cut off from the gods, once the sun was inverted and draining everything it had once nurtured to life, he'd be this realm's new deity.

"Jorin'otth Amnel of the Toreial Flats, you are hereby found guilty on multiple counts of disturbing the timeline for your own gain. Lay down your arms and surrender or you will be erased from existence!"

Meaius glanced at the bodies littering the floor. Shaking his head, he felt sorrow at their demise. He'd warned Ravion to stay clear of the chronomancer. Slowly approaching, he was careful to keep the hydralfar in sight. All it would take to escalate the situation was a single, quick movement.

Watching the duke approach, Jorin'otth counted the man's steps. He was nearly half way to him, more than close enough for what he had in mind. "You know, I never asked for any of this. It was thrust upon me. I simply had to make the best of it."

"Don't make excuses for your actions. You chose your fate. The consequences of those decisions are yours alone." Meaius knew the chronomancer was going to use the staff any moment. He could see it in his eyes. He was as ready as he could be. He'd been trained to withstand such attacks, as were all dukes, but an attack from the Staff of Ozmodius, it'd never been done before. There was no certainty his power could protect him from a relic of his god. Were it from a novice such as Jorin'otth, there was little concern. Being a duke meant he had time on his side. He could train and prepare himself until he was a master in all regards. The lowly chronomancer didn't stand a chance. But when that lowly criminal was powered by a godly weapon, how could he prepare for that?

His eyes followed the plated time warden. Hell was going to break loose at any moment. Jorin'otth prepared himself. He couldn't show any sign of action until he was ready. The dukes were trained to perfection. Any show of resistance and he'd find himself unable to move. He'd have to strike fast and hard, a single blow to end his oppression. Seeing

Meaius breech the crater, Jorin'otth dropped to a knee and let the staff free fall into position. Channeling the energies required to stop time, he let them loose.

The temporal energies gathered and solidified. Meaius twisted them to his own desire, warping the world around them. The dark chamber became a vast ocean. They were submerged beneath its crushing waters. It squeezed their insides, threatening to drain the life out of them.

A fear rose inside Jorin'otth. He'd hoped to stop time, but to do so in such a place would mean both their deaths. He had to do something and quick. Abandoning his intentions, he warped them again. The water disappeared, leaving them completely soaked from the salty substance. They were standing at the center of a pristine city, long before the walls crumbled and turned to dust. A grand temple towered over all else, displaying a large opal over the entrance. A moon and three stars hovered in its focus. It was a majestic sight to behold, but he had more pressing matters. Seeing the duke tarset continue toward him, he summoned the will to stop time again.

Meaius lunged forward, striking at the chronomancer. He was dismayed to see the staff knock the blow wide. He had to get them out of here. Such a period was beyond sanction. It was possible to see something that could not be unseen. Summoning his will, he wrapped them and hopped through time. Images of the past, present and future splayed beyond the wormhole. All was black and blue, and little specks of light could faintly be seen in the distance. They landed in a dense forest. Seeing the ruined city all around them, covered in thick vegetation, Meaius swung again.

It made no sense why the duke moved them. There was no harm in where he'd traveled. Izaryle hadn't been banished yet. Perhaps he could convince the dark god to aid him. Seeing the incoming attack, he realized he was too late. Moving the staff as not to chip the wooden device, but still deflect, Jorin'otth felt the sword bite into his arm. The sting rushed through his body, settling in the tips of his fingers and toes. It was everywhere, burning his insides. Then suddenly, he felt it grab hold and rip itself free. He felt as if his soul was being removed. No, not his soul, his magic. He screamed, feeling a large piece of himself disappear forever. Dropping to his knees, he felt a hatred he'd never felt before. The duke was going to pay for what he'd done. Summoning all his will, he lashed out, letting the magic of the staff carry itself toward the duke.

Meaius brought his sword around and prepared for another attack. The temporal magics were swarming around them. Whatever Jorin'otth had done, it wasn't going to be pleasant. But, maybe, if he was quick enough he could stop it before it ever happened. Lashing out, he let his energies envelop the chronomancer.

A stasis field erupted around him, slowing his movement. Time crawled to a near stop. He was almost trapped indefinitely. If he didn't escape before it closed, it'd all be over. He couldn't have that. He had a mission to complete. Using the temporal storm he'd created, Jorin'otth forced it through the closing crack. It surrounded the stasis field, sealing him in a field of his own making. The opposing magics fought for control, but he could see his was winning. Victory came seeing the duke's field dissolve. Redirecting the enraged magics, he launched them at his aggressor.

Meaius tried to absorb the magics flowing into him but they were too much. Even he couldn't resist the powers of a god. He felt his memories slipping, his body growing smaller, less filling. He was getting younger. Soon he'd be little more than an infant, and then nothing. He had to stop it before he forgot how. Closing his eyes, he recalled the books he'd read on the topic in the libraries of Panthum. It was on the edge of his mind, slipping away moment by moment. Staring helplessly at the chronomancer, he felt a word settle into place.

"Tesrat Ekud!" The energies fanned out, away from him. He felt the change cease, returning him to his former self. Every duke was taught a safe word in the event they lost control of the time vortex. It was a simple phrase that kept them from being lost to time itself and protected them from temporal energies.

"That's enough of your games, Jorin'otth!" Meaius swung hard, catching the hydralfar in the chest. It wasn't a lethal wound, but it should drain his abilities enough to keep him from casting for a few moments. Using the opportunity, he ripped them through time, bringing them back to the buried chamber.

Jorin'otth cried out. His magic was nearly depleted, but he still had the staff. It was certainly better to fight and die quickly than to experience the slow death of nonexistence. He'd only seen it once, the day his master was captured. If they simply removed you from memory, it'd be one thing. But to be erased meant more than never existing. It meant your family was targeted to the very first generation and executed. All in all, it was roughly forty-five minutes of excruciating torture, feeling your memories rip away one by one until the time distortions finally caught up and claimed you as well. It certainly wasn't a pleasant was to go.

Meaius watched the chamber settle around them. The three dead dreuslayers were right where he'd left them.

"Your choice has been made. Surrender the staff, now!" Pointing the tip of his bastard sword at the cowering hydralfar, he prepared himself for what was to come. It always came. They never went quietly for some reason.

The blackened sword was pulling at his innards, even from a distance. Jorin'otth could feel it weakening him, like that last hit hadn't fully disconnected. Tightening his grip around the staff, he pushed himself to his feet and took a defensive position. There was no way he was going to gain the upper hand fighting offensive. He wasn't a trained combatant. But maybe, if he was lucky, he could defend long enough to displace the duke and complete the job. Slamming the base of the staff into the shimmering red liquid, he felt it come alive. Energy rushed through it, empowering him. It reminded him of the first time he used magic. The feeling he got when the raw energies coursed through his body.

A smile formed on Meaius' face. He could sense the energy flowing though the hydralfar. He almost felt bad for him, yet he put himself in this position. The magics were going to be his undoing. Taking a lightning quick step toward the defensive mage, he brought his sword around. The girthy blade soar toward its target, aimed to cut him down permanently.

Jorin'otth prepared to block. He knew the staff was no match for a direct hit, and it'd be a shame to break such a wondrous weapon. He'd have to rely on deflection if he was going to avoid the blow. Stepping back, he rolled his wrist, letting the renewing wood connect with the back side of the blade. The added momentum forced the sharpened edge past him.

As expected, the criminal magician took the bait. Meaius spun around, breaking his sword free of the weak deflection. He was so close to the mage, he could have touched him if he so desired. Carrying the momentum in his sword, he drove the magic absorbing weapon into

Jorin'otth's chest.

A sharp pain erupted, spreading throughout his body. As before, it left no part untouched. Grabbing hold of his insides, it ripped them out through the wound, draining every ounce of magic the misguided hydralfar ever possessed. Jorin'otth collapsed in pain, feeling his body grow weaker. It was over. He'd failed. The physical pain was little more than a growing numb, claiming him slowly. That was minimal compared to the loss of his magic. It was gone. He could feel it. Not just a small part. Every last drop was missing, leaving a massive void inside him. Staring at the towering duke tarset, he couldn't stop the tears from rolling down his cheeks. "Would you just kill me? You've already taken everything else."

"I gave you that option already. You chose to fight. You know what fate awaits you." Meaius sternly explained, abandoning any remorse he had for the thief.

Anger grew with the words. If the duke wouldn't finish the job quickly, he'd just have to force him into it. He was dying from the sword wound anyway. What was the harm in finishing him? Lunging at the armored man, Jorin'otth drew his dagger, aiming at the man's exposed throat.

Meaius leaned back, seeing the approaching blade. Channeling his power, he shoved his open palm into the robed alfar's chest, launching him backward.

The staff came free, landing in the magic-infused dirt. It bounced once, reverting into it compact, bronze rod-like appearance.

Jorin'otth slammed into the wall and collapsed.

Reaching down, Meaius grabbed the disguised weapon, giving it a gentle flick. It extended back into its true form. It felt wrong, using his god's weapon without his blessing, but there was no other option. Only the weapon that did the damage could undo it. He turned, looking upon the bodies before him.

"You should have heeded my warning!" Meaius scolded, knowing his words weren't received.

Shaking his head, he channeled his will into the godly weapon. Time came to a standstill. And suddenly, it began to reverse. He could see the fight with Jorin'otth, only he wasn't in his body. It rushed onward, faster, showing everything and nothing at the same time, until finally, he found the point he'd been seeking. Forcing halt, he stepped through the veil.

Jorin'otth stood frozen, plucking an arrow from the air. He hadn't quite removed it, but it appeared he was getting close.

Meaius studied the frozen chronomancer. It was a strange thing, watching a time stop within a time stop. It was almost like looking into the sands themselves. But the veil hadn't lifted enough to offer sight. It was simply a small breeze into the nether. He could sense it more than anything. Taking a deep breath, he was ready to end this.

Approaching the frozen chronomancer, he gently placed his sword against the hydralfar's arm, letting the razor-sharp edge bite just enough to draw blood. There was no sense in inflicting unnecessary pain. He was going to experience enough of that already. Confident the magics were gone, Meaius took a step back and let the clock start once again.

Jorin'otth felt different. The temporal energies were everywhere. Glancing to his left, he saw the duke standing there, watching him, the staff locked in his hand. He knew it was over before he'd really begun.

The secondary time stop faded and the arrow sped forward, catching Jorin'otth in the chest. It launched him backward, knocking him off balance. He tripped and fell, landing on his back.

Ravion, Gareth, and Demetrix stared at each other, lost in the presence of the newcomer. A confused expression lingered on their faces.

"I recommend you get out of here. You don't need to see what happens next." Meaius calmly addressed the dreuslayers.

"Don't I—." Demetrix paused, searching the familiar figure's face, "Don't I know you?"

"There's time for talking later. For now, go help the dalari push the dreu to the north." Meaius refused to take his sight off the powerless chronomancer.

"Come on." Ravion guided Demetrix toward the stairs, watching Gareth make his way up, several steps ahead. The bald warrior apparently didn't have to be told twice.

Waiting for them to leave, Meaius let the staff return to rod form and tucked it away. Approaching the wounded chronomancer, he knelt down, getting as close to eye level as possible. He'd lost a lot of blood.

His death was not long off. But it wouldn't come soon enough. "You know what comes next. Don't let it be for nothing. Tell me, who told you where to find the staff?"

Jorin'otth coughed. Blood escaped his mouth. He was nearly gone. "Never got a name. He was cloaked. He had strange hands. That was all I saw of—" Jorin'otth fell silent. His cold, still eyes stared straight forward.

"You aren't done yet, Jorin'otth Amnel." Meauis plucked the arrow from his chest and held his hand out. A green light radiated into him, sealing the wound. Before the glow stopped, Meaius was standing in a hydralfar city. Nobles wondered the streets, minding their own. It was a bright, sunny day and the sky was the perfect shade of blue. Glancing over, he saw the petrified form of Jorin'otth at his side. He was white as a ghost, "Come on."

Jorin'otth's legs moved against his will. He never wanted to return to this place, yet here he was, obeying the commands of his executioner.

They passed through a tall, majestic arch, leading into what appeared to be a garden of some sort.

Seeing his target, Meaius let his energies blanket the area. All the alfar within sight froze where they stood, unable to think. Unable to breathe Unable to move.

Approaching a small boy, Jorin'otth recognized him immediately. He was the spitting image of the boy Tygrell had killed. He knew the boy to be of his bloodline. But to be a direct descendant? That was something he hadn't planned for.

As if he knew what was racing through his mind, Meaius offered word. "It's not him. This is his great grandfather, and the start of your bloodline." He corrected himself. "Or, the start of thirty-two generations of hydralfar that didn't make an impacting difference on the world."

Erasing someone was tricky business. You could only go back to a point where the timeline wouldn't be affected. If you removed the ancestor of a wicked tyrant, the world may be all the better for it, it still made a notable impact. Such alterations were not allowed. Additionally, you had to check the future to ensure no new prodigies were to be born. And if they were, you had to make arrangements for them to have the same life with a different family. The latter was much more difficult to manage. But being a duke was all about preserving the timeline. And if there was one certainty in this world, it was that time wants to happen, one way or another.

Pulling his dagger, Meaius handed it to the enslaved chronomancer. "Kill him."

"What?"

"You heard me. End his life. Take it and all those that are to follow, including your own."

"I don't kill children."

Jorin'otth felt his legs carrying him closer, despite his objection. He didn't want to do it, but it seemed his body offered little choice. Stepping within arm's reach, he struggled to keep the dagger away. It was no use. His hand shot forward, stabbing the boy in the throat. Jorin'otth felt a tear roll down his cheek.

The world shimmered and he was lying in the dark chamber, seeing the torches dance in the mild breeze of the tunnel. He felt his memories of relatives begin to fade into nothing. Within moments, he was all alone. No family, no friends, just him and the duke. And then, just like that, he was gone.

Levi Samuel

Chapter XXI
Where it Began

Cheers echoed from the hill top. The combined dalari and alfaren forces stood in victory over the fleeing dreualfar. They watched the last of their cursed foe scurry across the steep ravine and up the other side, dodging arrows, spears, and every other missile being flung at them. There was no need to pursue. They knew exactly where they were going, and the remaining armies were in wait, ready to finish this.

Gareth stepped through the doorway, noting the mass of alfaren soldiers mingled among the dalari army. Archers stood above the rest, perched atop the sparse parapets where the walls were still intact. He wasn't sure how many were present, but there had to be at least a thousand. Glancing at the settling battlefield, he spotted Trendal locked in what appeared to be a heated discussion with one of the alfar. This one didn't appear to be a mere soldier by any means. He carried a polished glaive, and towered over his compatriot. Neither his weapons nor his blinding, silver armor appeared to have any sign of battle mar. That meant he was either extremely good at staying clean while surrounded by chaos, or he watched from the sidelines while other soldiers risked their lives for his privileged ass. Hearing his brothers behind him, Gareth stepped out of their way and marched toward the commanders.

"I've already told you, such a conversation would be better suited when General Kashien is present!" Trendal declared, growing impatient with the alfaren general.

"It's a simple question. Why must your commander be present to answer it?" The hydralfar general held himself superior to the dalari captain, which was interesting considering he was trying to convince him to forego the chain of command.

"I won't say it again. Present your concerns to Kashien and I'm sure he'll be happy to answer any questions you may have. Good day, General Keal'neaus!" Trendal side stepped, abandoning the inquisitive general. Such discussions were above his pay grade, which considering his duty was to his people, meant he wasn't getting paid. Seeing Gareth, he approached. "Find out what they were after?"

"Yes. Jorin'otth is gone. We can end this."

"Gone as in dead? Or gone as in escaped?"

"He had an arrow in his chest when I last saw him. And while I wasn't there for his final moments, I've a pretty good idea we won't be seeing him again."

"Excellent. Are you ready to end this?" Trendal watched the other two dreuslayers approach.

"Give the command." Gareth marched toward the scattered army, finding the place he'd call his own during the march.

"Company, attention!" Trendal barked, watching the assembles forces snap, awaiting orders.

The hydralfar casually made their way through the ridged mass of dalari, forming into their own perfectly unified ranks. They didn't need a command to know what was to come. Awaiting their general to take the lead, they stood, sounding their boots on the ground in unison.

"We've landed a victory here today. And while the battle may be over, the war rages on. We march north to rejoin our brothers and sisters at the gates of Avlonwell. We do not know what awaits us there, but one thing is certain. This ends today!"

The dalari cheered, awaiting command to march. It was a six-hour trek to Avlonwell and they needed to make it before dark.

Sweat glistened off his pitch-black, muscular arms. His sword was primed and ready to deliver a killing blow. Catching his breath, Tygrell stole a glance at the carnage around him.

Dead dreualfar and dalari littered the once beautiful landscape. Many of the alfaren buildings suffered minor damage from the rain of arrows and the occasional magic blast. He was surprised they'd been able to break the walls without siege weaponry, but in truth, he'd underestimated them. He hadn't expected a full-on assault, let alone one that was so well thought out. Hearing the familiar rumble that shattered the outer wall, he braced himself.

The ground shook ferociously and two of the buildings collapsed, disappearing into a massive pit in the earth. The dalari roared forward, taking advantage of the distraction.

Tygrell picked himself up from the dirt. Bits of the dry, brown mineral, where bright green grass once grew, clung to his exposed arms. Dusting himself off, he turned, ready to engage the attacking forces. Raising his weapon, he blocked two swords. Twisting, he sent them into the dirt. Wasting no time, he plunged his blood coated great sword into the attacking dalari.

"General Tygrell, your armies are defeated. Lay down your arms and surrender!" Kashien's voice echoed over the sounds of battle, heard by everyone in the fallen alfaren city.

Searching the advancing army for the dalari prince, Tygrell found him, marching through the lingering dust from enemy boots. A knowing smirk rested upon his face, as if he knew more than he let on. Which was obviously the case. He wouldn't have been able to sack the city had he not.

"Kashien, you spoiled little pup, what did you think was going to happen here? You'd march in with your forces and take us prisoner? That's not the way we operate. The only victory in your future happens once the last of us are dead!" Refusing to wait a moment longer, Tygrell charged, raising his sword.

The dalari scattered, avoiding the larger dreualfar. Kashien had already laid claim to him and they weren't about to get between that fight.

Timing the advancing dreualfar's steps, Kashien silently whispered an incantation. He felt the magics leave him, settling on the ground beneath the enemy commander's feet.

The dirt around him turned black and oily, as if it had been greased. Tygrell stumbled, trying to catch his balance. His leather soled boots slipped on the wet substance, having trouble keeping traction. His speed was rapidly diminishing, which meant he was wide open for attack.

Seeing the dreualfar command slow, Kashien snapped his fingers, enacting a spell he'd practiced since childhood. It was little more than a reflex now. The oil coated dirt erupted in flame, burning brighter moment by moment.

Tygrell felt the heat surround him. He had to get out of the oil, now. But where could he go? There was a good twenty feet on either side of him and at least twice that long between him and Kashien. He had no choice. He'd have to run and jump for it.

Altering course he kicked into the dirt, feeling the first bit of traction since the spell had been cast. Shoving off, he took massive strides, covering the ground as quickly as possible. The flame was licking his armor and singeing his hair. He was out of time. Any longer and his body was going to start suffering burns. Tygrell leapt for the edge. Reaching peak height, he knew he wasn't going to make it. But he'd at least be much closer. His boots hit the ground, slipping from beneath him and he tumbled into the oily substance. It coated him, welcoming the flame to his flesh. Tygrell screamed, unable to stop the burning oil from spreading.

Kashien watched for a few moments. It didn't take long for the dreualfar general to stop moving. It wasn't the most honorable fight of his life, but they were at war. Honor, while important to maintain, had no place when the enemy had none. It was either win by any means or be extinguished.

Leaving the flames to burn themselves out once the oil had been consumed, he marched past the crispy general and toward the battle. They had the dreualfar on the run. Which was perfect, as the remainder of his men were in waiting to funnel them to the canyons.

The flourished leaves of the outstretched tree limbs swayed slightly in the afternoon breeze. The heat of the sun beat against Demetrix's blackened armor, forcing sweat to cling to his forehead and back. The salty liquid was beginning to drip, running dangerously close to his eyes. He was on limited time, testing his resolve against the burn that was sure to start any moment. He could hear the enemy's movement just over the ridge. But they had yet to show themselves. Patiently awaiting command, he stared down the shaft of his arrow. His breath shallow and stance solid. Finally, after what felt like an eternity, the dreualfar peaked the hill. Demetrix exhaled slowly, ready to loose his arrow when the time came.

"Archers, hold. Let 'em get a bit closer. We need to force 'em left!"

Lieutenant Razorius commanded from behind the line. Watching the dreualfar stagger into position. crossing the threshold, he waited a moment longer. He wanted a few more to cross. It wouldn't do any good to have them turn and go the other way. "Fire!"

Releasing the string, Demetrix lost which arrow was his in the flock. They struck with perfect precision, killing at least fifty dreualfar with the first shot.

"Fire at will. Make 'em turn!"

The dreualfar weren't sure how to process what was happening. Arrows were coming from the front. And there was an army at their heels. The only option they had was to turn and make their way down the rocky terrain into the Canyons of Alamar. Dodging the repeating shots, they quickly scaled the bluffs and paved their way to the base of the quarry.

Seeing the dreualfar take the bait, Razorius stepped back and pulled an arrow. The tip was wrapped in a piece of oil-soaked wool. Striking his flint, the sparks danced into the cloth and it flared to life. Giving it a few seconds to fully emblaze, he glanced up through the tree tops and took aim. Releasing, he watched it disappear into the sky.

"Save your arrows. Just keep 'em moving. If they stop or get off point, let 'em have it."

The flaming arrow soared through the air, reaching its peak height. Arching downward, it plummeted toward the earth.

Gareth stood ready, leaning against the jagged underground column, watching the overhead opening. Seeing the flaming arrow fly past, it hit with a thud, sticking in the moist clay, drowning the flame. "It's time boys!"

Pushing himself up, he grabbed the large mallet resting at the column's base and lifted it. Twisting with all his might, he brought the iron head across, knocking a chunk of stone from the natural pillar.

Several dalari around the cavern did the same, busting the underground framework. One by one, the pillars collapsed and the earth began to groan.

"Get clear, she's coming down!" Gareth yelled, backing away from the busted support. Reaching the escape tunnel, he turned and waited for the others to join him.

Dust and small bits of rock fell from the ceiling. Rubble danced on the ground, unable to remain still due to the combination of boots overhead and weakened structural support.

Seeing the last dalari reach him, Gareth pulled a fist sized stone from his belt pouch. Thumbing the unnaturally smooth rock, a blue glow formed at its center. Rearing back, he took aim and launched it into the cavern depths. It disappeared in the darkness, sounding off against the rocky floor.

"Get ready. When she blows, we're gonna' be surrounded by a mass of black-skinned bastards that need killin'!"

As if his words were the trigger, an explosion erupted in the darkness. An orange glow formed in the distance, moving rapidly toward them. The walls trembled and shook, knocking heavy stones from the ancient catacombs.

Gareth grabbed the small shield he'd been given for this very task. Lifting it overhead, he heard the rocks ping off, protecting him against the falling debris.

Daylight shot through the massive pit, displaying tumbling rock, dust, and disoriented dreualfar. Hundreds were killed in the collapse, but many others began to pick themselves up from the avalanching stone.

"Attack! Don't let a single one of these infernal bastards escape." Dropping the shield, Gareth charged into the fray, summoning his fist weapons. Without hesitation, he stabbed into the first dreualfar he saw, ripping him open. Trampling over the dying creature, he lunged into another, taking pleasure in each death.

The dreualfar struggled to hold ground against such an overwhelming number. Thousands had fallen, never to rise again. Only a few thousand remained, and they were battered and without command. It didn't help the dreuki and some of the stronger soldiers were arguing. If it weren't for the attacking dalari, they'd certainly be at war with one other.

Kashien stared from the bluff top. This war was already done. They just had to keep them disoriented. Signaling the unit to his right, he watched them spill down the hill, forcing the dreualfar resistance to huddle together. They were already trapped between the massive hole, the canyons, and his men. But it wasn't the time to get sloppy. Signaling to the left, hundreds of arrows took flight, raining down into the trapped dreualfar.

"All units, charge. Let's squeeze these murders and rapist between everything we've got!"

Stepping around the corner, Ravion let out a heavy sigh, seeing Gareth atop the mound of rubble, attacking anything that moved. Shaking his head, he marched toward the debris. They didn't have time for this. "Fall back. We have to seal the tunnels!" He called to his friend and brother.

Hearing the command, many of the dalari landed their final blows and turned the way they'd come.

Ravion rushed past them and carefully climbed the large pile if settled stone. Looking around, it seemed he and Gareth were the only ones left. Cautiously approaching, he stopped just out of range, not that Gareth needed to be within melee to hit him. "Gareth, you can kill more up top. We have to move."

Slicing an ear from one of the fighting dreualfar, Gareth caught it in one hand and drove his psiblade through the creature's face with the other. Turning, he smiled wide at Ravion, proudly displaying his trophy.

"Well done. You've mastered claiming them before they've fallen." Ravion's tone held sarcasm that no one could have missed.

"Efficiency, my friend. Saves having to waste time after the fight."

Hopping from the stone, Gareth reached the cavern floor and calmly walked toward the side tunnel. Seeing the shield he'd tossed earlier, he heaved it up and continued on. Just because he didn't feel the need to keep it didn't mean he wanted the dreualfar to have it.

Ravion and Gareth reached the surface. The dalari were already in position, awaiting them.

Turning to one of the dalari he recognized from the ACU, he reached into his pouch and retrieved one of the smooth, enchanted stones. "Are the charges set?"

"Yes, Sir!"

"Good. Blow it when you're ready."

Waiting for everyone to get clear of the blast, the soldier activated the rune and tossed it into the hole. A moment later, it exploded, collapsing the tunnel.

The sun lingered long after it should have, as if it wanted to see the final moments of the battle. By all accounts, it should have already reached the west horizon, but somehow it remained far overhead, creating waves of heat over the battlefield.

Kashien dodged a crude scimitar swipe, stabbing his attacker through the ribs. Retracting the blade, he thrust his hand forward, magically blasting several out of his path. Working his way toward the edge, he noticed everything was in position. There was no way they could escape now. He raised his sword, letting his words carry. "Force these abominations into the darkness from whence they sprang!"

The army roared forward, closing the gap around their enemy. The rear of the dreualfar army began to disappear into the chasm they'd created to contain them.

"Where the hell are the hydralfar?" Kashien said aloud to no one in particular.

He'd received missive not two hours ago that General Keal'neaus wanted to meet with him, but no reply followed his agreement. Shaking the thought from his head, he pressed on. There were more dire matters to tend than the absence of the alfar. It wasn't as if they were really needed anyway.

Seeing Trendal ahead, Kashien fought his way through the dreualfar. Reaching the embattled captain, a sense of pride came over him. So much had been lost since this war began. But few pressed on as Trendal had. He was a remarkable officer and an even better friend. Once this was all over, he hoped to make him the new colonel, if he'd accept the job. Seeing a familiar trinket on his captain's belt, he smiled knowing everything was going to be alright. Moreover, if anyone deserved to carry Kaileen's royal guard badge, it was his friend. "Trendal, I'm glad to see you made it. But why didn't the alfar come with you?"

"I don't know, My Lord. They broke away when we left Durnal Hill.

Haven't seen them since."

"It would've been nice to know they weren't going to join us."

"Aye, My Lord."

"The men are tired. We need to end this now. Take your troops to the left flank. Send word to Razorius. I want his forces to cover the right. We have to horseshoe them and close the distance. If we don't funnel them quick enough, the plan falls to pieces."

Trendal fought his way out of the line of skirmish and disappeared among the cavalry.

Kashien jumped back, avoiding an unseen stab. It narrowly missed his throat. Refusing to miss the opportunity, he lunged toward the creature and buried his sword in its neck. Spinning to block another incoming attack, he watched the creature's head come loose. Blocking the secondary attack, he signaled the archers, letting a blue bolt of energy fire into the air.

Seeing the signal, Demetrix grabbed the blue tipped arrow from his quiver. Nocking it, he looked down the line, seeing the others had done the same. Taking aim, he fired.

Hundreds of arrows soared over the dalari and into the dreualfar forces. Finding their mark, a thick smoke began to billow from the center of the enemy ranks, obstructing view.

Seeing the smoke, Demetrix dropped from his perch atop the rocks and made his way toward the rally. If they were going to curse the dreualfar to the shadow, he wanted to be there when it happened. Making his way through, he found Gareth and Ravion on the edge of the field, cutting a path through the dreualfar. More Gareth than Ravion.

Ravion chuckled, watching Gareth barrel over the dreualfar, forcing a small section to abandon their formation. It really was the little things that brought joy.

Demetrix approached, firing two arrows, one on either side of Gareth.

The bald warrior glared at Demetrix. He felt the breeze of the arrows on both sides of his face. Turning to see what he'd hit, there were two dead dreualfar behind him. One had an axe that appeared to have been primed and ready to strike. The other carried a rusted spear, but it seemed to have been knocked from his grip when he fell. Returning his attention to the younger dalari, he rubbed the stubble between his beard and ear, "You damn near hit me!"

"Relax. I wasn't even close. I had a whole three inches on either side."

Ravion couldn't hold back his laughter. Leave it to these two to argue during the largest battle of their lives.

A black armored man appeared in front of the group. It was odd, him being here. Like everyone naturally avoided where he was standing, yet nobody acknowledged his presence.

"I remember you. You were the one that rescued me when I was a child." Demetrix announced, seeking validity in his statement.

"That I was. I told you I'd see you again one day."

"You sure picked a hell of a time to honor that promise." Stepping closer, Demetrix studied his face. "You haven't aged a day."

"I assure you, much time has passed since we last met. I'm what you would call a duke tarset. We serve the god Ozmodius and regulate his domain. The entity you knew as Jorin'otth stepped beyond the laws of time and came to this place with the intent to alter history. I could not find him on my own due to a relic he possessed. Which is why I asked you to come here and flush him out. I knew he couldn't resist staying hidden once he realized you three were on his tail. For that, you have my thanks."

"First off, I never agreed to an arrangement with you. And secondly, if I had, I damn sure wouldn't have gone through all this for 'thanks'. I prefer to be paid in gold." Gareth declared, keeping his eye on the armored warrior.

Hearing the horns sound on both flanks, Kashien knew it was time to end this. Moving with his army, a familiar face caught his attention. Pausing, the dalari continued past him, displaying the duke in full view.

"Meaius?" Kashien gasped.

Seeing Kashien, Meaius gave a quick nod, acknowledging the dalari prince. "We need to be going now."

"But we haven't cursed—" Before Demetrix could finish his sentence, they were standing in a glowing white room. The walls were nowhere to be seen, yet it felt relatively small considering how open it was.

"This is purgatory. Time does not exist here. Being as you've done a great service for the world, I've arranged for each of you to be rewarded." Meaius reached into a black hole in front of him. Retrieving a winged helm made of the black ore matching that of his bastard sword, he handed it to Gareth. "For you, a darkstone helm of the Udurnie. Being as you've only one eye, this helm will allow you the see as if you still had both."

Relinquishing the helm, he grabbed another item from the hole. Handing it to Demetrix, he continued. "A quiver of Celnuntos. From what I hear, you've already started down that path. This will come in handy. So long as you never remove the last arrow, it will never run out. And lastly—."

He reached in one final time, retrieving a sealed scroll. Handing it to Ravion, he explained. "The Seal of Vascreil. This is the treaty of independence, signed by Emperor Vascreil during the first hydralfar dynasty. It's a magically binding contract between the hydralfar and the dalari emperors, declaring complete and total peace between the two races. It was written when the hydralfar declared their independence and segregated from the dalari. Fearing conflict between their peoples, the emperors wrote this contract as a means of assurance that no conflict would ever arise between them. The seal was eventually lost and its message forgotten. But all things lost, eventually end up here. When you're ready, march to the gates of Lorengale and declare your birthright. Present the seal to the emperor. He'll have no choice but to hear your plea, lest lose his throne for breaking the contract."

Ravion didn't know what to say. It was more than he could ever hope for. Clutching the scroll to his chest for fear of losing it, he watched the duke form a series of runes in the air. He couldn't hope to understand them.

A gateway opened, revealing a wooded landscape on the edge of Marbayne.

Recognizing it, Demetrix nodded his respect to Meaius and stepped through.

Ravion paused on the edge. "Thank you for starting me on this path. It never would have happened had you not brought me back."

Meaius smiled. "It's my pleasure. Now, go out and make your people proud."

Ravion stepped through.

Gareth stood there for a long moment, watching Ravion and Demetrix on the other side.

"Second thoughts?" Meaius asked, patiently awaiting the dreuslayer.

"What we did back there. How often does that happen?"

"What? Someone break the laws of time?"

"No. How often do the dreualfar gain a foothold like they did back there. And again, out there." Gareth gestured toward the magical doorway.

"Once or twice every few thousand years. Why?"

"Someone needs to be there to stop them."

"That's a dangerous road you're looking to travel. You understand there are rules that have to be followed."

"I do."

"That means when you're told to let someone go, you have to adhere. No matter what. Just because you want them dead doesn't mean you're going to be able to kill all of them. In some cases, one or two have to survive to set certain events into motion. Without a protected timeline, everything falls apart."

"I get it already. Teach me what I need to know and let me do my thing."

"Alright. I recommend telling your brothers bye. It's unlikely you'll ever see them again."

Gareth stepped through the gateway.

Ravion and Demetrix were standing there waiting for him.

"I'm not coming. I'm gonna' go with him." Gareth pointed toward the portal with his thumb, "Travel through time and take out the dreu where and when they spring up. It's not like I did much the last time I came back here. At least this way I get to keep doing what I'm good at."

Ravion stepped forward and extended his hand.

Gareth took it, gripping him about the forearm. Pulling him close, he gave him a solid pat on the back.

"You be careful out there and don't hesitate to come get us if you get in over your head."

"Please, I never get in over my head. And without such a pretty boy at my side, I've a feeling things are gonna' be a little less complicated." Gareth laughed.

"Yeah, this pretty boy won't be there to save your ass. I'm serious though, if you need help, don't hesitate."

"I'll be alright."

Gareth turned to Demetrix. Holding out his had as Ravion had, Demetrix took it and did likewise. "Don't do anything stupid."

"Please. Like I ever do anything stupid. Now, enough of all this mushy shit. You guys go live your lives. Have kids. But don't name any of those bastards after me. I'm not ready for that kind of commitment." Chuckling to himself, Gareth walked backward into the gateway. It disappeared the moment he was clear.

Epilogue
Rightful Place

Demetrix pushed the council room doors open. It was as if he'd never left. His cane laid on the floor beside the large wooden table where he'd dropped it. But something wasn't right. The dagger wasn't anywhere to be found. Walking into the room, he took a seat in his large, ornately carved chair and leaned back, putting his hands behind his head.

Ravion closed the door and found his chair. Leaning against the back, he stared intently at his brother. "We're the only two left. Are you still planning to go back to Irayth?"

"I am. But I need to see what that horator was all about first."

"Alright. As I said before, you have my support. But before you go, we need to fill the chairs. I'm going to have my hands full rebuilding our people, which means I won't have much time to lead the Order."

"I agree. We need some new blood. We have a niece training with the border wardens. Rayel. I believe her and William would make excellent additions to the council. Since you'll still be around, you can hold the fifth chair. If we agree to those two, we just need to find two more. Which I have some ideas there as well."

"Niece? Alexzandra had children?"

"From what Rayel told me. We left not long after I met her, but apparently she had twin girls."

"We need to see if she's capable of handling the job. Once we have a list of potential candidates, we can interview them and find a good team to lead the Order into the future." Ravion stood, pacing the length of the table.

"Agreed. But first we need to stop the attacks on the southern towns. I haven't been able to find out what their goal is. Right now, is just seems like random attacks with no purpose. Which means they're either looking for something, or they want us to think they're random as a distraction."

"Keep the border wardens on it. I'm going to travel to Fender's Spear and have the barbarians on high alert as well. Plus, it'll be good to let Senaria know I'm back."

"Have a safe trip, brother. And be prepared for a serious ass chewing. I haven't been there for a few months before we left, but I carried out your will. Technically speaking, you're no longer the Lord of Krondar. As you wished, that title went to her."

"She's a good leader. I've a feeling she'll do better than I ever could."

Pushing himself up, Ravion grabbed his pack and slung it over his shoulder. "Don't spend too much time worrying about the dagger. It's where it needs to be. We'll have it again when we need it." Refusing to give any further insight, he stepped out.

Fender's Spear was much larger than he remembered. Everything looked new and a steady flow of city guards wandered the street in their red and black tabards, depicting a broken spear against a round shield. Making his way down the street, now paved with brick, opposed to the dirt he'd last seen, Ravion found the keep at the city's center.

One of the guards, standing outside the door recognized him and snapped to attention.

"Stand down, I'm not the lord any longer." Ravion assured, smiling at the hulking brute, wearing chainmail under his tabard and a thick, redwood spear in his right hand.

Making his way through the arched entryway, he was both surprised and impressed. Many of the inner guards were composed of the mul'daron. It made perfect sense, he just hadn't expected it.

Continuing on, he found the throne room.

Twin rays of sunlight beamed through the overhead windows, lighting the large, castle-like chamber. The red carpet lining the center of the room was splayed out and inviting.

Stepping onto the liner, his boots were muffled by the thick padding. Approaching the throne, he fell in love all over again. The platinum haired woman sitting upon it at the far end, was just as stunning as the first time he'd seen her. To his surprise, she held a small child in her arms, nursing him. The boy couldn't have been more than a year old.

"My Lady, Senaria. I humbly ask your forgiveness for my absence. And I swear by all that I am, that I will never leave you like that again."

Senaria smiled, seeing her lost lover approach. Standing, she met him at the base of the dais.

"Ravion. I thought I'd never see you again." She hugged him as best she could, protecting the child. "I'd like you to meet your son, Rylan."

Ravion looked intently at the child. He could see the blue glow radiating from him. His short hair was blond-tinged red and his puffy little cheeks contained a few light freckles. "He's perfect!" Ravion kissed her forehead.

"Now, you'd better have one hell of a story to tell me." She playfully bumped him with her shoulder.

"Let's just say, with everything I've been through, I'm a changed man. And if you'll have me, I'd be honored if you would become my wife."

"This isn't some ploy to retake the throne, is it?" She smiled and kissed him passionately.

"No ploys, My Lady. In fact, if you can spare the trip, I have a larger throne to claim."

"But you just got back?" Senaria asked, concerned that he was going to leave right away.

"Yes. And I must journey again. But I won't go without you. You have my word on that. However long it takes, I'll be by your side."

Senaria stared into him for a long moment. She knew she could trust him. He'd proven that time and again. But there was something different about him, something hidden beneath the surface.

"Give me a week to make arrangements. At that point, we can go wherever you need."

"Thank you, my love."

The morning light was just cresting the tree tops when Demetrix drew the unique arrow from his enchanted quiver. Twisting it between his thumb and forefinger, he nocked it to the string and drew. Aiming into the sky, his fingers released and the thin shaft took to the sky. It flew up, past the clouds, little more than a speck in the distance. Yet he knew where it was going.

Slinging his bow, he broke into a sprint, charging after the slender object. He ran through bushes and thorns, meadows, and bogs. No matter how fast or slow he ran, the arrow always seemed to be just within sight.

Leaping over a deep ravine, Demetrix darted through a patch of thick trees he couldn't remember seeing before. *That was odd. There's not a single tree I haven't memorized in this forest.* Marbayne was his home and it was his duty to know every square inch of it. Yet here he was, in the center of a patch of some of the largest trees he'd ever seen. Even the great trees of Myrkwood were dwarfed by these giants.

Slowing to a stop, he saw the arrow lodged firmly in the ground at the center of the clearing. He clearly wasn't in Marbayne anymore. But where was he? He didn't remember passing a portal, but something mystical had to have happened.

A calm voice echoed over the clearing. "I see you're finally ready."

Demetrix spun around, seeing the man Kashien had introduced him to. More than that, several others stood on each side, wearing matching cloaks with the same hedge maze looking symbol at the broach.

"What is all of this?" Demetrix asked, confused by the cloaked figures, the massive trees, the strange arrow, and everything else unknown about the situation.

"We are the horators. Archers of Celnuntos and guardians of the realm. Very few ever learn of our existence. Fewer yet are invited to our ranks. Tell me, if you were surrounded by enemies and you were down to one arrow, how would you survive?"

Demetirx thought about the question for a moment before answering. "If I didn't have any other weapons on me, I'd stab with the arrow and use my bow as a staff until I had no other choice. I'd then look for a dead limb hanging from a tree, or some kind of trigger I could possibly shoot that would take out more than one. If none of that was present, I'd select the meanest opponent on the field and put my arrow straight through his eye. The rest I'd fight off with my bow. At least until I could take one of their weapons." Demetrix played with the sword at his side, recalling how he'd gotten the blemished weapon.

"Very well. A decision has been made."

The other horators walked into the tree line and disappeared.

"What? Where are you going?" Demetrix searched but couldn't find them.

The last remaining figure dropped his hood, revealing the grizzled face of an elderly myrkalfar. "They're returning to their duties. When a new horator is selected, it's our job to be present. But don't worry, if you ever need them, they'll return. Just as you'll answer if they need you."

"Yeah, about that. I'm planning to go through a portal and into another world. I'm not sure answering a courier missive is going to be the easiest thing to accomplish."

"Don't be foolish. We send our messages tied around an arrow and fired into your vicinity. And did you really think we weren't already aware of your intentions? That's part of why you were chosen. At this point in time Celnuntos does not have any followers in Irayth. Yet his domains are present. Once you've been trained in the ways of the horator, you're free to travel to any land you choose, so long as you uphold the sacred duties you agree to at the time of your naming."

"What sort of duties are we talking about?"

"We protect nature from unnatural forces. Demons, rampant magi—the occasional dragon trying to claim territory. Simple stuff most days."

"We'll, if you're going to train me to stand up to creatures like those, I'll need all the help I can get when I return to Irayth."

"Excellent, but be warned. That realm has not felt the presence of another god for many thousands of years. By accepting this mantle, there are those that will hunt you. It'll be your job to survive, and to train a new horator before your passing."

"Okay. How do I do that?"

The sea breeze splashed gently against his face from the bow. Ravion held the amulet, feeling the energy within guide his way. Seeing land just ahead, he signaled the navigator.

The ship groaned from the adjusted tiller and altered course to make port on the large, forested continent.

Ravion was surprised by how easily the mul'daron had taken to the sea. He guessed none of them had sailed before, but with a little guidance they seemed to pick it up fairly quick. It also helped to have a few trained sailors available to show them the ropes. But in the six months they'd been on the ocean, most could find themselves extremely cramped within the tar and wooden confines of a ship. He needed to wake Senaria. They'd be landing soon and he wanted to make sure she was ready for the last leg of the journey.

Quickly making his way to the hold, he rounded the corner and entered the private quarters. Slowly opening the door, he peeked in, seeing Senaria, peacefully asleep upon the bed. Their infant son was curled up comfortably beside her. Stepping into the room, he closed the door and approached. "Senaria, we're here."

Her eyes slowly opened, staring up at him. Careful to keep from waking the baby, she smiled. "Where's here?"

"Coriath"

"Isn't that just a big swamp?"

"It has a large swamp, yes. But that's just to throw trespassers off. In reality, the majority of the continent is a dense jungle. Our destination is a little over a week by horseback."

"How about by wagon back?" Senaria asked, clearly tired of the constant travel.

They'd gone from ship to wagon, from wagon to ship, and back again more times than she could count. If this was the final transition, she'd gladly thank any of the gods that would take the time to listen.

Ravion chuckled at her statement. Leaning over, he kissed her. "By wagon, my love, we're looking at about a week and a half. I know you're tired of all the travel. I promise, this will be over very soon. I won't ask you to stay in Dranar permanently, as I know you have responsibilities to attend. But there are some things I'm going to have to do to restore my people. That may take a few months, but we can leave whenever you desire."

"My husband, the thoughtful thinker." Senaria smiled and sat up, hoping Rylan wouldn't wake just yet. "So long as you're by my side and my people are taken care of, I don't care where we go or what we do. My responsibilities in Krondar were little more than a gift from you. Having managed them to the best of my ability, I don't believe they require my attention any longer."

"Whatever you decide, you have my support." Ravion carefully picked up Rylan, cradling him in his arms. He was already getting so big. "We should prepare the wagon and make sure the horses are ready to go."

Senaria took the child and kissed her husband once again, "Go. See to it. The quicker we get there, the better."

Ravion left the private quarters and found the stable near the back of the hold. The horses had been well groomed and fed the duration of the trip. He felt a little bad they couldn't exercise in the crowded confines of the ship, but it was for their own good. Horses and ships didn't generally mix well.

A human boy, barely old enough to be called a man stepped from the adjoining room and approached Ravion. "What can I do for you, My Lord?"

"We're making port soon. Will you see to it that the horses are harnessed and ready for travel?"

"Aye, My Lord."

"I also need the wagon stocked with feed and water. We have a little over a week's travel and I'd like to avoid having to resupply before reaching our destination if I can help it."

"I will be done, My Lord."

Ravion handed him a gold coin for his trouble. Climbing the ladder to the deck, he could see the large land mass much more vividly than before. She was beautiful in a way only nature could provide. They were approaching a long, wooden pier spanning out into the depths. That was good. It meant they didn't have to risk running the ship aground.

"Prepare to dock, port side!" The navigator called to the crew.

Men and mul'daron rushed to prepare the ship. The sails dropped, being folded up and stored away until their next use. Floating in on momentum alone, the ship rocked gently toward its destination. Two of the mul'daron sailors tossed mooring ropes to the pier and tied them off, pulling any slack they offered. She groaned to a slow and steady halt, secured by the thick ropes.

A mild warmth had settled over the jungle city. It was eerily quiet save for the guards and horses, which didn't seem to care how much noise they made. A thin blanket of fog floated through the air, restricting vision to more than about half sight.

Stepping from the simple coach wagon, Ravion held the amulet up once again, ensuring they were at the right place. He'd never been to Dranar before, and while she was beautiful, he expected there to be something more. Perhaps a living city. This place seemed abandoned and dead. The buildings and roads were grand in all ways, but the jungle had begun to slowly devour it. Vines clung to the sides of walls, and thick roots had cracked some of the elegant streets. Still, considering how long it'd been abandoned, she showed remarkable resilience. Stepping onto the city street for the first time, Ravion turned and extended his hand, awaiting Senaria.

She stepped down beside her husband and they walked into the city together.

Two of the mul'daron guards stayed with the wagon, while the rest followed after the pair.

Reaching the city center, guided by the mystical amulet, Ravion looked up at the massive palace. It was larger than he could have imagined. And from the way the back side was set into the earth, it was probably still larger yet.

Climbing the numerous, perfectly white steps, Ravion reached the unguarded doors. Giving a firm shove, they swung open with relative ease, allowing dust and stair air to interact with the sunlight. Turning to Senaria, he could hardly contain his excitement, "Do you wish to stay here? I don't know what's down there and I don't think Rylan needs to be breathing all this dust."

"He's survived six and a half months at sea, with several one to two week intervals in a wagon. I don't think a little dust is going to hurt him." She marched past her husband and made way into the palace.

The polished marble floors were lined in thick layers of dust. Several stained overhead windows allowed the light to faintly penetrate, leaving a dull hue over the massive entryway.

Ravion signaled the guards to remain. Stepping inside, he shut the door. He didn't need the amulet to know which direction to go anymore. He could feel it within himself. No sooner than he stepped into the corridor, leading deeper into the grand structure, the ceiling and walls flared to life.

Magically hovering sconces floated harmlessly near the walls, their brilliant flames danced in a nonexistent breeze, illuminating the towering hallways and gargantuan rooms. The ceilings appeared as the night sky, revealing thousands of speckled stars and swirling clouds of purple and blue.

Making their way deeper, Ravion glanced up, realizing he hadn't seen any windows for quite some time. He guessed they'd reached the underground portion, but it didn't feel as such. If anything, it felt as if they were floating far above the ground, closer to the stars displayed overhead than originally perceived.

Finding the door he'd been searching for, Ravion grabbed the platinum ring on the polished oaken barricade and pulled it toward him. To his surprise, the room was already lit. All the others had waited until he stepped into them before they flared to life. But this one waited prematurely. Sharing a cautious glance with Senaria, they carefully entered the chamber.

Making their way along the magnificent corridor, they could see the vast opening up ahead.

Ravion kept watch on the murder holes in the wall. All it would take was one missed ambush and it would all be over. Finally, he reached the end, staring in wonder at the magnificence around him. The walls and high vaulted ceiling were covered in hundreds of thousands of runes, each one telling their own story.

He couldn't recognize them all, but he understood most of their meaning. As best he could tell, one had but simply touch the rune to experience the story they told. It was a mystical picture book, using memories as the story. He smiled at the concept. What better way to preserve the past, than by saving it for the future?

The side walls were lined by huge statues, spanning up the ceiling joists. He'd seen those statues a few times before but never really understood them until now. The faces were in constant flux, shifting from one to another in the blink of an eye. But it wasn't until he saw Meaius's face that he realized the twelve statues were a warning to the enemies of all.

Lost in the decorative surroundings, he hadn't noticed the centerpiece of the room was missing. The dais was there, trimmed in the blood red carpet leading up to it. But the throne was missing. He could still feel the presence calling to him. But it wasn't in this room.

Senaria stared intently at the runes lining the walls. Running her finger over one, she was taken back, feeling the memories of the event settle into her mind as if she were present during their happening. But more importantly, it showed her this room.

Turning toward the dais, she marched past Ravion. "This way."

Ravion followed, curious as to what she was doing.

Senaria reached the rear wall, finding the pattern she'd seen in the vision. Quickly tracing it out with her free hand, the wall began to vibrate and suddenly, it slid open, revealing another door.

Smiling at his bride, Ravion walked past and approached the door. Easily, he pushed it open, revealing another, equally decorated, yet much smaller chamber. In the center sat the throne, an elderly figure resting atop it. Stepping in, Ravion noticed the twelve dalari standing around the edge of the room.

Many of them were younger than him. But they wore the same, matching armor, each one with a trident carved into the collar. Suddenly he knew who these men were. Or at least who their ancestors were. Returning his attention to the man upon the throne, he looked familiar. Approaching, he studied his face.

"Ravion, my old friend. I'm glad you finally made it." His voice was weak and hoarse from disuse.

"Kashien? What happened? You got old." Ravion was taken back at how aged the dalari prince, or emperor now, appeared. He felt like he'd just seen him less than a year ago. But the man before him was ancient.

Kashien nodded. "I've been waiting here, for you, for nearly twelve thousand years."

Kashien weakly removed the crown from his head and pulled himself to his feet. "Take your throne. I've one last gift to offer."

The elder dalari slowly made his way from the ornate chair, his feeble form unable to do so quickly. Turning around, he waited for Ravion to take a seat.

Begrudgingly, Ravion complied and sat. He was uncomfortable being the center of attention, but it was something he was going to have to get used to.

Approaching, Kashien placed the crown upon Ravion's head. "Behold, your new emperor."

The twelve dalari around the edge dropped to one knee, bowing their acceptance.

As the others, Kashien bowed as far as his body would allow. It sucked getting old. Pushing himself back up, he reached beneath his robes and retrieved a glowing blue stone. "This is what's kept me alive all these years. I trust you to keep it safe. Nobody can know its whereabouts. This stone, for all its glories, has the power to destroy our people." Raising it to the air, he released the magic within. "All dalari, return to Dranar. Your emperor has ascended the throne."

Ravion felt the words inside his head. It was then, he knew what Kashien had done. He'd recalled his people. Every single one that had been in hiding all this time, they were coming home.

Kashien handed the stone to Ravion and turned toward the door. "Be well my friend." Slowly reaching the doorway, Kashien stepped through, his body erupted as he went. With that, he was gone.

The full moon brightly illuminated the secluded grove, displaying thirteen cloaked figures. Two rested in the center of the group, one standing the other kneeling.

"Your time has come. Remove your cloak and be named the twelfth horator."

Demetrix stared up at the myrkalfar's face, trusting him completely. Dropping his hood, he let the heavy cloth fall down his back, displaying his shirtless form to the elements.

"Present your bow."

Whipping the reforged piece of enchanted wood around, Demetrix brought it up, holding his weapon horizontally in both hands.

"Repeat after me. I, child of Ur, swear my fealty to Celnuntos and promise to do all within my power to protect his domains from any threat, unnatural or mundane. For it is a horator's duty to serve the lands he calls home as the last defense against enemies both near and far."

Demetrix recited the words, feeling the mystical energies swirling around him.

"Llaf I llahs os, nrob saw I sa!"

A strong gust of wind picked up, encircling the two central beings. The energies began to glow green and Demetrix felt his left shoulder blade sting. Resolved against the pain, he held fast, watching his master disappear into the green sparks flying around him. Suddenly, the wind settled and he stood among his eleven brothers.

A dark green mark, matching the sigil of Celnuntos was embedded on his back. Getting to his feet, he lifted his bow and glanced around at the other horators. One by one, they stepped from the grove, leaving their new member to his mission.

"Remember my training, for a horator must never forget what he fights for. Now, go. Go and return to your beloved Irayth. Restore the blessings of Celnuntos to those accursed lands."

Demetrix felt the words inside him. He'd been told about the ritual, but hadn't fully understood it until now. His master was now a part of him. And one day, long from now, he would impart his knowledge on to another skilled archer. As was the way of the horator.

"You're sure about this?"

"I am. This feud has gone on long enough." Ravion stated to his old friend. Patting the hydralfar captain on the shoulder he continued. "My people have lost enough. If I don't do this, both our races will continue to suffer."

"I understand. I always have. That's why I took you in so long ago. But I urge you to err on the side of caution. The emperor may have changed many times since the decree was implemented. That doesn't mean this one won't still try to enforce it. I mean, look at the attack you suffered as a child. That wasn't some nobody giving the command. That order came directly from the emperor. It's a sad reality, but most are afraid of that which they don't understand. Sadder yet, are those whom hold positions of power. Their fear tends to blow everything out of proportion. I'm not saying don't try. Simply, be careful, what you're talking about is suicide."

"I ask you to trust me, as you did so long ago. Besides, I have many friends and resources at my disposal now. Your emperor would be a fool to attack me openly. Such a rash decision would display weakness in his rule and before long his line would be removed from power."

"You speak as if you hold the favor of all thirteen dynasties."

"Not all thirteen. But enough have heard my voice."

"I see. Just promise me you won't do anything foolish. You've come a long way since that boy I pulled out of the water so many years ago. I'd hate to see you meet your end today."

"You worry too much."

"And you seem to worry too little."

Another figure approached the pair.

Dropping his forest green hood, the myrkalfar nodded at them. "They're here. Are you ready?" Aldulrien asked.

"As ready as I'm going to be." Ravion replied, silently thanking the Evinwood King.

Had it not been for his friendship he wouldn't have been able to reach out to the dynasties individually, which would have made this meeting impossible without force.

"Lead the way."

Pulling his cloak overhead, Ravion followed the alfaren king, hearing the footsteps of his old friend and former captain at his heels. He was grateful both had been so accommodating. It was these alfar that gave their entire race hope for a peaceful future.

The group made their way through the grandest city Ravion had ever seen. It may have not been larger than Idenfal or Dranar, but it was certainly grander. The majestic colors and smooth contours made it feel tranquil and inviting. It reminded him of the brief time he'd spent in Adariel. Though there was a stronger natural presence there than he felt here. This place felt like magic. It was coursing through the columns and walls, serving as an invisible protector against any threat. But that wouldn't stop him. His kind taught the alfar about magic. If it came to open war, they stood little chance. But such threats held no place in his heart. He was certain he could settle this with words. But in the off chance he couldn't, battle would remain the last result so long as he lived.

They reached a large amphitheater near the city's center. The acoustics were fantastic. The alfar, collected at the base, were casually talking among one another, their voices little more than a whisper. Yet Ravion could hear every word as if he were standing right beside them. They made their way to the base, awaiting the emperor's arrival.

Taking position to the side, careful to stay out of everyone's way, Ravion watched them mingle. They acted like long lost brothers and sisters whom hadn't seen each other in years. Sure, some didn't get along, that much was clear. But they held a respect for one another nonetheless.

Hearing the echoing alfaren horns, the group silenced and turned to watch their emperor approach.

Six alfar, dressed in constricting, yet graceful robes of gold and white carried a large palanquin down the steps. Reaching the bottom, the front two stepped away, leaving the others to support the weight. One of the alfar got to his hands and knees, taking position beneath the door, while the other opened the smooth portal on the side of the enclosed cabin. A young boy stepped out, dressed in grand robes matching that of the city. Ensuring solid footing on the alfar's back, he gracefully stepped to the ground where he took his seat in a throne that had been placed for him earlier. "You called this meeting of the dynasties? I have more important matters to attend."

Ravion was taken back at how young he was. Even for an alfar, he would have expected someone in his hundreds at the least. But this child didn't appear any older than eleven or twelve seasons.

The alfar stood silent for a long moment, letting their emperor get comfortable.

"Spit it out. Who called us here?"

"I did, My Lord." Aldulrien announced, stepping forward and bowing deeply.

"And you are?"

"Aldulrien Quetalious Denarie, My Lord. King of Evinwood and Lord of the Eighth Dynasty."

"I see. And why did you summon us today? Would it not have been simpler to send a missive, rather than requesting each of us to travel half way across to realm to this—" The emperor paused a moment, looking around as if he was disgusted by the sights before him. "—place?"

"My Lord, Lorengale is not simply a place revered by our kind. It's the one site known to all alfar where title and dynasty hold no power over another. That's why all disputes, treaties, and matters pertaining to the alfar as a whole are conducted here. This is the one place where all voices are heard." Aldulrien explained. "As for my summons, I have a friend who would like to speak to you."

The myrkalfar king nodded to Ravion, granting him the floor.

Ravion stepped to the center of the amphitheater, sorting out exactly what he was going to say. This was the moment he'd been working up to his whole life. The moment when he would save his people. Dropping his hood, he heard a few gasps of shock from the assembled alfar. But he'd paid many of them a visit, asking their support prior to this day. He was relieved to see they'd come to honor their bond.

"My Lords, kings, emperors, and alfar of status. My name is Ravion Santail and I'm here to inform you that I am the rightful emperor to the dalari throne. For too long now, your people have waged a silent war against mine, attempting genocide each time we are found out. I'm here to tell you, that ends today. My people are returning home and you will not stand against them ever again. It is my understanding that you, Emperor Julien the Sixth, are not directly responsible for the atrocities that have befallen my people. That was the legacy of your ancestors. I hope a different legacy for you."

Reaching into his cloak, Ravion retrieved a sealed scroll. Pulling it out for all to see, he broke the seal and unrolled it, displaying the golden etchings on the page. "I have here the Seal of Vascreil. Signed by the first alfaren emperor, Vascreil himself."

Shocked expressions filled the area, amplified by the dish they were standing in.

"I ask you, will you continue on the path your ancestors laid out? The path that will lead to your destruction. Or will you honor your founders and end this foolish obsession against my people?"

Ravion laid the seal in the emperor's lap, allowing the boy to look upon it. Waiting patiently, he kept his gaze locked. He knew his words were a bit direct. Such a thing was a dangerous game in politics, but in this scenario he held all the cards. It only made sense to win without a fight.

The boy emperor reviewed the golden etchings. Rolling the seal, he handed it back to the towering dalari. "You've made your case well. From this day forward the dalari are to be considered our allies. Any attacks made against them will be considered an attack against me!"

Demetrix stood in the underground chamber of Eldarian, overlooking the ancient mirror. He was ready to go home. Ravion had taken the throne and demanded peace with the alfar. He was on his own journey. It was Demetrix's time to complete his.

Drawing a line in the floor, before the mirror, he could see the green rune come to life. It was the sigil of Celnuntos, bonding a link between worlds. When he reached the other side he was going to have to draw one there as well. Finishing his sigil, he took a deep breath and stepped through.

The air was chilly and uncomfortable. But the crypt remained very much the same as the last time he'd seen it. Perhaps more moss, but who cared? Quickly scribing his rune, he made his way from the hole in the ground and looked out over the gloomy world he'd chosen to call home.

The dark, rolling clouds collected in the distance. It seemed they didn't agree with him. But that was all right. He was chosen by a god, and that god, while lesser compared to Izaryle's status, would protect him.

Turning north, Demetrix stepped into the dead forest. The trees were barren of fruit and absent their leaves, if they could even grow them. This being his second time here, they didn't appear to have changed. Reaching the hill top, he looked as far north as he could.

"Elalon, my love, I'll be home soon."

While this book concludes the Heroes of Order tales, that doesn't mean the saga is complete.

Be sure to stay up to date with the newest Eldarlands books at http://www.levisamuel.com

Please leave a review at your online retailer.

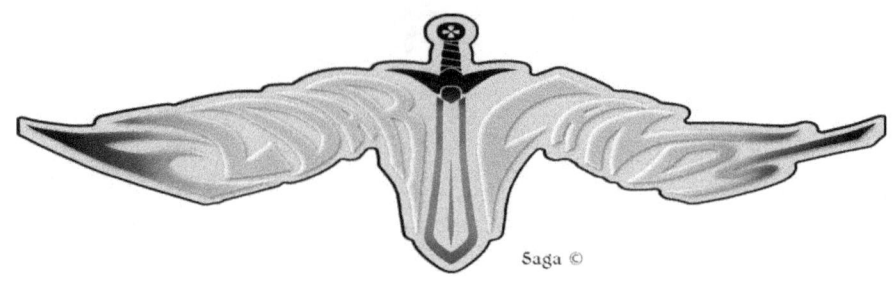

Continue the Adventure

NIGHTKING DUOLOGY · VOLUME ONE

RISE OF THE NIGHTKINGS

LEVI SAMUEL

Rise of the Nightkings

What was supposed to be a simple task quickly becomes a world ending battle as the vicious Nightkings march across the lands of Irayth. Little by little the realm falls to shadow. Friendships turn bitter. Love becomes lost. And possessing magic may as well be a death warrant.

Before long, only a spark remains in the night. And at the core of that spark stands Inyalia, a young elven woman who dreamed of nothing more than protecting her homeland as a ranger.

She got her wish. Will she have what it takes to live it?

Author's Notes

A book is an adventure. It doesn't matter whether you're the reader, author, editor, or some random person that finds it on the street and uses the pages to keep warm during a cold winter night. A book is an adventure for any whom come in contact with it. And while I hope you enjoy the story within these pages, preferable outside the need to burn them, I'd like to talk a little about the adventures I had while writing it.

I hadn't originally planned to write this book. Everything that's happened in story prior to now, yes. But this book was not intended as part of the original story. I was going to end it when Gareth and Demetrix stepped into the flash of light at the end of book two. Which if you recall that far back, I'd originally intended to be a single book. But things don't always turn out as we plan. And in my opinion, the story is all the better for it.

A friend of mine called after reading the original draft. He complained about the story's ending. It wasn't so much that he didn't like it. He was concerned about where it was going to go from there. I explained that I was going to continue their tale somewhere around book seven in my original plan. But I first needed to get the other pieces of the world written so it could all come together for that final chapter of the puzzle. Needless to say, he wasn't having any part of it. It was pointedly explained that book seven was too long of a wait for resolution. Apparently having your main characters disappear in a ball of light isn't a satisfactory ending. Moreover, he explained that if I didn't complete this part of the story before I moved on to the next part, not only would I have a whole bunch of pissed off readers on my hands, but he was going to come to my house and beat the hell out of me.

So, I did what any sane person who'd just been threatened with bodily harm would do. I started writing an outline. In truth, I wasn't overly concerned with having my ass kicked. Sure, he's quite a bit bigger than me, but I'm sure I'm faster. And while I doubt he'd actually go far as to hurt me over a book, he made some good points that required consideration. In the end, I decided he was right, and the fruits of that conversation is what you hold in your hands. (That is provided you're holding your reading device. For All I know you're sitting at a computer and reading from afar.)

I don't want to say the content of this book was made up on the fly. Quite the contrary. The elements of this story were planned since I first decided to write the series. And while the events that took place were sometimes not as mapped out as I prefer, every detail was a part of a bigger picture that I've been striving to relay since the beginning. I have numerous world rules that I keep in place. They help me shape the story. Certain elements are set in stone and cannot be broken. This keeps my stories balanced and making some level of sense, though clarity will continue to rise as the series continues, and more books are released.

In these books, you've heard mention of a few gods. Some have been a lesser status, some greater. And considering this story is somewhat driven by divine influence, this makes sense. It seems more gods are coming into the fold with each passing book. But what you haven't discovered yet is the fact that the pantheon is complete and fully functional. Every god (or goddess) is already in play. Some of them without anyone's knowledge at this point in time. I guess what I'm trying to say is that these world rules I keep around have been in play for years. I have an entire, functioning world in my head that I'm trying to bring to paper for your pleasure, and if you'll be patient with me, I plan to bring you many more books, packed full of excitement, adventure, magic, dragons, gods, war, blood, and perhaps even sex. But not too much sex as I try to keep my porn separate from my fantasy. Good luck finding any of that out there.

Now that this trilogy is complete, it's time to move on to the next piece of the puzzle. In that story we'll explore the realm of Irayth a little more in depth. There we'll discover how it became the dreaded world of darkness you saw in book two. There may even be a camo scene in there somewhere.

After that, we'll be moving onto the next trilogy, which will be more about the Eldar Races and their place in the world. But anyway, too much talk of the future, we're supposed to be taking about the now.

Those that know me personally know that I'm a fairly quiet and reclusive person. That is until you get to know me, or really if it's a small setting. I don't do well with groups. Where I'm going with this, once you get to know me, you'll discover that I'm always joking. I enjoy humor in many forms. When I have the opportunity to tell a joke, I seize it. But being an author means I can do one better. I can hide jokes throughout my work. And that's exactly what I did in this book. I sprinkled my twisted sense of humor throughout this novel, just waiting for people like you to find it. Some are plainly visible, others will take some looking, but I assure you, there are plenty for you to find. But don't worry, the story is still fully intact. If I dropped one, it settled with the elements around it. And I'll tell you, nothing gets you through some trying times like a good joke.

In my personal life, I ran into a string of deaths over the past few months. Too many people I liked and cared about passed to the afterlife, which can have some troubling effects. It's something we all have to deal with from time to time. And while I'm not overly effected by the prospect of death, it still makes one question life. Am I doing it right? Is this really important enough to sacrifice time with my daughter and friends? How do I make this happen faster so I can enjoy my life? These are just a few examples that have passed through my mind over the last few months. And while the questions are numerous, I've noticed the prospect of death makes me impatient and less calculating. I'm willing to take greater risks in order to achieve my goals when I start thinking about the loss of friends or family. But that's because I want to reach my comfort zone as fast as possible so I can live a full and comfortable life sooner, rather than later.

After one such chain of deaths and the thoughts that proceeded, I came to the conclusion that I was done working for someone else. I've never been fond of the traditional employment arrangement in the first place. It's not that I don't get along with them, simply that I don't agree with working as hard they require, for such little pay. It's that whole trading time of your life for small sums of money that I have a problem with. And depending on the industry you're in, you have to contend with injury or death, dirt, grease, or germs, not to mention all the time you sacrifice away from the people you care about in order to pay for a house you barely have time to live in, or the luxuries you barely have time to use. Yet if you don't pay them, it won't take long until you lose them. It's a broken system. We aren't meant work our asses off just to pay bills and die. Yet that's what our society demands we do to survive. And frankly, I'm sick of it. It's not that I'm lazy, or don't want to work. I just feel that if I'm going to work that hard, I'd rather do it for myself. At least then I can make full profit, opposed to making a few pennies from someone who's making dollars from my contributions. So, I decided I'd had enough. I weighed my options and came up with a plan. I had some money saved up for such a purpose and I decided it was time to use it.

I put my two-weeks' notice in at my job, using my writer's flair to write the most kick-ass resignation letter I could come up with. Seriously, almost everyone who read it had to complement me on it. I thought that was pretty awesome. Anyway, I breezed through the first week with minimal interference. It wasn't until the third day of the second week that the news circulated the entire company. The owner wouldn't talk to me, my direct boss wished me the best, though he wanted me to stay, and his boss decided I was too valuable to lose. So, he called a meeting of the managers and they came up with a plan to get me to stay. When I was called into the office, the day before my scheduled last day, they made me a few offers. I considered each one and added my own opinions. In the end, we agreed on a three-day workweek, which was enough to keep my regular bills paid, and allow me the time I needed to distribute my books during normal business hours, which I desperately needed. When you have to scrub your skin with a stiff bristled brush every day just to make it look somewhat clean, trying to do such things after work is extremely difficult to manage. I now had time to build my writing career beyond what I'd already accomplished, and I felt better almost instantly. I have much smaller paychecks, but I have more time to control my income with my books, which is the goal. And once I'm able to fully replace my income, I'm sure I'll reconvening my decision to step away. But for right now, things are working in a manner to keep everyone happy.

Anyway, here's to new and enjoyable books. I hope you enjoyed reading as much as I enjoyed writing. And if you'd be so kind, I would appreciate you leaving a review at any authorized retailer. Reviews are the new word of mouth, and I need your help to reach more people. Thank you for your continued support and I look forward to bringing you more books in the near future.

Levi Samuel
October 2017 - Originally Written
October 2018 - Revised

www.ingramcontent.com/pod-product-compliance
Lightning Source LLC
Chambersburg PA
CBHW070101030726
47506CB00002B/554